SALVATION
SHOWERS OF BLOOD

JAMES HENDERSHOT

Order this book online at www.trafford.com
or email orders@trafford.com

Most Trafford titles are also available at major online book retailers.

Printed in the United States of America.

ISBN: 978-1-4907-1488-2 (sc)
ISBN: 978-1-4907-1489-9 (e)

Trafford rev. 09/20/2013

 www.trafford.com

North America & international
toll-free: 1 888 232 4444 (USA & Canada)
fax: 812 355 4082

My kingdom grows,

My will grows

Lilith Series

Dedicated to my favorite RN, my wife Younghee,
with thanks for financially providing for our family during
my days of writing and to my sons, Josh and John and
daughter, Nellie and our publishing consultant, Love Blake

Contents

Sisters and Daughters

I now stand with a marble flat place, and as I look back, I can see the light bringing my sisters. I wait patiently for one to appear. It would be a burden beyond what I could bear if I lost them. This is to be their great reward, although what they did is nothing what my spirits do every day. As I float on these marbles, I wish while in the flesh for thirty-three years (I entered Auriel after she turned three years old) I could have walked on some marble. I can see where I may not jump in a flesh suit for some time. What a nightmare. It is accordingly strange that when you cease a painful activity, even though you remember the agony, it is no longer felt. I have so much work to do when I get back home, wherever that is. My home has been in my sisters who are blood of my blood and bone from my bone, which now lay for the Earth to recycle. I am consequently, happy that I did not have to be some insect or hungry animal. I can now clearly remember my daughters. I wonder how they are doing. I eagerly wait to see them also. Where are Sabina and Medica? Why is this place filled with so much solemnness? There are no birds, with nothing moving, being absent from all noise. I can actually feel my soul recharging, through this peacefulness. I can now see a large white stream of light defeating the dark whatever above me. This light is, at the present time, resting on the marble as some spirits start flowing out. Then I hear water for my thirsty soul that is lost somewhere in space. Voices ring out, "Ann; we are here we h you now." They form a straight line in front of me and call off their names, "Fejér, Julia, Mary, Ruth, Amity, Siusan the Harvey, Faith the Hyrum, Drusilla the Hyrum, Yanaba the Oakley, Máriakéménd the Stuart and the last one Heidi of the Eldom." I can feel the intensity of their love and loyalty. This creates within a generation of new power. They have me in their circle now. After we figure out the situation in this place, I will have to set my disciples on their sisterhood journey. I can feel them entering into me. I shall within me make a special heaven for them where with can share our new adventures and unite our loves. I shall have a river of love in which as we enter we all become the water in the river, united and together yet part of something bigger which will be the summation of our loves. As we feed off each other, my completeness is at the end of its journey. I left alone and came back with twelve parts of the new me. I shall enjoy the power of their consults as we rule my throne when I reach it. Hence, many memories in thirty-three short years with experiences that have reshaped me. I am now a stronger love powered and focused deity. My sisters are gripping themselves in my spirit. It is not a grip of fear for them; it is a grip of fear for me. I reveal to them, "Sisters, why do your souls protect me from harm?" They told me, "Master, we see not security thus fear danger for you." Then the light above us turned bright as a shower of yellowish orange rays flooded the heavens above us and the giant space gas clouds above us. This was to me a sign that something good was going to happen. I did not fear that anything bad would happen since I am in my dimension, and my throne blessed me with my sword of justice before I left. With that sword, I am invincible. Actually, I await more opportunities to use it. I can feel my sisters dropped out of my spirit and floating out onto the marble. Now the rays are concentrated by connecting one to each of us. We each currently appear in a bright warm light. Our waves deliver in each of us more peace. However, being up here somewhere, I remember my beautiful throne, so much, I longed to take back home. In my heart, I cry out, Miss you, miss you, miss you; everything I now do echoes with the laughter and the voices around you. For in you I find no corner, and remember every turn and twist, every old familiar spot, joyous songs how you are missed. I miss you, I miss my daughters, I miss my trinity, I miss my courts, I miss my angels; everything I do there are touching memories dancing in a row. Silhouette and shadow on every form and face, soul and reality everywhere displace. Oh, I miss you, miss you, especially my god Bogovi I miss you, Girl! There is a strange, sad silence when my mind remembers, the daily things I did, wait with me, and expectant for a word from you. Speak to me Bogovi, speak to me that which was, speak to my throne, and forget me not. My disciples look in amazement as millions of pure white angels now engulf the place we now exist. They fly back and forth, yet never hitting each other. Moreover, oh, how refreshing, they are making some peaceful noise as if each wing flop is programed to the nearest microsecond. Fejér now asks, "Oh master what do the angels want?" I tell her, "They only want to show us their love. These are newly created angels awaiting their first assignment. Ruth now shouts in excitement, "That statue is you Ann. Hurry and look." I look over and see the sky is now blue and white. Our marble world must now be on a planet. I can see a giant rock statue of me holding a sword and leading others into battle. The statue is so big that its base is higher than a human body. Why are we on a planet and now back into flesh suits? The sisters appear to enjoy it as they are running around this city of marble that we now have under our feet. As I look around, I marvel at the design of it. So many giant columns and temples surround me. I walk into one of the temples, which has no warm blood serving in it. I can see so many small statues of me and my wall of books. I see the feeding tables for those who are hungry and the tables with clothes for those who are in need. I can see the small stage where my temple's angel stands. My belief is that if you want people to believe in the spiritual world than having a real spirit for them to see. If I tell them, I am a goddess of love then show them love. They that see will believe and those who need to be pulled from the evil's grip will be pulled by me. I do the work of saving them.

They do the work of staying saved by living under my wing. I see that in so few deities. I am glad they are still in tune with my wishes. Likewise, of more importance, I am glad to be away from Earth, which in my current period is long gone for thousands of millennia. My sisters are all around my statue as Heidi tells us, "Master you look so powerful and mighty, beyond that which I can conceive." I then said, "My precious eternal loves, you are me and I am you, so please try hard to not call me master. My name is Lilith and I hunger, and to regain you as mine for your love. Will you feed me and let me feed you?" They all now bowed before me and said, "We do feed you Lilith and beg let we fed you." I then said, "Thanks my sisters." Then Siusan said, "With all our heart we surrender to your service Master ooohh Lilith." The sisters all surrounded her and started tickling her saying, "You must not say master oh beautiful Harvey." They were laughing as wonderful as I froze absorbing their laughter's into my soul like a mighty flood consuming me. We were now slowly walking to a giant temple that lay before us. It first reminded me of a nighttime vision; however, it was real, and the sky above it was different, as it silhouetted the temple enough to prevent walking past it. It had nice messages written on the marble floors as we walked towards it. My commandments and the verses that the Lights of Ereshkigal compiled for me now lay beneath us. I was always glad that the Lights made me look smart. I now see a message from me as we all stop to read it, "Bring unto me the sick, the hungry, the poor, the diseased, the naked, those who are lonely and let me get you food take you from your poverty, heal your infirmities, clothe you, and be with you so that loneliness may no longer trouble your soul. My temple is your haven for love and peace. Thus sayeth Lilith, your goddess promise onto the good." Ruth then said, "Lilith, how can you keep such promises?" I told her, "I have given my angels the power to do these things. I lay beside my horse on the beautiful pastures in my holy of holies sleeping with no worries. My courts watch their angels while they work so that we have no troubles as your old home had." The said Yanaba, "Wow" making her now a member of the wow club, as all laughed. I wonder if that is not our word that started the bond with us. Máriakéménd then asked, "Lilith, what is the truth?" In addition, I looked at her and said, "My love from the Stuarts, you are the truth." Then Drusilla asked, "How can that be and why is she the truth?" I looked at Drusilla and said, "My twin, for you are also the truth. All of you are the truth since we are bonded by our blood. Your blood surrendered to my blood and you and I became one. We are Blood of Our Blood. Thus, my truth is your truth and your truth is my truth. My truth is the law for my Kingdom and since your truth is my truth then does that not make your truth the law?" Then Julia asked, "Lilith, with all this divine power why do you share it with us?" Then I told them, "Our gods sent me to dwell in the flesh so that I could give my life and spill my blood so I could have the sword of justice. All here who see me know that I am their goddess. Yet when I was naked and hungry and lonely you gave me your free love and took my blood into you not knowing who I really was. You came and loved me giving me food and love and sharing your nakedness with me. You are the twelve that I needed to complete myself. Sadly, I cannot let you go since you are of me from my days of being in the flesh before my sacrifice as even Drusilla died with me and did not betray me yet demanded that she suffer as I did, not wanting life if she could not give me her love. I give you no power. I give myself the power and since you are I, you have the well to drink the water therein. I truly do not know this place, yet it must be part of my kingdom since the angels are singing songs to me. We shall discover our answer." I just saw no need to have them stay and Earth and teach about my kingdom. They cannot have eternal rest in my dimension; consequently, they have no reward. Sometimes I must keep what was given to my twelve sisters and me in must make complete and keep them. They are mine and I am theirs. Separated with our not complete however united we are complete. That is my new law" Then Faith asked, "Lilith what shall we do?" Then I said unto all my sisters who were eagerly also seeking an answer, "You will be called my disciples, yet your duties will be so much more, for you will have no duty. You shall go and come as you please. You will be me with you go. No one will know the difference as when you say your name my name will come out. What you bind is bound, what you curse is cursed, the laws that you give are laws, the love you give is Love. We are one, and unlike my trinity, which is always in me, you are always beside me. You of course must not enter Bogovi's holy of holies, as even the trinity must leave me when I am there, as I know you understand. That is his rule, not mine. I wish you could be there with me. Fejér then shared with us, "When she returns we can see every little detail." Accordingly, I said, "I strive hard to make it exciting for us." Then we had our first good laugh since returning home. That Amity asked me, "Lilith, do we ever get hungry now?" I then told her, while in flesh suits from my throne you never hunger. I had commanded on my way out before returning to earth to suffer my punishments that those in the flesh who give surrender their souls to me also be given these bodies that do not hunger nor have diseases and thus arrive to my throne later than their original date." Then Mary asked, "How do these bodies feed themselves?" I then answered her with my arms around her as I always did, "Mary, it is through some solar biological energy producing system that the Lights of Ereshkigal created. If at least one second of light appears somewhere near them they will recharge. We also have an internal micro battery fed chip that can produce recharge the battery for up to one-hundred years." Then Faith said, "No more number one's and number two's?" I answered, "That is the best part, no more body wastes that alert wild beasts where you are. Wild beasts feed off each other by tracking that way. When one must take in matter, to include the flesh of something else that once lived only to waste so much of the actual energy to produce the energy and regenerate decaying body mass, then dispose of it back onto the earth to help spread diseases it so foolish. I also hate the dangling of a carrot in front of a being telling them that if they continue to suffer and hope that evil does not destroy them that I will bless them after evil destroys them. I like giving them their reward beginning on the date that they dedicate themselves to me. I still must decide how that transition will be celebrated and verified. I will have my Lights ask our High Throne." Then Julia asked, "How do you know your high throne likes you?" I then held out my sword and answered, "Because their bosses gave me this sword in which no power is greater than those beneath them." Can now for another famous remark from Julia, "Wow." As all started laughing, I think this is a special treat for all of us. A little inside joke kind of thing while we walk around in this amazing structure. Then we walk into the big structure that my writings have brought us to. Inside we see many chambers along the circumference. In each nice chamber is a place to bathe and towels for us to dry the temporary flesh that we shall soon dawn. This bathe felt subsequently good as I could hear the happiness from my sisters as each bathe in such luxury. No fears could be felt as the legions of angels swarmed above singing, "Lilith has returned to her children." Then after a joyful refreshing bath, we once again joined each other in the center of this nice bathing temple. Then Faith said to me, "Lilith, ruling a small island with my husband was a giant misery for me, how you can rule so much so perfectly?" I told her the first thing I did, to keep it in terms you can conceive was to build a gigantic divine power source and from that power source all things are watched and all situations that need my response receive one. This way not one prayer goes unanswered, no one need that I have promised to fulfill goes unfilled, not one tear goes ignored, not one heart that needs my love goes unloved and with their new flesh suits, no child of mine hungers or suffers from diseases." Ruth asked, "How did you know how to make such a thing?" I told them, "The Lights of Ereshkigal or my divine mind created that for me. My mind is now a spirit that feeds off my divine power. It knows all my wills and my mind and feeds from my mind each day. This spirit will be with you in all things you do in my name." Then Drusilla asked, "Will all things we do be in your name?" I spoke to them saying, "No, for you will also be yourself and have your identity anytime you wish. I will be with you when you want me to be with you. I can enjoy myself in my holy of holies and attend special functions of my throne and reward the deserving children of mine as presented by the courts." Drusilla asked, "Are all your servants your children, sister?" I then said, "Twin, all in the flesh is. By being my children they get the level of divine love they should, not just having me sit back and enjoy watching them suffer and beg me for help only to ignore them, but guiding and helping them enter into my kingdom." Then Máriakéménd asked, "What shall become of us?" Then I said, "Many good things." Máriakéménd then asked again, "Are there any special things we must do?" I then told her, "Yes my daughters, yet even I do not know the details, be it for you to know you are goddesses and those in the spirit and flesh will bow to you and praise your name as you appear as you do to me." Let us walk in peace, as I know we shall give audience to someone soon. They were now starting to become more relaxed as we talked and joked about our shared pasts. Drusilla and I talked much, as now talking about that terrible time was of no significance. I told her to remind me someday for a wagon master fry as once I got back on my throne; I would select a few to punish after I got mommy and daddy here. We would do the inter-dimensional negotiations, which would mean trading prisoners. They were all frying, so it did not really amount to nothing more than recording it for history. The dimensions had apparently opened up a lot during the last thirty-three years. As I think now about how fast Medica, Sabina, and I rushed to get out of there for fear of eternal damnation, yet for me to hide there for thirty-three years is crazy. If only Fejér and those who resting with her in our Oakley camp could feel the seventeen years I was with Drusilla. In a way I am glad they are spared. Looking back now, I truly am so thankful to have been a part of her life and admire her power and strength. Drusilla and Faith will be good for Sabina. My trinity and throne must have forgotten me. All of a sudden, we saw a splashing light of many conservative lights. I can see a body emerging with some things behind it. This white, green, blue light continued towards us walking on the water clouds, for they were clouds when there was light nevertheless they are now splashing. We are all excited that we are finally receiving a visitor. To come so far so fast and then just have things stop is mysterious. Now the water or clouds are gone and before me stands one I do not know, so I say unto her, "Who art thou?" She answers reverently, "I am your servant

Medica and I have come to be with you my lord." In great excitement, I rushed to her and gave her a great hug and as I cried I kissed her face so many times, I thought maybe she would no longer have a face. I then slowly pulled myself together and asked her, "My trinity, why are you so formal?" Medica told me, "My lord, you have been gone for so many years; I fear you may now want to dispose of me." I then told her, "My trinity, you were with me when I received Ereshkigal. You were with me as we escaped the claws of eternal damnation. You were beside me, and I did not make you in me? How could I get rid of one who battled evil so hard to redeem my good children? You shall spend much time in me watching the price I paid for our divinity. The greatest throne of many dimensions made a new law, that whoever sits on a throne must be tested and sacrifice themselves for those who serve them. I have given my blood and we shall prevail. So tell me, why do you dress as you do?" Medica said, "To be free from the chains of clothing among so many of Bogovi's warriors was too much shame and too degrading." I inquired, "Why did you not cast them away?" Medica said, "It was long before we knew where you were and after we found our lord, you were gone again. We had a fear in our spirits that we would lose your empire, and then we asked Bogovi to take our courts and protect us. He did protect us and requested we appear as spirits with him, so he could protect us better. Many times evil struck at Sabina and me, however somehow we escaped. Bogovi saved us and a couple of times we were hiding in your nighttime world and often sent us back to you when he sensed danger to be near. You are here today and your kingdom is here today because of him. You were so wise to be with him when you declared Rachmanism. Today billions of planets are now free of evil. We have the new "no food needed flesh suits ready for you to examine." After we watched how so annoying and wasteful that process is, the Lights started digging deep to not only give you the bodies you want, but also produce and make available organs that can easily be installed if needed to keep the flesh suit operating." I then said the Medica, "Now that I have returned I need so much for my trinity to be with me as we ascend back to our throne. And I should make a long overdue visit to Bogovi." Medica then feed my curiosity by telling me, "The place we are at now is called Veszprém which is your holy place is which only you, your trinity, your wonderful sisters and our precious daughters. It is your sanctuary from Bogovi for he will never enter this place even though he created it." I joyfully shared with Medina, "I am so glad that you are close with "our daughters" for they will serve you with all they have and I do so much want to share with you the sisters of the trinity, as soon as either you or Sabina approve, for without a majority vote, they cannot be our sisters." Medica looked at me strange and said, looking at Heidi, it would be especially hard to vote no, nonetheless, if we did, what would happen to our sisters?" I then told her, "They are of my blood, I cannot live without them, and thus we would find a home in another dimension." Medica then, as she was hugging Heidi said, "I shall never be without you again, so I naturally want them so much to be with us for eternity. And if you decide to pick them out and live elsewhere, you must let me come with you and be your servant." I then motioned for the sisters to join us in a big cheerful hug, as I said to them, "Today, you are in the trinity, you shall be worshipped by my children, we will have a ceremony for this immense thing soon." Then Medica said, "Introduce me to the new treasures that will live inside us." I then asked our precious treasures to line up and introduced them, "Medica behold, Fejér, Julia, Mary, Ruth, Amity, Siusan, Faith, Drusilla, Yanaba, Máriakémend, and one like unto you Heidi." Medica then said, "Is Siusan truly a Harvey?" I then replied, "After so long looking she found me. This is a very special godsend, indeed. I shall ask the Lights to search all of our galaxies and then everywhere to find them." Medica then said, "Command them now, for they will answer your summons, just now appear in your holy Veszprém." I then commanded, "My Lights of Ereshkigal search you all places in a race known to me as the Harvey. You may scan Siusan to get the biological coding. Give me your results as soon as you get them no matter where I am or what I am doing." We then heard a voice saying, "It shall be done as our goddess has commanded." Medica now sat with the sisters and was telling them her history and about her love for me and for them. They all seemed to be hitting it off well, then one slipped up and came to me saying, "Auriel, will you talk to me?" I looked at Drusilla and said, "Of course my twin, how may I serve you?" Drusilla began by saying, "You know all things about me, because we have always been one, yet you were so much before me, I feel as if I know not my other half Auriel." I then told her, "Since you will be inside me you can learn all my thoughts, feelings, and adventures. You shall be more special than all the others to me shall because we did survive and go side by side, and you chose to snuff it with me and not betray me thus only you may call me Auriel. That name shall be our special bridge that no other my cross." Drusilla then said, "Having you to care for is forever all that I desire. Will you please instruct me how to care for you now? I served you when we were children, I served you every day that I lived in the flesh, how I could now not serve you, Medica then answered, "Our Lights and Bogovi's lights have created to connect power spirits that monitor everything every second. Evil can no longer focus an attack nor join in any task, for to do so alerts the powerful spirits. You and Bogovi simply give it your will. This power spirits can generate their own power reserves and can only be blocked by either Bogovi or you." I then reminded Medica that, "We are a trinity and each has its own will." Medica then replied, "I am sorry Lilith, we can present ourselves as a trinity in our personal parts of the throne, however anything in Bogovi, and your empire is you and only you. We are beside you if you need us, however most of the time we will be your servant of love concentrating on the holy of holies with your sisters and us together. Yet that which leaves our holy of holies is you, because you have paid the sacrificial blood price and you are the holy one." I then shook my head and asked, "My Medica, I made you a deity because I could not do it without you. I am confused because Drusilla also paid the same price I did. How can I rule without you?" Medica and Drusilla now came over to hug and pamper me, this so-called goddess of the universes, including our alliance galaxies. Medica, while holding Drusilla's hands whispered to me, "You never have to leave without us, just put us inside you. We will stay hidden when you are with Bogovi, for you shall do nothing that we have never enjoyed or suffered. We will build that special sanctuary that only you can access. Sabina and I always considered ourselves your sisters, so now you will have fourteen sisters. I will let Sabina know if you have approved our plea." I then shared with Medica, "As long as you are still with me, I care not what title you desire. If you wish for it, then I petition it. My sisters are I as I am my sisters. I ask for you to reintroduce our sisters to Sabina." Then as we spoke, the sky became filled with lights of many colors with the white light shining in the middle. That light was heading straight for us. This light also flooded our island with peace and the kind of warmth that coats the ankles, ooh yes. Then appeared before me a Hyrum, in which I pretty well know who it is yet need to act as if I do not. Thus I asked, "Who art thou?" Then this wonderfully slim tightly dressed in black and plastered with diamonds answered saying, "I am Sabina and I have come to worship my goddess." I then answered, "I never thought you would be afraid to appear exposed. Are you afraid of Bogovi's warriors?" Sabina then answered, "I did have to be careful, since they all wanted to have some Hyrum wine and even I did not have enough to satisfy the millions of them, yet the reason I dress today is to concede to Drusilla surrendering to her wonderful perfect breasts. I wish to drink all of her wine and give her my greatest service as her sister servant." I then said to Sabina, "I welcome you helping me with my twin. I do so much want you to love my sisters. I agree with you that Drusilla is wonderful, for she died with me when I surrendered my sacrificial blood." Sabina then said, "Medica told me that you approved as being sisters and me too so much welcome our young sisters and request that Faith walk on my left and Drusilla on my right. I hope the four of us can be in agreement with this." Drusilla and Faith both agreed saying, "If it is the will of our master than we shall enjoy the extra love and special relationship with Sabina." I was now filled with complete overwhelming joy. I then reassured all that our spirit could give everyone everything they desired at any time. My powerbase was beyond our wildest dreams now as it had regenerated itself so many times and we would not hold it back. Now, if we had a threat that a small pistol could handle I would blast it with a self-energy producing hydrogen neutron bomb or spirit eater. These weapons, as all in my arsenal expand then retract into their own black hole sucking any energy that they captured with them. Furthermore, with what my lights created combined with Bogovi's lights and our throne's lights produced weapons that none could match. The only delay in the process, which now is so nominal, is pulling the good souls out. I am now feeling a lot more at home having Medica's memories and Sabrina's memories inside me. I have my fourteen sisters now to enjoy eternity in our holy of holies. I have to work out a way to fit Bogovi into my life. This place called Veszprém is so well laid out. Columns running in rows as far as my eyes can see every way with marble. The cloud and on off seas are a great touch. The calm swarm of the angels swarming and stars east, west, north and south chase away the space cold and darkness. For our night, dark space gas clouds cover us. I should be so content, yet something is missing. My sky turns black again with blue now filling the middle. I see a big 'planet' blocking out a bright white light. I can see six smaller stronger lights with what could be another million lights in the distance. I look at Sabina and Medica and see that they are also captivated. The six smaller lights are now much bigger and rotating each other. What could this wonderful sight be? We all look at it with no fear and that is so good. We all are now holding hands, as this is the first time we will appear before something new as a sisterhood. Although this is Veszprém, my haven, it is the perfect place to fine tune any potential fears and turn them into opportunities to receive. The lights are here now and appearing before is something I have missed so much. Now I understand the millions of lights. I break our hand locks and rush forward as they stand before me, completely free from the chains of clothing as I they broke from my womb, my six top daughters. I can see Bodrogközi, Agyagosszergény, Cserszegtomaj, Sásdi, Adásztevel, and Kapuvári. They are not in their glamour flesh suits but in the suits they wear when they visit me in my holy of holies. I then asked them, "Daughters, why are you unclothed? Do you not fear Bogovi's warriors?" They answered, "We are daughters of Lilith, united, with fear for no one and love only for our mother. They tried to make us play games with them that we did not want to play. We united and attacked them as we would demons. Bogovi saw this and ordered his warriors to stop fighting and surrender. We thumped them some more and they requested a truce in which we gave them our terms and they accepted. We have never had any trouble from them and since so many of us have fought side by side with Bogovi's warriors. Bogovi told us that he could see our mother in us. We gave all so we could receive back our all and that is our mother." I then, with my famous by now tears in my eyes, thanked them and told them how proud I was of them." Their faces now glowed with happiness as each clan behind them emitted a different strong color. I then added, "We have so many trillions of years ahead of us. I shall bond with each of my daughters as they will bond with me and, their new blood aunts or whatever we shall call them. These extra fourteen mommies should be able to be a larger part in your lives and the lives of my Intimate Joy's Empire. I shall create another paradise solar system in which my daughters shall live, rule, and raise families if they desire. It shall be protected by our armies, who may be able to provide some mates for you girls to start your own destinies. Our Empire us based on good, and not the allowing of evil to torment and cause great sufferings. You daughters are an integral part of our new sisterhood, for you are with me. I shall now put a cup of my blood in this basin. My blood shall make the waters that flow into it one with it. All must now drink of this water. Have or summon all my daughters now." Ágyagosszergény was the first and she did drink a cup then she cried out, "Cserszegtomaj and Sásdi come to me and fill your cups for if this is the blood of my mother then I not only shall drink it, I shall shower in it so that I have my mother on my inside and outside." She then had her transformation, a spiritual cleansing, and a big dose of my love. As my blood tan down her body, my love filled every empty crack in her spirit. She cried out in such great joy that the marble shook. Her sisters did as she had and they all begged for showers in my blood. Each one got my baptism of love. All that unused power that I had in reserve was supplying their spirits being uniting with them into my spirit hence that I can be with them and them in me. As Adásztevel came up she begged for the same shower or baptism and she too received the same blessing. To my surprise, my sisters including Sabina and Medica started a new line, drank my blood, and baptized each other in it. I then took cups of my blood and poured them into many of my other fountains so that now we had many lines as each fountain also had many times. I filled one hundred fountains with cups from previous fountains and for each I added some new. I truly wonder how this "showers in blood" concept has evolved, yet my sisters and daughters are truly enjoying it. This is the unique function; which I must separate myself from the gods that give me sadness and make me angry. As my daughters are today celebrating a rebirth in my heart, I know they have longed for this day. My spirit, though not a part of me is divine. I can control it and command it. I would compare it to a separate planet in which in which my daughters and sisters may come and go as they please. This "planet" or power source will generate its own energy making much more than what it needs. The extra will go into the thrones reserves. Any sister or daughter that needs this divine wine may drink it at any time. This is divine wine and not heavenly wine. Heavenly wine is also available and can be generated by any using it. My daughters are soaking themselves to the point that with the sun's rays is baking their flesh red. They do not want to take the wine off. This is a great welcoming gift for me, to see all my daughters keep pouring in and they are leaving painted in my blood. That will cause some concern with the courts. I shall build another spirit for my saints. This spirit will be larger than my largest galaxies, so much that each can have a solar system. This will be inside a new spirit that will also be mine thus will not be visible to those still in the flesh. I will place this in the vast empty space between Ereshkigal and Bogovi's Galaxy. I wish he would name it, if not, I will, of course sweeten him up some. Either way, I do hope that his saved spirits will be able to join the group considering how much empty space is available everywhere. This way they can have access to my pseudo spirit, which is mine, yet only through a spiritual link and I have all that on auto mode with my Courts monitoring it. They will be a part of something and I can be apart from it. I have too many sisters and daughters plus Bogovi and my Courts to keep me hopping, plus Bogovi who will keep me busy. My daughters are now forming in small groups and staying here at Veszprém. A roar of happiness, singing, and laughter is so packed with love. My sisters to include Medica and Sabina are spending so much time with them as they each have such large audiences. As I look around, I can only see one daughter missing. She is not here. I wonder so much why. She is my beloved Atlantis. I will have to send some secret escorts to get her. I will ask Bogovi to help transplant her underwater cities to our many large planets with so much larger oceans. I also long so much for my special sister, one who bonded Mary, Ruth and I with Faith, Joy and Richard. That will repair our broken circle. Now that I know where I am and what I must now do, it is time to start some action. It is time to take my harem and head for my throne. I just have to wait for my blood to return to the fountains then suck itself into a black hole and then enter my spirit. I will have to make so much of this stuff. I want to walk on my throne, sit on my throne, and receive the love of my servants.

Queen Lilith, Holder of the Sword of Justice

A s I flashed through space with my tagalongs and rushed back to Ereshkigal, it all felt so pure. The space was free of the evil and pain of death graving demons. As can feel joy and life on the small white dots that scatter before me. All sainted spirits were living their reward and all evil spirits, including mine had been completely returned to energy and individual atoms spread through so many of our spirit generators to be used as a waste byproduct in the spiritual creation process. These demons were completely vanished from existence and fueling the creation of new good spirits. We were slowly working our way to Ereshkigal as our inter galaxy speeds were less than our dimensional jumps and my courts were making sure nothing bad would happen to me and my blood. Then my eyes beheld a sight that once was daily yet now has been absent for thirty-three years. My guardian angel was sitting on high, and above and being so majestic. He was the guard of the throne as no other could match his level of dedication. He so seldom smiled, yet he had a big smile on his face and wings now. I could feel the happiness in his wings. The entire throne and clouds packed around it was so heartwarming. This is my throne, built from scratch in a galaxy packed with evil that is now ruled by love and purity. This means so much now, especially after the twenty years of misery with what is now a source of love that I would suffer that again for Drusilla and of course all the adventures of other eleven sisters, yet twenty years sweeting each minute fearing something bad would happen to her cannot be swept under a rug. Sabina and Medica noticed a bond as they spend a lot of time with her, one at a time so as not to alert the others until I can explain this. Drusilla must be with me and I cannot throw away the power of our bond. It was molded by blood as I can think of no one who has bled more with me, or trying to save me. My daughters have revealed to me that everything I said "on the divine side" was transmitted back to the throne so they would be ready for their goddesses return. I always like it when they personalize it; such I am theirs for my spirit truly serves them. They deserve to have the promises made them to be kept. Sabina suggested that I send my blood ahead so that the spiritual powers could reproduce it in mass quantities and that I appear first as blood then put on my flesh suit. I also sent ahead that I wanted my head angels for a meeting. When I arrived, I saw my seat, transformed it into a basin, and filled it with my blood, then Medica, Sabina and my sisters and my head daughters circle behind my head angels and I then appeared and began speaking as all were bowing, "I welcome my head angels to our new throne today. Bogovi has done great things here, as you have served our servants so very well over the last thirty-three years. My love for you has not changed. I have created my blood spirit to exist with my throne spirit. Any may exist in both spirits, and I now hold the Sword of Justice, which nothing may ever conquer us. Our Empire shall rule forever and ever. Any who desire to be in my blood spirit must first be showered in my blood, which will always be on my throne. Whosoever showers in my blood shall live in me and I live in them, through my Blood Spirit, as my blood holds my spirit. I died that your Empire shall live. I gave my blood so my servants would not have to shed theirs at the hands of evil. I lived in pain so my servants shall not live in pain. I have made many new changes to our Empire so that we may serve our Servants greater since I will be spending much time with Bogovi. My daughters will now assume many additional duties. All my daughters shall be a part of my blood spirit. No human may come to me unless showered in my blood, which is the baptism into my Empire for eternity. Any spirit of mine that wishes to serve Bogovi may do so with my blessing. My daughters will have two new great tasks. They shall be in all my temples and shower my servants who want to be in my blood. All who are baptized in my blood that still are in the flesh shall receive a new flesh suit, one that never hungers, thirsts, or suffers pain. I shall keep the promise I made to my servants. A long life in flesh suits with no torment from their goddess. I shall be their sanctuary; not a torture chamber that sits back and allows evil to destroy them. Any god in this dimension that allows evil to harm their servants shall die by my Sword of Justice. Evil will not coexist with me, it shall not exist beside me or near me or far from me. I am the goddess of the good. My servants who are baptized in my blood shall be mine and I shall be theirs." Then my judges cried, "Oh master will you shower us in your blood so we may serve you better?" I then baptized them in my blood and they were transformed. I then looked among those who were before and saw something I wanted so much. There were two before me, which had to be showered in my blood. I called them forward to stand in front of me. I thenceforth yelled out, "Joy, will you again take my blood and be my sister. Will you release Richard to Bogovi who will shower him with great blessings? On her spiritual knees, Joy cried out, "Take me my sister, and put me before you on my knees that I may give you all my love and only you all my love, for I was in your blood before I met Richard. Your slave in the blood begs her goddess now. I shall release Richard. Richard departed unto Bogovi, showered in Ann's blood." Then Richard vanished. Then the Courts cried out, "Oh great Lilith, how can you let one call you by another name. Does she not truly know you?" I then said to the courts hear you this, "My sisters and daughters are my masters, they can call me anything, as long as we live together in our love. I also have agreed that all male spirits may go to Bogovi as his female spirits may be washed in my blood and serve me for eternity if they so desire. Our borders are no more. This is my new throne. I must thank Bogovi for his help."

This is the new heavenly chart for those who serve the throne in the heavens:

Bogovi, Lilith
Queen Lilith, Holder of the Sword of Justice
Lilith Blood Spirit, Throne Spirit of Lilith,
Intimate Joy's Empire, Enforcer
Lilith Blood Spirit
Intimate Restricted Sanctuary, Heavens for the Righteous,
Intimate Restricted Sanctuary
Sabina, Medica, Sisters, and Daughters, High throne's
sisters (later added)
Heavens for the Righteous
Living, Dead
Living
Daughters of the Temples Blood (new)
Daughters of the Peoples Flesh (new)
Dead
Great Heavens, Spirit Temple of Blood

Throne Spirit of Lilith
Guardian Angel, Saint of Faith, Court Angels of Lilith's
Messages, Aide for Destruction, Aide for Joy and Sorrow,
Judges of Lilith's Court, Courts of Ereshkigal Lights,
Lights of Ereshkigal
Courts of Ereshkigal Lights
Court Angel for Dimensional Travel, Court of Fun & Dance,
Court Angels of the Heaven's Outer Security
Court Angel of the Sky, Court Angels for the Unity of the Heavens
Court Angel of Power, Court Angel for the Dead
Court Angel for that Life Which Does Not Move
Court Angel of the Truth, Court Angel for Destruction
Court Angels of Friendship, Court Angel of the Future
Court Angel of the Holy Messengers, Court Angels of Fire
Court Angels of the Temple, Court of the Healers

Court of Death Angels of the Holy, Court Angel of the
Unholy Dead
Fertility Court Angel, Court Angel of the Family
Court Angel of Divine Wrath, Court Angel for the Righteous
Court Angel of Love, Court Revealer of the Blood That
Has Been Shed
Court Revealer That Seeks Knowledge, Court Revealer of the Light
Court Revealer of the Red Door, Court Angels of Punishment
Court Revealer for Those Who Have Heavy Hearts
Court Revealer of the Spirits, Court Angel of Harvest

I then added, "We are love and we will live in love. Hate, greed, sloth, selfishness will be no more when showered in my blood. My Enforcer shall help you in your quest for love and peace and above all compliance. We shall never stop looking for evil, as its seeds may someday rise. I go now with Joy to my Intimate Restricted Sanctuary where we will reunite her in me. Go ye now and rejoice for your goddess has returned." Then did one court angel ask, "Lilith, oh great and honorable goddess, where is our trinity?" I then answered, "We no longer have a trinity. This is the yearning of Sabina and Medica that they live in the Intimate Restricted Sanctuary and be a part of the sisters and our daughters, for they now are also their mothers in my spirit." Now I took Joy and rushed to my Sanctuary. Upon Arriving, I beheld swarms of my daughters leaving to set up the blood showers in my temples. As I brought Joy into my Sanctuary I had to tell her, "I have so much missed you have avenged your death. I shall welcome you by combining your heavenly wine into the holy river." She then fell before me and gave me her cup. The sisters all watched, eagerly awaiting their turn to enjoy Joy's wine. However, the wait was too long as we had not had any wine ceremonies in a while, thus we formed into seven groups, and the wine started flowing into cups. We could now enjoy the compassion of our rock solid relationships with my former trinity actively involved as Sabina comforts my greatest love Drusilla, and Medica molded into Heidi. They were so happy now by being a part of this special group. They did not like being goddesses. We would all enjoy so much more as my daughters were now serving in divine roles, roles in which they deserve instead of the evil roles the almost destroyed us. Ironically, throughout all my evil roles, I only feared punishment, yet when I became the Lord of so many good, I closed the ultimate living death. Bogovi has his hand over me now, so I have no fears about the evil dimension I escaped. His power was so great that he hid me there on Earth to do my special Penance for the Sword of Justice. Now with my blood all can be protected by my Sword of Justice. The sword demands the blood of the one who was sacrificed. Never be it that the Romans would not take advantage of sacrificing. The sisters and I bonded hard for five days when I heard a voice calling me, "Lilith, it is time to come home." I knew what that meant so I called Bodrogközi to lay in my place. One of my top six will always fill in for me when I go to bow before Bogovi, the god who stole my heart and has held fast to it for so long. I then departed, and to my surprise, my master was coming to take his treasure home. As a good treasure to be captured, I lay myself down on our altar as my entire throne watched. Bogovi gave his sword to one of his commanders, got off his horse and then walked over and looked at me as I lay there for him to capture. He looked at me and said, "Do you surrender that easy?" I said, "Why would I fight the one who stole my heart so long ago?" He then picked me up and gave me a spiritual intimate shocking that rattled every cell in my flesh. I now just lay in his arms a limber as a sheet of paper as he carried me to his horse. My throne shouted with great joy for they also had waited so long to see if indeed the legends were true. Likewise, they were; the great conqueror was taking his prize to their home with such a joyous smile. Then with a whisk did he, his loot, and armies return to Berettyóújfalui, which is Bogovi's throne galaxy. Upon arrival, Bogovi put on one of his flesh suits and welcomed the masses of spirits, which surrounded his new throne. He held my hand as we walked before so many as they shouted for joy. I was now feeling overwhelmed and actually filled with some fear since I had never been here. I could only hold on to Bogovi's hand and sense we were in the flesh

I could feel his compassion for me. We then stood before his wonderful throne, a dream throne as I asked him, "My master, this throne is as if it came from my dreams." Bogovi answered, "My Superior, your Lights gave this vision to me from your spirit. If it is a desire of yours, it is a command over me." I then looked at him with my eyes locked on him and my heart waiting to hear more words from him, "When may I confess my love for you?" Bogovi said, "When I surrender to you." I asked, "How may my master surrender to me?" He said, "I shall show you how. Let me introduce you to your servants." He then walked me across the stage and in the middle, he got down on his knees and said, "Oh great and honorable goddess of all goodness and love, may I surrender to you and be your servant for eternity?" I then dropped to my knees kissing the hell out of this romancer and cried out, "Only if I may be your slave." Then did a spirit of our dimension's throne appear. It was a she; I guess that I am starting to break the "good old boys network?" She is so beautiful with rainbows at her feet and her heart. She has so many power lights rotating around her. I asked her, "What is your name my love?" She then said, "My goddess, and the only one I worship, I am called Bácsalmás. I have been sent by our throne to receive your and Bogovi's oaths and for you to answer prayer of mine." I then said, "Oh precious Bácsalmás, how may I serve you?" She then said, "Many such as I wish to worship you as your servants and live in your spirit. Our throne has approved it, if it is your will. That is why they sent me to receive your oaths. Will you be our only goddess and allow us to shower in your blood?" I then looked at Bogovi who shook his head yes and I answered her, "Do you not know that your throne is so much greater than my little throne? I worry that you shall someday suffer because of your decision." Bácsalmás answered saying, "We only want to worship you, we are willing to take on flesh and suffer great miseries in your namesake if you so desire. You are our heart, you are the one we love and wish to surrender all that we have for you to enjoy." I then said, "How can I turn away such fine cups of wine. You shall be joined in my Intimate Restricted Sanctuary as my High Throne's Sisters. I shall serve you for eternity and after your Shower of Blood shall fill you with my love and shall take your love and bond it in my spirit. You and your spiritual sisters shall be loved in my intimacy and be as great as my sisters and daughters. Send them now to my throne to receive the blood of my sacrifice." Bácsalmás now gave her thanks and ascended before our throne with the grace and power that is from her throne. Bácsalmás said to Bogovi, "Will you surrender all that you have, and all that you are to become a new spirit that shall have in it your Lilith? You are to love and receive her love and defend her from all evils and let her keep her spiritual intimacy in her Intimate Restricted Sanctuary as long as no male spirit enters therein except for you by initiation only. Will you love her more than anything else that you surrender to her?" Bogovi once again sank to his knees and said, "I shall be bound by oath all that you spoke. This is the rock, which I live. I surrendered all, when first meeting her and never attempted to regain myself, forever to be lost to her. Lilith shall be my greatest and only love, a combined river of love we shall share with those who serve us. For I am now dying and wait for my new life to begin as a servant in Lilith." Bácsalmás then looked at me and said, "In all times that you are outside your Intimate Restricted Sanctuary and Holy of Holies will you serve Bogovi as his slave and be bound by his commands and love him with all that you can surrender to him? Will you give up yourself and lay your life before him to be reborn inside of him as one? Will you surrender all to him and love him more than anything else?" I answered, "I shall be bound by oath all that you spoke. This is be the rock, which I live. I surrender all and shall be his slave to do with me, as he so shall command. Bogovi shall be my greatest and only love. For I am now dying and wait for my new life to begin as a servant of Bogovi." Then did a wonderful transformation occur where his love flooded each atom in my spirit as we became united with only a small escape to my Intimate spirit. This felt so good, with no more emptiness! This was actually so much better than having Sabina and Medica in me as we all were searching for the same thing. I finally found what I was searching. I now feel as I have never truly felt before, for I am bound in love and good, as we shall continue to fight all evil and improve the living conditions for our living and our spirits. We shall be a powerful source of good and love, for we are loved. All who were at our throne was accordingly amazed even as spirits none had seen this. This transformation finally ended and we reappeared standing beside each other holding hands. Then Bogovi surprised me with his first command after our unification. He cried out, "All who are here today must be showered in Lilith's blood or depart. What say you?" Besides, they are crying out, "We beg that you flood us with the blood of the great goddess of good." Then did my blood flood them and they did transform yet I did not take them to my throne but kept them in our throne. Bogovi also had his old throne that was still functional. I do plan to visit there sometimes for nostalgic reasons. Even I felt strange with servants of another throne, or our throne being baptized in my blood. I want to be showered in the blood of Bogovi and him to be my master. This is a big change for me, as before I always controlled my lovers. I never want to control him but to support and serve him. Anyhow, yes, he can be on top of me whenever he desires. How can I convince him that I desire to serve him and belong to him? He then asked me if he could take me to a special place he created for our flesh suits. I told him, "My master, you may take your slave anywhere and do anything you so desire, for I beg to be a source of your pleasure." He looked at me and said, "I wish for us to do what humans do after they are bonded. With our flesh exploding as also our spirits exploding us both shall serve each other dreams." I told him, "Just belonging to you is my dreams come true. I am so surprised at my love for you, for it is greater than any I have had before. We arrived on our new planet, which is called Balatonberény. Bogovi told me that this was created as our planet of love and that when we were here the planet would be completely concealed from all. Our privacy was of paramount importance. He must know of the fondness I always had for the Eldom, as I have so often drank the wine of Heidi and Medica's cups. Likewise Moreover, I have lain before them with my wine bottle open giving them my heavenly wine. This time was so different for it has been so long since I have been with a male, I do believe the last time was with one of my humans. Bogovi was so special for I could feel his love and joy in giving me things. I myself wonder, 'What does a goddess give a god?' I then asked him, "Now that I have surrendered myself and most of what I have, only keeping my women, what can I give you that you will want?" He then gave me those milky eyes and told me, "I want only to serve you and share myself with you." I then said, "We are having like humans rather than deity." He told me, "Behaving like humans for is it not the human love that we need to survive so we should behave like humans in our love." I then, while slipping off my white gown, reached over and hugged him kissing him and releasing the words that were exploding inside me, "I love you, will you please overcome me?" He then took my naked body inside a home that was made for loving, nice soft rugs on the floor with candles and a nice fireplace. He told me to keep on my shoes for he did not want my feet to get hurt then his clothing vanished and his wonderful joystick started sliding deep inside me. I now felt on top of the world since I did not only want his family jewel in me as all my heart wanted him inside me. His strong hand held my breasts firm as he slowly went inside me and then out each time fulfilling all my desires. I never knew that being with a man could feel this good. When I was with Samuel, our lord took away his penis as a punishment and we had to rely on serpents going inside me. Oh, but this was so much better than a serpent. Each stoke slowly stretched and then contracted as he went out of me. All I could do was beg. I pleaded that he totally takes from me anything he desired and that he let me enjoy him with me for a long time. He stroked for three joyous days. I guess there is an advantage to being seduced by a god. Besides he controlled our time as did Henrietta and Máriakémend had done in for nighttime world, bringing us back to one second after entering. He totally controlled my complete body as it craved his hands and privates. I was so much embalmed in this god. I will indeed find great joy in worshiping him. I do feel so special. Each touch soaks so much love inside me. I am drowning in his love and I do not want to be saved since I want to feel it flood my lungs as I cross over the line completely filled with his love that will pull be back. As he kisses me he promises, "I shall serve your flesh anyway you desire. If you need our intimacy at any time tell me and we can come to Balatonberény and stop time returned the exact second we left, with all our love juices removed. It is my mission to be your intimate lover, so when you return to your sisters you will not be in need of their intimacy." I looked at him and asked, "You know about our wine drinking?" He said, "I do know and in our bonding vows promised not to take pleasure unto him pleasure and said to him, "I am so lucky to have such an understanding master. Yet I now fear that when I am with them, I will be only desired to rush back her and strip myself and lay my body down for your pleasure." I then gave him a special treat that loving me of great understanding do receive. We have a great relationship and he so understands, I can think of nothing to hide from him. I then as he blasted my mouth, since gods can recharge so fast, with his seed asked him, "Is there anything that I have hidden from you? I wish for you to scan my spirits as I will give you complete access for I want no secrets from you." He did scan my spirits and said in a joking, "My, you have been with fewer men in your millions of years than most of your holy ones, yet they have rejected enough Heavenly wine to overflow this planet." He then started laughing and swinging me. I so much enjoyed the way my naked body flowed into his arms. He is the haven of forgiveness. He then said, "If I had known you had blasted the throne of Earth, I would not have sent you there. Fortune is truly on your side as you paid your Penance in the absolute dangerous place you could have." I then said to him, "I am your love slave my master as my heart cries so hard to love you endlessly. Love things never made it reason to choose you. I cannot live with the pain of not belonging to you in the name of our love. Loving me first is the happiness of my soul, as we share eternity together as one in two, as I am your slave of early morning until we begin again on the next morning. I shall claim this woman shall do all that you desire. This is what love conscripted me. Tough it was love that defeated me, and made me a slave of love for you. I have always searched for the, what was to me, fantasy of this so-called love, that remained my unknown love. I find myself to be a stranger in own empire with my culture altered. Love can see easily make you beg be a slave of another. Of it is gentle, understanding, it shares, it lets you grown up forgetting all before it. Loved things, lovely things, nice to your heart are passed away along with the hidden emptiness and secret loneliness. Nevertheless, choosing to give self to your love because of the things you have are no longer wanted. Accordingly as long that one is capable of providing; we unite to fight no more, yet wave our white flags. Together we can reach the stars above far beyond our free birds. Still, we are not interested in the things of achievements laying our thrones at each other's feet. Forever looking the door, put all that was important in there, and casting the key aside. Nevertheless love the things that can educate my soul, learning freedom is but another word for nothing more to lose. Believing love is own to possess, no other can steal this, not even the love surrendered by others. Yet I am so happy to point at me and declare myself a servant to another and belonging to another even though I had fought so hard to be a slave of misery with the blood that flowed without the bonding of true love. I am so truly a stranger in my own land and can only see myself the slave of Bogovi's love, where just a whisper can have me begging for another command. I do not belong to my former self, since I killed it. Nonetheless, this love will render pains yet also provide the cure. I truly believed love was more than making love. However, true lovemaking is accepting the love given from another and surrendering your love, you make to the other. I so much never want freedom again. Please my Bogovi, bind me by your chains, and never free me for I belong to us. We now walked around the beauty that encompasses Balatonberény and started talking about how we can best care for our servants. We are now uniting the saints in a new heaven, much larger than three of our galaxies were. Since this is a spiritual haven, we have placed in the center of our most secure galaxies. We have sealed it and creating self-energizing heat and light spiritual world stars, which will maintain a perfect consistent temperature and constant light, as spirits of good do not need darkness and love conquers all things. Bogovi also told me that he was happier than ever before. I could feel that he had bonded with me and that he so much wanted me by his side. I had to know how he made such a beautiful planet. We were now around one hundred feet off the ground taking a tour. He told me that he came here a lot during our separation and that it hurt so hard when I was taken away from him and actually to be the one acknowledged as my savior was. He confessed to me that he had nothing to do with it, and was only given a few opportunities to speak with me, not knowing if the message would reach me. To have everything yanked from you was as if razors were cutting you into pieces. I told him his memories were blocked from me for so many years and these memories were replaced by emptiness. I was actually reborn as an infant in a body that required matter is put in and matter be expelled. I was put in this newborn with no memories of my past. Yet I have learned how to bond and depend upon others and the others here were my parents who stood up tall and strong. They knew my heart and my mind. That was strange, yet later became wonderful. Even now, I cannot fully explain the beauty of it; however, I can tell you that it even now requires that I surrender to you and melt in your arms. I can truly give my heart to you and let it live in you as if it were living in me. You must decide all that we do, since I am along for the ride at your side. He then said, "I must be sure to keep our car on the correct road." He then showed me another surprise. This male is something else, even after he gets what he wants served to him on a silver platter he keeps on giving. We were now in the middle of one of our oceans with one of the close moons orbiting beside us casting its warm romantic light upon us. He once again made his move and found me still to be as putty in his hands to use as he wished. It is not nice to be in complete surrender trusting that your master will fill you with his love. Just lying there while he drops one pleasure bomb after another understanding how this flesh was designed to function and knowing that he has all the keys to unlock any door and they permitted to enter any room. We enjoyed fine dinners, already prepared of course, with so many warm candles and campaigns created in the furthest corners of our empire, actually I want it to be his empire since he a man that deserves that title. He came in on his knees and walked out with holding on his legs begging to surrender more. This is so wonderful. I now belong to him. I want to belong to him. I will beg each day to be his servant. The great Lilith finally was laid. No more dominating, although enjoying the peace of being dominated was a giant leap forward. From the sounds of his tender voice to the charming fragrance, that drives me feral. I will never endeavor to get him out of her head. His presence lightens my day with instant sparks led me to stay. Bogovi's compassionate eyes held no lies, which penetrated through my soul testifying to me that he truly cares. Those eyes keep no secrets and are like an open book telling a tale of our young love. His masculine arms hold me with ease while so easily keeping me away from any harm. The knowing that I can run into his loving arms shows how much he in fact cares. Oh, how wish to harbor in his arms and release my tears as the run down our bodies. His response will always calm and polite "Everything's going to be okay." He is simple and sweet knowing all the right things to say while speaking the words that warm my heart. Hearing his name spoken among our great thrones, sounds like beautiful poetry, as I always became lost in his nurturing eyes. Showing me his feelings are true, as I now finally realize I am experiencing a crazy thing called love that had eluded me all my days as all attempts to find it when their various ways. Love found me and shall no longer escape this crazy, joyful, and rewarding thing called love. After joyfully traveling Balatonberény, for two months enjoying so many numerous stops are final day had come. As Bogovi returned us to the second we left our time he now prepared to show me our Empire. I was completely flabbergasted when he told me our Empire ruled over 1,000 galaxies in our universe and had alliances with another 1,000 not annexing them until he could effectively manage them. I then looked at him and said, "Why would you share this with me? You could have given me three galaxies, then conquered them and taken me as your slave." He looked at me with his tender eyes and said, "I would prefer to have one with you rather than thousands without you." That was another arrow, which went through my heart, setting it on fire. I then asked him, "My lover, will you stop time and seduce my soul for a couple of days?" He then jokingly told me, "Sorry, unless you command me to, I fear that you will quickly grow disenchanted with me." I then told him as I wrapped both my arms around his big muscles, "Will you promise to lay me any time you feel the urge?" He shook his head up and down with a grin of a child that just got permission to open the cookie jar. I can only imagine that a thousand galaxies would me mean billions of planets. I asked him, "How did you conquer this?" He said, "I always lead my soldiers into battle in the name of Lilith, let us bring Lilith home." I then replied, "I owe these soldiers so much." Bogovi updated my statement by saying, "We owe these soldiers so much." Then we again kissed. How shameful, to be the king and queen of billions of planets and asking like children who kissed the first time. I then became aware that we had to have the love of a child in order to rule our empire in the name of love and good. It is as good gets older it turns to worse. This is sad, nevertheless too close to the truth. We had to stay as youngsters and burn the fire of the love in our hearts to heat our Empire. I think that can be arranged. As we entered, again to stand before our courts as these courts were dedicated to each of us as one, as we both still had our original spirits and courts. After all, someone has to do the work while he is enjoying all the fruit I can give, nothing holding back. Our courts looked at us strangely as a new glow emitted from us. Our halos were united as he stood strongly behind me with both his arms embracing me. Then the chief guardian angel blew his trumpet and cried out, "Empire, behold the King and Queen." I guess this stream was broadcast to all of our billions of planets so all could see. I so envied Faith when she was crowned Queen of England, yet today was my day. I was glad that Bogovi did not set up many ceremonies since I over did it on the ceremony side back at my old throne. It felt so good standing in his arms before our servants knowing we had abided by the same rules we wished that they did. We could stand with honor and dignity. My temples were a favorite place for my servants to marry and eventually we had to build extra "marry only" halls onto our temples. I wonder now how they are keeping up with the showers of blood ceremonies. Bogovi has been receiving male spirits from me, however not many wanted to leave. The opposite is true on the female side as so many are leaving that we had to stop the immigration. We decided to build a "husband and wife" gigantic heaven and this way we will pull all couples in there and allow other married couples that have been separated to join. A married couple can agree not to spend eternity together, as many do, especially those who had multiple husbands, however females go to me, and the males go to Bogovi. Joy and Faith are the only married women who have no choice. Those wine cups belong to me . . . Sisters I share not. I do not want to speak to anyone around this throne, not for anger but to show total submissiveness to my master. I thus left up my head and swing it back as he lowers his ear, and I give him my input. No matter how he answers, I will show our unity. Many times, he flexes his muscles telling me he wants to talk to me. He likes my input on many things and does get mad if I behave like a 'yes girl.' He tells me that he married a goddess not a mortal. He does not want one of us to choke out the other. If we do not go down the wrong road then we would not have to work so hard to find the root of the right road. So, I tell him how I truly feel and ask him to get to the decision he feels best with telling him he is also my idol. I am hence amazed as to how our throne is now equipped to rule so many galaxies. To leave with Ereshkigal, which was within itself a tremendous battle with evil gripped in for the long haul and having to be pulled out one nail at a time, and the promise of two more, five more if married was within itself overwhelming. When a battle rages hard, evil will run away. This is the fear that I told Bogovi I had that evil just simply collapsed into a black hole to return another day. He assured me that was not the case. The massive storage pits of such advanced cultures added to the creation of better faster tools to destroy evil. Any evil that Ereshkigal found, it destroyed. I told him, I had little concern about Ereshkigal but the other 999 galaxies. He then held me firmly and told me that our new Empire was also named Ereshkigal, the place where he was conquered by a female goddess. I lost control of myself and immediately swung my entire body around and wrapped my legs around his waist and started kissing his face everywhere. Our throne now cheered with such a joyous sound that roared and roared as so many millions of angels and spirits were rushing to see their divine couple kissing. As all knew, a male god can control his emotions; however, the true emotions of a goddess will be revealed in front of all. This was the case, he was mine before he was theirs and I was his number one servant. They had to stand in line behind me. The throne was so excited, because with their gods united, the prospect of good reigning was increased by a magnitude. Bogovi offered the other gods their galaxies, yet they chose instead to divide into large sections and administer their district as servants to the Ereshkigal throne. This gave them more assurance against evil and actually only added one more visible layer in their chain of command, plus the advantage of having more galaxies to aid quickly. Bogovi now took his war booty to another new part of the throne, the Hall of the Gods. This also was on a mysterious planet where no flesh could ever touch. Its surface lay under 500 miles of burning gasses with only a secret portal in for the gods. I approached this humongous temple made of pure gold with a throne stage in a room that was ten cubic miles with rainbows from the surface reaching their climax at the doors of this temple. What an amazing sight. Within an instant, the gods and a few goddesses arrived. Bogovi walked me down the red lane that was only for us. He led me up to the stage and wrapped his arms around me as once again I melted and started kissing his hands. He told the council, "Ereshkigal, behold your king and queen." Then did they all bow down and started worshiping us. I asked Bogovi, "Why do they worship us?" He told me, "Because of the great things we have done for them. We earned their ultimate respect." He now told the council, "Hear ye the words of your Queen, Lilith." I was stunned, how could he put me on the spot like this, yet he told me 'in mind talk' "Fear not for I will help you." I then spoke to them saying, "I am so sorry for being gone for so many years, yet the ultimate heavens demanded a penance for my Sword of Justice. Good must be purified by the blood and sacrifice to conquer evil. I have given my blood so that we all may live free from evil. I also have laid at the feet of Bogovi begging to be his slave and him be my master. He instead took my love and gave back one hundred fold. Our spirits are strong and shall give you all things we promised. You now are part of the great Empire of Good ever to exist. Evil no longer has a safe home for we continue to hunt down evil and destroy it, for as long as one servant suffers from evil, we will never stop, we will never grow week and we will never coexist beside evil. This sword shall fight hard to keep evil away from our Empire and to give you and your servants the good they have been promised by me, for me thank you and worship you for helping me give you the riches you have earned. I belong to you and I challenge any to come to my throne and demand I worship them, for that I will do. You give me the ability to fight evil, and I cannot exist without you. I also have another great special request. I search for this race, the Harvey (I showed them the video stream) so that my sister Siusan may take on flesh and live a life among them. I desire that all my sisters take on flesh and die in our dimension, so they can cross over into the spirit world from within and never be bound to another dimension, a fear for me, with only Bogovi's love is pulling me into our Empire. I shall also request that you each screen my sisters as I have granted each of your access. I truly wish to place all of them in good worlds, so they can marry and give their children in marriage. This does also include Medica and Sabina. Please help me give our sisters a better planet to live in." I now walked in front of Bogovi and fell to my knees worshipping them crying, "I pray that you will help me rule your Empire and let me help you. I pray that you will stand by me, and punish me if I do any evil. I do so much love each of you." The council of the gods was shocked. Never had they heard a speech like this. The greatest empress who had the greatest weapon that was the most powerful in all the dimensions was now before them, her servants preying on them. All rose and sank to their knees crying aloud, "Our goddess is Queen Lilith and we shall serve her and Bogovi with all we have. We swear to surrender all to our throne." Bogovi did not even expect this and whispered in my ear, "I should have known, you would conquer them also. I am only glad that I became your slave first." The power of their prayers shook the entire galaxy that we were. Bogovi then cried out, "Behold the one I worship, the honorable Queen of Ereshkigal, holder of the Sword of Justice." They cheered for three weeks, as Bogovi had to pull us back in one second after their arrival. The Empire would be in danger with so many gods out of thrones. As we went to leave the six goddesses came up to my altar and begged if they could have a private audience with me. Bogovi just shook his head and said, "Another one of those women things, go and care for your servants even as they are goddesses. As we went into the private chamber, they fell to their knees and began, "Oh monumental Queen, we wish to serve you with our souls and bodies and become a part of your Intimate Restricted Sanctuary and also serve and worship your sisters and daughters and the thrones angel." I had to ask them, "Why do you want to be in my Intimate Restricted Sanctuary, which is not as pronounced as your heavens?" They then replied, "For we have not the ability to love you with our intimacy." I was somewhat puzzled and asked, "Is not all our love with intimacy?" They agreed yet added, "We want to be your slaves that you may own us and we dedicate ourselves to you." I then asked them, "Do you know that my Intimate Restricted Sanctuary is my private sanctuary and that once you go in you may never leave. Also, if I tell you anything about it and you repeat it to one who is not a member you will perish." They answered, "We will serve you, and only you in any way you wish." I asked them, "Will you wear the flesh suits we wear and live in nudity at all times in the Sanctuary?" They said, "That we will so that you may receive joy from what you have created for us." I then told them, "Those who are in my Sanctuary must share their heavenly wine with me and also drink from my cup. Do you agree and submit?" They all swore their submission. I then added, "If you are in my sanctuary I will be your servant and serve you. Love demands that the greatest in a group bound by love must be the servant to those she loves. Will you submit to me being your servant?" They did submit. I then apologized for not knowing their names and ask that they give me their names, I am your slave Bárdudvarnok, I am your slave Tamási, I am your slave Békéscsaba, I am your slave Ceglédbercel, I am your slave Dédestapolcsány, I am your slave Jakabszállás. They all remained on the floor bowing to me. I then joked with them, "With so many gods being slaves, wonder how are slaves introduce themselves?" I laughed alone, especially since we had no slaves in my Empire and these girls were surrendering their hearts. I could now feel that hope that they were barely hanging on to, so I then asked them to stand. I now fell down on my knees before them and kissed each of their feet. When I was finished, I asked them, "Do not I get a hug from my new sisters?" They all swarmed canoodling me everywhere. After a few minutes, I said to them, "My new loves make sure you save enough of me for my master, lest he be angry." They all continued to hug me and laughed with joy. Join me on our stage as I stream back my command to my courts, yet first let me ask my master so he will feel like he is a part of this. I told them, "It is time to play good little humble innocent girl." I then had them follow me laughing not looking sad and soft. I then said to my master who was receiving praise for giving our empire such a great queen. I then asked two boys if I could have a small audience with my master. They readily agreed, as Bogovi has to walk away with me with his pride intact. He so much deserves that from me. If I am his prize then I want to be his prize. Males must hold onto their pride for without it they will stumble and the one that stands beside them must understand this. I then asked Bogovi, "Master may I have these six goddesses for my play house?" He then laughed and said, "I shall never understand you women, why would six of my only goddesses want to hide in your sanctuary?" I told him, "The same as Sabina and Medica, the fear of not having such a strong master such as I have. Life is not the same for us. We must have our other half to be strong?" He then asked, "How were you so strong?" I told him, "I had Sabina and Medica plus so many daughters."

Bogovi then looked at their sad and humble faces then replied, "No male could ever turn down such humble females, except for one who has been the victim of their anger. If it is their will, you may have six more toys for your sanctuary." I then thanked him and jumped in his arms wrapping my legs around him and kissing him nonstop. All our gods and my six goddesses gave us a standing ovation as I slowly fell to his knees. He lifted me up and said, "My dear that which you must do, do quickly so that others may enjoy the richness of your audience." I then ran back to my new wine cups and told them; follow me to the stream chamber. This chamber had been set up in case emergencies were to occur in our universe. As we rushed in, I spoke, "My courts, your Queen Lilith, Holder of the Sword of Justice calls for your attendance." They responded and I gave them my command, "I now command that once they have given their galaxies to a new god, they serve in my Intimate Restricted Sanctuary. These are my new personal sisters, "Bárdudvarnok, Tamási, Békéscsaba, Cegléanbercel, Dédestapolcsány, and Jakabszállás. This is the command from your Queen." I then told them to return to their galaxies and submit nominees to my courts, once they approve or select another, and your throne is ruled you may come to my throne and the courts will give you entry. I shall send this stream to my sisters. Go to prepare you wine for me. I then rushed back to stand in my master's arms as all were introduced to me. Somehow, they all just clicked with me. I felt so natural talking with them. So many marveled at how the six very strong goddesses in our Empire are now my personal servants. I then reminded them that they came to me so I could serve them and I so much want to serve them. They are now my sisters and soon shall be showered in my blood, having also once existed in the flesh for their throne. I also told all, "We can make our Empire the home of the good and the death sentence to evil. We must never stop fighting for somewhere out there is a good soul that is being tormented by evil, such as was on Earth that is no more. United we stand and fall. None shall fall without us with them fighting. "Glory is to Bogovi, the King of all Good." This time I fell into his mighty arms and cried on his breast as he petted my hair. The throne was now on a solid unification road, even though Bogovi had it under his control. I guess the big thing is a unified bonded King and Queen always creates the shield of security no matter if it is on a small island in a small planet belonging to a dwarf galaxy or such as us with 2,000 large galaxies wanting to be a part of our giant empire. Whatever it is I am now among 1,000 or more, gods and they are dedicating themselves and declaring me their Queen. No matter what Bogovi and I declare unless, they give their allegiance our Empire is a house with broken walls. Allegiance given always overrules allegiance conquered or taken. It is our will, that we protect and serve our family of good and that we shall do, as all know that they may secede at their will and keep all we gave them and still be in alliance if they so will. That is what makes an Empire strong that all belong because of wanting to belong. Each must also be appreciated, as I so know the pains of not being appreciated as was I when Lords of New Venus. It is a real pain and fills the soul with hate and revenge, the seeds of evil. I once ran endlessly through a buffet of what life has to offer, yelling, screaming, kicking, pleading because we do not get what we want, anytime is fine, unless the time's is right now, never was able to get the master I wanted, we know that's not allowed. Making sisters out of what no one would take a chance on. Anything will do right now under the right circumstance while teetering towards a heavily weighted decision. This is what causes the opposing forces into unification. We knew what many felt should happen, but Bogovi also knew what was in his heart. Entering this mode of thinking, he felt, "This is why they all thought this way right from the start." "Winning" could bring about closure, but it could also bring proper exposure. We were jumping for joy because all our thrones were on the same page. Every single god was an actor on eternity's stage. Never mind what had made them different before, King and Queen we now all, with only the whole universe to explore (and beyond) ours forever more. Insight made everything feel right and all the gods now did bond. Nights and days, rang out cheers and praise for all and the stars within, seeing to be true what was always seeking, the utopia of love. I cannot imagine a love greater than ours, and an

Empire so filled with personal joy to live atop and see a storm of love falling on them. We were now beginning our road to happiness and more battles with a weakened evil scarcely available. Lilith has come home lying in submission while my master strives so hard to give me all that I hint at wanting. It is so easy to receive from one who is offering to give and more important to give, without even the hint of wanting to receive to one whose heart and soul carry our love. This is without a doubt a crazy thing called love and I care not about the foolishness in which I now behave. I want to be as week as I can be so my master will do with me what he so desires, for it, my master desires it then so do I. I know the weaker I appear to myself, the stronger my master and I look to others. United and bonded in the quest for happiness and life ruled by good for all whom we serve. This thing called love does talk in circles because those, which love throws into its pit can see neither the beginning nor the end.

Chapter 03

Planting Siusan and Evil's Strike

As Bogovi and I were relaxing in our new Holy of Holies around this magnificent throne with over one million angles with their courts buzzing in and out as our spirits gave them what they were in search of to keep the wheels rolling for this heavy wagon. Bogovi is one who enjoys nature and wildlife, which is tamed of course. After all, no one really wants to see lions walking around with human parts falling out of their mouth. My master had another gift to shower upon his favorite little humble servant and as the courts brought this beautiful creature out for me to see my heart stopped beating. I asked him, "Where did you find this fine creature at?" Bogovi answered, "That does not matter, what matters is he is yours." I was so excited that the next thing I knew was that my bare body was trotting along in fine style with my new horse. He took off for me very fast as we; both enjoyed each other's company. A smooth warm coat oozed against my legs, as if meant to be my clothing, a familiar, inviting smell with a soft shoulder to rest, body, and head on, and in the mist, inviting sweet smell. A smell that is like no other filled with the speed greater than a lion and yet so gentle passing through the air like a dove. An undying service for which, they choose to give judgment free love chained by loyalty and the truest of friendships. They surrender their speed and spirit so their master can race through nature as a king or queen. An unbreakable bond in addition to an unspoken promise coupled with unbearable sacrifice by sharing their master with other smaller and weaker humans. They bear such gifts as the indescribable feelings of flying without wings, a hug that can ward off the darkest of storms climaxed by a carrot being muzzled from your hand by velvet lips. The power of a wholehearted gallop creating smiles and laughter brought on by unmatchable memories. The thrill of meeting the goals of personal conquests condensing into the moment of connection when you stop being two and start being one, a half beast and half human. Moments of sheer uncontainable bliss, moments in which you want to live forever as these are always the joys of my horses. Some events defy logic. All horses defy my logic, something about these beasts charge me. I feel that charge releasing me in my servants. Notwithstanding I now told Bogovi, "I shall now be both hearts a sad heart some times, for I have 'Spirit' here and my two white horses in Ereshkigal. No matter where I go, one shall be without me and the other(s) without me." I then wanted to know why this horse was black, since all the horses, the Bogovi and his warriors rode were white. The answer was so that all could see which one was the queen or 'master' in the group. All I could think was 'silly master.' He was so creative like a taste of heaven in everything. As he rode beside me on his white horse it felt as if night and day, the opposites uniting. We are now trotting down a stream with shallow banks and a mountain valley inviting us to go forward challenging us to top it. I fear not the snow for Bogovi will keep me warm. I fear not the water, for he will put life back at me. I fear not danger for he will save me. I can hide under his feet as he walks, for he will not walk over me but stop and pull me up tight with his arms pressing me to share his heart. I can give him a knife and beg him to kill me and he will steal the knife from me and beg me to live. The list can go endlessly. I now ask him, "Why do we spend so much time in the flesh?" He told me, "So time will go slower and we can touch and feel the same togetherness. Our spirits explode inside with our flesh keeping them stable and strong." Somehow, I could understand the love in that reason. We do not desire to spend all of our time in gigantic gold mansions. We want to sleep under the stars, or sometimes in the clouds free and open. Oh, how silly we are. We know everything about each other yet some parts need to talk to heal the wounds. Everyone is hurt at one time or another. Not all pain is caused by evil. The interactions of so many different variables will accidently trigger a bond that later things pull apart. Such is the physical realm. This place is so unbelievable. So much endless beauty fills this wonderful planet. Bogovi always likes planets because they are easier to protect and are not flat. I now asked him, "What is the name of this place?" He told me, "Birkerød which is our holy of holies." I now asked him, "Can I create some of my Seonji and bring here to care for this Birkerød?" He declined the offer saying, "I have created a spirit that is made from both of us that cares for all that is here. When we are here, we shall be alone." I asked him, "If you are not here, can I bring my sisters?" He said, "Do as you wish and please have them go when I return." I looked at my master and said, "Oh yes absolutely, for I will not share you." I then thought what a stupid question that was, because it may be a long time before I visit with my sisters, although I hope to start planting them for their lives to begin and thus wait for their sacrificial return. Luckily, they would not be required to die a painful death and they would not, for my spirit will be protecting them with them all the days of their lives. I know there is much work to do, and that I must get started on it. I eagerly await any news about the Harvey. I know they came to New Venus from Earth's universe so there should be a similar version in my dimension. Thus far, our Empire has come up empty. I thought for sure we would have something. How can a species be so rare unless most died out long ago yet I cannot accept that since they are identical internally as humans so if we made it they should have made it also. I now received a message from one of our courts suggesting that we enlist the help of our alliance galaxies. That would give me another 1000 + (and increasing constantly galaxies) so I readily agreed and commanded that they begin the negotiations and search immediately. One by one, they started to turn up empty and finally the final report came in. Not the 'we found a colony report' but the 'none discovered report.' At least I had my master beside me who worked hard to keep my disappointment in check. It was not the end of my life. I should be so thankful to have my 'blue' Siusan. She was such a great blessing and won the hearts of all my sisters, especially Sabina and Medica who remember the legends how they were erased from the sister's tribes. That was another time and place, without them, I would have no Medica, and Sabina, thus something good did come out of such a bad thing. I guess she will have to be recreated in the choice she desires. I will have to start looking at the options I have available. We rested alongside one of our oceans; Bogovi loves the oceans, as do I, as the cool morning light fills the blue sky we behold a rainbow. Bogovi tells me, "My love, I did not put rainbows in our program because there is to be no rain while we are here unless desired. I need to ask my spirit why we have a rainbow in our sky." I told him it did not really matter because a few surprises add some adventure in our lives; however, he places a great emphasis on obedience, which he claims creates a safe and secure empire. "When things do not work as they are made then they need fixing" are the words that flowed from his mouth. He walked down the beach from me and I saw some spirits join him, and afterwards he ran back. He told me, "My precious gift from the heavens, you may receive some good news today, for soon we shall have a guest from one of our galaxies, "the god Tarrós wishes to give us some new information he has." I then told him, "Have him appear when you desire my master." Then Tarrós appeared before us and bowed to his knees with his royal robe on. Bogovi required them to be in royal clothing when they were in our holy of holies. Tarrós began by saying, "Oh great god Bogovi and goddess Lilith, holder of the Sword of Justice I have news for you today. One of my servants returned to his home planet after being on a voyage in one of our neighboring alliance galaxies with a long time trading partner. This trading partner told him of a planet where the people are blue and have legends about ancient travels to other dimensions. They live on a planet called Sásdi, which is also the name of their solar system in the galaxy of Balatonföldvári. Their god is called Tápiószolos, who has fought in many battles with and for our King Bogovi." I sprang up from my master's arms, gave Tarrós a big hug, and asked Bogovi, "My master, how can we talk to Tápiószolos." Bogovi then told me, "I shall have our spirits arrange it. We need to go back to our throne now and let you meet everyone." I asked, "Master, will we be in spirit or flesh?" Bogovi said, "In the flesh so all can see the wonderful gift I have received." He then looked at Tarrós and said, "We thank you for your great news and for taking time to share it with us." We then shot through space arriving at our throne surprising so many. As we arrived, our courts briefed us that Tápiószolos had verified the blue people and would love to host us for a verification visit. I then asked Siusan to be brought to me as soon as possible. Then within a few hours my little bundle of blue joy appeared before me on her knees crying out, "Oh great Queen Lilith, holder of the Sword of Justice, how can your servant serve and worship our pure and filled with good goddess?" I looked at her and said, "Siusan, it is I your sister of blood and love, serve me with your love, now get up here, and sit on my lap with me on our throne." She rushed to me and melted in my lap as we hugged, cried, and kissed while exchanging our salutations. I then, while holding her tight as if I were her mother and guardian, introduced her to my master. He then replied very warmly, "I can see now why my master is filled with so much love." Siusan looked at him and said, "I love my sister more than my life and will suffer anything and all things to protect her and even for her pleasure. Her pleasure is so much more important to me." Bogovi then walked over and kissed her cheek saying, "I will worry about her pleasure, you just keep that love flowing in her heart, ok my sister." Those really made me feel good now in that my master had accepted them as also his sisters. I thanked him saying, "Oh praise my master for allowing our sisters to be a part of our family." He looked at me and said, "A god would be a fool to pass up some wonderful beauty that apparently runs strong in your family. Siusan, it is a pleasure to finally meet a Harvey that she adores so much." I knew now just to keep quiet because it is impossible to overpraise him and it is so fun allowing him to get the last word. We now proceeded to our physical throne room. Bogovi likes physical because it is easier to concentrate and easier to control those appearing before it and how they depart. He asserts that the human quality of it allows for more justice as spirits are so often bombarded by so many external interferences. We must have looked strange today because my master sat in one chair and I forced my sister to sit on my lap with me. This actually puts many off-guard as they actually could now see Siusan as no recorded history documented a blue species so close to human. She sent a few running out by growing like a lion to them. I was afraid that Bogovi might get mad, however he laughed with the both of us. All were briefed about Siusan when they entered, yet the seeing part through them a curve. To walk in and see the new Queen with two heads, one blue, one white and four legs and arms would ponder anyone. I was sad that I had to do this and told my master that I cannot let her loose. I requested that we retire from the throne seats and wait for him in our waiting room. He requested that we stay with him saying, "Families must stick together." Siusan told me that the sisters missed me so much and so much wanted to visit. I told her that I soon would be collecting their lives, and would plant the seeds within. She marveled at our new throne claiming that she thought nothing could be better than Ereshkigal. I also thought the same thing until I arrived here. Bogovi was wise to make a new one for us, since our old ones would trap us with so many old movies. Siusan told me that Queen Mother of Ereshkigal Queen Клеопатра and her daughters Queen Dceralásky and Princess Maharashtra all send their prayers to serve you. I then said, "Queen Mother of Ereshkigal Queen Клеопатра?" Bogovi told me, "Your courts requested it citing the wonderful relationship she now had served her daughters." I thought about it and then said, "Absolutely, for she is now much more worthy than her first appointment." Siusan then told me that Sabina, Faith, and Drusilla were so fond of them and often spend much time with them in their mansions. I told Siusan I could understand why. Siusan then told me, "I am amazed at how great they serve Princess Maharashtra and her undivided loyalty to them." I then also agreed saying, "That was indeed a mighty wedding and great day in my throne." As we were now finishing our business for now, Bogovi told us, "It is time to Balatonföldvári." Siusan asked, "What is in Balatonföldvári?" I told her, "My love, it is a surprise we have for you. Let us follow my master." Siusan then asked, "How can you both be the master, for which is the servant?" We both answered as fast as we could, "I am." Siusan just shook her head and said, "Oh you silly love birds" and laughed. I then asked her, "Would you not want to be a love bird?" She answered, "Oh so much yet who would want a Harvey?" I told her, "We will have to work on that." She now lay beside me as we raced through our empire in one of our royal flash ships. Her eyes always melted me as she would lay there looking off into another world and time. Something is missing in my precious little bundle of love and I so much hope I can get her into a newborn's body and let her live a life with her people and spread her seed into their blood, then come back and live with me for eternity. The thing I really enjoy is the softness of her skin and the way it should pleasure sensations into my soul. No other has her soft touch and I will eagerly wait to touch it again after our night in this flash ship. We have a good plan, she is to start crying, and I will take her into one of the ships vacant rooms and we both shall drink some wine. I cannot survive maybe eighty years without my Harvey wine. I do of course have an option to sneak over every couple of years. Our bonding memories in Buckingham will ring in me throughout our universe for eternity and on for they all return from their lives they each will be given a very divine position as soon as I work the details out with my master who now is yelling that we are entering into Balatonföldvári's area. I fail to believe that this is one galaxy. Bogovi assures me, "This is one galaxy, it has many new stars forming and that it contains over 450,000 solar systems. All galaxies way out here are extremely large. The yellow cluster to our top left is the center of this galaxy and the throne of Tápiószolos since he wants to be a shining light in the empire of the good." I asked him, "Oh master, I do not recall hearing that name at our meeting with the heroes in our Empire." Bogovi told me that this galaxy is one of our allies and we will be allowing them to enter our empire until we have things running smooth." As we approached, the space of Tápiószolos one million high-speed powerful warships escorted us. I asked Bogovi, "Why are we escorted by so many ships?" He told me, "My love, Tápiószolos is still dangerously close to evil and our host will take no chances with your safety." Then Siusan gave me one more thrill as she looked out her window saying her famous words, "Wow" at which time I rolled on the floor laughing so hard that Bogovi feared I might be hurt the in flesh suit I wore. He asked me, "Does she say that often?" I told him, "She only says it when I least expect it as I was rubbing her hair and kissing the top of her head." Bogovi once again shook his head and said, "One would think with Quadrillions of females serving me, I would be able to understand them, however that being so wrong. I only know that to live without them is sad and to live with them is confusing. Not much hope for us weaker members in this dilemma." We both walked over to him and started kissing and wrestling him. He begged us for mercy, yet Siusan told him, "You do not sound sincere" and started to tickle him again as I jumped right in there with her. He then gave us both a hug, kisses, and told us, "It has been so long since I had a family, I do believe having fourteen sisters will bring some good times. I wonder what our hosts think about their big King being conquered by two females." Siusan told him, "They will envy that it took two of us to get you down." Bogovi shook his head and looked at me saying, "I hope the entire Harvey do not have her powerful wisdom or we all could be in deep trouble." As we landed in our dock and the doors opened, I looked out and saw some strange looking people. Behind them was a giant that stood twice the height of his comrades. I asked Bogovi whom the tall one was and he told me that is Tápiószolos. Bogovi put his royal robe on and I asked him if Siusan and I could remain undressed. He gave us permission. I told him it gives me the edge in my dealings as Siusan carried my Sword of Justice for me. As we went to meet our hosts, he explained the escort was required because of evil activity in his neighboring galaxy. I asked Bogovi if I could have Siusan join me and destroy them. He looked at Tápiószolos and said, "Can you spare a few to take her to the danger?" He then refused saying, "We have waited too long to have a queen thus how can I put her in a battle that even I fear?" I looked at him and said, "There is no evil stronger than me." He then said, "If it is the kings will." Soon we were on a small ship with two female crewmembers surrounded by 1,000 warships. We soon departed from Balatonföldvári at which time I ordered the other ships to stay back and told them I was serious. They did as I ordered considering that I was, indeed divinity. My two-crew girls became scared as we headed to a violent yellow red and blue chaos. I was at first taken back by this, yet kept my cool disposition as my sister was drinking my wine. The two-crew girls at first were uneasy when they saw this however grew relaxed because Siusan and I were so much at ease. Then we heard a large voice speak to us as a hand was trying to squeeze us. I immediately destroyed the hand and set up a barrier so no one could escape. I then yelled out with my divine voice, "Who is the fool that speaks to me?" The voice pounded back as I took each pound and thrashed it back. The voices now replied, "We are Athabaskan, the Empire of Evil, and who dare enter without worshiping us." I then transitioned back into my spirit and answered back with a thunder that shattered all the evil spirits, "I am Queen Lilith, and I have come to destroy you." They then answered, "How can you be foolish enough to think you can destroy us when Bogovi and Tápiószolos cannot destroy us?" I looked at them and took a spiritual form of a woman. They all laughed when they saw me and said, "We shall capture you for a great reward shall be ours." I then started laughing, pulled out my sword, and said, "In the name of my sword, the Sword of Justice I destroy all evil that is in this galaxy and all who belong to your evil empire." Instantaneously the space was calm and reflected stars behind them. The chaos was gone. All evil in that galaxy was no more. I then spoke to the people on all planets with a vision in their skies, "My children of good today is a great day in your journey to be free of evil, for I am Queen Lilith, holder of the Sword of Justice and evil is no more in your worlds. Go now and share your love and goodness with all your people. I shall return someday to give you my spirit and salvation." I could see bright lights exploding all through this galaxy so I returned to my flesh suit in our small ship. I then told my crew, "I believe it is time for us to return to Balatonföldvári." The two crew girls asked me, "Oh great goddess of god may we serve you in your Intimate Restricted Sanctuary for you are the greatest goddess ever and me now wish to live serving you. We hope you do not become angry at Siusan for telling us of your great love and Sanctuary of Good." I asked them, "Do you know how to drink heavenly wine?" They both answered, "Siusan let us practice with her." I looked at Siusan, said, "I am proud of you my sister, for you know how to optimize an opportunity," and kissed her. I asked them, "Would you drink my wine and give me your wine to drink and let me serve you?" They answered and said, "We will do whatever you desire us to do for you, you will be our only goddess and we will put our lives and future into your hands to do as you wish." I then asked them for their names, "I am Almásfüzito the Eldomite and she is Bükkmogyorósd the Eldomite." I then promised to ask for them when we returned to Balatonföldvári. As we approached the Balatonföldvári space, border all our escort ships were rearranged in a space parade format with their special emergency space lights rotating. As Almásfüzito flew us to the front of the parade, we headed for Tápiószolos and half way there another two million warships were flashing their lights and preparing to form behind our parade. Our space was clear that night making it easy for many of the planet to see us. I could hear great cheering on many planets. As our ship docked and my crew escorted me out with Almásfüzito and Bükkmogyorósd, each wrapped tight around Siusan as my sister carried me. I really did not want her to carry me, yet I could not take this great glory from her. As we walked to the dock's entrance doors Bogovi and Tápiószolos were standing together and once I saw them, they both saluted me. As we approached, Siusan let me down however Almásfüzito and Bükkmogyorósd wrapped themselves tightly around one of my arms. Siusan walked beside me on my right side carrying my sword. Bogovi then said to me,

"All shall now know that you are the greatest fighter against evil. I will stream it to all our empire's and alliance galaxies. All shall hail their mighty queen and will know why I so wholeheartedly serve you." I walked over and gave him a kiss. He looked at my two escorts and said, "My Queen, I do believe you have two more fans." Tápiószolos then told me, "Oh great goddess, I know not how to repay you for I have fought that evil chaos for millions of years and you went before him without your warships and only three females and defeated not only them but all in that galaxy. How can I repay you?" I then said to him, "Will you give me Almásfüzito and Bükkmogyorósd to be my personal servants?" He looked at us and jokingly replied, "I have no choice for I fear they will not let you go. Almásfüzito and Bükkmogyorósd, will you serve our Queen?" They both jumped for joy and cried out, "We will serve her with every ounce in our spirits." Tápiószolos looked at Bogovi and said, "My King, I do believe they may have practiced this." Bogovi then told him, "When our Queen asks me for anything, I always say yes, for I know she was preparing herself in case of a no." They both then laughed. I then asked Tápiószolos, "Will you allow Siusan to live in the flesh on the planet Sásdi?" He then sadly replied, "I fear that I cannot grant such a request because we are not a part of your Empire and fear forces me to consider the danger that could befall upon your wonderful precious sister. I do hope you can forgive me." I looked at Bogovi and asked, "My master, can we bring this wonderful galaxy and the one I freed from evil into our Empire?" Bogovi then answered, "My Queen, this is also your Empire and if you wish to add alliance and freed galaxies your answer is what you wish to do." I then walked over to Tápiószolos and shook his hand while sitting on Siusan's shoulders and said, "My god, welcome to our Empire. Will you also send a mission to inform your neighbor that they may join if they so desire." He then told me, "I shall do that, as soon as we get back from Sásdi. I am confused, why had you mistakenly called me your god?" I then looked at him and said, "Any god who is in my Empire must let me serve them. I am your servant for the greatest among us must be the servant if good is to reign throughout the ages. I request that you allow me to put some temples on your planets and your neighbor's galaxy planets." Tápiószolos then told me, "Oh great Queen, we have already requested many times for your temples nevertheless the requests were denied each time." I now looked at Bogovi and he answered, "We have yet to put your temples on all the planets in our Empire." I then asked him, "Will you please publish a waiting list to include our alliance galaxies and I will have my courts help and I shall tell them to start here in Balatonföldvári and his neighboring galaxy Skørping. I explained that first we would build theological universities to produce priests locally. My servants are much more at ease with one of their own guiding them. I shall also increase by tenfold the number of my priest's universities and soon we will be able to have temples that share the great love of my master and me as these temples teach and indoctrinate in the name of the King and his servant Queen as our servants need tools to defend against evil." Tápiószolos then told us, "You may now view sights from Sásdi's throne planet." Siusan then asked me once again with both of her arms wrapped around me while kissing on my neck, "My sister what are we looking for on Sásdi?" I now hugged her and rubbed her beautiful blue back telling her, "A very special gift for you." Siusan then replied, "Master, you do too much for me." Her new sisters Almásfüzito and Bükkmogyorósd now also helped massage her. She was so limber with a smile now to go with her distant look then suddenly she leaped up and said, "Master, I hear my heart singing and can smell a smell from my dreams of long ago." I could see a light starting to shine on her. As we started to make our descent Tápiószolos then spoke, "My Queen, you have many fans here to welcome you. Siusan and I looked out the window and she started crying for joy and kissing her two sisters and me. She now looked into my eyes and cried out, "I love my master and sister so much, so much forever and ever." Out mighty host and Bogovi were now fighting back tears of joy as her love was flooding our ship as no-one of us could get enough of it. As our ship landed, we all got out and stood on the landing stage. When the crowd saw Siusan get out they at first were stunned, then they started clapping giving her a powerful ovation. After about thirty minutes, Tápiószolos raised his hand to signify he was to speak, "My servants, today I break our policy of the isolation per your request for I bring you great news. We have here with us today your King Bogovi and Queen Lilith, holder of the Sword of Justice and her sister goddess Siusan the Harvey." The massive crowd now cheered in hysteria as Siusan stood out as I and Bükkmogyorósd each held one of her hands and raised them for a sign of unity and power. The King of this planet, King Lesenceistvánd came out and welcomed us into his Palace. The people now chanted, "Showers of Blood" repeatedly. I went outside and cried out to them, "I am the goddess Queen Lilith, holder of the Sword of Justice and I ask you today, Will you serve me and worship me and make evil your enemies?" They all cried out, "Queen Lilith is our goddess and we pray that she will shower us in her blood." King Lesenceistvánd came running out with all in his palace and cried out, "Oh great goddess, may we also be baptized in your blood?" I then shook my head yes and had them fill up the stage. I then said, "Today I will shower you in my blood as they we may be of the same blood and me inside you. I shall protect you from all evil and my spirit will give you my unconditional and eternal love for today you will hunger no more, you will no longer suffer from diseases. You will be one of the blessed people since I shall put the spirit of my sister Siusan into one of your wombs and my sister and I will live among you. She will give birth too many children so that my seed which is in her will be forever in your gene pool." The people now stood quiet as a large red cloud appeared above them and was quickly descending. As it was almost upon them, it stopped and unleashed a heavy rain of blood. The rain baptized all who were there. When the rain stopped, they all saw another cloud, this one being white descend upon them. This cloud did not stop but divided itself into all who were baptized. The large crowd now glowed in white for about five minutes. When the glow evaporated, the crowd was made up of new reborn people. I now called for some courts to send angels to build a few temples and start teaching the new priests. We walked back inside to rejoin Bogovi and Tápiószolos to start working out the details for Siusan's rebirth. Tápiószolos wanted to know why this was important the Siusan reincarnated. I told him, "For she is from another dimension and her death would mandate her spirit return to that dimension, however if she is born here and die here her spirit can stay here." Tápiószolos then asked, "Were not you and your sister Drusilla born and died in another dimension?" I answered him, "So true, however mine was for spiritual penance and a test in order to hold the Sword of Justice. Drusilla also died beside me; having the freedom to forsake me, she instead created a wrath that gave her greater pain. As she was dying, she worshipped me, her sister who had been beside her all of our days. She thus died inside me as she was baptized in my blood. The great God declared her death to be in my death and thus I was able to keep her for my sanctuary." Tápiószolos replied, "That is such great news for all have heard of your sisters." I then said, "Many have heard yet few will see for these are my toys whose bone is my bone which I will not live without." I now looked at King Lesenceistvánd and told him, "The spirit inside Siusan shall be reborn in one of your people's womb. She shall grow, live and love with you, she will be given in marriage, and she shall bear children so that she will always be with her people. She is a Harvey and was my sister with me during much of my penance. The love she gave me shall be rewarded by me for her eternity. I will keep her flesh suit and when she gives up her old body, I will bring her spirit back to me to rule with me in our heavens. When she returns she will be the goddess of Sásdi and her spirit shall protect her people against all evil for eternity. Her people will be blessed by me for she shall give them to me and we shall serve your great race forever and ever." King Lesenceistvánd had now fallen to his knees and worshipped all who were in the room, especially Siusan. I felt accordingly proud of her as I could see new life and a stronger fire burning as her distant far off look was no more, for she had found something to fill that emptiness. I had stopped the shame she had in her skin color as I am still puzzled why people would hate someone who was such a packed bundle of love just because her skin is blue. I was almost too embarrassed to tell James about it and have it put in my books; however, he felt that such things needed to be put out in the light so people can see how stupid it really is. He is a male, so I know that they are strange about their lack of ability to reason. King Lesenceistvánd now started to summarize the sad long history of Sásdi for us. "Our history goes back to a time that no longer is recorded. However, we did start keeping records about six millennia ago. We have always lived in our Sásdi solar system and began as many people did as a wondering who lived in caves and hunted for food. They eventually started to domesticate animals and gather food forming into small settlements. They rarely left their small areas. This proved to be disastrous as strange aliens were feeding off our planet's people. They would also take them to their space ships, do experiments, and return them to Sásdi. This was the beginning of our taming wild animals to ride for transportation and help move large trees. Within about one decade, most settlements were warned. We built large forts around our small communities and learned how to fight. Our favorite weapon was the slingshot, which would sling the extra hard and razor sharp stones. These stones when slung would cut into their space suits and expose them to our environment, which resulted in death within about five minutes. Everyone carried slingshots, including children and women and trained on them until they were experts. These stones when slung at their ships and making contact at an angle on sensitive areas would create small chips or cracks on their outsides. If the crew tried to fix them, the settlement would pick them off one by one. Many times when the ships were leaving our planets the pressure would turn the cracks into large holes and cause explosions. As the number of ships and raiders returning started to decrease, their invasions started to be concealed, and concentrate on experimentation. They wanted to brand us in such a way that all would know who we were." Siusan listened to this with all her precious heart as I soon walked over to her and wrapped my arms around her hugging her very tight. I had now learned to cherish her soft blue soft skin and always found myself wanting to hold her. She has now learned about who she was, although it did not matter except for her peace of mind. She had absolute faith in our relationship and knew our bond was sealed for eternity, yet she also knew she needed the joy of being with child and someday seeing her grandchildren being born and later giving birth. Bogovi, my new sisters, and our host god were outside now, as I could not depart from this wonderful story. Siusan was such a huge part of me and I needed to know that and from whence it came. The King smiled at us and continued, "Siusan is the first Harvey to become a goddess and many future generations will worship her or . . . I mmmean you." He was looking at me, in which I shook my head no and pointed at Siusan replying, "All Harvey shall serve their goddess, Siusan the Harvey sister of Queen Lilith who holds the Sword of Justice." Siusan turned her head back and gave me a ton of kisses as I joyfully swung her around. The King continued, "Surely, Siusan is of the gods." I looked at him and said, "She is a goddess with the greatest gods who love her and serve her." The King began again saying, "Siusan you are the greatest Harvey to ever have existed, for none has ever been greater, than you. Your people now have pride and hope, something that we have lacked our long history. Back to our past, they decided to brand us by changing our skin pigments and for five centuries, we had more colors than a rainbow. Eventually they decided to give us our current color. They then told wild stories about us throughout the universe. Karma finally caught up with them and they contracted a deadly virus, as so many advanced empires did at that time and became lost in history. On the other hand, the damage of their stories was just beginning. As inter-galactic travels was now a thing that was a distant past travel inside galaxies began to accelerate with new smaller Empires beginning to travel in space. The over rated legends about us gave rise to space race hunting as ships would stumble in, discover us and openly hunt us. We were able to fight many off as our slingshots had advanced to go along with the rich supply of our explosive chemicals that we learned to harness. We could now propel sharp razor stones into the ship shells and watch them explode as they departed. Each victory for us increased the drama for others to come and hunt us for sport. Our planets also have a rich supply of bacterium and viruses that we are immune to and so many other races have no immunity. This was translated into the concept of a curse as many would die on their trips back to their home planets with their ships arriving filled with carcasses and releasing the stronger well fed viruses and bacterium into their environments exploding with plagues that wiped out so many. This was known as the "blue curse," and prompted revenge from so many. Over time, we were able to collect a rich inventory of these invaders space ships. We sent out exploratory missions to seek out and find new worlds in which we could survive. Any mission that was sure to fail was ordered to crash land in a big city on a planet in that region. We empire's that we took these ships from were blamed for the assault and many wars started, which bought us some time to get more ships and explore. We were able to discover the gift that spread our species. Our planets were part of an ancient Star gate network that allowed us to jump to other parts of our universe and other dimensions without the constraints of time. This was a double-edged sword as it did give us some hope and a way to travel without advanced ships. We mapped out our gate network and within one century were able to bounce around with a high degree of confidence and security. We spread ourselves into small communities throughout our universe and planets in other dimensions to include your ancient 'New Venus.' Unlike the other vast number of humanoid races, we were never accepted. Siusan is sad, the first successful space explorer to return not only accepted but also respected and honored. We have studied this problem so much and can never find out why most were completely destroyed and bitterly tortured." I now said to the King lowering my head, "On my New Venus as their lord, sainted tribes joined and destroyed the Harvey that shared our planet. Evil demons took on the form of blue people creating a very negative reputation for the blue peoples. I discovered this unexpected evil too late and the stereotype put on the Harvey. I have lived with the shame of my inability to save these very special and private people. I did punish all who hurt a Harvey by casting them from my heavens. That is when I promised to search out, find, and amend this terrible wrong. Your people will never fear again for I will allow no one to hurt my blessed gift, the wonderful Harvey Race. This time I will come through with my protection as none will be able to defeat Siusan." The King continued, "Do not have shame, for our curse has always had a way to avoid any available protection. We have also been victims of raids intended to save us with absolute good intentions. Somehow, the ball has so many times failed to bounce our way. A ball finally bounced our way when the god Tápiószolos decided to study us to verify if we were a danger to Balatonföldvári. Upon his discovery of our inner good intentions covered by a will to survive, he entered into a treaty with us. He would hide us and protect us, as long as we did not leave our solar system except to punish a raiding party. This light now filled our skies. We had always feared that others would take our planets because of its wonderful scenery all year round. The one strong blessing of our blue skin is its insulating effect that allows us to occupy harsh arctic regions. Our solar system has twelve planets, all within your Earth's distance from our one star. Ten of these planets orbit in the last orbit or the equivalent of your Earth's orbit. This historically made it easier for us to move from our planets. Tápiószolos also worked hard keeping us a secret to the other galaxies and solar systems. This made it possible for us to increase our population as our daughters did bear many children as their fathers gave them in marriage. Recently our entire solar system and galaxy received new hope as your Empire of Good came through and destroyed so much evil. We actually now felt comfortable in controlled trading and asked Tápiószolos if he would find some trading parties for us. For the first time we felt accepted. When we learned that our Queen had returned rumors started floating out of Ereshkigal that one of your sisters was blue skinned, we were able financially to motivate a few traders to report they had seen some blue people. When you asked Tápiószolos, he had no choice but to confess. He told us you are good and that without you; the evil would still be a strong force in our universe. Our excitement became exotic when a court of Tápiószolos informed us that the King and Queen were to visit us.

We never dreamed that such mighty gods would even know us, much less visit us. We are so thankful for our beautiful lands the produce abundant food and peaceful waters to quench our thirsts that you have allowed us to share in the community of the good." I then told him, "Oh great and good King, I give you nothing that you have not earned and have a right to expect from the ones who created you. The love given to me by Siusan can never be equally repaid, however I shall have great people also to try. Your people now have deity. Your history will not be repeated, for as your children go to enjoy opportunities open to all. You shall be respected and cherished by my servants as I pour my love on all." I must now take my Siusan with me for her secret rebirth. I know how traumatic this event can be, thus I shall accompany her. I now thanked the king for his information and returned to the spirit distribution center to line Siusan up with the next baby to be born. I decided to monitor where she went; wanting her not to be in the extremely rich or the extremely poor. She would go somewhere in the middle and not in any geological danger areas or potential battlefields. We now jumped into the funnel and the process began. Spinning and flipping I held her hand so tight dreading the minute that I would have to let her go and escape. I knew she had to be let go if I wanted to keep her in my Empire. The moment came and went in a flash. She was now being fed into a newborn baby as I recorded the transfer and then pulled myself up out of the funnel. Siusan was now breathing and starting on her road to being a real member of the Harvey planet in my dimension. It was now time for me to return to my master, yet first I wanted to witness my sister's second birth. She was such a beautiful little blue baby girl, born with a head of dark hair and rich blue eyes. I was stretching myself as thin as their concentrations exploded like large firecrackers. They were now everywhere as this was like dropping a bag of small pellets on an uphill road. I was now spinning around starting to get dizzy as each I popped more were in front of it. As I started to lose hope of containment now and leaning towards a long hard hunt, something jabbed me in my side. I looked down and saw my sword. I was so tied up in catching the flies that I forgot about my friend. I pulled it out and screamed, "Evil is no more." The sword sent out millions and millions of laser beams as I could feel so many vanishing. I was now pulling myself back together at one time being spread out over twenty light years cubed. Almásfüzito was holding our sword for me now. Soon the sword slowed down to a few long-range lasers beams and then reported to me that about twenty percent had escaped. Darn, what do I do now? I am not going to let them go. I asked my sword, "What shall we do to destroy them?" Sword then recommended that we follow a few light-years above them dropping relay units to do the random attacking, keep our location camouflaged while reducing their numbers, wait for their reunion point, and follow them to their base empire. This was a wonderful idea. Occasionally we would discover a group of them and with our relays blast them from doing many angels they had no idea what was happening. This was fun and productive as we waited for their reunion. When they joined in one large group again we dropped location sensors in each spirit so if they spread again, I would not have to stretch myself then. The smell and voices of frying evil are so unique and eerie. They beg for mercy, promise to reform and then release the voices of the good who begged them as they killed, is very consistent among them as if a part of their substance. Any slight smell of mercy will elicit a full escape attempt from them. My sword out of nowhere is burned hot. We are close to their base and set back while they start to assemble. Then a multi-army force charges out in the opposite direction for an apparent raid. Sword lets them get about ninety light-years out and then vaporizes them erasing them from existence. Another crime of evil destroyed. As the absence of their reporting signal hits the base, billions of evil come rushing in. We are now completely stealth as groves of them keep rushing in. Their base must be extremely dense as it now in dropping through space. Within ten hours, the returns are but a few insignificant dribbles. I now hold up the sword and command, "Destroy what you must so good can reign." It then blasts into the core of the dense evil base and exploding a burning vaporizing gas that prevents them from leaving while sucking them into its vaporizer.

Within one minute, trillions of evil spirits are erased from existence. This will make it so much better for about thirty galaxies in this area. With so little, here to clean up it is time to go back and see how my Bükkmogyorósd is doing. Thus, Almásfüzito and I head back to my Empire through our alliance galaxies. We are about one day out so I suggest to Almásfüzito that we drink so wine in which she quickly agrees. I hope to get to know her a lot more during this next day. We are going at a safe high speed so my capsule can stay in tack and at now scatter us throughout the universe. We are going a comfortable universe speed of 250 light years per second. I had not realized how far we were out. A good feeling knowing that it will be some time before evil reaches us again from this sector. Almásfüzito tells me her story, "When I was a child, my parents sold me to some evil worshippers. They did all manner of evil to me; I prayed for only one thing, that I could surrender my young life and thus die. I tried to commit suicide so many times, yet these evil people have evil spirits that warned them when I was going to attempt suicide. Then one day, an army fighting evil came through and freed us. So many people were free, and now wandered our planet searching for food, and other necessities of life. My search ended during a storm in which I died. As my soul went to my reward, it was stolen by an evil and put in their prison for the good. I suffered in there for over 500 years until Bogovi came through and destroyed all the evil in Balatonföldvári. Tápiószolos then went through collecting the good spirits and preparing them for transport to the Empire's haven for the good saints. He also needed more saints for his heaven's courts. While selecting saints he discovered me, really was impressed, and thus put me on his thrones court to his palace. This was as lucky for me as he is truly a servant of good and had fought evil unsuccessfully for so many millennia. They just kept coming in. However your (to me) Empire freed us all and gave Tápiószolos what he needed to protect and keep secure good in this galaxy. When I heard of you arriving, I could only hope to be your slave and serve the greatest power of good ever known." I then told her,

"I came back with the Sword of Justice, yet Bogovi did all the hard brutal fighting to chase evil as far as he could from our empire. He probably now worries very much for us, since we are still so far beyond the long range communicators."

Chapter 04

A Time for War

Bogovi and the Empire he shared with me were very confused. No one could understand why I would take poor little innocent Almásfüzito and leave zips else behind and zip off into the dark deep universe never to be seen again. Fejér and petitioned all that there must be something wrong. Notwithstanding Medica and Sabina stood up for their Trinity saying, "Our Queen will never leave us. Let us prepare for her return since she was last seen chasing evil. Evil will suffer with our evil-killing Queen chasing them." Yet as time went on, this argument became less believable as many charged that Bogovi had angered his Queen forcing her to abandon the Empire. This caused many gods to become angry with Bogovi and to avoid or shun him. He eventually retreated to Balatonberény, the planet of love that he and I had enjoyed building our relationship. The Empire was sad, yet had enough safety networks to continue functioning strong. Then, to my Empire's delight, their long-range sensors picked me up about fifteen minutes out. We had now been in the decelerating stage for about one hour. A decelerating stage is required so the ending point can absorb the landing without any atomic chain reactions. As word spread of my ship, returning to the courts alerted Bogovi who sent out messages to my ship where he was and for me to visit him first. My war ship had a streamer that had all my adventure recorded and had made to edited highlights that we now being transmitted throughout the universe. I had destroyed three times as much evil that had been destroyed in building our empire and alliances. Their Queen was a dedicated evil killer. As we landed on Balatonberény, I asked Almásfüzito to stay with me in the event that Bogovi was angry. Luckily, he was not angry at all but to the contrary very proud of me. When I saw him Almásfüzito and I fell to the ground, worshipped him as he ran to us, and fell on the ground worshipping us. I told Almásfüzito that this did not make sense so I asked Bogovi to hug me. He leaped up and hugged me saying, "I was lost, and so sad thinking, as did the Empire, that you left me forever. When I watched the stream that your ship shot back, I could understand why you had to go after this evil. I do hope that evil understands that when it attacks us, you will pursue to their end, as will I." I thanked him for understanding and added, "I hope it does not happen frequently because even though Almásfüzito is good, she is not as good as you." He laughed and said, "You have a strange sense of humor." I knew that was the time to get it out and asked, "Would you hate me if I drank their wine and let them drink mine." He said, "That must be a woman thing that I do not understand nor care to worry about. Do what you do and always come back so I can also serve you, ok." I kissed him and told him, "Baby, you are the best." Almásfüzito also gave him a kiss and added, "Her sisters and I also thank you for sharing her with us. We will insure that she returns to you better than how she came to us." He shook his head, winked at her and kissed her cheek saying, "Now that is a good deal isn't it." We all hugged and laughed as I told him, "My master, when you touch one of my sisters, you are touching me." He then said, "Darn, you would tell me that after we planted Siusan, some of that blue might have been interesting." We both kissed him as Almásfüzito was squeezed between us as I told him, "Oh master she is, and she will return to us someday in which you may enjoy as you wish." He then told me, "My queen, you will have to give me time because I am still getting used to your wine and still want so much more." I responded, "My master, my cup is for you and shall quench your thirst whenever you so desire." We were once again happily reunited and even better, my sisters we added to our family, not only my family but also OUR family. Things would be so much better now, for I know a relationship, even for deity, cannot be good with secrets to trip one up. Truthfulness must go with good for lying will plant a seed of evil to grow. He worked hard to build a great Empire and opening share it with me. When I was first taken to do my penance for this dimension, we had just been rewarded with six galaxies. I had barely seen his and still had many introductions remaining for my galaxy as the smoke of the war against evil was vaporized. When I returned, we had over 1,000 galaxies with another 1,000 wanting to join. We would have them all in our Empire soon as all the courts and support networks were being finalized. Our militaries were already united and new stations planted along our border in place. We know of no other Empire close to our size and since space is infinite, we will never know. As long as they do not know us, things will go along smoothly. Bogovi recently, actually during my temporary absence, launched a new network of extremely deep stations, which were controlled, remotely by an extended leapfrog network, which would monitor itself and the next layer close to our communication limits. This network was four layers deep. That is how they were able to detect my return and report it back. Our lights and courts continue to work on new ideas. The theory is to plant maybe like twenty layers of bouncer stations in between each network layer and give us a forty-four max range each layer defense network. We can be mobilized and ready to fight and meet the invaders at the mid twenty layer. Moreover, like all technical ideas advancements will continue to be made. I trust and have faith in our lights and courts. Good things will continue to happen for the good. We can only hope that other powerful good Empires are also fighting Evil although to think that evil will someday be defeated is foolish for evil will always be. I remember during my evil days how we would retreat far from our prey and wait for an opportunity to destroy became available. The important thing now is to maintain our security layers and plan future deep universe raids while continuing to add new galaxies. Good must stay united and grow in not to do so leaves innocents in the miserable grips of evil. It ironically feels like so much work building good and so easy for evil to destroy it. We must learn to live with the same love and enthusiasm for good as evil is dedicated to its hate and enthusiasm to destroy. I depend upon my priests and temples to help with this important mission. Many who wait for us to save them question the time delays, however we are a 100% humanoid Empire, thus all the galaxies that we allow to alliance and join our Empire must be transformed to Humanoid and after my shower of blood transformed free of disease and the need to take in physical matter for energy. All my blood servants are solar feed. I need for all of us to be the same species and speak the same language, which is now Bogovi's language. He earned that honor. Even though all who are in flesh share the same species, little things like skin color and the resources that a rejoin has can lead to hate and war. In any war, both sides are punished for we have one law that is always enforced and that is if anyone attacks immediately petition your temple to call upon the throne. We will join them, judge the situation, and give our recommended course of action. It is recommended because they or even one side holds the option to repudiate our recommendation, and be destroyed. This may be cold yet not as cold as years of bloody killing and utter destruction only to be friends a few decades later. Compromise and survive giving your children a better future than one of asking, "Why did my daddy die?" Sadly, if your enemy has surrendered to evil, they will fight until their deaths, and then continue unless put into a punishment area or erased. Now the question continues, 'How did they get Bükkmogyorósd and fling her within our territory with ease?' Our courts will need to work on this. Bogovi and my spirits' record every action in our Empire so the Courts can review each little detail and discover not only that glitch but then again maybe other future ones. We will never stop all of them; however, it will be very rare with revenge as I can let my sword go with my armies so the revenge will be deadly. Now I want to move on to something more important and that is the planting of my sisters. Fortunately, not all will need to be planted. Bogovi has given me some great news; he is revamping a special planet, with his special touch for design and 100% security and privacy to be my new Intimate Restricted Sanctuary which will also include a copy of my holy of holies maintained by my Seonji with fields to feed my three horses which will be together. We will also have a special court that will monitor my friend requests including my Hyrum Queens. It is as if he can speak it into existence straight from my mind. A part of me fulfills any of his requests for information. I just cannot hold anything back from him nor do I ever want to. He always seems to accept and understand. I really do believe his mother had a great part of that in teaching him that females have different needs and views and I guess just about everything. He never really expected to find one with a hate for evil that actually fought evil. It is not that I want to be a man; it is my love for my servants and wanting them to have a deity that loves, understands, cares and is personal. One that does not have to threat with punishment yet does punish when required. This is the revenge of the good and just. I have seen how extreme evil can be and this just cannot be permitted. They tell me that I place too much emphasis on it, however who can there be love if hate is waiting to destroy it? Hate can so easily divide those who love. When marriages break up the one-time lovers now tend to become violent and hateful of each other. As deity we must look at the causes why a family would break up and try to fix the ones that we on the outside put on them. My temples are very active with families and children, giving them a place to burn off all the extra energy and bond with me. The families discover more what we can and will do for them. Miracles need to be daily and not at the point of total disaster. When they are showered in my blood, they get their new bodies and no longer hunger and have diseases, which take a lot of stress on the family. The next thing is extreme taxation or letting the government take all the money. I rule my governments. There is now division between my temples and the nations that surround them. Every nation was born that has ceased to exist. It is that simple. When nations die, so do the families in them. That is not a pretty sight.

Speaking of pretty sights, "Where are my wonderful sisters?" Bogovi is taking me to our throne so we can reunite Almásfüzito and Bükkmogyorósd and watch an edited with highlights only on my last whipping on evil's nests. The courts did a great job of making it exciting and strong and even had a few scenes of Almásfüzito gripping me in her fear and me comforting her. That was a nice touch, showing me defeating a horrendous evil nest and caring for my sister at the same time. The ceremony was long and exciting as everyone was celebrating the Empire's great victory. With their Queen winning, it was their victory. I like this. Their King and Queen fight for them and their sanctity. We earn their worship. Bogovi took the risks and made the sacrifices to build it and our sword, which I shall dedicate to our Empire when we do our consolidation of our alliances. I will be going on another mission cleaning up galaxies that border us, which probably will not accomplish much since we will still be surrounded by evil. I will be going on many campaigns over the next couple of millions of years expanding our Empire and alliances. The first thing I want to do after our Empire finishes celebrating this great victory over evil is to get my sisters planted. That seams now may be a while, because now our flesh servants are celebrating throughout the entire Empire and even our alliances. I never realized that the small dense hit by my wise sword actually puts such a hard blast to evil's base in this part of the universe, yet I will never be foolish enough to think there is none going the opposite way. They are everywhere. Even though our servants have been freed from evil, the memory of that pain appears never to diminish. I guess OUR recent victory put another coat of faith in the power of good over the smoldering coals of evil inside them. They all look so happy, as many have been showered in my blood or are now being baptized with my (OUR) last victory giving them the courage to accept the temple's commands. We are pumping out so many improved flesh suits as those who were old are now running with their great grandchildren, those who were in hospitals getting ready to die are now in the temples worshiping me. No more killing wild animals for their flesh, however the temples are now neutering and fixing all animals they can get hold of the prevent massive overpopulation, which would then require they sacrifice them to me. Although I do not really care much for sacrificing, the act does power my spirit reserves, which I use for blessing my children, so in a way it comes right, back to them. We are working hard to bring each planet into its equilibrium. Correspondingly, we are moving more outer frozen planets in the life supporting orbits so when land resources become limited, we will be able to set settlements on them. We may discover many surprises on these planets as they may have orbited a previous star that exploded maybe a few billion years ago and since everything is a cycle, Bogovi and I will be keeping an eye on them to get an idea of what to expect when we go into that phase. We shall now speak, or I shall speak with scary cat Bogovi at my side, "My children, we must celebrate today as a beginning, a new beginning of attacking evil and no longer victims of being attacked as was my sister, your goddess Bükkmogyorósd. These attacks will result in a massive strike against evil with a demand of billions of evil spirits to be erased. We are the strongest known empire of good, yet I truly hope one of the smallest in our universe. Our deep searches will tell us someday, as we are continually searching the depths of our endless universe. Each day we grow stronger. Each day you grow stronger and not weaker as before. The days in the flesh shall become closer to the life you will live in our eternal homes we have made for you. United with the same flesh and language and dedicated towards moving closer to a utopia of good. Our Empire shall now be known as the Empire of the Good and holders of the Sword of Justice or EGaSOJ. Today we add all our alliance galaxies so that they may join us in our fight against evil and share in our love for prosperity for all, as we are known not only to love our neighbors but those who hate us. We do this to be greater than evil, for even evil loves evil as evil hates good. As they perish before our sword we can love seeing be erased by justice and good. The Sword will now join with your thrones spirits and be able to detect evil from the depths beyond our new ten-layer deep defense perimeter. United Good can survive, divided we will fall. That is

James Hendershot

why your King and Queen crave to serve you so much, and thank you for allowing us to serve those whom we love. We shall always stay in your hearts." The courts closed the stream and I now motioned for Almásfüzito, Bükkmogyorósd, and Fejér that I wanted them to meet me. Fejér instantaneously appeared before me. I introduced her to our new sisters as they all hugged each other. The courts reported that the royal couple was now actively involved in 'royal family duties' as the servants loved the humanizing of their deities. I next asked Fejér to help our new sisters settle in and that I would be there soon, I had some wife duties to take care of on Balatonberény. Fejér and our new sisters vanished back to our new Sanctuary and I now turned to my King and asked, "Oh great King, may I serve you on our Balatonberény?" His smile was great as we joined hands and went to our favorite planet. The beauty of this place always blows my mind, as it is one hundred times better than any Garden of Eden I ever existed. My king actually molded this place to be a reflection of the good in our hearts. Endless fields of beautiful flowers that even looked good at ground view. This is our power of love base. We live as humans here as we get cold when it is cold and hot when it is hot. We still keep our divine transportation powers so when it gets cold or dark, we can zip over to the other side and find a lighted warm place. I do enjoy floating in the sky with my King as we enjoy the great beauty of this large planet. I now felt much more relaxed in EGaSOJ having seen so many changes so fast in my short time here. It was time now to let our temples and spirits keep the show on the road. Bogovi had started adding me into his temples as he was added into all my temples as our divine master and King. I have no desire to compete with him on this issue and would just as much wish that he had all the temples so I could slide into my sanctuary, yet we know I am far too restless for that. For now, the important thing is to build in Bogovi and eventually into our servants that my absence is to fight evil and that our relationship is solid. My sisters and I decided to create a special private room for Bogovi to stay in if he wishes to visit me when I am in my sanctuary. I want no secrets from my understanding master and King. This will give me more time with my sisters as he can run the throne from within my Sanctuary and thus by being with me keep, the courts calm. The main problem I have now is leaving this magnificent place. Bogovi reassures me that some of the highlights of Balatonberény were put into my new Intimate Restricted Sanctuary. He also tells me that my old Intimate Restricted Sanctuary is still functional being maintained by our spirits. So for now just layback, rest and relax, and let the master enjoy his slave. Oh yeah, somehow that statement does not correctly reveal greater gain for me. I am now truly a joyous servant. I do push my spirits to work with his spirits so he can have more time to relax especially now since I doubled and almost tripled his workload as we now have 2,844 galaxies in our Empire. I lay here resting knowing that by giving up little I have gained so much. My will on New Venus was to have a good planet, yet evil just kept on raining and raining as the blood just never stopped pouring yet even in that chaotic disaster produced three heavenly queens. In anger, I lashed out packing a hard punch and exiting into the unknown now to have trillions of planets and so many people freed from evil. The horrors of seeing what evil does are too painfully gripping on my soul. However, everyone freed will create the need to free two more, so I have a ton of work to do, someday. It might as well just lay back and please my master for the time being. I am so thankful that Bogovi loves being in our flesh suits as much as I do. To breathe in the air that is a part of me is such a wonderful sensation and to drink the water our spirits created ads to this sensation. In addition, the most important for me is to stop and baby makers from hitting my eggs. If we ever decide to have children, we will speak them into existence since I am not in that reproduction process. My servants do not know about the pains of giving birth as I have eliminated that. They are making new servants for me, and thus that is a divine gift for me. Why should they suffer giving a gift to me? As I have said so many times before, I get NO joy out of torturing the good and no god in my Empire had better ever gotten any joy in it, or they will experience it. I have zero tolerance when it comes to my saintly servants. Speaking of tolerances my sisters are going to burn me at a stake if I do not visit them soon, so I grabbed my master's hand and said, let us go to our sanctuary. My sisters must be hot because he offered NO resistance and in fact, got us there faster. Upon arrival, I was so shocked that if I had had pants on, they would have dropped. My master has outdone himself. If I were ever to have sons, I would want them to be like my master. Even though he creates females, he knows that little spark that can ignite a fire in the right parts of the soul. I can so much better understand why my sisters have been staying in the sanctuary without complaint and why Bogovi put a workplace for him here, just in case I could not break away. He does not have to worry about that because the master will have his slave anytime he wants. Nothing has ever been greater for me. I have heard the argument that since we are a deity, we are both equal however, that is hogwash. Bogovi was born divine, and I was not. I was made divine by the gods of this dimension, which now I learn is a small section in this universe, which is still so very much. I was given an opportunity to serve as deity whereas Bogovi is deity. However, knowing this he ignores it and puts me on a pedestal. He is such a fine example of true deity, and that is why I serve him and give him all the glory. He quickly rushes into his private chambers and starts working spiritually with our courts. I sit my sisters down and explain the law of death in another dimension. It is where one is born and not where they die that determines where their soul rests so in order to spend eternity with me; you must be born here. Accordingly I now list those that must be born in this reality, "Garden white Fejér, Julia, Mary, Ruth, Amity, Joy; Harvey Siusan already planted; Hyrum, Faith, Drusilla with Sabina staying for her death counts as here since she was part of a trinity; the Oakley Yanaba; the Stuart Máriakéménd; the Eldom Heidi, with Almásfüzito Bükkmogyorósd having died in Balatonföldvári and Medica having been part of the trinity.

Those staying with me are Bárdudvarnok (Empire goddesses), Tamás, (Empire goddesses), Békéscsaba (Empire goddesses) Ceglédbercel (Empire goddesses), Dédestathe (throne Empire goddesses) Jakabszállás (Empire goddesses), Bácsalmás (from throne), StuartMáriakéménd, Eldom Almásfüzito Bükkmogyorósd (from Tápiószolos's throne) and Medica (trinity) and Hyrum Sabina (trinity). We still have not decided what to do with the angels who came from our throne and those who died in my previous reality. With over 1,000 of them, Bogovi wants to give them very high positions in our expanded courts, especially since the dimensions throne will be willing to help them without hesitation. I will talk to them about that. Either way, I keep Bácsalmás since she took my oath to Bogovi. She also holds a special place in Bogovi's heart as he always gives her the best protocol he can when seeing her. At least, I will have eleven strong ones to help my Master and me during the departure of my divine penance sisters. Bogovi and I now sit down with my eleven of my twelve original and start making plans with them. I remind Drusilla of my promise to her and asked Bogovi to bring her up last. This time rather than going through the local gods we went straight to the mothers telling them that the child in their womb was a sister of the divine queen and that many legions would be protecting the child. We would tell the sisters their identity when it is getting close to bringing them home. Bogovi recommended that they not be placed in a home such as, I was because of the risk of being an international influence as was 'Ann' having an overzealous granddaughter to start the famous "Salem Witch Trials" which instead of fighting evil ended up killing innocents and of the numerous general officers to populate her family tree. We do want good things for my sister's descendants. However, they must be treated as equal as possible thus when the sisters return they will remember nothing. They will keep their race, they are now since that is a part of their identity. As each is planted, we arrive at the planned last one, which is Drusilla as she totally loses it begging Bogovi not to send her away. Bogovi looks at me and I start explaining, "Drusilla accounted for the majority of my penance time and just about completely my entire poor slave suffering time. We were raped, beaten, and made to do all manners of things to anyone our masters so commanded. Through all of this Drusilla not only suffered as I did but also worked as hard as possible to protect and care for me. She has loved the true me, the part of me that is nothing additionally than a smutty slave is, even further than she is. I cannot be apart from her, and I cannot send her away; however, I know I must because she owns me for eternity. What shall I do?" Bogovi then responded, "Indeed I do know the great debt that I also owe Drusilla. Drusilla comes forward so I may hold you and tell you of the love your King and Queen have especially just for you. I shall petition to our throne an exception for you since you gave your life so to such an extent not to be apart from the love you had in faith for your goddess. Furthermore, since this was your Queen's penance death, and you were beaten without mercy, as was your Queen, I do think, we will be able to work around this. You shall join us as we go to our dimension's throne and petition with you. Then we once again traveled to our dimension's throne the same as, I subsequently vividly remember the last time we were here and the shocking surprise we got when we returned. That was history and with any luck, we shall return with the news, we very much hope. As the three of us stand before the throne, we petition the courts to grant us an audience with the judges. They then petitioned, and the judges granted us access to their court chambers. This time it was somewhat less formal than our first time, as I think maybe to have over 2,800 galaxies may have something to do with it. Bogovi reassures me that he had nothing to do with it as the judges have a false concept of being gods themselves. They then ask us, "Why do you wish to speak to us?" I then stepped forward and said, "I wish to petition for the eternity of my penance twin sister." They then tell me to state my case. I then show them the highlights of Drusilla's and my lives as twins during my penance. The stream shows our join suffering plus the additional suffering that Drusilla took just to stay with me. It then drastically shows our final hours together as we were both severely beaten to death and as our spirits united and exiting back to our dimension. The judges remained stone-faced as they watched the video stream and when finished began speaking, "We knew not that penance in another dimension could be filled with such pain. We shall keep your master in our dimension for his penance. Do you have anything to add?" I then asked, "What do you mean by my Bogovi's penance? Being united by you, would not my penance be for each half of me?" The judges said, "Sorry. However, not so in this case as both must have penance to save your servants." I then asked, "Why do you not make the evil suffer equally?" They then answered, "We make them suffer also when we can, and they tend to evade us rather skillfully? Suffice it for you to know that his penance will not be filled with the pain yours had, as we will be monitoring it very closely. Back to your petition before us now, do you wish to add anything?" I then started to add, "Drusilla never lived a life for herself only existed to serve and protect me and in total faith at the end of our lives worshiped me when I confessed my real identity to her, which, in reality, had no bearing on our situation that was at hand. She has proven to be my faithful servant and solitary longing to love and worship me. I feel that to exist without her even, that one day would be a great pain, especially now that you talk about taking away my master for three decades. Drusilla gave all she was expecting nothing in return from me except to allow her to love and protect me. I wish for her to be granted an exemption from the must be born here and die here exemption." The judges after that retreated to consider the petition. They then returned almost immediately using time shifting so as not to keep us away from our thrones too long. They then gave their verdict saying, "Goddess Lilith, holder of the Sword of Justice, Drusilla may stay with your throne for two reasons, the first since she suffered with you equally in your sacrifice and was joined with you as you came back home her death counts also under the provisions of a penance. The second reason is related to your designation of all your sisters as deity namely goddesses. None of your sisters must live and die here, and may be recalled anytime you wish. Simply replace a soul for your sisters' souls that you bring back. It is better than their seeds do not live to exist in any gene pool except for the Harvey. They have suffered so much for so long and so vitally need a hope and bond with deity as they have not until recently received the favors they so richly deserved." At this time, we rejoiced as we started to head back to our throne, as I wanted to get some quality time in which my master on Balatonberény before our sick throne with their invading selfishness takes him away from me. I will have to grow up fast, which means some of my planted sisters will be returning rather quickly. We relaxed and recharged our already steaming hot bond. No one or thing has ever given me so much and worked so hard to make me not his shadow but his glory. That is naturally so special. I just hate it that every time I try to advance a doctrine of good I must surrender to pain and misery. My revenge shall be cold and swift. In the meantime, I will have to stand strong for my people so that they can have the lives I wish so much for them to enjoy. I guess since they are not suffering we must suffer in their place. Such a sick system yet we must give in until we find or create an alternative. As we are so completely enjoying the fruits of our bond, we receive an emergency message from our throne. We grab Drusilla, who I am not letting away from me for a couple of millennia if possible, and rush back to our throne. Upon our arrival, the throne's courts start blasting us with reports of powerful unexplained forces disrupting EGaSOJ's communications making it impossible to monitor the safety of our servants. We are driving our ship blindfolded. We know not where our Empire is going. I thus pull out my Sword of Justice and command it to repair our communication network, notwithstanding my sword informs me that this is not the work of any known evil. That is all we need now, a new form of advanced evil to fight. Then suddenly darkness filled our throne as we have now been truly blinded. Even our spiritual eyes could not see. This is not good. How can be evil continue to become so advanced? I once again ask my Sword of Justice to give us sight, as my sword tells me more confident that this is not the work of evil. That is a big relief as I definitely do not want evil to be able to do this. This is not evil then it must be good. Oh no, I just had a dreadful thought as I reach around to see who I can touch. Holding on standing strong beside me is my Drusilla. I ask her to help me find my master. We search to no avail as I then ask my sword "Is my master here?" My sword answers, "My Queen the King is not adjacent." I then command that darkness to depart from my throne as it does immediately. I afterwards ask the courts, "Where is our Master?" Within minutes, our communication network becomes functional again as an Empire wide search for our King is in effect. I now sit alone on my throne with Drusilla sharing my seat holding me and trying to comfort me. The King is gone. Then a loud voice speaks to all in the throne, "Fear not fighters for good, your King, as was your Queen, now goes to pass the test of penance, so he may return a greater force of good and justice. He shall return in the same number. of years as your Queen served her penance." I now order my courts too, with prior approval from our throne, to recall Fejér, Julia, Máriakémend, and Faith being that they have the strongest leadership abilities. I will try to allow the others to stay in the flesh to balance their karma and have a chance to live a more complete life. It is now starting to hit me, as I am alone on this throne (having no master) and with recent additions now having 3012 galaxies in our Empire. I shall depend so much on my sisters and am now thankful that they have to see the special side of our master. We are blood of our blood. There is no need to compete with us, as I share all things with them to include my master to his delight in theory yet hidden so well. The one thing that I am so thankful is the insight of Bogovi, as he knew the challenges, he experienced without me, and thus set up our spirits existing in multiple functions, such as our powerful spirits and our servant's spirits, thereby our temples will still have both of us to care for the Empire's servants. I guess the important thing for me to do is keep the Empire from falling apart before his return. I do believe that my sisters and I will use our cleavage to keep our courts hoping taking into account that even though they are spirits their base in the flesh was male or female. Our females want very much for this to work for their self-pride, as we shall faithfully reward them, as we will all who strongly serve us. This I hope will be our additional motivator. However, I must not overdo it for if we reduce it when our master returns could create rightfully great disappointments and feelings of not being treated fairly. I command my courts to set up emergency security in the even some galaxies overreact when I announce the temporary absence of our king. Sixteen goddesses will help our King and Queen spirits protect and guide the empire. Once the security is set up, I will make the announcement. Of course, the security was set up extra fast. Thus, the courts set up the video streams and announced the Queen had a message to share. With no choice, but to share, "My Empire, your Queen must now share some news about our King. The highest of thrones had taken his soul so that he may also suffer in the name of good and thus give to his servants the greater good as I do. The King's spirits still are with us and rule our Empire with my absolute support and protection. I still shall seek out and fight evil. I suffer the greatest, having not his soul to share my love on our Balatonberény. I am not alone on your throne. Our master has worked hard establishing strong courts and powerful spirits to guide us closer to our ultimate glory. Prior to his departure, he moved our Intimate Restricted Sanctuary beside our Empire's throne and renamed it our Royal Deities Sanctuary. This was to allow our sisters to share in our desire to serve you in our preparation for another penance trial. I am with you always as we strive together to make our universe a safe haven for the good." I then stopped the stream. The real job was to begin now. It is now time to fly high and stretch our wings for those who need us to protect them. Máriakéménd and Fejér, Julia, Faith and my Drusilla shall be in my chamber group who will be with me at all times. My six Empire goddesses along with Sabina and Medica shall work with our spirits in organizing and controlling our security and raids against evil and all divine duties that require a goddess. I plan on staying in the background and working on supporting Bogovi any chance I get, as did Bogovi in giving me Fejér, Máriakéménd, and Julia who are now bonded to me so I can jump on any possible leads that may arise. Bácsalmás, Almásfüzito, and Bükkmogyorósd shall run our courts. They have excellent administrative skills, are familiar with leading courts, and once the courts see that my spirit and Bogovi's spirits are with them things shall run smoothly. I shall now take my chambers and stay on Balatonberény. I shall have Berettyóújfalui completely restored, not changing anything except to improve its original looks so when

Bogovi returns he can spend some time with his courts to get his focus restored. I shall also build another Veszprém so that when my master returns he can have some time to reorganize himself before I capture him, as I plan to reward him greatly for the sacrifice he is allowing himself to make for our Empire. I must face the fact that we shall be separated for some time. This is so sad considering that we were just starting to work strongly together instantaneously as if we were of one mind and are spirits are now so mingled that even the lights are not able to tell where one ends, and the other begins. For now, the battle to keep my sanity begins for I am separated from my master, the first that I have ever given that title and power, and it is difficult to handle. I want to hold him and to love him with all my heart. I can still love and hold onto our memories to build in me the faith that will keep our torch burning until his return. I want to tell him every day that he is special to me, and I am even so his devoted servant. He is my god forever and ever, as my heart is missing the other half. Seeing your smile calm my soul and longing to hear his divine voice shall be like music in my ears. However, the one main pain that I cannot handle is not seeing my master personally. Sorry, I cannot help it, for I will do anything that is not evil just to see him because I am burdened with real love. Sadness shall now dwell in my empty heart. I never knew a shattered heart could keep on breaking. I keep on sending you my love yet no one is there to take it. Rivers of tears keep a steady flow; nevertheless, no one is there to know. It is my master, who you want to know every day; you are whom I want to see. All of what I think and feel is that I want you here with me. Not a day goes by without wishing for a hug a kiss, a laugh, a cry and jump through the skies, a visit to one of our many galaxies or playing with our angels, for soothing hurts, tucking our vast Empire into bed, or just a simple touch. Not a night goes by I do not miss you too much, or my heart does not break just a little bit more. Slivers turned to ice constantly falling to the floor. I do not believe in this need for punishment, yet still I humbly beg to hope to expedite somehow someday your return back in our lives for always and forever. Moreover, we will never let each other go again. Never!

This burden is causing me to lose all that I am, for I gave it to my master to keep safe and keep on him and now he is gone so I wonder where I am. I now feel as if I am only a safe haven for pain and hurt. Hurt and pain. There is so much to gain. Peace and love, it is all the same. Confusion and doubt, and am not without. I weep, I cry, I plead as do my thrones weep, cry, and plead. We give all we have for our master. We try, we laugh, and we smile only to be hurt by one last try. Life is a lesson, as we learn it well. Maybe one day, we can tell this painful tale without tears. I now must try to fight back the memories of my life before surrendering to my master. I was so aware of my sadness and loneliness having nobody to comfort me so I wore a mask that always smiled to hide my feelings behind a lie. After so many millions of years, I had many friends; with my mask, I was one of them. Notwithstanding deep inside, I still felt empty, as if I was missing a secret part of me. Nothing could hear my cries at night as I had designed my mask to hide the lies even from others who lived inside me. Nothing could see the pain I was feeling since I designed my mask to be laughing. Behind all the smiles were the tears and behind all the comfort were the fears. Not everything I thought was everything there was to me. Day by day, centuries of centuries, millennia by millennia I was slowly dying. I could not go on, there was something missing. Until now, I no longer search for the thing that will stop my crying, for the one who will erase my fears, for the power who will wipe away my tears. Until my master's return, I will keep on smiling, hiding behind this mask I am wearing knowing one day I can smile and until then, I will be here waiting. I must be strong and show faith, for I have many sisters now who are all alone trapped inside flesh suits as they do walk their journey through the experience of life they so richly have earned. I lived once so very long ago that even the memory of it has vanished, but not being a grain in the sea of my life. Just a little faith can light your path. When everything seems dark, it is only faith that can push you forward to reach your finish line. Some believe just a little faith can move a mountain from its place, which is true for my servants who have faith in me. My temples teach them that just a little faith can assure that they face the challenges before them. Just a little faith can give the courage to reach a dream, and can restore confidence and self-esteem. Just a little faith can allow one to soar above the sky and can make them never give up, and try, try, try. Just a little faith can pull them up, from rock bottom, straight to the top. Just a little faith can make a dying person once more living. In a universe, which before treated them as though they were nothing, just a little faith made them survive. There is a cost for such a universe as Bogovi previously paid and I now must pay. I will hurt; I will suffer; however, the love that fills me for my servants and their master will put me on top of that mountain as I survive throughout the ages as Queen Lilith, servant of King Bogovi and the holders of the Sword of Justice. I shall portray the look of power and focus of deity with the far off look that sees in the future. I am so lucky in that with my sisters I have kept back with me, especially my chamber sisters; I shall receive much consideration. I may have to entertain the idea of pulling Heidi back although at last resort for her, above all others needs to have a life of freedom, even though Faith gave her all the freedom that one could have and Heidi begged to be made the slave out of love, a binding that now so much better understand. She was so far ahead of all of us in her concept of total peace of mind and heart. I can agree so much with my master when he told me that our sisters were true blessings that would so much enhance the lives of our children. My master could see this and even though I also knew it, I was somewhat selfish in wanting to keep all that pure love for myself, a vice that I will fight to keep as millions of years push us deeper into eternity. I thought I was complete inside, yet I knew I was missing a big part of me as my memories of my master moved into their renaissance inside the timeline of our eternal journey. My chamber sisters do not need me to put up a shield of pride nor will they allow it. They have no fear of me. They will fight me tooth and nail for my good. I can lie down and release all my worries, as they will labor endlessly for me as I would for them. We are blood of our blood and I have been baptized by them. They are the part of me that holds my master inside me. They are keeping that shell preserved by turning it into steel so that I cannot change it in any way. Moreover, when the joyous day comes that I can fill it again with my master the life in my veins will give my sisters access to that shell and help them turn that steal into vapors that will vanish. Although I did not know this day would overshadow me when I selected by sisters, I do know that I selected them because they love me more than I love myself. Now that is the kind of hands I need to keep from crashing into the sea like a meteor into a planet causing extra suffering to those who must stop it. I so often search their minds to determine why they have such great love for me, especially to first twelve and my new sisters; many gave up heavenly thrones with the remaining surrendering high secure positions operating a celestial throne to function as my play toy. As I continue to search, I have joyfully discovered that they consider me the well of love and fountain of good and that by serving me they are serving themselves. I am so blessed to have servants as rich in morals with loyalties as these have. My master and I allow them open access to our power spirits without any hesitation. They hesitate to exercise such options for fear that evil could find a way to profit from this privilege. As we now decide to relax on one of your spongy concrete patios, Drusilla is working very assiduously to help bring me out of the dumps, as we had so many times fought sedulously to pull each other out of our depressions. Somehow, this little bundle of joy has the secret keys to unlock every door inside me and make me respond in a manner she wants, which is always in my best interests. I am so fortunate to have another person who studied me inside and outside of loving each ounce of me inside and outside. We held each other's beaten and raped flesh excessively many times. I find myself so many times just turning off when Drusilla is beside me going into total remote control with her. This gift is rarely found in others. As I think, it may not even grow between my master and myself. Each time her hand hit the surface we are both now on I feel something new inside me surrender. I shall not allow anything inside me ever to exist that can resist her. She is my twin sister and shall be forever and ever the absolute my favorite as even my master now acknowledges being the closest creation of a child between us. Bogovi even allows himself to fall under her innocent and caring charms without trying to resist. He can feel what she has done for me and feels he owes her way too much for the great love she has given us. A true gift that made every second of pain I suffered during my penance for the good worth it for that experience cannot be created for the millions of experiences and ability to predict each other is something not made but flowing from the depth of an unconscious soul. I was so glad that destiny brought us together and with her painfully at my side as those beasts beat us to our deaths I had something to hold onto as I returned to my eternal existence. The fact that I was nervous was known by only one other spirit, that Drusilla; still held on to her faith that I would keep us together. If there was a kingdom before us, she did not care for to be slaves again as long as together was all that she needed. She had to care for that twin sister that was beside her through so many horrible experiences. Faith, Julia, Máriakémend, and Fejér all stepped aside as the queen of my soul was crawling towards me. She now stopped and raised her body up with her hands supported on her legs and feet forming a cup as if to also be ready for me to rest my head sandwiched, as she would give me her most sacred fruit. Drusilla was also very popular among the sisters as she reverently worshipped each one even though she was my favorite and thus had the highest position. All the sisters craved her and struggled hard to please her, yet all who look into her eyes know that something is hidden deep inside her and that is her devotion to her twin sister. I never in any way try to remove myself from that position as when my master comes around me I melt and when my twin sister comes around me. I melt as my head is now being pulled by love to rest on her ankles as my arms brace her strong legs and she starts to penetrate inside my soul and plant happiness inside all those now empty rooms. My other four sisters in the room join Drusilla as they work to make me strong again. I can completely surrender to them having no shame and fill myself with my love. They have stored away for me in case a day such as today were to come again. So much has happened on this day. However, our Empire, with both its pilots out of their seats is pushing strong ahead on autopilot. This is when the depths of our courts and deep insight of our lights shine the brightest. Everyone believes in our mission and loves our mission. They are the arrows that fly from our bows. I do know that I must search out another large evil nest and destroy it to energize our Empire; however, now is not the time at all will be watching their throne as their source of love and protection. This is where Bogovi's and my multiple spirits play such a major role. Other gods need the thrill of being served and worshiped and testing their servants to determine their love. My master and I do not need this, as we prefer to be the servants. This has played strongly to our benefit as it instills a strong willing loyalty. Moreover, the harder their throne works for them the deeper their loyalty is installed, and a very productive ecosystem is formed. Each element has its part in keeping our living mission alive. In addition, we struggle hard to ensure that the part is made to feel worthy and appreciated for its unique and special contributing function. I have Drusilla now to thank as she once again paid the price to get me back on my feet and my chamber sisters and I am now rewarding her as each of us eagerly seeks a part of her to give our special uninhibited reverence and worship. I just love seeing her like this and that is being rewarded for her self-motivated loyalty to her twin sister and all that she loved. She does not worry if they deserve love or not, her twin sister loves them so she will not only love them but worship them giving thanks for the love they give the part of her that keeps their heart. Her eyes are, without question the greatest power that we have for she can cut or build with them. My feet become weak when she looks at me yet by some miracle, she is always able to catch me before I hit the ground. Someday I hope to make clones of her and make these my sisters their twins and give them ten years living as slaves. They will not be sacrificed however will live through some tough times. This would give my sisters that something extra deep inside of them to hold on to when they face future tribulations. Like I said, this is a maybe something someday for them, for as we now stand they have me to hold onto. As I now stand up again, my chamber sisters can see the power in my eyes once again. I shall now walk around my throne and reinstall confidence back into my courts and lights. The Queen is back and she is ready to smoke some evil and bless her servants. My courts are giving me their reports emphasizing the number of new temples and schools for priests to go along with the temple's angels being produced in our now 3,485 galaxies. I ask them, "What is the factor that has these galaxies deciding to join us?" My lights now tell me, "Our great Queen, we have assimilation requests from over 10,000 galaxies, that we have given alliance status how and are activating them as fast as we can properly secure and care for them." I then told them, "Produce and reproduce what you must bring them into our Empire as safely and securely as possible. For when our Master returns, I want him to see that we have worked hard to make what he gave us into much better for his name's sake. You may use our Sword if needed to accomplish this. I want as many children of good that want to serve me are given that opportunity so they can have great faith and security in Good." The courts and lights all said in unison, "As our Queen as divinely commanded it shall be done." I now gracefully walked around the beautiful throne that Bogovi had built for us. I never really had any time just to walk around this powerful nerve center that travels in a 100 planet rotation and rules now 3,485 galaxies and over one Septillion (10^{24}) planets based on our current data. The lights have just begun a 500-galaxy sectors chain by establishing a throne for each 500 galaxies, each with direct access to Bogovi's and my spirit and its own lights and courts. These thrones are further divided into fifty galaxy sectors, and these thrones are divided into seven thrones with seven galaxies each, with one receiving eight galaxies. Then, each galaxy has its own throne with a receptor spirit that is linked to its next higher throne and so on up to this wonderful center whom I am now enjoying the actual magnificence from it. From the person who worships in their temple at the time that is filtered up to my thrones court is less than one second. This recommended solution is most times approved. However, sometimes it must be rejected for the better good of all concerned. The response and anything needed to implement it is less than one second that may also include a special presentation by our master or me or both if that are what the servants wanted. The perfection in this process is continually being improved. Our military force, both flesh and spirits are more advanced than I ever could have dreamed. I often think now, what am I doing here, except enjoying my flesh cravings? I continue to enjoy my nudity as it at present gives me pleasure to give those who enjoy looking at me with some additional excitement. It does help remove some of the mystery of what is underneath the clothing of the opposite sex for young boys, as all Empire Buildings have a large painting of me and Bogovi standing beside me in his robe. Most of the society that is in my empire has now taken a lenient view of public nudity, since trying to enforce it always elicits the argument that their queen is unclothed. I enjoy the power of sharing myself instead of hiding it as my shame. If there is a defect, I will simply fix it or wear one of my other flesh suits. The thrill of moving through large groups with the power to be both different and showing the great comfort and hiding no shame presents the appearance of being so relaxed as if being in my private chambers. The self-conceited notion that what I have if so much better or different or of more value than the half of my servants that share the same sex or that it need to hide it to get a better capture from the other half is just as foolish. I got the master of what someday will be over 13,000 so how could I ever get more. There must be the point of contentment as I was with the concept of joining Ereshkigal with Berettyóújfalui and then the shock of receiving four more was a terrifying thought crippling my return. My master has left me with over 3,000 galaxies. When he returns I will lay at his feet over 13,000 galaxies. I want him to know that his servant was working hard for his Empire. Oh, I now subsequently miss him. It seems that my time is always spent with one of my three lives, the servant to the master life, the life of a Queen and the life of a sister. This is such a wonderful dilemma although I feel that each part hurts when I go to the other part. Bogovi did well by creating such a wonder haven for our Royal Deities Sanctuary where we all can go. He gets the joy of being able to concentrate on any issue in his mind and being a part of a large Divine family. With such a large collection of former goddesses in our family, we can send them out on our behalf. We always send two out at a time since my master and I go to the throne together most times. This gives our lights the added belief of a solid divine body to serve them and our Empire. My eight divine sisters are now zapping through our Empire verifying the installation of Bogovi and my new power spirits as we are now creating so many more. My ultimate goal is to have each throne beginning at the five galaxy thrones all the way up to my current seven 500-galaxy thrones. As we will soon have these in places, each one can respond to a foreign attack immediately with the same punch as from the throne I now walk. What is so nice about these thrones is that they are ruled by hologram clones of my master and me. Not even their lights or courts can tell the difference, as they are real time with the throne I now walk. I am everywhere, yet I am also independently in the now completely comforted flesh suit that is being loved by Drusilla and my chamber sisters. I am the same me as I was before, yet my spirit has been reproduced into so many more by my power spirit. Amazingly simple, yet so complex, that I would have to dig deep into my subconscious for a glimpse of this massive process. The one thing that I do know is that it always gives the perfect solution that is based upon my master's and my desires. It is nice to be everyone at the same time, especially for my servants as they can see and hear me serving them. We are also expanding our flesh military by adding the technologies of the Empires that are joining our family. This is nice in that they all get a feel of something unique to them with the added security of seeing such massive forces dedicated to their security. Each force also augments our long-range exploratory forces. These massive forces work beyond our ten-layer deep security zone. We do not enter any area or zone when notified that its beings are from another throne. We have never fired in the strike mode against those who are not assaulting. Our ships will not fire in these situations, as the weapons systems will shut down. There will be no killing of the innocent. As long as we notify the other force that our mission is one of peace and ask to retreat without anyone being harmed I am happy. Yet sadly, some foreign governments are ruled by greed, consider non-aggression as a sign of weakness, and have to take advantage of a misperceived opportunity for victory and fire upon my ships. Our shields always reflect the shots back to the attacking force causing some damage. As standard procedure, we demand that their fleet retreat first so that we may retreat safely and that failure to comply will result in the complete destruction of their force. We always stream the highlights of this encounter to the planets the force represents. Then those who decide to fight are completely rendered dysfunctional and at that time, we depart securely to our next exploratory position. We cannot accept alliances with these galaxies as they are excessively far for our security abilities. We are mainly searching for any evidence of an evil stronghold at which time we will activate my Sword of Justice, which will verify if evil is there and if it is wise to attack them or to trace them back to a larger nest. I do have fleets that are tracing their evil prey back to their nest. The more nests we pop the safer we all will be. We do have to be careful which ones to destroy as evil nests have different goals and functions. Some are not concerned about deep universal aggression and those we want to lightly quarantine for to destroy them could allow a very wicked evil nest to appear. I have now decided to drift around Ereshkigal and see how things are going. Everything is moving accordingly peacefully as the servants are producing for than enough for themselves and sending the excess to those galaxies that need it. It takes some time to bring a new galaxy into a productive state, nevertheless my baptisms help remove the disease and hunger problems. I truly am so impressed at the work our spirits are doing. To think about one Septillion planets that worship my spirit is absolutely beyond anything I ever imaged. My master sets everything up so well which allows us to concentrate on building the love and unity expected from a divine royal couple. The thought of so many people living healthy lives as their children train in our advanced universities existing in peace as they raise the future generations. My temples also conduct many family activities because of my belief that families who play together are so much stronger as their societies build the required infrastructure for an advanced life with all their modern Empire's assets available. Even though evil does not exist here, there is always a threat that someday it may try to plant a seed and that seed must be dug up and burned by one of my septillion stars although I have my eye on having over one octillion stars and planets when my master returns. It is so important that I prove to him that his faith in me is his greatest conquest. That may be mushy; however, I am still me at the core. I hear a strange noise and wake up holding Faith in my arms. I do so much enjoy holding Faith, yet I thought I was holding Drusilla. I ask my chamber sisters where Drusilla is and they tell me she stepped outside doing some exploring, as she is never quite comfortable in a new place until she has completely studied it. I remember she was that way when we were kids however, her opportunities were very much limited. She always wanted to know what was around the bend, more for my safety than hers was. She was able to relax when Bogovi was here since she completely trusted him to care for not only me but also all of us. She considered him the umbrella that was above all of us at all times. I now had Faith braced in my arms holding her as tight as I could as she was wiping away my tears. I had not really felt this close to her since she left for France to return as Queen. As I was draining my misery into her precious Hyrum, body we were hit with a big psychedelic star flashes that left us all temporarily blind. My lights immediately got us back some temporary vision while they worked to rebuild the eyes in our flesh suits. We looked around and could verify everyone, except for Drusilla who must now be blind and alone in the beautiful forests that fill our sanctuary. I needed to have someone to verify that she is ok. I called for my Seonji to help as I had built them with special eyes that could see a dime five miles away and run like a deer for hours. I gave them their new mission and off they went. An hour went by yet still no word. Drusilla could not be that far away. I now called upon my spirit to tell me where she was. My spirits responded back, "Oh great Queen Lilith, holder of the Sword of Justice, the goddess Drusilla is not in the Royal Deities Sanctuary and we know not where she is." How can this be, my spirit is everywhere in my empire. How could they not know where she is? I called for my courts and spirits to meet me on the throne. I posted a giant image of my Drusilla and I asked, "How can this part of my heart just vanish. Do we not have a security force that can protect a goddess in my most sacred part, my Royal Deities Sanctuary? Find her and bring her to me, and those that captured her for my judgment . . . Now." This is now starting to bug me. My master vanishes and now my closest sister is gone. How can parts so close to I just vanish? I have the greatest security known in the known universe and my closest loved ones are vanishing. This is not going to happen. I must find a way to stop this. I know every safeguard from the highest throne in this part of the universe as programed into our security safeguards by my sister Bácsalmás. The search is now on as even my local throne is assisting us. My deepest security forces are reporting no sign of the Goddess Drusilla as even our deep range exploratory forces are reporting with no news. There can be no way that a spirit can just vanish and leave no traces. We have the ability to trace any particle of my twin sister. I now have the thought that she could be gone, as I even; there is still no proof where Bogovi is. We knew that his penance would have to be tried however now that I think about it, the time is too soon after our reunion. I think that allowing us some time further to build our expanding empire would be more important than playing their stupid pain games. Is it that important to them to get the maximum suffering from this stupid game of deities suffering? I mean, when I think about it, dividing us just before we were to set a fire on a new eternal love was a sick sense of timing. Yet the time they select is always a mystery. The greatest value of my empire is that we do not play the 'throne must make you suffer' game as the throne above our dimension does with its penance games. I suffered because I knew that by playing their stupid game my servants would live better lives. It is so important to add those new10, 000 galaxies as fast as I can so that the higher throne above this dimension will be cheated out of the joy gained by watching innocent good beings suffer. I know they are getting joy from me now as I am suffering. The loss of both my master and Drusilla is so painful and just as Drusilla had put me back on my feet after she soothed my soul and buried my face deep between her wonderful legs. An absolute taste of heaven that has just been taken away from me and I hope not without a big fight. Every second they are reporting that they cannot find her. I wonder now if this is not some kind of internal empire game, they are playing in order to shake me up while my master is away. If it is, it will not work. I will stay strong for the one who was always strong for me. I am now beginning to have my spirits starts some shaking on my lights and courts and armies and all this advanced spiritual and flesh power and get me some information. No one can be allowed to enter the Royal Deities Sanctuary without invitation, and much less enter and still a goddess, especially my beloved. This cannot be allowed, as I am now placing my Empire on full war alert. We are going to give somebody or something a powerful punch as I am now posting war warnings and also, just in case posting them in other dimensions as well. It is time for war. My throne is off limits. That which takes from me shall suffer endlessly. I am tired of these stupid games. Then we all heard a crashing sound as I felt myself being lifted up. I could feel my spirits fighting hard to hold me back as they were making sure to keep a link on me. I can also see my armies fighting hard for their naked red haired queen. They are fighting accordingly hard as I can feel this force starting to weaken. Then I hear voices telling me, "Fear not Queen Lilith since we will do you no harm." I then ordered my Sword of Justice to attack and destroy an evil that is trying to capture me. Yet once again this worthless sword tells me, "Oh great Queen, you are not being attacked by evil." I then told it to attack that which is taking me." The piece of shit tells me that, "I cannot hurt that which created me." I then said to it, "As you cannot protect those who you promised to protect. First, my master, then my most sacred lover and now me, now the question is how many more will you let this creature take away. I guess my armies will fight and protect me." My armies are packing a tremendous punch in both the spiritual and natural worlds. We are now moving out of my dimension and my armies are beside me as I continue to be trapped inside the collapsing vacuum. I now hear the greatest voice in my eternity saying to me, "My master, please call off my armies for we are in no danger, yet if you destroy them you will not be able to see me." I then immediately told my armies, "My master has asked me to hold off our attacks, proceed beside me, and yet hold your fire in both realms." They did stop firing, as my body was now totally limp. I had heard the voice of my Bogovi so I did not care where I went. If I must call upon my armies will pull us both out. Time would tell how large this war is going to be because for once I will get what I want out of this stupidity. My limp body floated like a ball of light as I was now in a place where flesh was not permitted. Then slowly did my spirit lay down before a giant throne that had many beasts of stone before it with large columns that held up a glass roof with the ending one holding up giant angels. I could barely identify one, sitting between two large stone beasts. An entire kingdom with a mighty golden city behind it was now vaguely before me. As I went to stand up the stone beasts turned into spiritual beasts. I then said to it that was on the throne, "Do not try to make me angry or cause me to fear for I have many armies ready now to destroy this place thus I would recommend you stop your stupid games now or die." They then said to me, "Do you not wish to speech to Bogovi and Drusilla?" I then stomped my feet as initial attack hit parts of the city behind him and I then repeated myself, "Do not play games with me, for you are thieves in that you tried to take me yet when you were failing to have to have my master beg on your behalf. I then decided to give you a temporary extension on your existence however I do emphasis temporary because if I do not get what I want I will fight a war as never seen between two dimensions." They then asked me, "Why do you think you will win." I then ordered more attacks in the area as I could see a lot of scrambling behind him. I then repeated myself, "Give me my master and Drusilla and I will spare a small amount of you to be my slaves and I do not think I can defeat you, I know I can and will. You have two strikes against you, so to save a small amount of your beasts give me my demands now." Then I did look over and saw Bogovi and Drusilla (both in the flesh) as I then dawned my flesh suit and we ran together, hugging and crying and kissing. I would kiss one then kiss the other and told them both that we would be going to war to punish those who did this to them. Bogovi then told me, "They brought Drusilla here to care for me and help fight away my loneliness. She is also my twin sister in our little home." I then said, "I hope she does not have to suffer as she did with me." Bogovi then told me, "Actually she will die a painless death as I go to college and then she will live in my night time world." I then clarified this by saying, "That is what these beasts that take people are telling you, if one can steel they will also lie." Bogovi then asked me, "My fiery little master, I beg that you give them a chance to explain to you why this must be." I then told my two lovers, "This does not have to be, and a war will prove it." They both then stepped to the side as the throne asked me to appear. I was very angry and screamed out, "Where do you think you get the power to tell me to appear before you. I will wipe this little piece of junk that you call a throne from existence." They then said, "We petition you appear so that we can show you the importance of your master's mission." I then walked before them and told them to start talking. They first asked me, "You are the greatest Queen to ever rule as you rule more planets than a large lake has sand yet you give into your servants wonderful clothing and you walk among them with no clothing allowing you servants to gain pleasure from your personal parts. Why do you do this?" I then answered, "Because my servants are my children and should not a child be permitted to see the body that brought them into existence. I hide nothing from my servants and can only hope that what my body has can bring them pleasure for I want them to be happy and have hope and to know that their Queen is eager to serve them." They now asked, "Then if you wish to serve them why do you want to put them in war?" I answered, "For it is forbidden to take a goddess from the Royal Deities Sanctuary as it is even more forbidden to take their King. All, to include myself will die for our King. If we lose our King then we will fight to the last person. That is my law and my law is enforced by the love inside my empire and war outside of it." They then asked, "Do you love your servants?" I then said to them, "Are you stupid or were you born dumb, I told you that I not only love my servants, I also serve and worship them and give them all that I can include sharing my shame with them as they may enjoy as they wish." They then responded, "You do truly rule in a special way, yet to see how loyal your empire is to you is shockingly refreshing, as we do know you suffered your penance and was awarded the highest honor that a goddess could receive." I then said to them, "I think this take a god and smoke them to trash and then return them for some sick higher deity is so wrong and is based on evil, for it cannot be based in good. They took me, as I was to surrender to my master whom I worship still each day, as I worship all that is around me, for I want to be the lowest and weakest for that is when I learn who is truly good. You took my special love, the one who has the key to my heart and I am now learning the key to my master's heart from me. How is that just?" They then asked, "Does it anger you that the goddess you love the most is also cherished by your master?" I then answered, "I want all my sisters and all my female lovers to lay before my master and serve him as he so desires. For all that is mine is his. That is why he now has a home in our Royal Deities Sanctuary. For when they lay under him, it is the same as me lying under him. I will have nothing that I cannot lay before my master." They then said, "We must confess that we did not know the love between Bogovi and you would grow this strong this fast. That must be the result of planting a love in an Empire of Good. You and your master are clearly the greatest royal deities ever to appear before this throne. We all cheer the unbelievable Empire you shall someday rule with millions of galaxies. You almost make us wish to wear flesh suits so we could feel our hearts beat caused by our eyes being locked upon your beauty, as our flesh servants now worship you and your beauty as they can now feel your love and kindness and have no fear of your large warships hovering above them." I then said to my physical army, "I am your servant Queen and I pray to you that you go in the peace time mode and do not hurt anyone in the flesh, but show them that we are an empire of love, kindness, and caring. If you see any in need and can produce what they need, please share it with them. Fear not for us for our spiritual armies is also here to protect us." The one on the throne now said to me, "I must hasten our visit so that my servants do not leave me to worship you. We have brought Drusilla at this time to care for Bogovi's loneliness as you were given twelve sisters he does not want to bend or expand his realm of some new people so in order to keep him on his path to a greatness he has never had before. W honored his request and brought Drusilla here since we are forbidden to take a King and Queen at the same time." I then looked at Drusilla and said, "My twin sister, worship are master and tend to all of his needs. Lay down your body for his pleasure, as he so desires. Prepare these in the name of our great love my special goddess. Remember all that we have and are being given to us by our master and we must give to him what we can to keep him strong so he can continue to be our god." I then looked at Bogovi and said, "Take my greatest love and enjoy it as you would me for she is me as I am her. By taking the woman in question, you are taking me and by denying this girl, you are denying me. Please do not forsake me my master as your servant Drusilla now lies before you for you to take and enjoy." I now looked at the throne I was standing before and asked them, "Do you now have great joy that I have given my master to my greatest lover? Does that grant you great joy in knowing how you have tried to push our bonding with a desire to cause suffering? What you try to do will not work because my master is the master of all in our empire. We serve him as he so gently and kindly serves us. We will not let evil destroy our throne for we must stay true to each other and serve only one master so we can be the sanctuary for the good. I still believe you act in such shame by taking a master from the ones who love and worship him and cast him down to undergo pains that we fight hard to prevent our servants from ever suffering. We as their divine gods will have no pleasure in watching them suffer. We will keep our faith in their love as they keep their faith in our love. It must go both ways, as we will fight those who only receive and demand that their servants suffer greatly for the pleasures of their gods. It is by the name of good that gods must love and give to their servants, and thus their servants will gladly give all their love to feed the power starved divine spirits and allow them to produce much more than ever dreamed of. This has worked as our Empire now has over 3,000 new spirit power sources that are all overflowing. I do not stand her in front of your boasting of a theory that might work. This does work and will give me the power to destroy all here for this great evil." The one on the throne now spoke to me, "My great Queen, and you are my Queen for me have surrendered myself to you in total agreement and shall someday move the dimensional wall between yours and my Empires and I shall lay all that I have before the feet of the one you call master. It is reason that we will work hard to insure that he meets all the penance requirements as set up millions of years ago by our divine ancestors who ruled in a time of great evil. Moreover, they wanted to make sure that only the strongest of the good received the great powers such as you received with your Sword of Justice. So many gods have pleaded and tried for the great gift that we hope Bogovi qualifies for yet all have failed. So far, he has been strong yet his love for you is defeating him. We want you to believe that this painful process is required by the judges so long ago when great empires also ruled yet their eternity ended very early by evil. No matter how much evil you destroy, there shall be twice as much evil, which will try to destroy you. As your empire of good continues to grow, evil will mount a campaign against you, as you have never seen. This is why your master must suffer through this penance so that we all can have security as we someday fight the war that you so eagerly wish to fight now." As I heard them speak these words, I called off all my forces and told them to leave me a small ship with my chamber sisters about it. I would need no protection. Nevertheless, I knew that they would hang back and that was to be expected when the servants love their masters. I then decided that I knew the tool to help Bogovi to pull through. I then spoke to Drusilla in mind talk telling her that I would change her into me in the eyes of Bogovi, so for her to only be with him when he was alone. She is to stand behind me as I now explain this to him. Bogovi did not have his divine powers and could not hear me talk mind talk to Drusilla. I then went before Bogovi and told him, "My great master I have great news for you. They have agreed to let me stay with you as long as we keep it a secret so that no penance spies catch us. I will be at your feet serving you as my god." I could see tears of joy pour out of his eyes as he held me saying, "With your love I shall be able to survive, for we are one and shall always be one." He then held me tight as I slowly put him to sleep and the then gave a small invisible and a networked copy of myself inside Drusilla. This was networked as atoms mixed with Drusilla's all through her body. Thus she should not be able to be detected by penance scans, for the network was only activated when Bogovi and Drusilla was alone and only targeted for Bogovi's senses, as they reached out to study the surroundings and returned to his perceptual network to tell him what he was experiencing. I just had one more precaution set up and we would be screwing the heck out of me to rebuild his manhood for another trial in his penance. Drusilla helped me lay him down as I told her, "Fear not for he will be seeing me as you are now giving to me more than I can ever repay." Drusilla then gave me that big sister hug and then asked me, "My precious twin sister, if I enjoy seducing him as much as you do will you let me get some in the future when we return?" I then kissed her and told her, "My twin sister, you belong in my bed with our master and that is where you shall rest for eternity." Drusilla said, "I will seduce him so that I may be with you as much as possible for it is only you, which I need. I believe that by doing this pleasurable task for you I shall be beside you or even below you just so I am with you always." I kissed her again as I knew so well that I flowed in her veins and that she would do anything for me as I would for her. I then told her, "It shall be as you have said since I will worship you in my bed for eternity. I am so sorry my twin sister; however, I must go now so that you can finish your work and return faster. I shall ask about your night world also so that I may enjoy some of you before our master gets it all, if that were possible." I then proceeded to the one on the throne and spoke, "I hope you do not get angry however I had to put him to sleep so you can return him to his mission. I have instructed Drusilla to stay hidden as much as possible so as not to alert the penance scans. Is there anything else that you ask of me?" He then told me, "I ask only that I may serve you when this is finished. We will provide Drusilla protection from the penance scans as we also would be in great danger. You may of course visit sometimes as we will sneak him up here however I hope you do realize that this could be painful for him." I then asked, "When will you set up the night world? They then told me that last three or four years of his time here. Too early is dangerous as too late is dangerous. We will consult with you when the time is approaching. Also you may at any time come here and watch him as we did so many times allow him to come here and watch you." I then offered my thanks, "He never told me that, guess he thought that was too mushy, however I shall come and worship him from time to time. I do so much feel shame in my anger when I arrived here. I shall replace and repair all things. I will send some of my power courts here." The one who sat on the throne then said, "I do so much understand the reason for your anger and applaud you on your desire to talk before destroying. That is a great gift as is having the one you designs your flesh suits. When I look into your eyes, I can feel your warmth and desire to understand and share. I shall have a fleet escort your small warship back to the wall of this dimension that I shall remove when your master has finished his journey as I will be at your side when evil becomes foolish enough to attack you." I then walked over and kissed him as my breasts rested on his chest. I asked him, "Please help protect them as they are my greatest loves." He then said, "As my Queen has commanded it shall be done." It was now time for me to turn around and watch them return my master and my twin sister back to the penance journey. I now walked out into the open area of the giant court that seemed to run on forever and wait for my war ship. In order to keep their attention I made sure to do the female wiggle so that what they saw would keep them looking as they put before me a giant ring like the one we keep on our throne with a nice powerful fire behind it. This was truly amazing as it reassured me that they did indeed respect my bond with my master. As I waited for my chamber sisters to arrive, our hosts departed as I now stood alone on this stage with my ring of love giving me comfort. This ring brings to me great joy and peace of mind. The one on our throne is 1,000 miles from turning side to turning side and over 100 miles thick throughout the entire circumference filled with spiritual armies. It shall now be graced with great flames of fire with the writings of the penance court. Subsequently they are subordinate to the ancient throne that demands penance as a method to burn all evil out of the good. I wonder if it truly works, although my greatest love is with my eternal master now and these were loves, which were cultivated through penance. At least with my master being with Bogovi, I do not have to worry as much with him bringing home twelve male disciples to chase me around the throne and trap me in some room for some spiritual enlightenment, which usually is surmounted by me lying on the floor. I would much rather Drusilla chase me, that way I could run slow and let her catch me many times. That will be a game a few decades down the journey of my eternity. My war ship is here now and my four loves or for now officially my chamber sisters exit and guide me safely and gently into our ship as I melt before them. In my weakness, they guide me into our space chamber as I hear a voice whisper in my ear, "For truly you are loved by your servants, as in your weakness they become your strength. You are a blessed goddess who receives better worship from a galaxy that other gods get in ten. May your trip be safe and your many return trips be rewarded with great joy. We were now inside at which time my sisters positioned themselves as if part of a rehearsed plan and I ended up as we lay on one of our viewing floors, which are always nice in that you feel as if floating in space. Máriakémend now anchored herself beside me and slowly started to massage my privates. Her fingers always felt so soothing as would move them up and down and then slowly insert a few of them in her special in and out motion. My insides began shooting heavenly wine as Faith, Fejér and Julia rushed over to insure the spiritual wine was drank, and not wasted. Now their six hands roamed over my body exciting every nerve sensor that I had. Máriakémérd now took over massaging my bosom as Julia anchored me and brought her hand forward to pet my wine bottle keeping it wet and warm. I am very relaxed now as my chamber sisters have everything in me running full speed. I am totally at peace with their tongues, hands, and fingers. They have my entire flesh suit crying and begging for more. They know how to take care of their goddess even as I have ordained them all to be goddesses. As I am now at the point of total climax at the master hands of Máriakémérd thinking nothing better could happen, I was wrong, for Faith had been living with Drusilla and learning everything she could from her and as her fingers warmly went up inside me it felt as if it were my twin sister. As she slowly kissed me, I could feel us sinking in the river of our heavenly wine. My spirit was being recharged with the billions of small soft charges exacting us to surrender as Drusilla. I began to lose control. I flashed to the top of her kissing (or shooting spirit charges) blending spiritually with any part of her soul that was near. This was higher than the heavens we were zipping. She then whispered in my ear, "Anytime you want something done right, you need to get a Queen to do it." Then it hit me, this was my Faith, my lovely Queen Maria Henrietta. I then rolled her over to be on top of me now and held her tight in my arms saying to her, "You are a wonderful sister, for even as a Queen, you were willing to learn from a beaten slave. I am impressed at your wisdom." Faith then said to me, "Oh, my Queen, the beaten slave had the greatest gold in the universe and that was the skills to please my master. Oh great master, was I not naked with but tearing rags to hide what I had to share to keep my sisters and I from starving? Were we not cold until you warmed and fed us? How can I ever repay such a great debt except to search for ways to please you? I shall worship and serve you as my goddess for eternity. I was created to be your servant, in both flesh and spirit, yet both times, you gave to me the same as you had. You own me and I will never let you free me. Never, my goddess!" I could feel the power of her words as they pressed through her wonderful breasts against mine. This was a perfect time for a testimony. She was based on good, for a wise greedy being would have captured me and made off with my powers, but not her, she chose instead to serve harder and not see my shame but see in me a lack of love from her. What a fantastic reward for this holder of the Golden Sword. I have been hit hard twice and through the power of my sisters, I am now whole. I have now issued orders for my spirits to send all my sisters back to me. I want them, I must have them, and this is my greed and need for I am with them as they are so much in me. The send them out is as sending me out. I must keep as much of me in me during this important phase in the struggle to save my master's kingdom. This is my weak time so I must stay in my power and my power is my sisters. They have studied every particle in my soul and learned how to serve it beyond what I could ever have dreamed. Besides, my greatest treat was yet to come, is the senior sister to all of us, the aristocrat Fejér that is completely home with the new flesh suits, as hers exceeded Queen Mother of Ereshkigal Queen Клеопатра and the goddess Sabina. In your heyday, even Drusilla would lately just lay down and marvel at her creation. In all my misery and heartaches of late, the greatest gift is they, and I must keep them where I can protect them. I know they will be beside me when I make that lonely landing back at my throne. I hope all my sisters that I sent out have returned. I am accordingly excited about drowning myself in them and hoping that no air reaches my lungs and they become filled with their great loved. I must currently rest this very much drained flesh suit, and I am fortunate in that I get my favorite position on my oldest sister who did so much for me in my first half of my penance as I often testify helped give me the strength to hang on for Drusilla. I at present move over to Fejér as the other sisters' move away, and I lay on top of her as she spreads her breasts putting one against each ear and slowly starts to rub my back and muscles. As usual, I start to drift off speedily asleep at most saying to myself, as I fall away swiftly, "My Empire must go on, and that it shall as I can merely hope the surprises are ending." Nevertheless, the surprises were only starting to begin.

Chapter 05

Surprises with Family Ties

As our luxurious war, ship glides through the universe dimension as if going through regular space astonishes me. The man on the throne had, at least for me proven that he could control dimensional walls. At this time, we can see a message come through saying, "We have a pleasant well deserved surprise waiting for you as you return to your HOME. Farewell and see you soon." I am starting to get off on this "person to person" and personally using flash technology. It is considerably better than standing on top of each other's mountain and yelling back to forth, gets results so much faster because misunderstandings and misinformation cause unspeakable destruction. My spirits and courts work so hard to keep the unknown known to my children for this is what kills. What is more, I hate to cause any child of mine to suffer along the battlefields as even I am quick to take arms, yet smart enough to recognize whom I am fighting and why I am fighting them and more importantly try to determine if a reasonable solution is available. Social existence, even for gods must be based on compromise. Compromise is not a sign of weakness but a sign of power because you have the strength and honor to understand that the needs of all are different, and what you give up today will be received in another encounter someday. During all this indoctrination through my temples my children still fight wars. That is the path of the flesh, which shall never be forgotten, as even the obedient fight righteous for holy reasons. I just make sure it is not to have vital resources just to survive, for that is when I step in and give them what they need to survive. In my Empire, the deities serve their servant's needs, for I made them to need these things and thus I must do what they need to exist in the world I put them on. So much for all that my spirits do, for I continue to play around with my lovers and enjoy the exotic and sensual side of existence. For when the base or core of a deity is filled with love its spirit picks that up and generates to divine power needed to accept the worship from our servants, which is the food of the gods. I have discovered that I possess many empty rooms, or even filled rooms that are locked. I marvel that this is still so complex even as I have worked hard to keep myself so simple. At least I have an eternity to clean house. I often wonder if I have these issues then why my sisters not have them. I just must try not to create more issues until my master and twin return to me. At least I can feel that the one on that throne is taking or trying to take great care of them. As I look around, I can see that we are deep into my Empire now. We should arrive at my throne soon. I wonder if I can sneak in and jump into my sanctuary with my chamber sisters. That will be my next challannnnnnn . . . Forget it, they just picked us up on their radars as my escorts have alerted them. I guess a goddess especially a Queen does not sneak in and out which is to my benefit. They are very protective of that little naked redhead that hangs on or in our master's arms. We all give each other the most we can. That is what builds a powerful throne to send that power to our servants. I have been thinking too much about my philosophies. I need to think about how I can care for all my children and sisters. I do love all my servants and want to be the greatest Queen goddess they could ever dream of and spend their eternity in our reward for them. Our soul heavens are so massive now as we allow our servants to travel to whichever they want as my master and I have combined their eternal resting places. Security reasons force us until we keep them protected in the central areas of our Empire. They have a choice to volunteer or not to volunteer in the defense of our Empire. They appear to be a ready to volunteer at all time, which pleases my master and his Queen. The truth of the matter is that most of the spirits fleet that escorted me to meet our master was from the eternal heavens. Bogovi is so big on letting them help, as long it is volunteer. He feels that to keep them in the total rest can make their eternities a living hell. I agree, and it is so good to have a vigintillion (10^{63}) souls ready to defend. It would take an unbelievable evil force to defeat them. Anyway, they come and go as they please especially since we have established my spirit courts from their ranks that create challenges and thrills even my deities cannot create. This insures that their eternal rest is as it was promised. As our ship is now docketing I see one who I cannot identify right off hand, highly decorated in front of a giant army waiting to meet us. I have a feeling about this host as if she is a part of me; nonetheless, they are all parts of me so let me go out and allow her to receive us. As I go to hug her, it strikes; she is my Medica. This is great, as I must now ask her if all my sisters have returned. As we hug so tightly I can feel the sharp edges of her decorated jewelry cut, however, I do not care for the short time they were deployed was too much for me. I just want to get them all into our Royal Deities Sanctuary for some serious strategy improvement. My Seonji will be off great value in this process. I must first ask Medica why she is as specially adorned whilst she simply tells me, "My goddess Queen, as I am representing your awesome power, I wanted to all appear as a goddess." I told her, "You are, as far as my heart contends you shall always live inside me as part of our trinity." Medica replies, "Oh great goddess, I need to be your servant in order to be at peace inside me, for I wish only forever to be the ground that you walk upon." I then told one of so many truly devoted servants that I am lucky to have worship me, "As my ground Medica, you hold me up as my support so that I may stand. No one can endure unless he or she has a strong foundation, for when you no longer give me that firm foundation, I shall pass. Thus I must beg you to please allow me to stand so that I can keep the rain from you." She then took her hands, wiped as much blood from me as possible, covered her face, and licked her hands. I sometimes wonder if I have created, I then healed the bleeding so that my armies would not be alarmed. I also had to be careful not to create a stampede for my blood. I then asked all my sisters to line up and to be free from the chains of clothing as I am since we are the humblest servants in this Empire. My Empire's Sister Goddesses are now standing with me. I always kneel before them and then I sit on the ground in front of them so that all times they are higher than I am and introduce them, allowing an ovation for each one. The galaxy goddess Bárdudvarnok, the galaxy goddess Tamási, the galaxy goddess Békéscsaba, the galaxy goddess Ceglédbercel, the galaxy goddess Dédestapolcsány, the galaxy goddess Jakabszállás, the penance guardian goddess Fejér, the penance night world goddess Julia, the penance countess goddess Mary; the penance countess goddess Ruth, the penance love goddess Amity; the penance countess goddess and first to die in my name Joy; absent currently serving her penance for her people's salvations the beloved goddess of the Harvey Siusan; the Hyrum penance goddess Queen Faith; absent currently serving our master during his penance for our great Empire the Hyrum my twin the sister who gave her life as I lost mine to end my terrible penance, the goddess Drusilla; the penance Oakley goddess Yanaba; the Stuart and bearer of our heavenly wine the goddesses Máriakéménd; the Eldom goddess the penance Queen's chamber maiden the goddess Heidi; the Eldom goddess as among my trinity of Ereshkigal the goddess Medica; the Hyrum goddess as also among my trinity of Ereshkigal the goddess Sabina. I shall now hope that you will join me as I worship these great goddesses of our eternal Empire." I know bowed before them as all the courts, armies and spirits and flesh from all our now over 4,000 galaxies saw from our throne's streams. As I finished bowing and worshipping these fine heavenly goddesses, that each could easily be a Queen to this empire, I still cannot understand why they worship me. That is more than enough to drop me my knees before them and especially now if front of our Empire. They had never received an official introduction from me as the courts had introduced them. This now puts to rest all doubts; these are my sister goddesses as I now once again drop to my knees and crawl before them kissing each foot of each magnificent goddess. I do not know if the applause is from me kissing their feet or the rather exotic exposure of my fleshly privates as viewed from behind, yet I care not. I still marvel at the excitement they receive over seeing a thing that is created the same among all of them, and has been as such for my ages. I know this, as I am the one who kept the old Earth carbon based style and give it to all of them. They search to see that which they have seen. Maybe we should have given them more access to their brains. I could understand if they were created differently. They only can see what I have given to my master and these goddesses although so many of them who applaud are commendable. I hope they understand that even I must obey relationship rules and customs. I left my sisters and clung to my master yet he being that one in a novemdecillion, (10 followed by 114 zeroes, to mix up the method I use to report these numbers to you) which is totally understanding and not only allows my love for our sisters to continue yet even moved them here. This prompted me to give him our open door policy, since most men get bored quickly hanging out with females as we do the fun things that they, by design, do not enjoy. He thus spends most of his time shaking up our courts and running our empire while I lay on or under our sisters. Maybe that is why they call this place heaven. Our sisters do naturally show themselves very friendly to our master and that helps his ego immensely especially since they know that my shield is available if they need it, yet they would never think of using it. They wholeheartedly do faithfully serve him as is Drusilla surrendering all to him in the hope that he can return to us. Destiny did me good when it puts these wonderful creations in my path. I cannot really push the blood of our blood theme anymore since all were now showered in my blood. Now is the time to show the power of that blood. In addition, a power of love speech would now do that. I have no fear of showing emotion before them since most are concentrating on my pubic hair giving me the power edge to drill my message into their hearts. Mother Nature has a way of creating interest in a patch of hair so small and not on the beautiful well-groomed long red hair, which supports my crown. Such are the mysteries and powers of the ages. I cannot blame my children since they did not create these impulses thus, I shall, as their Queen goddess, work hard to demystify them. The core of my deity is not to make them with defects and watch them beg to survive and their loved ones suffer. The thought of half the people being killed from terrifying diseases and not being labeled as a murderer or killer deity is repulsive, then try to criticize me for sharing all I have and not hiding myself from my servants still mystifies me. If a deity is mighty, enough to create them, then why create a virus or bacteria to kill them? Is that anyway to treat the ones that were created to serve us? I think not. Anyone who sees the magnitude of this welcoming crowd here today and their total allegiance to their crown would have to agree. They serve because they are served by those who made them. They know that if they give to their gods, they will receive from them. None of this 'starve yourself' or 'suffer great loss to be' sound worthy doctrine. My doctrine is, "I made you, and I love you; I will earn your love" They have the choice. Now we can get back to the mystery of the 'lusts between the sexes' and why I have not removed that special feature from Mother Nature, and the reason is consequently, modest. We must have the birds and the bees if we are going to have the babies, a simple foundation for the survival of the species. With such beautiful goddesses standing on this throne, I can feel many species that are begging to multiply after seeing our show. A line must be drawn between the levels of testosterone, and other enzymes needed to keep those babies dropping and the extreme as I suffered immeasurably with the Romans, when the need is satisfied by perceived divine right and thus subject to above. Thereby, the time has arrived for me to speak. I hope by the diversity of the backgrounds from whence came my goddesses. They should have learned my appreciation of the races when they saw me kissing their feet, without any honor, pride, or robes, purely for my love that I have vested in them. My sisters pulled me up with their grace and charm and stood at military attention behind me with their arms splashing the cosmos above their heads. The

throne now ceased all noise as all looked upon me. I currently took
the opportunity to let my spirit do a power show for my
introduction. As my small free from the chains of the clothing
body walked out to the middle of my stage, I waved my hand for
my spirit to stop the power show. The time is presently to feed
them the news they have so eagerly awaited to hear. As I walk out
in front of our golden curtains that cover our silver walls, I raise
my hands and begin by saying, "Let us give praise to my twin
goddess who is at present with our master keeping him strong. Let
us also give praise to my chamber sisters who gave me the strength
to care for my master's Empire until he returns. Let us give praise
to the sister goddesses who were keeping our borders secure until I
could verify that our master was in safe hands. I have journeyed to
the penance throne that is in another dimension from ours. I have
spoken to the one who sits on the throne. I threatened war with my
armies at my side as we prepared to strike. Even so, he who sat on
the throne fed into me the words of wisdom from the ancient gods
of Empires a trillion times larger than ours. These empires ruled
while this universe was yet to be born. For even though our space
is infinite in all directions so is time. Even gods would have to
travel back in time for ages yet could not find this great counsel of
gods. I was so pleased when it was revealed that they also were a
power of good. They furthermore fought with great powers of evil
such as, we optimistically will never see. I do not believe that you
have a desire to worship gods who can only hope to protect you.
Nor shall your gods not take every action to ensure you are
protected. These ancient gods had inordinate tools to fight evil, one
of which is the Sword of Justice; I now share with my Empire.
They want to warrant that the god, which ensures great tools, is
truly from those of good pronounced accordingly that is why our
master and I must be test through penance. You also must know
that your gods have been tested through great sufferings and
miseries yet refused to serve evil but held on for our just cause and
our love for all of our servants, flesh, or spirit. Deity can never fear
or lust pain, as lust fear reduces safeguards and fear creates the
extreme in safeguards. The power I gained through my penance

will allow me easily to keep our master's kingdom waiting for him. Our Sword of Justice shall help to defend us, as evil will try to attack us. What our Sword cannot defeat we shall defeat. We shall survive. You are my people and we are your gods. Fear not for your future for your master will return with greater powers than any evil that we discover. Any evil that we discover I shall give our Sword of Justice to defend us. Those that sleep in my empire shall awake the next day. We shall continue to work hard bringing in our new alliance galaxies. I want to be their goddess, and show them that heaven is even closer than a prayer away. You have your work to do, as I also must do my missions. Our master's spirits and my spirits shall continue to attend the needs of our servants. May our works bring glory to our master and let us all pray for his swift return. We know not when he shall return. We fight evil, yet most of the evil we fight is the evil created in those who are in the flesh. This evil cleverly attributes its true source as spiritual. This mystifies, and may in the minds of some even justify, these evil acts. Punishments and fames may be also altered by shifting this true blame. Many of the borderline flesh servants can be saved by removing the temptations caused by lack of satisfied basic needs. Hunger and terminal diseases are a few of such needs. Lust and greed can be altered by available alternatives and fair distribution of available resources.

We must be ready for our master's return, and I pray that his servants are also prepared for him." At this time, my sister goddesses and I slowly vanished from the throne's stage and reappear in our Royal Deities Sanctuary. As we, all now exchanged welcomes, hugs from the excitement of being reunited again, except for Siusan, Drusilla, and Joy asked me an important question with tears in her eyes. "My masters, at this moment since we have returned, without dying in the flesh, will you not permit us serve you for eternity?" I told her, "Joy and my other penance sisters, we have been granted immunity from this rule, since many of you suffered by me during my penance, and our master received permission to bring you here, considering that dimension can be expected to exact great punishment to you for being associated and worshiping me. You shall occupy eternity with me." Let us now walk together throughout this beautiful sanctuary for the Empire's goddesses. We all had straightaway discovered the easy ways to get around including swimming in the air and thus like birds go to the mountain tips, rest, relax, and then go to our next desired point. Even I cherish these moments. The strange thing is that when we existed in our flesh we wanted to do so many things and go to so many places, yet even in the heavens it is hard to find time to go see the so many more truly great places and do the so many more truly great things. However, as when we were in the flesh, it is fun trying to do these things. We are except for two together again. That is the important thing as we all are up in the mountains, as if to create the appearance of solitude, yet within one breath the my entire Empire can be before us. Every Empire has its showcase and this is ours, the home of the goddesses, the Empire ruled by a master and served by goddesses at the throne level, not to count the thousands of gods at the galaxy levels. Yet all know that if we want something, we know how to get the master's ear as the master knows how to get ours. The important thing is that our powers and spirits are focused on our servants, so our little wonderland here has nothing to do with them. This can only be a deity private playground hurts or takes nothing from our servants. We do not even let them understand what is in here, not in spite of our courts. We come adjacent, get pointless, act stupid, and brainstorm reaffirming that the 'thought' is the most powerful tool of existence, flesh, or spirit. Actually, all thoughts are from the soul as spirits can leave them repressed and ignored. Our goddesses' spirits work hard to remove the repression while in the Sanctuary and hope the thoughts that are floating can be seized. Thoughts, being either in the flesh or not, act as landing strips for the thoughts, hence settle if given the clear sign from the receiver. All the lights throughout my Empire are constantly searching for thoughts and running them through their systems searching for new ways to improve what we are doing or even fresh ways to do things. Subsequently, as many times as something is released to my servants, an improved counter enemy method is being developed. This works great. I had never thought about thoughts until our lights briefed me on them. They are powerful tools for divinity to use in guiding their servants. They are so easy to plant, and the servants think they are theirs. That is the unique thing about thoughts is that the servants believe they are theirs. Evil will, if available use thoughts to cause great pains and suffering. Evil does not need to know the servant, since most painful things are generic, including feelings of sadness and depression. Few things are worse than being gloomy when you should be joyful. Evil's thoughts can be shot through space as in a laser form seeking out populations knowing that when it explodes it will make many suffer. Taking into the account of my experiences, evil must have been suffering along with controlling sex in its attempt to achieve gratification. The control must know the victim has no power to deny, and it unconditionally committed to the evil one's pleasure. We now have special detectors that can catch wicked thoughts, turn them green, and quarantine. Currently, the method used to detect the alien thoughts is the space matter that attaches to them during their vast journey through the universe. Thoughts are based on an element that attaches and induces things to it, thus making it easier to land at its destination. All space along their journey is altered enough to alert our sensors. We sojourn about 100 each day, which based on the area that we are protecting presents a rather low threat; however, it is what one thought can do that presents the problem. Many times our entire lives are judged on an action that took less than one minute. so many relationships will be forever destroyed on just a few words spoken or one contradictory action. Thus, true happiness for my servants must also be based upon protecting them from the invasions of evil thoughts. The matter at hand now for this beautiful group of goddesses is how we can best lead our Empire. We know not to break something that is working well nor to search for something broke when there is no need to do so. For the time at hand, we can appear our strongest by staying calm, united, and secluded. We can hope that if they do not see us, they will think we are being strong. I seriously doubt that they will leave us along for too long, because I have too many sisters that are involved in too many activities, which is so good for when many find additional avenues to the throne a more suitable deity is presented. Sabina is now calling for me to join her, which is always a treat. This former flesh priestess always presented wonderful options when times were weary. She came through for me when my children were leaving the garden on New Venus; she was with me during my revenge strike at my former throne, risking her future as long as she would be allowed to serve me. As I sat down beside her, she wrapped her arm around me. I lay my head on her shoulder as she petted my hair. She began by saying, "Oh mighty master of my soul and eternity, I think there is something that I need to show you. One day while walking with Drusilla and Faith we discovered a very strange creation in which we had verified by the lights to be genuine. It is about one day from here. Will you allow Faith and me to share this wonderful detail with you and our sisters?" I then told her, "We shall follow you. Sister Goddesses, let us now follow our ancient priestess and Queen so that they may share with us a new fortune." We are a special unified group. They do not care what we are looking for or where we are going, their only concern is 'someone is going somewhere and am I invited.' Within a few minutes, we have all formed into smaller groups and into our own worlds. We are moving steadily laughing and chatting along the way. I am so glad that I continued to create my females with vocal cords, for not to do so could have caused great suffering to them and given great pleasure to their counterparts. There is no mystery where we are, and that surrounded by itself is wonderful. Now we are singing a song, which always adds warmth to my heart and soul. We all have such varied backgrounds yet share the same solid sense of values. We serve each other and surrender all to each other. We tend to refuse something that we cannot share, I am making the greatest exception is bonding myself to my master, yet now he is shared as my Drusilla is serving us with her powerful heart and soul. My sisters love our master because I love him. They can refuse to serve him and hide under my wing, yet they chose to do what they can do in order to serve me better. I can so easily love them for loving them is the same as loving me for I am with them so deeply. That is what makes being a goddess so special especially the higher I promote them, the more they surrender to me. Our golden bodies are now covered in good hot sweet, the kind that is ordinarily obtained when my master is rather exciting and feeling like a conqueror or even when some of my sisters here get excited. The moisture on our skin is absorbing the special sunlight here to give us nice tans. At least we do not have to worry about bikini lines. Being strong women, our respites become a nice chance to find something to sit on, and chat being thankful that no one will see us with our wet lifeless hair. I believe it important to keep the menial female traits, which add to the life of our flesh. As for me, I could enjoy this for a month. Overall, this enhances our mythologies and enables our servants to relate more favorably with us. It is so nice to be a tired member of an exhausted happy group.

Our current rest bequeathed us with some beneficial hours ahead of us, and then I guess we will find a place to sleep. I hate making a small town that would distract from the beautiful scenery, nevertheless if I know my sisters, we will be laying on our backs with our eyes looking at the stars we rule and slipping off into our dream worlds. For now, we are holding each other's hand as we continue our mystery mission. Sabina now tells me that we are close to the secret place that Drusilla had discovered and that it would be best to stop here and visit it first thing in the morning. We shall now find a good campsite on one of these nearby hilltops and enjoy our wonderful view. We lay beside each other, stretch our happy tired legs, and try to recount all the thousands of things we talked about during the day. I can no longer hold it, get up on my knees in front of them, and tell them, "I do so very much treasure your love in relation to the kingdom above that we rule. I do so much love each and all of you." Moreover, being a normal mushy female, I break down into tears as they form around me and begin crying. Now this would baffle the wisest of men, the most powerful goddesses enjoying a nice all day hikes in a heaven our master made for us not being bothered by anyone and here we are crying.

Time stood still for us, thus we never gave the pressure of time an audience. Specifically, these tears are tears of ecstasy, which any rocket scientist would be able to deduct. A god cannot make this kind of love however will strive for an eternity to find it. Great loves come when something great has been lost. We lost, with no guarantee of return, our master, and my twin sister. We will continue to hold on to what we have and fight for what we may lose. When it comes to losing my Empire I will drop this pretty shy helpless little girl image and stand as tall as the highest mountain and hit with the force of millions of nuclear bombs. I guess that is to be expected as most mothers to fight hard for their children. Thankfully, today was not one of those days, but a goddesses' day out. I do very expect Sabina will make this all worthwhile tomorrow even though I now understand it to be worthwhile. My back feels so good now against the soft surface that is now beneath me, and the warmth radiating from my sister's flesh suits floats past my skin that settles into my bones. I am so thankful that Lamenta had this style of flesh suits and that this style was favored by the planters of the cosmos. To put the icing on the cake, Bogovi also favored this style, as did his ancestors. There are so many other styles available throughout the universe. In order to keep our Empire strong we replaced all other prevailing styles with our style. This way we can feel closer as I have also kept us with one language. This adds to the unity and uniformity that is needed in my Empire as we expand so rapidly. All other languages are now dead in my empire and erased from active speech. If they do not see it, do not hear it, and do not say it, then they will not want or miss it. I do not have to fear my servants uniting and challenging my throne. We have a 'thank you and good bye' reply to any galaxy that wishes to leave my Empire. I simply move them very far away from if they want their independence they can fight to keep it. I do not want to see that bloodshed as freedom is just another word for nothing else to lose and I never want to be free from my children since they are something very important to lose. Looking up to the sky and seeing these stars knowing that I rule each of them and stars so far beyond them. I created the flesh that dwells on the planets that rotate those stars. The important thing for me to remember is that even though my Empire is so big and growing so fast, there are larger Empires out there somewhere and I must stay humble in the flesh that I created and promised to protect depend upon me. Just like them, a day's walk makes my feet hurt. I actually enjoy this feeling since when I float around in my spirit nothing hurts or can produce a sensory response. Flesh suits are still quite popular in our saint's heavens, although they can only be worn in controlled environments meeting the necessary temperature and breathable gas requirements. I need to harp on this another time. For now, I am with my sisters and that is all that counts. To know that all who live on those stars above us are dedicated to protecting us although few know we prefer flesh suits, however that does not matter because they worship more willingly when that which they worship is not alien to them and when they can conceive an empathic relationship. It is as if I dangerously place my heart in their hands. I never recommend my servants love on this level, however my priests often do as Sabina has provided them with volumes of how to manuals on the process of serving with flesh embalming spiritual empathy. Sabina has been the foundation for the massive enhanced priesthood that we have. I have created trillions of Sabina power spirits to continue this fine tradition. The priesthood is the link between living with the people and showing them the keys to our kingdom thus getting them into my temples where my angels can initiate their spiritual journey. I always add the most important element concerning the success of my relationship style I have with my servants and that is my power to do so. Some consider this a waste of power, yet to hear the servants stories as they cross over to dwell in their eternal home as compared to the stories that were told by those before my Empire saved them are as different as night and day. Even the righteous suffered too much and that is a pet peeve of mine, the righteous are not to suffer. That is the jog of my guardian angels. We all have activities that others do not agree, for the old saying, what is meat on one man's table shall be cursed from another holds to be true more often than not. Many do not agree with the relationship I have with my sisters and that for the most part is why we try not to flaunt it in front of them. Even though they cannot do anything about it, there is no need to put them through such a challenging tribulation. Actually, it is to my advantage that they disapprove, thus that leaves less competition for my sisters who are mine. They are the air that I breathe when wearing these flesh suits we enjoy sharing since these actions are not possible when we exist in our spirits. The major conflict I could see that would stop this would be from my master. When I bowed before him and offered myself to serve him as his Queen, I gave him that right. I do not condone the fact that I first tried to let both loves coexist, however I applaud my master for learning all about me prior to accepting me as his main intimate servant. Since he now approves of this, I feel comfortable in sharing my gifts of love with him. Each sister is truly a gift of love and I often am saddened that I selected or adapted so many, however at least I did not adopt the entire 1,000 that Bácsalmás wanted me to bring in from our dimension's throne. I strategically created the Queen's Angels for them as they act as a special go between with my Empire and the Royal Deities Sanctuary. They often represent my Royal Goddesses in many of my Empire activities especially in my alliance galaxies. And they do command my armies in my name when the situation dictates as I never back down from an opportunity to serve and protect my alliance galaxies, which even if I were on the farthest star in the sky above me I could not even see those stars from their nighttime skies. This is such a small part of one dimension's universe, one of over thousands of dimensions. I do not even want to explain that. Accordingly, children are being raised in good families with positive futures ahead of them. Notwithstanding, I wonder where all my daughters are tonight. I also wonder how many stars this mother will have to count before she falls asleep in Sabina's arms. My morning greets me with a slight chill, the ones that allow you to feel your bones and adds that snap to your touch. The air hangs heavier in your lungs and even, at times creates a crispy sensation with your taste buds. As I twitch to get my blood flowing again, I am comforted in the modifications I have made with these flesh suits that allow the flesh to be more attune with its environment as long within range limits. Too far on either side does force permanent shutdown which is required since combining the modifications to withstand either extreme causes more hardships than the benefits received. There is no value in causing billions to suffer while only saving a few. I do make exceptions where the population is concentrated in a specific environment, such as living under the surface on sub artic planets. The good news for me now is that one of my suns will be sending me her warm rays very soon as I have ordered my winds to sleep. Good morning Empire, your goddesses are sleeping on the mountain, except for the Queen. As I look at each one in their peaceful state of rest, I know that for selfish reasons, I must wake one of them. This is the right of those, who are awake, to share their current state with one who is still trapped by the time-consuming sleep monster. My heart is being flooded with the peace that a mother receives when she looks upon her children sleeping. As I walked in front of my sisters, once set of eyes opened and with a smile looked at me. I could feel the glow of her spirit reflecting front our surface back to her. This is a sister that I have not had a chance to spend a lot of time with as she was added to supplement Máriakéménd in our night world to smooth the transition from the exposed Henrietta. She revealed her evil in the end, yet when I first saw her, I knew she was evil, nevertheless as she started telling me good stories and was in my head chasing off bad dreams I became dependent on her. Enough said, "Henrietta no longer exists as even Faith has moved on from that love lost. As we started to bond with Julia, our visits to the night world became too dangerous. Julia was so instrumental in saving us and proved to be well prepared for every possible contingency. I always admired her for the wisdom she had which was beyond her years for the flesh suit she wore. We all continue to speculate where she accepted the flesh suit that she now wears. Every little curve is perfect and every move appears to elicit a smile. She must have a sun inside her as she always radiates heat. My scans of her always report that she is a model consistent with the ones I create. She was created by our master and from one of his galaxies. We have never discussed it, as it really does not matter since she was showered in my blood while I was still in the flesh and made a disciple during my penance. We all love her and no one ever questions the advice that she gives. Her specialty is giving advice only when asked unless an emergency dictates otherwise. Thus with this in mind, I begin our conversation, "Well good morning Goddess Julia, how was your sleep?" She replies, "May sleep was wonderful my master for you allowed me to serve you and that always becomes heaven to me." I then looked at her and said, "My goddess Julia, you have been and I foresee that you will always be a faithful and loyal servant of our master and myself. I often marvel at the master's perfection in discovering you yet I do not know your story, as I know our other sisters. Tell me so I can know how to better serve you." She rose up, gave me a wonderful hug, and whispered in my ear, "I cannot give you what you ask for." This surprised me, as I cannot ever remember a servant openly disobeying my request. I thus said to Julia, "Oh my master's Julia; I foolishly thought you were my servant. Please forgive me for my error." Julia then fell to her knees and cried out, "Oh great Queen, you are that which I worship for eternity. I shall always obey all your commands even if it leads to my damnation or death. Please, I beg of you, keep me as your servant. I lay here now for you to enjoy as much and in any way you desire. I exist only for your pleasure. I beg of you to destroy me if I have made you angry." I then bent over wrapping my arms around her to help lift her up and then said again, "I do not know your story as I know our other sisters thus I do not know you. I so much want to be your goddess and enjoy the pleasure of your worship. Tell me your story so I may know you." Julia fell to her knees again and wrapped her arms around my leg and the tears of her sorrow flowed down my leg. I now said, "Oh Julia, trust me for I cannot let this sorrow stay inside a sister of mine. I must free you." She replied, "Oh master, I do not cry for my sorrow, I cry because I cannot give you what you ask for." I then started kissing her beautiful face and ask, "My servant, why do you withhold this from me?" Julia then answered, "Oh master, how can I withhold what I do not have?" I then questioned,

"Why do you not have the knowledge of your past?" Julia answered, "I only know that when we master found me he took all my memories from before and put them in one of his scrolls that only he has the key for and through the scroll into his Sea of Forgetfulness. He told me my book would be rewritten as the servant of his goddess. To go and prepare myself for this mission by swimming in the Sea of Wisdom, and live on the Island of Knowledge, eating the fruit from therein until he called me for my mission. I only know my great life as your servant and the joys of surrendering all to you. I can only speculate that based upon my reward to be permitted to serve at your feet and to share our heavenly wines I must have been a great saint." I then looked at her beautiful eyes and said, "My Saint, will you guide me to a nearby stream where we can wash away our tears and where I can officially dedicate myself as your goddess. For eternity, even as my blood flows through your veins currently, my breath will flow through your soul and I shall take your spirit to be with me forever and ever." Julia then said now with her lovely warm smile back, "Follow me master through this field of flowers and I shall drown in the water you put me in for I want to be no more but to have you in me and you be my life and the source of my devotion." We then went to a stream and lay down our flesh suits in in our spirits I performed the spiritual bonding ceremony. My spirit of power and spirit of love come upon us, forming a new flesh that imbibed Julia and me inside it. We both shared the same heart as my blood flowed through us singing songs of joy and peace. We could smell so many great smells and all who entered to sing before us was pure white, the white equal to royal white. I could see no blemishes and could see mountains of purity and love serving them. It was now that I realized that we were traveling in my spirit of power. There was no empty space between the planets, and the mountains had no tops. I could only see them rising and rising and they had no bottoms. The rivers flowed up and down and they had no water, only my pure blood as all the vegetation and animals fed from it, for the blood went to those who were in need. As we floated up this one mountain and as we looked out I could see what must be twenty vigintillion (10^63) mighty strong warrior spirits, for there are so many they pack the space between the planets of burning blue and white planets that sail maybe 100 miles above, as the mountains feed into them. I see rivers of love gushing out of the sides of these bottomless mountains. Then I hear the sudden sound of octillion trumpets sounding and a large voice speaks out, "Who goes there?" I spoke out, "I am the goddess Lilith, and with me is my new soul sister, the goddess Julia. Why have you tried to take me as your prisoner? The trumpets stopped playing; now these sparkling pure spirits started playing harps, and the music was so wonderful that Julia and I drifted inside each other. Then the voice said, "You cannot be captured by yourself oh mighty Queen and holder of the Sword of Justice. You have been brought here to show you one of many quadrillion giant power spirits in which your blood flows. Your bonding and deification of Julia is now recorded in the scrolls of the goddesses for eternity since she shall serve you with your power for the glory of the Empire of the Good. Her spirit no longer has knowledge of evil, for she is now pure white inside and protected by your blood. She will never betray you and will serve your master and you in both spirit and flesh, for she has been reborn in your image to bring glory in her divine King and Queen. Do you wish to give us a command to serve you?" I then said, "Yes, I wish to speak in private with you?" The spirit then made visible to me a video stream of Julia being returned to her flesh and put back to sleep with her sisters. At this time, I asked one of so many of my power spirits, "I know not the story of my sister Julia; will you tell me her story?" My spirit answered saying, "We are so sorry of the great Queen Goddess and the holder of the Sword of Justice, for we cannot tell you her story." I asked, "Who is the "we" you speak of?" My spirit answered, "Oh mighty goddess, the "we" is all your power spirits for what one does we all do thus allowing us to be at all places at all times." I then thought, "How can this much power not know about my lovely Julia?" I foolishly did not realize that my spirit could naturally read minds, to include mine in my mind, as its mind. My spirits told me, "Oh loving Queen and the holder of the Sword of Justice, we cannot tell since it is your law that any scroll thrown into the Sea of Forgetfulness can only be revealed by the master." I then asked, "Must I wait for my master to return from his penance?" My spirits said, "Oh no, greatest of all goddesses, your master is your master and our master is you for we serve your master in your honor and glory." I then, now perky and feeling like I might find an answer to this now great mystery said to my spirit, "My spirits, I am so honored to have you in my name for then you are truly the wall of good saving our children we serve. Where may I find this Sea of Forgetfulness and how may I find my sister's scroll?" My spirits then told me, "We can take you to the cave on the planet Gråsten and you must be in your flesh suit when you arrive, as no spirits may go there including even our great King and Queen. We cannot protect you during this save. You must bring your Sword of Justice for without it you may not return." I asked them, "How can such a place exist in my Empire and where is this place?" They answered, "We know not where it is for we will send you to a place they tell us and they will bring you to them. This place exists by your law." I then told my spirits to tell my courts that a new law shall be made, "No law can exist that does not have a safe access provision for the King or Queen, and anything that harms the King of Queen shall be punished as an act of evil against the Empire. Get these laws on the books before I arrive there. Return me to my sisters and when the laws are on the books and the Sea of Forgetfulness is notified tell me so I can tell you when I can sneak out for I do not want to put my sisters in harm's way." I was now lying asleep with my sisters. I do believe they got better looking in the short time I was away, as I may be like them today and sleep until noon. That mountain climb, even in my spirit was exhausting because of all the massive power radiating everywhere. Soon, Drusilla wakes me and tells me it is time to head for the mountaintop. I immediately thought, 'oh my god, not another mountain top', yet my eyes proved to be my salvation as I could see the top of this mountain and a clear sky leading us to it. As we form our hiking line and begin today's long list of chatting topics that will solve nothing except lay a rich foundation for tomorrow's topics. As I look out at the beautiful bay of blue water from the sea I see what must have been created by my master's finger. He puts so much attention to anything he creates for me, such as Balatonberény and Veszprém. I can only look in amazement as I travel in his creations for us. It is so tempting to jump off this cliff and enjoy the view as I would slowly descend, yet that would take the natural adventure out of this long hike. Before I know it, Cegledbercel gets me tangled in a girly conversation as I gave up all attention to my surroundings. Cegledbercel like the other goddesses that joined me from our Empire's Galaxies are such great conversationalist as they have had so many experiences in the millions of years they have lived. They have taught us all so much as my penance sisters soak every word that comes from them thus adding so much more depth and experience or training in our sisterhood. Then after about three hours into our walk, Sabina asks all of us to rest beside an orchard while she goes ahead to make the reception arrangements. As we sat underneath the wide assortment of fruit trees with berry bushes covering the hillside behind it, we all got busy and ate some fruit, more to enjoy the taste since we did not need it for energy. We all then began to take advantage of the shade trees as we quickly went to sleep. Then Sabina returned with a great smile and eyes saying, "I have seen the Mountain of the Rødovre." I looked at her and said, "You have seen what?" Then did the goddesses Dédestapolcsány reply, "I have searched this Empire inside out for the Mountain of the Rødovre as told in the old tales, and could not find it thus dismissing it as an old legend." Julia then added, "For I too thought it to be an old legend and could not be so." I now screamed out, "Ok goddesses, do you not think it is time to free your Queen from her stupidity?" Julia and Dédestapolcsány both did bow to their knees and said, "Oh great holder of the Sword of Justice from whence from the mighty Rødovre, we shall tell you. We know this to be true for the glow on Sabina's face from which the Rødovre cry out to us. They have requested that all the goddesses of the Throne to accept their invitation that they may help in the battle against evil. We have no fear, although we may travel into an area that has great evil forces trying to destroy."

Then Julia and Rødovre fell upon the ground, turned into a white light, and vanish up the mountain from which Sabina had just returned. I yelled out, "Who dare take my sisters from me? Oh spirits find them for me." My united spirits replied, "Oh great Queen, you have lost no sisters?" I screamed back, "I have lost the goddess Julia and the goddess Dédestapolcsány?" The spirits then answered, "Oh great Queen and holder of the Sword of Justice, you have never had sisters named Julia and Dédestapolcsány." I chill now came down my back. This was something I had never thought I would have to deal with. Either that mighty network of spirits who go by my name now had Alzheimer's or I was now matched against something far greater than I could have ever known. To add to this shock now Máriakémend, who was Julia's closest friend said to me, "Master who is this Julia that you speak of?" I then asked the goddess Bárdudvarnok and the goddess Tamási, two of the galaxy goddesses who joined me with the galaxy Dédestapolcsány and the other three galaxy goddesses, "Do you know of the galaxy goddess Dédestapolcsány?" All six bowed before me and answered as one voice saying, "Oh greatest Queen Goddess of the ages and the holder of the Sword of Justice, we know not this goddess Dédestapolcsány that you speak of." Now this was definitely from a power greater than what my master was, and I had. I do not know what to do. Then Sabina said to me, "My master will you follow me to the castle on the next mountain over from us and we shall solve this great mystery that you now have?" I then agreed. Sabina then told us, Oh great sister goddesses and our master, no flesh may touch the mountain or castle so we may only enter as pure white lights. We shall leave our flesh suits here as they will be guarded for us." All looked at me and I just shook my head yes, as if I had any other choice. From a night of seeing the greatness of my spirits and having the confidence that someday my master and I would rule the greatest Empire ever to now inside my Royal Deities Sanctuary to have two of my sisters erased from the minds of goddesses is one mighty roller coaster ride that I should not be on. No matter how much greater my power may be something jumps in front that is always universes ahead of me. Furthermore, the thought that something could be inside my Royal Deities Sanctuary, which is a place that my goddesses and I may live in the flesh, that forbids me to wear flesh is also very disturbing. I feel so humbled now, I worry that after this will I ever again regain my confidence. That will be within itself interesting to discover. We are now floating to the castle. As I look behind me, I see another great mystery. Our sanctuary is being sucked into a hole, as a mighty force of which I do not know is now consuming it. What a great time for my master to be lying with my twin sister. He should have built greater safeguards for I do not really know if I exist much longer or drew into that thing that is taking away my sanctuary. As we get near to this magnificent castle that sits so well protected on a mountain that it supports a powerful force pulls us deep inside it as we are all together beneath my sanctuary which has nothing below it, so where we are I do not know. This show keeps getting better and better. Then a voice rings out, "Oh evil goddesses, bow before me so that you may be purified." As we prepare to bow I ask, "Oh unknown thief that steals from me, why do we need to be purified, for what evil have we done?" The voice then shakes the underground cavern that we are in and says, "I know what you have done, and of your great deeds, for you have paid your penance price, yet you must bow to have that which you have recently lost be purified or that which you have lost will be no more." I immediately fell to my knees and cried out, "If you can purify me that not only purify my soul but purify my spirit also so that I may not know evil, pride or lust for greatness." Then inside me, I felt a power change me into something so much better, and purity is not a thing of gray. It is either pure white or not pure. I could also feel two new lights burning inside me as they rushed out. I could now feel Julia, Dédestapolcsány, and this brought within me such a great satisfaction, for I was humble and saved that which I lost. As I looked to both sides of me, my sisters who were bowing were now standing up, dancing, and shouting for joy, as they also were now pure white. I then said to this whatever it is, "I know not how to thank you for this gift of purity, and for I did not know that I was so far from being pure. Will you please tell me who you are?" It answered, "We have found great favor in you Lilith. We are the Council of Nykøbing Mors, the greatest power of the Rødovre. We have one more demand upon you. You must worship us to save the lives of your servants." I then fell to my knees and cried aloud as my pure white spirit was now stained with love tears, "I beg you, who are my masters to punish and torture me as your slave for our eternity, if you will but spare the lives of my children or as you call them my servants. I beg as my spirit has now surrendered to you. Take me as your slave." I now lay crying and pleading for my children and with a flash my tears and words were gone. I now hung in a cloud of so many warm colors such as I have never seen. There we so many bright lights that had white beams extending to the four corners. I fearfully saw a black hole in the middle on my left that sank down and flowed into a large cavern as a powerful white light stood between it and me. I also can see two lights inside it as its depths are so great. I cannot remember ever seeing something this great. I can feel each light to be at least one hundred tredecillion ($10 \wedge 42$) times the size of my Empire. How do I know such things, yet I know them to be true. My Empire is but a grain of sand in this infinite giant ocean. I can also see what looks to be blue veins flowing out of the large hole in the middle. I wonder what is in those giant veins, the widths to be greater than the giant lights. I have never even dreamed a place like this could ever exist, and I can feel it will be a great place to be a slave. I can believe they will protect my servants so much better than I could ever have. I do not feel a loss of an Empire but the gain for my servants and that is all I could ever hope to have. I shall miss my sisters and my master. I then see a voice, which speaks in lights yet my spirit, understands as it shines, "Why will you miss your sisters and your master?" This is a dimension so far forward thinking in ogles my mind. I then shine back, "Have I done an evil to you by missing those whom I loved?" The light shines back, "Do you know longer love them?" I shined back, "As I am your slave, I will love only whom you allow me to love?" The light shined back, "Oh foolish child, you are not our slave, but our cherished guest. Your sisters are being well cared for as is your master in penance.

Your children or servants, however we agree to define them, shall be protected by our powers from all evil for eternity with you as their sitting Queen and your master as your sitting King." I then, now bowing in open space, as I could feel myself going into the middle large hole, shined back, "Oh great ones, I am not worthy of such a great honor nor can I ever care for them as you do. I know not what to do. Will thou help me and guide me that I may lead them to you?" The lights shined back, "Oh Queen Lilith, we have found that greater is in you than that is in your universe. Your Empire shall someday have over nine hundred centillion (10^600) galaxy clusters with each cluster being one centillion galaxies and yet it shall continue to grow the greatest size is too far for us to see in the future. We know that your Empire shall join our lights here as among the brightest." I then shined to them, "Will my Empire continue to love and serve our children and be free from evil?" All the giant lights shined back, "Queen Lilith, it shall always be pure." I then lay limp crying spiritual tears of joy, for my spirit was now so happy. Then it became evident to me I was now somewhere else. I could see only blue lights flowing into a center brighter blue light with so much darkness before me. I cried out, "Oh mighty Council of Nykøbing Mors, have you forsaken me? Have I done wrong, please do not leave me, for I have surrendered to you." The blue rays now shined back to me, "We have not lost you, oh faithful queen, you are being sent back, for nothing that was born within the last eight hundred sexdecillion (10^51) trillion millennium may enter within. You have journeyed farther than any before have ever journeyed. We wanted you to know and see where your Empire shall spend its eternity in the far future." I then shined back, "Who ever created the number sexdecillion must have had a mind much light mine. How can you be from so far back?" The lights shined back, "In the beginning was only good, yet in all galaxies within all over an undecillion (10^36) dimensions, most of which all the dimensions that you know of now will never be able to discover, evil has evolved from. When all were created, only one third progressed ahead. One third remained at the beginning and we were among the one third that traveled back in time. Thus each day to go forward, we go back one day. We are both on journeys that will never end." I then shined back, "I am so blessed to have found you and for you to have found favor in me. One of my sisters told me that you gave me the Sword of Justice. I hope this to be true." The lights shined back, "We did not give you the Sword of Justice for you earned it. You took upon yourself flesh and sacrificed your body in great pain for good. We have blessed your blood with a power never known in your universe, for no evil may ever touch them as no evil thought may ever enter your Empire. You may use your Armies to build for the people. If evil even mentions your name, they shall perish. Your master will return to you, for he too would have suffered greatly for his servants that we did not need to test him as severely as we did you and Drusilla. He will return with the Sword of Freedom. Be it known to you that Justice may never live without Freedom. Freedom requires great sacrifices to be made. The Sword of Freedom will remove the need for those sacrifices as only those who do not accept Freedom will be required to make sacrifices. As we return you to your current time, we also want to applaud you on your great love to give all that you have and hide no shame from your servants. As they walk among you in great rich garments, you and your sisters walk among them with no shame and hide not the purity of your flesh. We know this to be so hard on the designs of your flesh and the fear that you live with daily just to be the servant of your servants." I then shined back as they returned space light flesh to surround my spirit, "I have worried about this many times as so many judge me to be wrong for doing so. How is what I do not wrong?" The council shined back, "It is that which is inside your heart that provides the innocence and purity of your action. If you were to flaunt your nakedness to personal gain and power over the males, you would be judged as evil. You shall now rejoin your sisters as you all begin a new journey of prosperity for all in the EGaSOJ." Then they vanished as I landed in my rebuilt and purified Royal Deities Sanctuary with my sisters as they were sleeping while waiting for me. I thought it to be good if I also slept, for the roller coaster I have been on is made of pure gold as I now enjoy a confidence and feeling of purity that I have never known. What a great reassurance that something so great is protecting us. My life was now changed, no more fear of my prior dimension taking me. I am the power of the good. I now started getting light messages. These lights would put in my mind a thought and a demand. I never worried about the demand, since I am also in a faith relationship. I must act in faith making visible the light they have given. As I returned to our camp, I saw only Fejér and I asked her, "Where are our sisters?" She told me they were in groups praying for my return, and that she would summon them for me. Soon they came rushing to me shouting cheers of great joy. Even I became excited knowing what they also have experienced in this great discovery and the joy of being reunited again. As we gathered and all were among us except for Siusan and Drusilla, I prepared to share my news with them. I began by saying, "It is a great blessing that Drusilla leads Sabina who lead us to this place, which is no more. The Mountain of the Rødovre has been returned to the Council of Nykøbing Mors, for they have become our masters for eternity, as someday our great Empire shall be a light among their eternal haven. They were at the beginning of time and now exist in a time that we could never travel to nor shall we since we are to spend eternity there. They asked me to call my spirits here today and to speak these words unto them with you as a witness, as these spirits also exist for your power and glory. I now called for my spirits and spoke the words that the council gave me to speak. To our utmost amazement my spirits all turned fiery orange and yellow as my spirits grow so large they filled the sky as one by one they shot off into the depths of my Empire." We did not know what was happening as soon my lights requested permission to enter. I granted this since I too wanted to speak to them. They showed me how large and dense my spirits were now, so large that they had to shift galaxies to find space to occupy. I asked them, "Are my spirits unharmed?" The lights answered, "They are unharmed. Yet now they are over 850 nonillion (10^{30}) times more powerful and growing in power each second, oh great goddess, how can this be?" I looked at them and said, "It is a gift from the Council of Nykøbing Mors." The lights flashed erratically for some time as a reply came back to me, "Oh great goddess, the Council of Nykøbing Mors was spoken of by the Rødovre who are the most ancient tales that we have known, yet even they speak of the Council as an ancient tale. Why do you believe you have spoken to a Council that is so deep into ancestry that it would take you twice the known time at the greatest reverse time travel speed to reach them?" I then said to my lights, "Behold my spirits. I did not go to the Council, the Council found me. They have given me the greatest power in this universe and no evil power may ever touch me, or even think of me for it will perish. I am devoting all my military powers to rebuilding a great home for our servants. Our master will return someday with our Sword of Freedom. No other Empire shall be greater than ours." The lights then spoke back, "How can we exist with no Army?" I then flashed back to them in light language, "I am the Army." The lights flashed back to me, "How did you learn to talk light talk?" I answered, "I did not learn it, for it was given to me by the Council." I then touched my lights in which once again, we were amazed beyond our wildest dreams. All of our lights beginning with the Lights of Ereshkigal the ages as bright as ages beyond ages of advanced knowledge were stored inside of them. This became so bright that all in my Empire and alliances were awakened. I then said unto my spirits and lights, "Let us join all alliance galaxies today and give each planet a rich supply of my blood so that they may be showered in my blood and I become their goddess. Secure you all my borders and speak out my name so that all evil that hears it will be destroyed. Take you command of my armies and let them serve our servants building new temples, schools and roads and factories to make our new deep space warships, as we shall destroy all evil that we can find. As I have commanded, let it be so." My lights now left the Royal Deities Sanctuary as I now rested with my sister goddesses as we all now knew to prepare for a greater tomorrow. We would prepare by resting, playing, and sharing our heavenly wines today. We can now assimilate a requesting galaxy in just a few minutes now. Likewise, yes, if they wish to join they must be assimilated, for just one grain of sand left open for evil can produce a mountain. I will not even entertain the notion of an evil seed growing in my garden. My lights now tell me that we have over 21,000 galaxies in our Empire now, as so many more are requesting to be joined. My spirits are now attacking evil in parts of deep space that I never dreamed we would ever go. They are transmitting my name to the maximum range they can and reporting large clusters of evil be erased from existence. I am so glad to hear that the Council of Nykøbing Mors installed so many safeguards in our systems to prevent over expanding and not properly protecting and providing for our servants. They have even provided a layout for the building of our advanced new civilizations. The dawning of tomorrow is today. Our cities are self-contained and can survive on any planet in our galaxies. This allows us to mine for precious resources on planets that have not supported life since early in the universe's life. I do know that the planets will rotate in with the central ones being thrown off into space to join a new solar system. I will see this many times in my future. My greatest concern then is to recycle and change all wastes back into its basic elements. This should prolong the lives of these planets. Not one atom will ever be wasted in my Empire nor will it be lost. For my kingdom is our glory. My spirits are not only everywhere at all times as I only record positive actions and negative actions. The individual's spirit records all things and uses that for its defense in needed to be tried by our throne. Most spirits are admitted immediately as death is simply changing residence. Within a few centuries, I will no longer create new souls. I will recycle evil souls that can be purified. If the soul cannot be purified it be completely reduced to the basic elements and then converted into empty matter. This prevents that model from ever being formed again. I see no reason to torment those evil souls for eternity, since I almost feel to be part of the blame. I should have discovered the "Rachmanism provision earlier and then evoked it, yet I now even wonder why should I have to evoke it, in was not the one on the universe's universes throne. Flesh now is proving to be nothing but an obstacle. My special cities that can now exist anywhere in my empire erase most barriers for the flesh. Even though they can exist in monstrously hot burning stars, I still have a small phobia against fires. Something those 1,000 years of burning instills in someone. I envision a future empire, which all spirits will have human forms that can become solid, or be a gas or even a light, instantaneously. I enjoy breathing, walking, running, loving and of course hours of endless chit chat with my sisters. I like my thoughts being tied into my lights and spirits. Many times, I am getting what I wanted before I knew what I wanted. That is because we have an added feature to my spirit being everywhere at once, it is also everywhere at selected points in the future. Thus, foolish accidents are prevented before they happen. Any foolish invasions are stopped in their planning stages. Any nation or flesh empire that tries to take from my other children is stopped dead in their tracks. Now, for the first time life in the flesh so closely represents life in the spirit, as the structural differences are being merged and moving towards consolidation. I plan to have so many more heavens available for my souls that the old travel to the other side of the universe when under attack by an evil threat no longer exists. As l lay myself down to sleep with my sister goddesses, as we all know we have many welcoming missions ahead in our future. For now, I can only wonder how much greater things will be tomorrow on top of a perfect day such as this. I could cheat and ask my spirit; however, I am so used to the surprises. As I lay asleep, I heard voices say, "Awake Lilith for you is safe now to travel in the cave on Gråsten." As I started to awake, I asked, "Who are you and what is the cave on Gråsten?" They all looked at me as if surprised that I would not know this and then replied, "Why do you not know?" I replied, "I think maybe since I just finished meeting with the old council in the history of our universe, my mind may have been goggled some, so explain how you got into my sleep. You also may never address me unless you use proper protocol, as maybe a couple thousand years in one of my lakes of fire may sharpen your obedience." Then one of the females with a voice as soft as honey and eyes as blue as the skies answered, "Oh great Goddess Queen Lilith, member of the Council of Nykøbing Mors and the holder of the Sword of Justice and servant to the master who holds the Sword of Freedom, you ordered us to notify you when your laws made it safe to travel to the Sea of Forgetfulness, which you forgot my savior." I looked at her and said, "What is your name faithful servant?" She bowed to her knees and wrapped her arms around my leg as I lay on the ground and with tears hitting my skin said, "I was called Långå before I angered you." I told her, as I caressed her hair and swabbed away her tears, "You have not angered me, to the contrary you have pleased me greatly, and I wish to keep you as our servant of the goddesses in my throne if you will accept." She jumped for joy and said, "You are my goddess and I will serve you for eternity and be your slave giving you all that I am and shall ever be." I then looked at Jakabszállás and said, "Let us find a home for our new love servant Långå that she may dwell in the land of the goddesses for eternity. Jakabszállás did as I asked as the sisters did mob her with excitement, as she would now learn how to talk for hours saying nothing. We call that heaven. I now told my remaining guides to take me to the cave on Gråsten. My empire was now undergoing so many improvements as the gases and clouds were creating new heavens as all the good souls from my new galaxies were being offered new homes if they so desired. Any time I was to travel now, my lights wanted me to be in white, thus all would know the Queen was passing through. We then slowed down as we started to rotate this dark white planet with its moons hugging it in the middle of nowhere. The planet was white from millions of years of ice. It now had very little atmospheric gasses as they have been frozen. The planet would attract stray gas patches, pull them into its atmosphere, and freeze it. This planet, which was naturally growing each day from the frozen gasses, would someday be a nice source of raw materials for one of my ambitious flesh empires. As we were now being readjusted to this new part of my Empire, the rude guide started breaking the ice by saying, "Oh Great Goddess, my name is Skive. As you can see out here, we may only get away once in a couple thousand centuries. I do hope you will forgive me." I told Skive, "I shall forgive you, as I think of you a trip to a lake of fire would be a reward from such a cold freezing dungeon such as this. I truly did not know you were out here like this. This does not meet the standards I have for a quality life for my servants." The female with him, Haderslev then divulged unto me, "Oh great Goddess Queen Lilith, member of the Council of the Nykøbing Mors and holder of the Sword of Justice and servant to the master who holds the Sword of Freedom, our master has created for us a wonderful world deep inside this planet as well as we do rotate with other crews and thus spend a life in her part of galaxy and then return." I told the both of them, "We can now skip the formal titles and work as a happy group on the mission at hand, for I do believe that Skive will think himself lucky to protect two free from the chains and shame of clothed women." Skive replied, "Indeed, among the luckiest ever to be created." I then spoke to Haderslev saying, "As with Langå, you have such a wonderful voice. Why did you not speak in the Royal Deities Sanctuary?" Haderslev replied, "For I have been Skive's wife for over one million years now." I then looked at both of them and said, "Why do you still live in your flesh in an environment that would be painless for your spirit?" They answered, "For our master offered this as a reward for our loyalty, as we have no pain." I then looked at them and said as we passed over a moon that was so close that our orbits had to orbit it also, "You have the bodies I wish to make for both our living flesh and eternal saints. I shall have my lights discuss your lives with you in more detail in the near future, if you so agree." Skive then answered, "Queen Goddess, we agree with all you say and ask for we are your servants." I told him, "I understand; however I want this to be an opportunity for you to sell what you like about this destruction proof flesh suit to our lights so that my future servants may live a great life." Haderslev replied, "We wish to do as you have asked oh great savior." Skive then informed me that it was time to land and drill deep into the core. Even though they had drilled out, the holes become sealed immediately. We now turned on our pain free switches and started bouncing all through the inside shell as we drove deep into the surface. We would stop at times, they would place their hands on their screens, and after a few lights flashed, we would once again be on our way. They told me that these were security stops, and that if not passed total destruction would be immediate. They had had thousands of invasions yet none had ever succeeded. I wondered why any would now try to invade since all this wisdom and knowledge was no longer of value except as a starting point if we ever would need it. As we started to approach the core of the planet, which I suspected would be hot as turned out not to be the case. The core was an empty world inside this planet. Our master was very creative when he set this up. We were now flying through the thick sky at a medium speed. Haderslev explained that this place had among the greatest gravity anywhere in the universe. Thus, unless equipped with special unique features, an invader would be pinned to the surface. I looked and saw two advanced pyramids as tall as the nearby mountains that touched the clouds. I asked my guests, "Who lives here?" They answered, "We do, plus many of our master's greatest scrolls are saved here." As we approached, a giant opening appeared and we were quickly inside. They started to give me a tour of this magnificent structure that I would have to keep secret. I saw so many scrolls as this building was infinite in its inside width. My guests explained to me that this was because the inside is so dense that to an intruder it would appear to be solid rocks, which cannot even be blasted through. I now started to wonder why my master would have so many scrolls. I now asked Haderslev, "Why are there so many scrolls here?" She answered, "Oh I am sorry my Queen Goddess, we thought you knew, however I can understand with all your penances and no opportunity to settle in why the master had made the embarrassing and hard to explain the explanation. We only know that the name of the father to our master is Abaúj-Hegyközi and we have found no record of his mother. Their Empire had almost two thousand galaxies and his father wanted more so he made a deal with an evil empire to defeat with 500 galaxies separating them. As the wars turned out to be fierce, the evil empire pretended to have internal problems, thus could only supplement Abaúj-Hegyközi's forces in order to hold their current stations. This Trojan horse proved to be the end of Abaúj-Hegyközi's Empire as they sabotaged his armies stealing what they could and killing the defenders and their ability to fight before returning to their evil empire. His armies collapsed as he lost the war. The evil empire quickly came in from behind and capturing many of his galaxies before making a truce with the empire they had attacked, in which they later rescinded and destroyed them forcing them to survive with only one galaxy. They were able to capture Abaúj-Hegyközi's son our master. Over time, this divine group lost their galaxy as a new throne took control. They needed a god, yet none was available except for young Bogovi. They finally made Bogovi their god, as this young deity was still impressionable. He fought so hard for so long against the evil in his galaxy. As he would clean one area, another would fall into evil. Yet he never gave up, finding great favor with our dimension's throne. We honestly believe that the reason you were given Ereshkigal was for your fighting spirit and devotion to love and good. The rest of this story is your story. We want to add that we have no proof that Bogovi knows his history, thus you may wish to go fishing in this topic before diving in." As tears now filled my eyes for the loss of Abaúj-Hegyközi who so much reminded me of my master and he would have been such a great god for all of us, if he had not made a deal with evil. I know what happens when we deal with evil, for I at one time was the evil making the deals and I would never ever deal unless it was guaranteed the other party received nothing and was destroyed in the process. This simple game plan works every time with no chance of failing. Play on their greed by justifying it as a need and work on their pride. I do believe that to be the thing that saved me from the Council of Nykøbing Mors was the total dismissal of my pride and willingness to humble down for the good of my servants. Evil will never make a deal for the good of your servants for fear that it may have to do good to at least one. Pride is truly the root of each evil. I really justify my nudity as the absolute freedom from pride. I do not need fancy garments to show my power. My power is my servant's love and faith in me. Let them see whom they trust their eternity. Let them feel greater than me. That is a good thing, for they will be more at ease to call upon me when they need my spirit.

I do not spend much time sitting in my throne seat, as I enlist my sisters to fill that position most times. They keep each other in check with love and that is the bond, which prevents an opening for evil to enter. Hate opens the doors for evil. I so much wish to spare Bogovi from this past, as I know it would haunt him. Thus, his most loving servant will be the gatekeeper on this one. This topic now gets me thinking about my mother from so long ago. She did me no wrong, as I shamed her beyond any chance of forgiveness and I suspect she has erased my bad chapter from her history. I sometimes wonder why I am such a proponent of good, seeing that I was once a mighty queen of evil. I tried to be a good lord, which led me to great heartbreaks. I resorted to evil as I pulled in two saints, (Sabina and Medica) to destroy many who were innocent and I even may have destroyed sisters that I miss so much. That was history, as I can only do one thing now and that is to prevent a beast like me from arising in this empire. Now that I see the pain and emptiness that now fills the secret parts of my master, I worry about his attention to detail on pleasing me in all things. I can now understand why he needs Drusilla so much now as he goes through a purification penance, that empty part of him with only maybe distant memories of his mother, which I vaguely remember him mentioning before with a saintly tone, crying out inside of him. This also could explain his being completely at ease working secluded in our Royal Deities Sanctuary, as he may be sensing the comforting silliness of females enjoying each other. He also stood strong for my daughters, protecting them in every way as a father would, during my penance. One priority task upon his return, along with the dodecillion (10^{39}) priorities is to get away with our (since I have also surrendered them to my master) daughters and let them get a feel of their new and last father. We will then reproduce some of his powerful spirit to be dedicated just for them, as they are free spirited girls and love to explore, yet I want them to explore with our master's name and my (to protect against evil) name. I am not in the mood to loose anymore, as I must humble myself every way I can to get Atlantis here. She would love the many giant and rich oceans in my thousands of galaxies. I had better start thinking about why I am here, and that is to discover the maybe sad history of Julia. I have so many things I want to do and even though I can do them all at once through my spirits. It takes away the thrill of sharing spiritual energy, such as seeing the joy in my daughters' eyes as we bond as a family. Conclusively, the secret humiliation of getting ready share spiritual pleasures with Haderslev only to refreshingly discover she is Skive's wife. Oh well, only the normal excitement that accompanies the adventure of trying to start a new relationship. I adore having passion in the air; it keeps the heavenly wines flowing. I am now just wondering around the halls here picking up a scroll here and there to glance at it. This gives me that extra charge of knowing that I must be a greater goddess than the god who filed these scrolls since only greater can view, yet that also comes with intent, as I have to intent to hurt the master I worship. His father had it all; the Empire was hence to the same degree strong as he did dwell with his servants. That may have been the problem in that he dwelt with his people and became as they. That is one reason why when I find someone I want, female of course since I am owned by my master, I bring him or her to me. They dwell with me and we dwell in a protected private place only leaving to do official divine tasks, or nose around as to the same degree I am now. That is another part I love about being female, not only can we talk about stupid stuff as I am now, or we can be nosey and are general forgiven as being victims of a sneaky male who forced us out of our comfort zone to search for the truth in of coarse pure innocence. I also get the joy of watching James type all this. He is being blessed by seeing things that no other Earthling could ever dream of seeing. We might even see me, oh wait, here is a scroll with blood pouring on the floor. I have never seen a bleeding holy scroll, yet again I now know all too well, there are many things I have not seen. I must open this scroll. As I touch it, my mind is flooded with screams of great pain with so many horrifying noises. Live humans, children, parents' young old male, and female are being fed into these grinding and chopping machines. This is endless, they are stripped of their clothing, and all their hair is cut off and then lined up and forced into these death machines. Millions and millions of them and they are offering no resistance. I cannot believe this, a complete genocide. I thought this only happened in that haven for evil called Earth. Trucks are pulling in and herding these people to the choppers. Trains and I mean mile long trains are coming in from all directions. No original person who lived here is being spared. The most horrifying part is whatever was being done with the ground, and chopped flesh, it is being packaged and loaded on large freighter spaceships, and I can see them selling this meat to non-humanoid species. So many lives are being ended and destroyed not by these chopping machines but by their loss of hope. As I look around these galaxies, I can see these human cleansing everywhere. Yet no other galaxy has stepped in. These dimension's thrones are allowing this. This is a testament to the power of evil, as no one can stop them. They found that little hole and through it flooded the galaxies. Evil must hear those screams and cries for mercy. A thought now hits me that since everything revolves in circles through time, something like this may happen again. I now fear dissolving my armies. I think I will go half way with twice as many. I am on my knees now crying. This is destroying my heart to see so many innocent suffer. I cannot even bear to see animals suffer like this. How can one species eat the flesh of another living thing? Why is it ok to eat the flesh of once living animals yet go to war after seeing the same thing happening to people? Even I do not know the answer to this, yet I do know that it is, for what I have seen here today was so unexpected and does show me one thing. If my master and I screw up, our servants will suffer. The only consolation I have is that I was told by the greatest council of good, which still exists at the growing away beginning of time that my Empire would rest with the others in their heavens. I do know that I must work hard to receive that reward and after today, I want only my blood being showered over my children as they receive my blood they become blood of my blood and that means whatever attacks them is attacking me. They are my body since I will flow through every part of them delivering the gases needed to keep the breath in them and the manna from my blood to feed their cells.

That is how deep I want to be in them. I must be involved with every part of their life. I am so glad that I provide the energy for their blood to distribute throughout their body. The animals in my galaxy live without the fear of dying for their flesh. I have made extent all beasts that kill and eat others. I am shocked at the sick deity that ever came up with that sick blood sucking game. They must get a lot of joy watching the lives leave these animals. I do not allow their populations exceed the limits that their ecosystem can support. I feed my animals also. My body is shivering as I have seen how lust and greed can destroy so much. If I were losing my hard stance against evil, I have now regained it and am going to jump back in this battle with some new weapons. I must know each day that I have many spirits fighting at the outer depths of this universe killing evil. Every time evil is destroyed, something good begins to live again. I have snooped somewhere that I should not be. I have enough infrastructures to keep us on the right road to the greatest Empire ever to be. I am now running and screaming out, "Skive and Haderslev where are you?" This now brings another thought in my minds wherever they are that when in danger, all the Women are equal to Men turned into, Men are strong and where are you. I fight hard for women to have opportunities, yet I am thankful the equation does have some muscle available when needed. Ironically, I was angry enough at Skive just a short time ago to threaten to cast him into a lake of fire, yet now I must see in his eyes that I am safe. This is why I love staying in these flesh suits. Instead of just "beaming" into safety, I can feel the blood rushing through my body as I fight for air and try so hard to keep my sanity at the same time I am pushing my legs. I look ahead now and see two sets of eyes looking at me. I see the little one crying and rushing to me calling my name out with 'her' soft voice if my ears and eyes are working properly yet this is not the cue I need to pull my anxiety back to where I can control my senses. I need to see calm on the big one ahead of me, and from what I am detecting 'him' does seem to be calmer since he is allowing the little soft one to rush out to me. I think I am going to make it. The first thing I may do is chop off my nose for getting me into this kind of trouble.

I can now identify Haderslev as she is wrapping her soft warm arms around me and holding me so tight. I now hand limp in her arms telling her, "Please hold me to my love." Now Skive comes forward with a bucket of warm soapy water and a cloth and has Haderslev release me as I hang on to her hands refusing to let them go and now a rare thing is happening. A male is washing my body, removing blood from my breasts and all parts of my body. I would guess this is okay as his wife is now helping him as she broke one hand free. She tricked me by kissing the top of my head one of my hands relaxed and she slipped free and started helping her husband clean me. Once they cleaned me, they both fell on their knees before me and started worshiping me. I looked at them and said, "How can you worship a goddess who you just saved?" Skive answered this fast and easy with his calm deep voice that was feeding my nerves, "Oh great Goddess that is so easy, for you are perfect in all ways." I then kissed each on their foreheads and said, "I do believe I am only perfect for my servants are so strong and perfect and always there when I need them." They each grabbed one of my legs and continued to praise me. I am such a lucky goddess. Haderslev asked me if I was able to continue to the cave on Gråsten. I shook my head yes, and we then jumped into one of their commuters and headed into a long dark tunnel that kept on going and going. It seemed like forever. I asked Skive, "Why is this tunnel so long?" Skive answered, "Our master did not want too many visitors to enter the cave. My goddess, please reconsider, you may not find the answer you are looking for. Let sleeping dogs lay idle. I told them, "This is a trip that is more focused on being prepared to serve my sister goddess if need be. There cannot be too much dirty laundry since she is so perfect in all ways." Skive then asked, "What if she has done something so terrible you cannot forgive her?" I then told him, "How can it be that bad if my master cleaned her and gave her to me to be one of my sisters? I must also remind everyone that I too was evil once." Haderslev then asked me, "My goddess, would you wish I went with you and serve your needs?" I looked as Skive and said, "You have me thinking on the edge now, I think I could use her help if you allow her to serve me." Skive then told me, "You created her and you are her goddess, you own her heart and soul, so by all means something we can do to serve you will be our great honor." I now wonder how that light is always on just around the bend from us. My master is truly amazing in his details and security precautions for this amazing place. I now asked Skive, who I seem to like a lot now as a big brother, "What prevents others from going down this long tunnel?" Skive told me that, "Every 100 feet are sensors and they must be his or one of his two girls. Except now I must replace Langå and code the new girl's genetics into these sensors." I had better be careful for I think I am getting nosey again. Then all of a sudden, we stopped. I looked in front of us and saw a large dark cavity. We were positioned beside a bright light that helped reveal what was ahead of us. This is such an eerie spooky place. I wonder why it has such a zigzagging path of our tunnel down to the sea. I asked my host, "What are those large strange rock carvings that cover the walls?" Skive answered, "Those are the forgotten people from a forgotten time. We know not what they were just that they were mysterious. A race of wizards or demons, we only know they have no life and are in no danger." I then added, "If they were alive once they could be reborn. That is a danger that should not be overlooked." Skive reassured me, "Our master's lights studied this mystery in great detail. We could find no evidence even suggesting the danger of evil, yet evidence of something different that is here for a reason and may someday even save us. This is an abandoned cavern that we discovered by accident while looking for water. We do not know how many more are hidden in planets throughout the universe. This is another one of those ancient advanced civilization circumstances." I guess we should keep an eye on them then. Haderslev then motions for me to follow her, and Skive bids his farewell and vanishes. I look at the empty space he had occupied and asked Haderslev, "Where is your husband?" She tells me he has work to do so he returned to their base. I then asked, "If we could have traveled the light and got here, why did we travel through the tunnel?" Haderslev replied, "For we do not know how to program you to travel these beams. We only know how to code inhabitants and do not want to chance injuring the Queen Goddess especially with the master gone. Let us walk down to the sea since we have a nice small cozy fort there where we will be comfortable and safe. After we rest 'some' tonight, we shall start the search tomorrow." She then reached out her hand for me to hold. I then asked her, "Why would we only get 'some' rest tonight, are there dangers here I should know about?" She looked at me and said, "Oh no my master, for my husband will not return for a few days and I know you like heavenly wine, I thought you may wish for me to serve you while I worship you tonight." I then raised her hand to my lips and kissed it saying, "I so wish that you could live with me in my Sanctuary for you are so dedicated to serving your goddess with all your heart, love and mind." Haderslev answered, "I too wish it; however, I made an oath to you for my marriage that I would stay with my husband until death." She had me by the law on this one, for I do require that bond before I join my servants in marriage I my quest to keep the family strong. She has so legalistically labeled our love tonight as her love to her god or goddess. No one would ever question this as disloyal or evil, for a servant must be loyal first to his or her heaven then to that which he or she has given him or her. Works in my favor tonight, as I study how wonderful soul and heart and enjoy her loyalty and devotion. As we enter the fortress, I notice the flowers are well kept. I ask my little pumpkin, "Who cares for the flowers?" She tells me that they do not know. Darn, it might tough betting some sleep tonight. Our night actually starts out well as we were tied up in some good girl talk. Considering that she is alone so much, her topic range and depth are very impressive. She then confesses to me that she many times take long swims in the Sea of Wisdom resting on the Island of Knowledge. Although it deals exclusively with a different age and people she would just go with the flow and soon was able to understand much of what was going on. She called it her in the past make believe world and enjoyed it because it is interactive. As I begin my first day of searching, Haderslev gives me some tips on how to search and what to look for. She does not know where Julia's scroll is since it was tossed in before she arrived. She said she arrived a few days later as a replacement for an original girl who mysteriously vanished. Day one and in I go. Not as dark as I thought it would be and at least there is not a lot of vegetation under here. Haderslev had taught me so much about this last night. She cannot search with me since she does not have our master's permission, and rather take a chance on getting her in trouble I allow her to sit out this search. In order to save time in this long process I switched my oxidation process to gill from lung so I do not have to keep doing up to the surface. Soon my body adjusts to the cold water. There are so many scrolls down here. I wonder why they wanted to forget about so many things. Although so tempting, I dare not open any of the scrolls since I got such a big awakening with the last one I opened. As I am swimming along, I accidentally scratch my leg on one of the underground rock formations pushing some rocks to the seabed. Strangely, as these rocks hit the seabed rocks start moving and a special pedestal rises up. This catches my eye as I switch back to see what it is. I look down at it and it says in fancy ancient lettering from an ancient language, "The secret scroll of Julia." The bound large book is sealed inside a special case to prevent any damage. If I had been in this freak accident, I would have never found this book. It is so much larger than any other scroll down here and made out of very high quality materials. I very carefully bring it up to the surface, leaving it under while I slowly swim back to our little fort. I have Haderslev lower a wooden pail under the surface and book and slowly bring it up allowing the captured water in the pool to keep it submerged. Haderslev remarks that she has never seen a special scroll like this before. I told her it was sealed in a special container under the under scrolls and that I found it by accident. Haderslev is so taken in by this that she appears to be hypnotized by it. I tell her I fear opening it without special equipment. Haderslev tells me that we can see if Skive knows of something to help us. She then calls for Skive to appear and he appears, with food stains all over his clothes. She yells at him for being messy yet he tells her that is a special privilege husbands getting when wives are away. We both know this to be true so we address the issue at hand. After he studies the situation for a few minutes his eyes get brighter and he says, "Let us search the Sea of Wisdom and if that does not work, we shall go to the Island of Knowledge." I am too embarrassed to admit I did not think of this first. So simple it had to have come from a man. Therefore, off we go hiking back up the path to the entrance where we get into our shuffle and after traveling for about five-minute stop. They punch in some codes and some lights start flashing and the top of our tunnel opens and up goes our shuttle as we now travel a new road. We soon find ourselves at another opening as Haderslev tells me, "Behold the Sea of Wisdom." I notice a similarity among many of the tall spiky rocks here as with the ones in the Sea of Forgetfulness. This sea looks much more transparent than the sea I was traveling. It looks as if this bed is made of lights and is much deeper. Skive recommends that I dive in with the book and ask the lights if it is safe to open it. He also added that I can ask that question anywhere in the water. In I go with my pale and book in it. I begin by asking, "Sea of Wisdom, may I open the Secret Scroll of Julia without bringing harm to it." The Sea answers back, "It is such an honor to have once again a Queen in our waters, are you Julia?" I was taken aback by this replied, "No, my Julia is waiting for me in my sanctuary." The Sea then answered, "You may not open this ancient book for it will forever hide its knowledge. We can however research the tales and stories in it and rewrite them for you. What we will tell you will be what is in this book, however we may miss a few details along the way. If you need those details, we will get them from the Island of Knowledge for you, since no knowledge is secret. We must ask you another question, if we may?" I told them to ask away, "They then said, "Why do you not want the Books of the Gyor-Moson-Sopron? Julia was to send Bogovi back to collect them." I then told them, "Julia forgot this request as Bogovi rewrote her book for her beginning her on a new chapter. I will be glad to give the books to my master's lights so they may determine how they may best serve our master." The Sea then said, "You must be one of the little Bogovi's best servants." I answered, "I strive to be the best." The Sea then told me, "Allow us to reestablish the Secret Scroll of Julia for you." I thanked them and started nosing (I mean looking) around to see if I could find something interesting. This is a place of much wisdom. They keep it under this lighted water for its protection and since water and light beams reflect, they receive the additional protection. I now wonder if Bogovi could have built this, as it does not have his flair. I ask the Sea, "Whose wisdom is this?" They answer in unison, "The only wisdom that being of Abaúj-Hegyközi who compiled this, yet did not take it to heart himself." I then answered, "That is so sad, as so many innocents suffered." The seas then agreed and went back to work. I felt a lot more comfortable here as this was based on wisdom and thus things that civilization wanted to remember. Soon Haderslev joined me. I asked her if she thought this to be wise. She answered, "If one cannot be wise in the sea of wisdom then where she could?" She got me there. Anyway, she added, "Skive said it should cause no harm, since I already had the scroll." That made sense so we started shopping around together. The sea then asked, "We all know about little Bogovi, yet are you his lost sister?" Haderslev replied quickly, "That she is, for she only wants to protect Julia and still remain lost." The sea answered back, "That we can understand, since there is much to be gained by living in secret." I started to think about these strange conclusions that wisdom kept putting together, yet I guess when you think about it, Julia is living in hiding. Wisdom applies this very so naturally. That is why I like dealing with lights because if they get too bright, I can turn them off. The sea then said, "We found this pic so you can see the bride of Abaúj-Hegyközi." We both marveled at the elegance and the portrayal of another custom. I felt good at seeing a queen also of a multi-thousand galaxy empire. It was nice of the sea to show us this picture so unexpectedly. I since that she was a stylish yet not glamorous queen, thus I still am wrestling with King Abaúj-Hegyközi's fall to greed and pride. There is something so eerie and mysterious about this picture. I am getting a strange vibe from it. It must be from being under the water so far below the surface. I hope that a good night's sleep will fix it. The sea now tells me they have finished the story however sadly the images did not materialize thus they must dig them up from the stories from the Island of Knowledge. This will take a few days, so they will return to scroll back to the Sea of Forgetfulness through an underwater tunnel that links them, and add the graphics to my working copy within a few days and asked me not to leave the Sea of Forgetfulness until we have all verified completion of this work. At least I can study the image of Bogovi's mother while learning about Julia. Skive takes us back to our little fort at the steps of the Sea of Forgetfulness as he returns to work. Thus Haderslev and I snuggle up in some very comfortable bedding I have provided us since all this dampness and darkness has put a chill in my bones and she starts telling me the stories from the Secret Scrolls of Julia. Her story began in a small planet ruled by her father. He was an extremely rich man and had a very large army. In those days it came to pass that King Abaúj-Hegyközi was fighting a war in their section of the galaxy and asked the father for his help. He agreed to help if Abaúj-Hegyközi would grant him one request and only if they won the war. The King agreed and the father's armies fought hard and won the war. The king asked the father what reward he wanted. The father said, "That you take my daughter to be your wife." The King joyfully agreed, and soon married Queen Julia. After hearing this, I asked my little love bundle, "Did you say Julia?" Haderslev then calmed me by saying, "It is very common to name children after great Queens such as you were during your penance times on that small island on Earth. You have apparently stumbled over the book of Bogovi's mother as Julia could have been named after her explaining the desire for our master to protect her. Do you want to continue this scroll or rest and start searching for your sister's scroll in the morning?" After thinking I answered, "It is hard for me to make choices, thus I wish to do both, considering that a better understanding of Bogovi's mother would help me serve him better." Haderslev then leaned over, gave me a kiss, and said, "That is why I worship you so much, yet let me plead for my life by saying if you do not leave any of my breasts for my husband, he may kill me." I then smiled at her and said, "Thus I would have to resurrect you then my dear." We both laughed as her heavenly voice continued this ancient tale. "Nevertheless, the King did take Julia to be his wife in anger for he loved another whom he wanted to be his queen. Yet her beauty and grace captivated the empire as all praised him for his wise selection. Inside he did burn with anger, yet outside collect the praises and rewards that others were bestowed upon him. One night, while returning from a long battle and finding his mistress with another in anger he did kill her and became killed by strong drink and led by Julia who as in all things served her king the best she could. It was upon this night that the great gods did plant inside Julia a male child of the king. When the king discovered that, his wife was with child he became very angry and cast her into prison where she did bear his son. The king's anger leads to great foolishness, as he soon became a slave to evil. Queen Julia promised to stay in the dungeon as long as their son was given to her father. The king kept this promise, as his anger and greed continued. He would have her chained to a wall without clothing and beaten for all to enjoy. He would have people pay to see a queen beaten. He then discovered he could make more money by selling her sexual services. Daily she was beaten and raped. Then one day an angel appeared to Abaúj-Hegyközi telling him that she was once again blessed by the mighty throne gods, and would bear him a daughter. He cursed the angel who warned that if he did not escape from his evil empire would pay a great punishment. That night the garrison army freed the queen where she was taken into hiding. Her father took his daughter and the young female child into permanent hiding where they were never again seen or heard of. He had to leave the young Bogovi so that what was salvaged of the empire would have a king, yet they kept him in hiding so evil would not kill him. The empire was punished as was the king who burns in a lake that no one can ever discover." We now starred at each other with tear-filled eyes. I cried out, "Why would I be given the wrong scroll? I must erase this from all memories of all times. It cannot be forgotten, it must be destroyed. Will you help me my love?" Haderslev said, "I will do anything for my goddess to include give my life in death each day for eternity." I told her, "You must never die and if you do, you will be mine to have and to love forever and ever. This is the commandment of your god." She then replied, "The greatest god ever to rule humans." I knew the next day was going to be hard, yet I also knew it was time to give this hunt up. I would wait and ask my master someday. I have stirred too many assortments of problems already. The next morning we took the remade scroll back to the Sea of Wisdom and I asked them to, "Destroy this scroll for it does not have the Julia I am looking to find." The sea then asked, "Do you not search for the Julia who is currently living with you in your Royal Deities Sanctuary that your master gave to you with a new book and chapter?" I looked at them and answered, "Yes, however that Julia is not in this scroll." The sea then told me, "She is the daughter that was taken into exile for her safety." I asked the sea, "Does my master know the history of his father's great evil?" The sea answered, "Oh by no means great goddess." I then told them, "This scroll is to be erased from all existence as no one else is to never know this, especially my master to whom someday I wish to bear him sons and daughters. I cannot ever let this hurt befall him as even I could in foolishness try to revenge him someday. I want another glorious history recreated and I demand all knowledge of this be erased from Haderslev and myself." The sea then told me, "We know not if we have the power to erase it from you oh great goddess." I then cried out, "Hear all, I give this power to the sea of wisdom for I shall erase it and you may never let me again discover it." The sea of wisdom told me, "As you have command it is." I looked at them completely puzzled, "What is?" They told me, "We have finished preparing the Secret Scroll of Julia." I now snuggled in beside my precious Haderslev hoping to enjoy some wine with her and slowly lightly nibble on her beautiful nipples while she reads this story to me. "It was in the year of the great raids when evil empires tried to destroy the last foothold for good, a small empire ruled by King Abaúj-Hegyközi and his wife the great goddess Queen Julia. The queen spent her days raising their young son, the god Bogovi. The family was blessed by the great saints of the good who petitioned the great heavens to give unto them another child this time a daughter who would resemble like her mother. During the days of her pregnancy the King's Empire came under great attack as many evil armies from around the universe did attack them. A day came when the king could no longer save his people and thus gave his life trying to postpone a sure loss. Members of his court smuggled the pregnant queen and her son out in the palaces garbage fulfilling the forewarning, "A king shall arise from that which they threw away and create a great Empire for Good that shall be blessed by the fathers who existed at the beginning of time." As they made their way out of the galaxy, some new armies of good came from a galaxy far away and freed the small galaxy that was yet to be captured. These freed people cried out for a god to worship. Queen Julia in tears gave them Bogovi as he did belong to his father's empire. She then went into hiding where she did bear a child that she also gave her name. They lived a simple life, staying hidden in the mountains for fear of their lives. Yet their hiding was in vain, as did one day some evil merchants discover them and sold their location to some evil demons. The demons captured the mother who has hidden her daughter. The demons destroyed the mother in revenge for the victories her son had over them. The young princes remained hidden until one day soon a poor married couple discovered her and raised her as their own. Poor Julia's fate would not be decided that easy as one day a wizard discovered her and sold her as a slave to some evil merchants. These merchants wanted to capitalize off her beauty and made her their sex slave. As they became rich and famous from Julia bad luck came their way and they lost all their riches as no one wanted to enjoy her sex anymore. For this, the evil merchants beat her endlessly. One day some angels heard her cries and called out to the spirits, "Who is this that cries?" The spirits told them, "It is the goddess Julia who is the sister of your master. He must never know she is his sister, for the pain of losing his parents and also discover they have hidden his sister from him could do him and Julia harm." The angels then asked, "Can we tell him she is an escaped saint that was captured and tormented by evil and beg for him to give her a new life and a new book?" The spirits then agreed and told the angels they would also tell this story to Bogovi and that someday a better time would exist when her book may be opened." Upon discovering, Julia Bogovi's heart grew very warm towards her. He gave her a new book and said, "You shall be blessed among women, for you shall be a disciple for my precious love who is now serving her penance. For you knew so many things about pain and even though I erased these pages from your book you shall have a secret skill for guiding our Queen through her penance." I was now so excited to discover that Julia is indeed my master's sister thus also my sister. I always knew there was something special about her. I did not make her a goddess for the reason that she was born a goddess. Once again, I am being worshiped by the best. This is rewarding to know that Bogovi has a sibling. That will help make him feel more at home in our Sanctuary. We will of course use discretion when playing with Julia however; we pretty much use discretion all around when the master is present. I am so excited about having a real sister in law. This is someone who has absolute ancestral blood right to intervene. She was born from the love of her mother, which any way you slice the cake deserved much better. Julia is the manifestation of my master's mother a woman whom I have the absolute respect. My mind is somewhat foggy over my master's father; however, my birth mother never mentioned my father, so that must have been the style then. I always, by instinct kept my daughters away from their fathers. With so many of my daughters, dying at birth it just was not fair to watch a man suffer for my punishment. How do you tell three males, your babies are alive, and then turn to the other three and say, "Sorry Charlie?" That can also escalate into other problems as some males take the treatment of their seeds personal. I think after my daughters get another ten or twenty million years under their belts in this empire, things well for stable and the shaky beginning forgotten, especially since they now have a wealth of aunts and even an aunt from our master's side. It is always better when your in-laws are your friends first, that way the relationship is not flirtatious and political. I have found the answer to the question I came to seek. I am also having the sea of wisdom edit some of the identifications that could be derogatory to my master's family and we will publish the bleeding scroll I discovered. It will be mandatory reading in my "gods only" library. I want them not only to see why we fight evil but also to feel what is at stake. If we need to fight someday, we must fight hard without mercy, and understand what treatment to expect from our enemies if we lose. This trip will also have another painful memory and that is not to have the love of my servant Haderslev at my feet. I will have my lights figure out a way to get more in their rotations so that they all can also have some quality lifetime. Haderslev may someday wish to have a family. I think modifications can be made to support family life there. Haderslev is holding my hands while we are drilling into the surface. I so wish there could be another way to enter and depart, however the lights will have to discuss that with our master once he is settled back in from his penance. As we reach the surface, I say goodbye to my two faithful servants and tell them, "Next time we meet at my house, Ok." I now am seated in my royal seat on this rocked war ship as we prepare for our trip back to the center of my Empire. I so wish Haderslev could have gone with me to my throne and returned to her husband; however, that would be unfair to Skive, and forced her into a sad return trip. I just did not know being divine can have so many emotions, yet then again, many divine do not allow emotions to enter their spirits. I do, the bonding through tribulations build memories and emotional experiences that I think it is hard for even gods to reproduce. There is now a locked room in my spirit with the name Gråsten written on it. I am off course moving Gråsten to a more secure part in my empire since the historical content there is of great value and should not be forgotten. My lights can figure this out for me. I have a royal family business to perform. As I land in my throne, I call for my courts to meet with me as I prepare to brief them if I can stay awake. I begin with, "My courts, I have been to the Sea of Forgetfulness and Sea of Wisdom and looked out to the Island of Knowledge. There is so much history there as I cannot tell you that they were primitive to us or us primitive to them. I do know that all the gods of my galaxies shall view the scroll of blood. I also wish to enhance the living conditions there for our servants. We shall relocate it beside our throne so the skills of our ancestors will be at our hand if needed. I am tired now and have business in my Sanctuary with a future announcement coming from there. Oh, yes, by the way, please do not embarrass me with complaints from our Empire that there requests to share are ignored." The lights then asked, "Who did we ignore?" I told them, "The Sea of Wisdom for they wanted you to help them store some old books." The lights then replied, "Oh great goddess, which books?" I answered once again, "Ahhhhh, let me think something about the Books of the Gyor something . . ." All the lights replied, "Not the Books of the Gyor-Moson-Sopron?" I answered, "That's it, see what they need." Our Empire lights all lit up now and they replied to me, "Oh great goddess, those were the books in which the Council of Nykøbing Mors lost during a major war and was never able to find them. Those books have many of the secrets to the universe in them. These books will greatly enhance your Empire's power since they have the answers to all questions." I looked at them and answered, "So that means you plan on picking them up? When you do, be sure to use precaution when trying to open them." The lights had now called in the Courts who wanted to verify my findings. I told them, "The verification will take place after we have the books." The courts then asked, "Oh great goddess, wilt thou ask the spirit to make a great library for these books and to keep that library in your spirit?" I told them, "I will think about that after I rest, for my spirit is strong yet my flesh is weak." I still do not know what all the fuss is over those books, if they were so great why did the Sea of Wisdom not use them? I am sitting here now making some decisions that only my throne can make, as my master and or I are the throne. This is a busy place today. Guess my sisters have not been here recently. Even though my spirits have already made and implemented the decision, one of the goddesses or us gods must sit on the throne and visibly order it so. Makes for a possible boring day; however, we do have ourselves programed for key words, such as good, evil, hate, love, kill, war, etc . . . . Therefore, that way insures our wish is being served. We also have alerts to warn us to reevaluate something. This is the way of the ages and is important for an Empire not to be 100% automatic but to keep that element of surprise and empathy in the decision process. As I sit here watching these presentations, I can at least be happy that I am not the one giving the presentations. Today is for the most part receiving gifts from our new galaxies. I am somewhat of a bitch on this one in that the gifts must be of nominal value, and made by the children in that galaxy from inside my temples. Exclusively they are to have children give the presentations, as we always have those go first. Whoever is in the 'hot seat' stays because we just cannot get up? These children are randomly selected by my spirits as they do the initial scan in the new galaxy. They are brought together and trained by their governments in my temples. I now motion for the representatives of these 1,000 new galaxies, as they have been presented by the 'fifty-galaxy consolidated thrones.' Some day we will have to give these thrones names, however for now I will keep the numbers in it, tends to feel more personal. These twenty presentations were as usual wonderful. Today, I just wanted to say something extra to these children as they all line up before me. I began by saying, "I do wish we can give all the children who perform in front of us official welcoming words. However, we cannot nevertheless today I am granting an exception. My Empire is built upon the family unity with laws that even I cannot break. Husbands and their wives serve as in one body for their families, such as your master and I serve in one body. From this union comes forth our greatest product, the purpose of our Empire and that is our children. All in my Empire and my throne serve you, our children. My dream is now alive in that you shall live in an Empire based on love and good. Evil shall never live in my Empire. You are children of the greatest Empire ever to have flesh on its surfaces. You will live lives of love and peace and not in hate and fear. I bless you as you return to your homes and ask that you work hard to keep our Empire good. Thank you." At this point, I did vanish as the courts cleared our judgment and reception area for now. I need to return to my Sanctuary and rest. To my relief the goddess Bárdudvarnok is now here to perform our divine duties. I have now entered my Sanctuary and call for my sisters to wait for me and I take Julia off to be alone with me. I feed her the secret scroll (revised) in her name. As she digests it, a fear begins to flow down her cheek. I ask her, "Why do you cry Julia?" She then answers, "For I am no longer your sister." I told her, "Julia, you are now even more my sister for our master and I are one and you are not only blood of my blood but you are blood of our master's blood. You were born a goddess as your brother was born a god. The truth is that you are a real goddess and I am a promoted spirit with all powers given to me. Your powers are not given to you, for you are your powers. Let me be the first to worship you." Julia then cried again, "Oh please my master; do not force this upon me, for it is my will that I serve you. I will curse this power if you forbid me to worship you." I now held her and asked, "Oh Julia, why is your heart so heavy now? This is truly a great thing for both of us, for when you love me I will know that a true goddess loves me. May I wash away your tears and will you give me back your wonderful smile with you to keep me in your eyes and let me read inside your soul once again." The way she looked at me now was so very special since I could tell she loved her goddess. I feel so bad in that her ranking now is higher than mine is, yet she refuses it. It is her birthright as my master's number one servant I am to stand at his left and Julia, as his blood sister and not wed is to stand to his right. Once I give birth to a child of my master, I then shall stand to the right, in between Bogovi and Julia. This is because of the importance divine law gives to making new gods. I do not plan to be standing on his right for some time to come. My spirit is now releasing the scrolls to our sisters, except for Drusilla and Siusan. For now, I will just hug my poor scared Julia. I cannot hold back my words, "Julia, you do know the greatness of my love for you and that I all things I want so much more for you and my sisters. Each of you is a gift of love. Your special gift was coming as a new book from our master. He must be told that you are the daughter of his mother and both of you are from the same father. I can feel you know this to be true. Our master has been alone for way too long. He was taken away from you and your mother to continue the work of his father. Too little was given him and you belong to the same blood that he belongs to. My blood in you is the blood of faith, for that shall always be with you, the true blood in your veins is the blood of the gods and as such deserves its place among the deity. I would be breaking every law of good if I were to deny this from you. I will not deny or hide it from you. Your will is your will and if that is at my feet, I shall have you as mine. Yet you must know that I will be worshipping you. If you forbid me this then you destroy the rights we have that allow us to be the gods of our servants. Any power that makes gods worship their servants is evil." Julia then, as she was kissing me she said, "What you say is true, yet remember you have us walk around our servants nude, to show them we have no shame or hide nothing from them and to show them we want to be their servants. It is my eternal love for you, for you made me your sister and your sisters made me theirs. The love here cannot be found elsewhere. You are the only thing in me and serving you is the only thing that gives me a life. You are my goddess and I shall never worship any other. If I must worship you in hiding, so be it. You cannot forbid me to worship you and that you know to be true." That which she said was true. I figured she did not want to be left alone and feared rejection from us thus I told our sisters to treat her the same as always. It is a fearful thing to treat a real goddess as a sibling. Predicament, I will either have to do this, even as Bogovi's sister or mine. As we are all trying to wrestle with this new change of the status quo, Julia comes stumbling out in front of the group and begins to cry as she falls to the ground. Máriakéménd runs over to her and holds her. We then form our group around her and the sisters start reassuring her of our love for her. As each one of us kiss a tear and hold onto whatever is in reach we can feel her start to relax. She then cries out, "Why does my closed book come back to haunt me? I have here more than any goddess could have. I want nothing else. I beg my sisters to let me be their servant. Fejér once again proved why she was our unofficial leader by saying, "Well, in that case maybe we should live in here where we make the rules." You could see the excitement in each sister's eyes as the lights came on. We never cared if something was right or wrong; we only cared about what each of us wanted. In this situation, we all felt that Julia was justified in her position. That part of her life had been closed, even though the one who closed it made a big error that does not matter. It was closed and she was happy in her current situation much as Faith was happy as a countess before evolving into a Queen. Faith had to move on because that book was not sealed. Why Julia should be punished because her Queen had to be nosey, we could not answer. I never thought trying to help someone could end up being such a painful ordeal. Where we stood on stage never mattered, for Bogovi appeared many times with my sisters. We just did not care, more of who is having a good hair day ordeal. At least by now having his sister on one side and me on the other we can control who is around him, which weighs heavily in my favor. Julia is more concerned about her world, and now that she is officially a goddess by divine ancestry, it is her world in here. I guess there are worse things than having a goddess worship you, for me that worse thing would be losing that bottle of wine. I can truly see the divinity of her wine now, as I would worship her just for her wine, although she is worth more than that. Her powerful wisdom and ability to anticipate so many possible outcomes and be ready for them saved my little ass a few times. It was not just a few major times; it is in all things, no matter how trivial. It is now starting to make sense, for only a true goddess could to that. She knows her brother has the right to know there is one in existence created with the same building blocks as he was. We will all stand up and tell him, "We shall share her with you, yet she owns us and she is not selling." He wills most likely shake his head and makes a comment such as, "Oh someone has mercy on me, and it is running in my family now." It will be just so good to hear him say, "In my family now, instead of the empty lonely way he tries to hide when he says, "in your family now." For now, it is time for some fun, so here we go, "Hay Julia, big sister has a yummy yum for you." Now they are all laughing like crazy hyenas. The ice is broken now, Julia is back where she wants to be, as she is crawling towards me saying, "Hay big sister, where is my yummy yum?" We all pounce on her hugging, crying, and doing all that other stupid stuff that blood sisters do. Leaves little to wonder why she wants to hold onto what we have. Think about it, each of us walks out of this sanctuary and can snap a finger and galaxies move yet come in here for the security of our universe shaking love. Soon after we become quite exhausted, we bundle up in our rotating pairs and fall fast to sleep. If the universe could hear the snoring in here now, for when we have enjoyed an exhausting day we sleep hard. Early in our morning, we hear large alarms sounding asking the goddesses to appear. I then call for my lights to explain. They tell me we have an urgent message and a gift from our dimension's throne. Darn, guess I had better take this one. The lights also inform me I am to bring Julia with me. Accordingly, I go over and pull her sisters off her; you would almost think they thought they were going to lose her. Then I whisper in her ear, "If you love me you will arise." Up she pops even with her sweet eyes still closed. Ooh, how I wish I could laugh now, however we need to get on the throne as soon as possible. As we arrive, we see angels and courts packed as far as our eyes can see. There is no path for us to walk to my throne. I then take Julia's hand as I think about reappearing in front of my throne. This place is incredibly crazy right now. I refuse to reappear and demand that my army commanders meet me in my throne chamber. It is here I demand some explanations. I tell them, "There shall never be a situation where I and if escorted by other gods cannot walk to my throne. I have created and given my Empire the greatest streaming equipment in the histories of our universes. Every one to include all children can see and hear this event. We cannot permit chaos around the throne. The throne is a judgment seat of gods, and will be treated as such. Now lead your armies and bring order to my throne." As I gaze out, I can see them having some trouble so I decide to energize it for them by having my spirits clean up the area. I can understand their excitement; however, this is not the first time we have been visited by our dimension's throne. This is not an opportunity to show them how weak our Empire is when controlling its souls. I punish our servants in the flesh when they misbehave and the same shall be true for my spirits. I do not call relocating them to a safer place, with of course ample access to the streams as a punishment. That is the difference in the rational for wrath from gods and goddesses. I now take Julia and proceed to our welcoming area for our guests. They are both male, from the throne does not send females to me anymore since they all want to abscond to my empire. They explain that the lights of the dimension, upon discovering Julia to be the daughter of Queen Julia had in its possession the Bajánsenye Heart, which was made from the jewels and crown of Julia's grandmother and had been kept in secret, as it is only to be worn by one of her female descendants. It was made by human hands and took over one hundred years to make. There is no other known royal jewel to match it. As I look upon it, I can feel how many killed and destroyed for greed in order to have this. I cannot remember ever seeing anything like it ever before. Julia sees how it brings great pleasure to me and takes it, falling to her knees lifts it up to me and says, "Take this my goddess, for I only want you to have it." I look at her and say, "Oh know Julia, I want to see how beautiful it looks on your divine beauty. This is from your grandmother so please honor her so that she may find pleasure in you and not hate in me. Fear not, for your sisters and I will babysit it from time to time for you," as I hooked it onto her necklace I had given her when we celebrated her first birthday in our family. I then hugged her saying, "I am so proud of you now let's go out there and let our guests give this to you so our servants can see it before they destroy our throne, okay tiger." She then winked and gave me her kitty cat roar and hand in hand with the jewel in our guest's hand to the stage. This amazing piece of jewelry was actually comprehensive, a collection of fifteen pieces including some that fit inside the large center heart. The middle heart had an internal light, which we later discovered would shock any who touched it except for Julia. Thus, that would be her heart. We all tried on the hearts as it added a unifying decoration to our style. We jokingly wondered what it would look like on Siusan, yet we had some time before we would, if at all, cross that bridge. For some strange reason we all felt strange around this amazing piece. Ceglédbercel was able to pinpoint it to the lighted centerpiece. We did not want to say anything about it in the open for fear of disturbing Julia. Nonetheless, later in the day our small harem received another surprise. Sabina came running into our camp yelling, "Master follow me, I have found a surprise you must see." We all jumped up and started running behind her. Any surprise elicits a response from all of us as we discover together. It is so nice to have so many sharing the same anticipation. For one to see us from outside they could hardly believe we were all goddesses, now with one actually being born one. Even though many of us were deified by the current dimensions throne, it does not match the ancestral heritage as Julia is coming, as did her brother, our master, an empire as great as ours did. To go back past her grandmother would require going back to the Council of Nykøbing Mors to discover her great-grandmother and that is only possible for her mother jumped out of the loop, if such a thing is possible. She died or gave up her flesh, yet I would suspect her spirit, being divine would be somewhere since the sea of wisdom never told me she was "made no more" which is a punishment reserved for evil deity such as Julia's father. I hope Julia searches for that answer because nosing around has caused me enough headaches. She is much wiser than I am so she will become curious someday. Even three generations, such as Bogovi, Abaúj-Hegyközi and his mother moves the timeline back past the beginning of time and pushes so deep into the reverse of time. Sabina now shows us what made her so excited, and a sight truly this is. Before us is a nice simple pond in a heart shape. I know I have never seen this before, for something like this, my master would have shown me to collect the appropriate award for such a place. I do notice there are no trees around this pond and the grass is very short. It does not blend with this Sanctuary, however does have the same stylish touch. Maybe my portable brain is being overloaded; however just in case I am on to something here, I will ask my spirits. As I go to submit my transmission, it is bounced back and we look into the sky and see a heart shaped cloud. I now call upon my spirits and they have appeared before me. I ask them, "Who made this pond and what is that heart-shaped cloud?" My spirits answered, "The heart is the symbol of Queen Tompaládony whom is the grandmother of your master. The darkness inside it is her son King Abaúj-Hegyközi. The hole beside the outer tip of the heart is her son's wife who vanished. The four holes directly below it represent other loved ones she lost in the spirit wars. The two headed, with one head upside down towards the bottom, represents your master and Julia whom she hopes someday will turn into the white of the heart." I then ask, "How did Queen Tompaládony enter my sanctuary and create these hearts?" My spirits answered, "She is a queen of the ages, and her act was one of love and revelation which we do not detect." I am now wondering how many more billions of exceptions allow others to visit this sanctuary. I tell my spirits, "I never want to hear that something can enter this sanctuary undetected. Anything before that I have not approved enters here then I will be notified. Can you store that in your highest memory as a law for me, sorry not can, you will . . . Also, I wish to meet with Queen Tompaládony." My spirits told me the arrangements would be made. Then we could feel a storm blowing towards us. I cried out, "Storm is still and give us warm sunshine." Consequently, it was so. My spirits now told me, "Master, we have the Queen ready to enter." I then said, "My god, let her in. I told you I needed to see her!" I may have to have my spirit's IQ checked. They will let in total strangers yet keep out someone I told to let in. Is there any hope for any form of security protection, or do they all have to let in what you do not want in and keep out the things you tell it to let in? Then before us appeared a beautiful woman with a magnificent crown and royal green robe with a royal posture, something that we do not have. I must admit it does carry some elegance with it. As she appears, we all bow and she begins, "You may all arise. Which one of you is the servant to my grandson?" I arise and tell her, "I am Queen Lilith, greatest servant of King Bogovi. All in this Empire are servants of Bogovi." She asked, "Where is that little Bogovi?" I then told her, "He wished to be a penance god like I am a penance goddess. Thus, he is now serving his penance." She replied, "Oh poor baby; I hope you have someone to be with him for he is so tender." At this, all my sisters started chuckling. I looked at her and said, "Your poor little baby is now a strong and loving King. I did give him my twin sister to help him if he so desires." She then looked at me and said, "You are a good servant for him. Our throne speaks very highly of you, saying you are the greatest goddess since the beginning of time. I am fortunate to exist on the other side of the timeline. It does my heart good to know that you are here to serve my grandson and to let my granddaughter serve you." I then told her, "When the sea of wisdom told me Julia was my master's sister; I did beg her to let me worship her. She refused to allow me to worship her, for her love was too inordinate for me. I know not how to serve her for my love for her is equally important pronounced to deny anything from her." Queen Tompaládony then replied, "I know my child, and I thank you for your great love for her and to ask you to allow her to serve you. I fear that if she were to exercise her ancestral danger could come to her." We all stood up and surrounded Julia as I answered back, "All that you see here before you are willing to die or suffer misery for eternity to keep Julia free." As Queen Tompaládony scanned each of us, she replied, "I envy my granddaughter since she is among a greater love here than I have ever seen." I then said to her, "Since you are my master's grandmother and thus have ancestral rights to this Empire would you enjoy staying with us for a while?" The Queen looked at me and said, "I would very much enjoy staying yet I have not the strength to appear before others nude. I need these great garments to give me the power to appear. Also my daughter, I want no ancestral rights to this Empire; for I was not there to save my poor little grandchildren after the war, thus I should be punished in shame rather than be greeted with honor as you have so foolishly done." Julia and I with our other sisters following went over and hugged her. I told her, "You are blood of our blood and your heart is of good now. In this manner, together we can fight evil. As I was once the queen of evil, my wrongs are greater than yours are, yet this dimension forgave me and made me a goddess. You have all the rights as the master's grandmother here and my throne will deify you. You may abide here in the Royal Deities Sanctuary with the other goddesses of this kingdom and your granddaughter will sleep in your arms during our darkest hours if you so wish. We shall now worship you." Furthermore, we did all bow to our knees and worship her, for this was also a great pride for us as she was an ancient goddess with the knowledge and powers of the ancient as we so hard struggle to get back to where they were. Time will judge us on our efforts. Queen Tompaládony now had our knack for crying as she cried. Her cries sounded so good as her happiness flowed into Julia. She looked at me and said, "I have detected your appreciation for my beauty which as a goddess never goes away. All you who are here shall keep the beauty of your youth for eternity." I then asked her as we all laughed, "My Queen, does that apply for gods also?" She looked at me, for the first time started laughing, appeared so relaxed, and said, "Yes my daughter, your master will still be your prince charming for eternity." We all laughed at this and then Máriakéménd started one of her old Stuart songs as we all did sing and laugh. After a few songs, I asked Queen Tompaládony, "Our new love, would you enjoy taking a walk through the Valley of Giant Flowers with your newfound granddaughter?" She answered as she had now picked up our courtesies, "If my grand-daughter would permit me I would enjoy it so much." Julia then jumped up and grabbed her hand and off they went. Furthermore, they did go to the Valley of Giant Flowers where Julia's brother did enjoy me as he did wish. I am starting to get excited about the way our royal family is formulating as I now am thinking about Prudence and Edward and how as a baby they would sing beside the fireplace and sing songs to me. My penance did give me two childhoods, one with love the other with pain yet even out of the one with the pain came my greatest love of all Drusilla who I now suspect Sabina may be missing also. Accordingly, I called for Sabina to walk with me and we did talk. She did confess that Drusilla and she were very close and that she so much did miss her. I must admit this is good news that they are so close to I have been so busy with so many other things that I have neglected Drusilla excessively. I then asked Sabina, "Do you think I have made Drusilla sad by neglecting her and now placing her in the bed of our master?" Sabina reassured me, "Oh no Master, she understands and is just so glad to see you being happy and loved. She would never be angry at you for putting her in the bed with the one you love so much. Anything she can do for you is as a blessing for her. She will return your master to you when his penance is finished and fall to your feet worshiping you and only you." I gave Sabina a kiss and thanked her for helping our Drusilla. I then also apologized to Sabina for not spending as much time with her as I once did, even though she lived inside of me and filled a big hole. I told her I missed having her inside of our old trinity and me. Sabina then told me, "Master, I was born a priestess and not a part of a trinity. Now I can live here and enjoy our sisters yet still serve you as a goddess when your spirit needs me. This brings me great joy and I beg that you not take it away from me." I then answered saying, "You have served me well, and I believe you will always serve me well. That which brings you happiness also brings me happiness. Let us now bath in the relaxing waters as we have before." Hence, we did bath and return to the camp in time to take our afternoon naps. As I awake I notice Julia's heart is beside me. The mystery light is shining bright enough that I do believe it did wake me up. As I look deeper inside it, the light began to grow. I then wondered why this light grows. I asked, "Who is in this heart?" Then a voice came back to me, "I am Queen Julia, the mother of your master. I have come today to share with you a warning. My daughter is not safe with the evil Tompaládony." I then asked her, "Why do you say she is evil?" The Queen, as I now wonder if we are going to have more divine queens here than just your regular goddesses answered saying, "For she has chased me for over twenty dodecillion (10^{39}) years trying to avenge me for the death of her son. I am innocent of that blessing for his death was the blessing that gave me a chance to save my children. I had Julia carefully hidden here until you discovered her identity in the sea of wisdom. I then went into hiding in this jewel or my Trojan horse to bring my daughter back to safety, however when I saw that you sensed something in this jewel I was given a message from the Council of Nykøbing Mors to trust you." I then remarked, "Wow, you know the Council of Nykøbing Mors?" She laughed saying, "Remember child, we queens hold our age real good. I roamed the universe fearing for my life so many ages before you were born unto your mother, and unlike you, I have only one daughter to love and protect, yet I feel she is harder to protect than you with all your daughters are. You are so lucky." I could feel the sincerity of her anguish and thus reached out to hug her. She hugged me and chuckling said, "I do not want you to think I hug every free from the chains of clothing queen I see." I kissed her lightly on her cheek and said, "Really mommy?" She answered all of a sudden seriously and said, "My god, I lied to you honey, for you are the only free from the chains of clothing queen I have ever seen." I then told her, "Ahhh, that's ok. Let me ask my spirits how we can keep Julia out of danger, for if anyone were to take her from me, I would go to war. Unlike you, I share the armies with your son, my master." She then told me, "The Sea of Wisdom gave me many streams of beauty of your relationship with not only your master but the servants of your empire. I do believe that if I had been given the chance, I would have followed much the same path as you did. You had the dimension's throne to support you while my father's kingdom was only a few galaxies, one of which you and your master exchanged your vows." That really hit me with a great sense of honor. I am still so amazed at how the three of them resemble each other so closely. I asked my spirits, "What shall I do?" They answered back very fast, as if for a change their brain was working, "We shall give Julia to the highest protection in our Empire, and if she must travel she will do so with many armies. Both queens shall be monitored at all times for security purposes. If they do not agree, they will be banned from your Empire. Also they may no longer see into the future on any matter relating to Julia." I asked my spirit, "Are you going to protect her better than you do at keeping unknown queens from entering into here?" My spirit became quiet as I looked over at Queen Julia and she replied, "You may of course monitor me as long as Queen Tompaládony is not given the information for my security purposes unless you wish to join those who hunt me?" I told her, "I saw the original Secret Scrolls of Julia in which your innocence is proven. We will protect you as your son and I do for your daughter." Queen Julia then asked me, "The Sea of Wisdom told me they destroyed that manual and erased it from your memory." I told her, "That is true; however my spirits recorded it and have it secured where no one can ever find it." Queen Julia then looked at me and said, "Very wise young queen." I gave her another kiss and said, "I had better stop kissing you or others may be confused as to which one of us is your daughter." She looked at me and started kissing me checks saying, "Nonsense, you belong to my son, thus you are my daughter also, am I not correct?" I gave the only true answer, "You are indeed correct, for you are our mother indeed." I suggested to her, "Let us go find them so we may talk." When we appeared alongside them in the Valley of Giant Flowers, I was somewhat amazed by their reactions. Being court women of the ages they first immediately changed into somewhat palace royal informal gowns and after staring at each other, Queen Julia broke the silence by asking, "Oh mighty Queen Tompaládony why do you hate me so? Did I not do my duty and give into your son two fine children?" Now, surprisingly, all four of us had tears flowing like rivers from our eyes. There will be some planets getting rainstorms today, as the old tales would suggest. This is so heartbreaking, a mother who only struggled to save her children now on her knees being their grandmother to stop trying to kill her. That is the depth of true love and I think if we can keep the Queen here, we will have available one of the richest wells of deep love ever to be created. Then Queen Tompaládony, "Dear child, the evil I have done unto you should never be forgiven. I will give myself to be your slave for eternity. I command the heavens upon this day to take all that is mine and surrender to my new master since I am indebted as her slave, that if I shall ever disobey her command I shall be punished 10,000 times all her suffering each day. As I have commanded it shall be done." We were all so shocked, for she now appeared as a naked chained slave at our feet. Her power was such that none of us could stop her. She no power yet only held the chains up to Queen Julia saying, "You may beat me if it gives you pleasure my master." Queen Julia cried back, "I shall never harm not even I hair from your body, but worship you for making the seed that gave unto me two such fine children." She looked at me and gave me the keys to her chains and soul saying, "I have never nor will I ever hold another as my slave, you know what I say is true. I hold no ill will towards Queen Tompaládony as I told you; my fear is only for my children. I never knew her to be filled with love, thus I never trusted her and ran from her taking my two babies with me. Did I not also take her babies? Could she have some cause with me? How can I make her pay for a crime that I might have made even somewhat justifiable for her? This punishment is too much for me to bear. As you worship your servants, I shall worship mine." She then fell to her knees and worshipped the now human, Queen Tompaládony. I cried out to my spirits, "Spirits, can you help me now?" My spirits answered, "We can help our master with this as long as you know Queen Tompaládony has the divine right to punish herself." I told my spirits, "Please do not give me the divine rights speech, can you help me?" My spirits answered, "Queen Tompaládony's enslavement command was given from your Royal Deities Sanctuary from which only you may command. What do you wish to command now, oh great Queen?" I looked at Queen Tompaládony and said to her, "Although I do like you better nude, you sexy older female, in my Empire we can have no slaves. If you were to be the slave than you would have to be our master and I am not ready to have a new master, especially one related to my current master. One master per family is the limit. That will keep my new children from getting confused. However, I command you now to promise never to bring harm or take action in anything that could bring harm to my Julia and master and Queen Julia." She looked at me and said, "That is the easiest promise I shall ever make, for they are the three I love the most. I forbid myself ever from committing such a crime, as I extend this to also include all who serve them." I looked at Queen Julia who rose up wrapping her arms around the now free from the chains of clothing Queen

Tompaládony and said to her, "My goodness, I did not know your skin felt so soft, I should have kept you as my servant and enjoyed your spiritual fruit. I do hope you will once again be my mother, wilt thou?" She agreed as they hugged, saying sassily, "You are the cheater in this group you non-nudist?" We all did laugh, as I asked her, "Where did you hear about the fruits?" They looked at us and said, "Do you foolishly think you invented everything, after all children, we were once searching for love in all the wrong places also." I then asked them, "Would you think it evil if Julia shared her spirit with the other goddesses here?" They both looked at me and said, "She is your servant, do with her as you will, but please love her in doing so." We all jumped up and cried out, "We love you Julia." This surprised me how I do believe I had a sister hidden behind each flower as they all now came out to confess their presence. Queen Tompaládony now stated, "Julia, you are so lucky to have the love from so many goddesses. Your accomplishments rival that of your brother." Julia then answered, "The only thing I rival my brother for is the love of my master." Queen Tompaládony then said, "Oh, what are we going to do with this younger generation always wanting to make someone their master." At this, we all did laugh so loud I would suspect some planets received the thundering waves from our great joy. Now we would have to arrange for how we would live, for I do not really relish the thought of sleeping steadily with my master's grandmother and mother, nor do I want them seeing us enjoy Julia's heavenly wines. I do not want to let Julia far from our sight as she does belong to all of us, which is her wish. Will probably sit them up with Queen's mansions away from my master's mansion for I do not want surprise visitations when I am receiving a cherished surprise. We will of course establish rooms for them in our mansion, which is more of a sign of true relationship for our courts, and I will set them up with quarters beside Bogovi's here in the Royal Deities Sanctuary, as they are indeed a royal deity of the highest faction. We will work on that tomorrow, with all of today's excitement I think we shall all be sleeping well tonight. I am so amazed at how much has changed in the short time my master has been gone. He will most likely return to an Empire that he does not recognize that as much did I. Tomorrow our Empire shall receive one of the greatest shocks ever, one beyond its comprehension, as its foundation shall be rebuilt. That will be tomorrow unless any more of my master's family appears. I shall ask that good question Queen Tompaládony. I begin by saying, "Is this fair, that Julia gets all the new fruit in our garden?" All my sisters answered, "It is fair, for she is the fruit from those trees and it was those trees that gave us her fruit yet again today." I answered, "That is true, now I may ask, "Will we be visited by anymore trees?" The two queens chuckled and then said, "Not unless you are expecting your master tonight." I then looked at them and said, "Oh that I do so much wish could be yet once again my night shall be filled with prayers of his return and be awakened alone." They looked at me and said, "Relax young child, you have your master's family here to care for you as it should be." I then leaned over to give each a kiss on the check and said to them, "That I shall give great thanks for." Then Julia grabbed my face with one hand and gave me a solid kiss while massaging my breast with her other hand. At first, I was somewhat surprised, yet her powerful touches dropped me to the ground as I lay beneath her. Then her mother said, "Now Julia, save some of that for your brother." Then Queen Tompaládony said, "The hell with your brother, save some for me" and she joined Julia as soon Queen Julia also did. Now all our sisters were standing up and make a circle around us singing, "Our master is sharing her wine tonight, sharing her wine tonight . . ." Then soon they had stopped and each new Queen whispered in my ears, "Your master is lucky, for he does indeed eat from the tree with the greatest fruit." I thanked them, for this made me feel so much more at home with them. They trusted us enough to enjoy me in front of my precious sister Julia, yet then again, all my sisters and now Queen mothers are precious. I think I might actually enjoy having my master's family nearby. As I lay myself down to sleep, I call upon my spirits to receive a new command. They arrived and I did say to them, "Prepare the Empire for a great ceremony tomorrow as we shall add two more to the royal family. All of our alliance galaxies shall also see. I wish for this to be streamed to the deepest parts of our galaxy. Tell none their names. None shall work tomorrow, as all shall enjoy this great day. No child shall attend school (*as this would create a lasting memory in their minds*) and there shall be great festivals, as food shall fall from the skies. All places shall be filled with great music from the heavens. Every spirit, be it in the flesh or not shall see this ceremony through our advanced streams. I shall present these new goddesses at the tenth hour on the morrow. Remember to have a clear path for us to enter the stage this time." As I awoke in the morning a saw beside me another Queen Tompaládony style surprise, singing hearts dancing above a somewhat strange shaped red cup. I looked up above her and Queen Julia as I noticed Julia standing there with a small blade. I asked them, "What is my loves up to this morning. Then Queen Tompaládony explained, "Julia told us of the blessings that came with being showered in your blood, thus we beg that you shower us in your blood till we are covered completely and it soaks deep into our souls." I then looked at them and said, "Should not I be asking you to be showered in your blood?" They both replied, "Too late child we beat you. Is not the servant you hate the most worthy of your baptism? Then should we not be worthy?" I could see that I would have to get up very early to get a jump of these old super brains, thus I said in Julia, "Cut my skin deep so that your mothers may receive much blood from me." She did as I said, and I did fall into a sleep. This sleep was short lived as my spirits repaired my flesh suit and refilled my blood. The two aged mothers received the greatest spiritual baptism that my spirits could give them, with it being such a great honor that two of such great ancestral honor could request such a thing from a newcomer on the block as me. They were born so much before most galaxies in my Empire, with the only exception of Bogovi's rogue galaxy, which could easily be labeled the Galaxy of the Eternal Gods. As we all finished our hair and scrubbing each other down, because no servants want to see a dirty goddess we pride ourselves in the natural care of our bodies as we so much stress to our servants, Sabina comes running in with some news. She yells out, "Master even the birds above the sea honor Queen Tompaládony." As we all look up in amazement, even I am impressed. It is good to know that even nature can detect the importance of such a homecoming. Sabina further tells me that the spirits are telling her that birds from all planets that can support them are flying in these love formations. This pleases me, as I know now the mystery searchers of the heavens will be studying our streams today to discover what the heavens are saying. Who knows, someday they will discover that this throne gives all its information to its servants. I see no need in having servants try to guess our doctrine. That only leads to division and gross misinterpretation of the doctrine. It also gives servants more ability to profit from an interpretation of the doctrine that serves their best interests. My doctrine is presented in clear simple language formats with references to all matters judged on that issue. My spirits clear up the misinterpretation while in the temple. Any who seek an answer may come to one of my priests in my temples and they will be given an answer, even if it must be given by my spirit. As we now proceed to fly to the throne, Langå who will be getting a surprise in the near future yells out, "Oh great goddesses look at your path to the throne." As we look out, we see a large river of flowers flowing towards my throne. I guess it is time for the vegetation to give their praises. This is a first for me to see. This would be nice to keep. I will ask my spirits if they can preserve this. It would be nice to float above a river of flowers on our casual Sunday afternoon trillion light-year joy rides. We cannot resist the beauty of the flowers as we now decide to run through them. I am glad we got an early start although soon our flesh will tire and we will fly in the space as if lightning striking. I so enjoy watching all playing in the flowers as even Queen Tompaládony and Queen Julia are behaving as children. Queen Tompaládony as she runs by me gives me a kiss and thanks me for this presentation. This catches me by surprise forcing me to ask my spirits, "Oh spirits, who gave us these flowers?" My spirits tell me they are a gift from our dimension's throne. That removes any doubts or hesitations I may have had about today's ceremony and adds to the true majesty of a road we are about to travel upon. As we approach the throne, we start to feel the excitement that is flooding the throne. My spirits have done so well on this one. The armies and courts are celebrating vehemently even though they know not what the day is to bring for them. Many of the goddesses are now descending from the sky towards the throne as they wait in line to be introduced. The Empire is sensing the gravity of this day, yet they still have no hint what we have for them today. I hold back Julia, as I will introduce her after I am on stage as she will appear after her ancestors and will be the second to last surprise today. Sabina and Medica now join the line as they always receive extra applause since they came from the trinity those to all the temple scholars were born from their master. They always rejoin the line in separate places showing honor for the other goddesses. That is nice because it is our display of unity, which allows us to rotate on the throne giving the rest of us extra time to fulfill our other divine duties. Now with our Empire at 15,000 galaxies I do not believe we can ever have too many gods. The first and I feel most important one is their specific galaxy god. We work hard to insure the people get the one they love the most, which the overwhelming time is the one currently reigning. The tricky part is when we allow joining the multi-galaxy thrones. I require that each galaxy have its own divine throne in which we supplement them as needed. The system now being used is five galaxies form a five-throne and then five-thrones from a fifty-thrones and ten fifty-thrones make a 500-throne and ten 500-thrones from a 5000-throne which are now called arch-thrones and we will make further adjustments as the Empire continues to expand. To me it is important that we are able to respond to all needs in a divine process and that we have administrative control as situations may flow up fast and down fast. Many times as a presentation are being made to the five-throne it is simultaneously going to each throne above it. This offers an excellent check and balance system, as we must keep control at the galaxy level. The system is working good considering how fast this event today was planned and implemented. As the courts prepare to announce the Queen and the honored guest's six horses come splashing through the clouds above us. This is a true sign of a great event as one of the courts yell out, "Oh mighty Empire behold the Six Great Horses of Ancient Council of Nykøbing Mors. For our Empire is truly a part of the glory of the ages." The goddesses on stage now bow as the horses thunder through our heavens. The courts, armies, and saints all now bow as we cease all activities until the passing of this one in half an eternity special visit. I must now pull myself together and review the stage world created today for me by my creative spirits. The time is now as my spirits unite me with them as we shake the heavens for my appearance. My spirits wanted us to be, as one on such a glorious day as all my servants will see whom their Queen is, as my spirits will also add some special heavenly effects for the flesh dwellers. The spirit dwellers know who the boss is so for them I can strut around as a little redhead with a nice set of knockers to excite some of their former memories or maybe even current ones as I do allow them to put on flesh suits with each other. Notwithstanding, they may only dawn flesh suits in my temples at a priest's request when appearing before flesh dwellers. I do not want the flesh dwellers to get so excited about crossing the line between the flesh and spirit worlds that they start committing mass suicides. This is one great benefit about my sisters and me appearing in flesh before them. This reduces the fear or the glory of the spirit world and presents their heavens in a somewhat familiar form, the form by which I created them. I like today's surroundings as I sit on a rock in the middle of a flowing stream with the sun shining from behind me. The sun adds to my red hair as the red rays explode behind me as the land reflects back a rather awkward red ball to my left. Time to start our show, "My heavens and servants, today is a day that will be recorded in the history of so many of our Empires. My travels in the worlds of the Council of Nykøbing Mors and scraping deep into the mud on the floor of our Sea of Wisdom and the Sea of Forgetfulness have now been rewarded with greater gifts for our Empire. Our master's Empires began her in the galaxy that holds his throne, yet we now have discovered this galaxy to be the only remaining of the Council of Nykøbing Mors on this side of the beginning of time. We have recently been the hosts of two such goddesses ordained by the Council of Nykøbing Mors and to discover one who reigns with us to also be a gift from such an almighty ancient Empire that we shall someday, as promised by the Council join them for eternal love, goodness and peace free from any possible danger. So many great Empires beg to join them yet so few are chosen. We have been chosen with the only delay being we have so many more galaxies to save ahead of us, as we cannot rest until our work is finished. I shall now call forth the two greatest Queens in the battle for the good, both ordained and coroneted by Council of Nykøbing Mors as preceded by their Six Great Ancient Horses, Queen Tompaládony, and Queen Julia." Now they all gave great applause as my spirits gave a stream of their great coronations and the great days of the grandmother's Empire. They omitted any negative times, as we see no need in stirring up past trash that can have no possible value to this throne. The Empire is now absolutely exploding in excitement as I can feel many are glad that these new queens are among us yet cannot see the significance or relevance to this Empire other than a gift from the ancient Council of Nykøbing Mors and even that is stretching it since I have cemented our destiny with them. I can since a growing suspicion that I may want to leave the top of the throne. I know this must be suppressed before it causes too much confusion. I now walk out on the stage and give each a hug. I stand in the middle of them and motion for my spirits to pause their breathtaking presentation. I am now continuing my introduction, "Their great accomplishments may never be duplicated, yet I am glad that they may try to do so for us. My spirit tells me that many are wondering what makes these two ancient queens so special. Let me now introduce them with their relevance to our empire. First I introduce again, Queen Tompaládony, the mother of our master's father and second Queen Julia, the mother of our master." This sent to attention monitor through the ceiling, as this indeed was reason to celebrate, since most mythologies include extended family members of their master. My spirits continued their presentations with highlights of our master as a young god being cared for by his mother and grandmother as edited. Now all the courts and high councils of the saints gave homage to these new Queens, as one would be called the Queen Grandmother and the other the Queen mother. Divine rule always gives the throne to the master and the one he selects as his Queen. They will be important for diplomatic actions that require the master or any queen to the throne. Both the grandmother and mother are Queens to the throne, which takes some more pressure from me, for when they support what I do it, is the same as the ancient gods supporting it. Now it is time for me to give my first surprise introduction as I now call forth my sister Julia, "Goddess Julia, will you come forth now?" She comes out of the sky and walks on my stream heading to the stage. I wanted her to share the same entrance to set the stage for something special. She comes forth and I motion her to my right side as this sends shock waves through my Empire and courts. She stops beside me, and I give her a kiss and then to my throne I say, "Behold Queen Sister Julia, the daughter of Queen Julia and sister to our master. I discovered this secret in the mud beneath the Sea of Forgiveness as hidden for eternity by our new royal Queen Grandmother, in which both her mother and grandmother bear witness to her true being. She shall split her time between our master's mothers and my sisters, as she is the bonding link to all who are on the throne. I now bow to my master's sister, mother, and grandmother and so long for the day when he returns to discover so much of his being here to serve him as none of us lay claim to his throne. Let us worship now our master's ancient family as they shall give unto us a greater and deeper master." Likewise, all did give their highest reverence in thanks for our master having his ancient powers magnified to the depths of the universe. Our spirits now began the ceremonies again as we all left the stage. After a few hours, my spirits notified me that is was time for our last big surprise today. My sisters all now reappearing on stage and are close to being in their positions, which is always random so the courts do not read anything into it. All three Queens appear with them, and are in random positions. Queen Tompaládony and Queen Julia are the ones who are so easy to identify in that they are dressed in royal robes. We explain through my spirits that ancestral divine law prohibits a grandmother or mother goddess from being on their son's thrones nude. No such provisions exist for the sisters, as many were made spousal servants to their brothers. I guess I was lucky to have come along before his sister. I now walk out my staged rocky stream with Langå as few recognize her. She is still rather nervous and feels awkward. I tell my little bunny rabbit that all will be ok as I have never led her into harm nor ever will. She laps those milky eyes on me as I can feel her great faith grab hold of my hand and follow me. As we come to our positions, I now motion to my saints that the time has come for me to speak, "I once again appear before my Empire with a joyous task on a day that has been flooded with so many wonderful events. We now charge forward with a stronger, wiser and so much more experienced godhead for your Empire. Each event is as driving another large nail into the dying head of evil. Yet today may not have been possible without the great loyalty and devotion from Langå at my side and Haderslev, her sister who cannot join us, as she must fulfill her marriage vows as her oaths to me force her to do. Langå had spent so much of our eternity holding fast the Sea of Forgetfulness, Sea of Wisdom, and Island of Knowledge with other powerful achieves that shall add to our glory as the ages continue. Langå has found great favor in me and my fellow sisters and Queens as we all acknowledge the great sacrifices made for our glory. It is for this reason that we command that no other appropriate award would be suitable to the saint who has served us all so humbly than to exalt her as one of our sisters. Our ancient gods hide her with this vital part of their future Empire's body knowing that with the wisdom they had made available that we would restore this part in our divine glory once again to drive a giant nail into the head of evil. Langå, you shall never be called by that name again unless spoken with your true glory. As a goddess of love and mercy and humility in the greatest godhead known throughout our universes and one that someday shall give its servants and eternal sainthood with the Council of Nykøbing Mors who used your great soul to bring them to us and bond us with them. May we all now bow and pray to our new sister in my master's throne." Goddess Langå new omnipresent spirit appeared in all the skies throughout all my planets so that all see their newest goddess. Her complete dramatized by my spirits history of accomplishments are now also appearing in all my temples as a statue of her now appears alongside her sisters and in the same lineage as the four Queens. We now slowly and gracefully make our way to my stream as so many thrones, courts and councils of the saints wish to make their oath to serve her as we accept and give them blessings. We finished two days later as the other three queens had to appear to receive their honors and pledges. This has been such a wonderful chapter in the power of the showers of blood. I honestly cannot think of how this could get much greater, but I guess I will hang James by a thread over one of my lake of fires and get his fingers and brain flowing again into what will be more excitement even if I have to help old slow fingers on his keyboard.

Chapter 06

Honor Thy Mother and Father

My heavens and servants are now pumped up with a new sense of joy and hope as our spirits are working so fast that I have now joyfully forced the expand all the goddesses" spirits and hopefully that will buy some time to increase the mass expansion the lights are currently engaged in with my spirits and Bogovi's. We are now building spirits that only help create new power spirits as I can see someday our spirits approaching that of the Council of Nykøbing Mors. One thing that is helping us now is a small group of courts that have been trying to digest the Books of the Gyor-Moson-Sopron and the preliminary reports are now enticing more courts and even a great number of the "Councils of the Saints" to join them. I wish more could be devoted in what is appearing to be what we will need as we move towards a multi-million galaxy and so far beyond. We will need something more since I must keep the familiarity of the godhead with the flesh dwellers. I will be a part of their life and not apart from them. I do not need to test them with temptations unless I give them the power to control it. Pain is pain and it hurts. I know that this godhead is now amazing you with her great knowledge; it let us look a little closer to what we just talked. Pain is pain and it is not in the normal function as created. Pain has no benefit for my flesh dwellers. It teaches them nothing. Oh, it keeps them from sticking their hands in a burning fire. If this is true, then why do flesh dwellers still get their hands burned? Pain actually reduces the flesh dwellers ability to control the actions they are performing and if that is in the production of so many of our advanced products they now enjoy, then that lack of attention will increase the probability of defective productions and thus the likelihood of defective products harming my flesh dwellers. Pain is a punishment from the creators for living and as I have seen a perfect tool for evil to use to decrease its miserable grip on these flesh dwellers. Sometimes we must get serious, if I say I am the good guy and I give you pain and I tell you the other guy is the bad guy because that guy takes away the pain what part of that is true and what part is the lie. To say one is good and to give the flesh dwellers, who should be their children, pain is not valid. If you give or allow pain to your loved ones, then you are not good, simple short and sweet. As I am now on this subject for pain, why would intelligent life forms think that our beasts and animals would not suffer pain? When they have injuries, they do bleed and some of them take serious steps to get away from the source. You hurt their leg; they try not to use that leg the same as flesh dwellers that have invisible spirits inside of them. Hurt is hurt, however for animals the pain aspect is needed more for their self-preservation, yet only as a learning tool to keep them out of trouble. Since I have removed the stupid need for input only to leave output as a dangerous position identifier in the animal kingdom thus no hungry, no kill each other to eat their flesh. Flesh dwellers were made to live beside and with their animal flesh dwellers in peace and harmony. Let me reassure you, a nice white lion to snuggle against on a windy or chilly day hits the spot perfectly. Rubbing up against that soft coat of fur with the animal's body heat soaking into your bones is a nice treat from my nature. Things should be this way, and all my galaxies are converted. First, the servants take their oath of allegiance voluntarily. Any who do not pledge their allegiance are relocated by others, who do not want to join in secure areas and quarantined. No punishment, life as they know it, pain, hunger, disease, and all those stupid things they must hold onto. They are quarantined since their lifestyle provides the necessary requirements for a bed of evil to grow, and that is when they are no more. I will not allow any situation unsecured that can invite and excite evil. It is so hard to talk since my little kitty cat is licking my face so much. That is something else I copied from the other creations and is the love our animal friends can give us. They give it to the flesh dweller regardless of how that dweller compares to others. Most times, they will actually ignore or avoid the other dwellers and concentrate on the single relationship. They have the same needs as do the soul dwellers. Flesh is flesh, as hearts are hearts and only my blood is the power blood. My animals exist and then they do not exist thus they need no showers of blood for eternity. I made the skies and decorated them, the mountains, and trees. The rivers I give you provide water for life as even my non-eating flesh must have water since it does so much for cleaning and regulating heat. Beauty is the harmony of moving life with non-moving life or even moving non-life such as water. Everything is given a function is the so complex thing called worlds, solar systems and even galaxies. All things must contribute to the movement's mission and sing the song that our Mothers of the nature's signs. I have seen excessively much the last verse when the song must end. It is not a pretty sign, as my spirits tell me; we are on the road to solid harmony with all our planets as our technologies repair the stains of greed from recent generations. As I prepare for my new surprises that shall befall my throne let me explain this in another way. I love the animals I created for my soul dwellers. Live with them and love them as the system is designed to function. Mess with my animals and play this spoiling my land with blood other than mine and I will fight back. This will not be the little shy free from the chains of clothing redhead that hangs on our master's arms but one who stands taller than the mountains and walks on the rivers. I will stretch up my hands and the spirit of death shall come forth from me, as those who would not hear will not hear now. I am so fortunate that threats as they are not needed for my servants but are needed for the dormant seeds of evil that hide in the dark spaces of my planets. They shall hear my words. Our days can be great days filled with joy and happiness if we flow with the system and nothing disrupts that flow. My job is to keep the disruptions from occurring and that is a fun task. Spread the love and happiness, which is so much more of a turn on for this godhead than spread the pain, blood, misery and tell them they are loved. I shall sink my feet just a little into this calm river so I can feel the water cool me. I should be getting back to my goddesses as these nice nature trips sometimes take a lot of my time. They should be starting to get up in their small groups as they prepare to look beautiful for another day in the heavens. Their beauty adds to our throne as it magnifies our diversity and devotion to purity. Although beauty is not pure and vice versa, beauty does imply or even make believable that, which is before them is pure. It also adds to our master's bragging rights with the boys; however, that works. My spirit mother always told me so many millions of years ago that you must give your master his pride with other masters. This bothers me not for I do not want to hang around my master's friends, I would much rather allow one of my sisters to occupy my time. As I now walk along our special ocean beach that has so much cool late morning air I see Sabina and Faith with a couple of our other sisters playing in the water along the beach. I have wanted some special spiritual time with Faith, and now see how she is molding in our group. She appears to be the center of the show this morning with Sabina behind her with her far off stare. This happy union help project our unity to our servants. The Seonji greet me and say that the three Queens will be going on a VIP welcome tour today hosted by the Lights to visit many of our established older gods. This will help give us a click to them instead of them feeling a bunch of naked girls is making a joke out of the heavens. By having the Queen Sister Julia free from the chains of clothing with them, it shows their acceptance to this new love and sharing style of divinity. I hope to have some time for our new goddess Langå today and reassure her of the permanence of her new position in glory. So much dedication and sacrifice in so much loneliness and darkness forever now to be rewarded in heavenly fashion at the top of all lights. As I lie down to snuggle close to my goddess Langå who is justifiably resting after such a laborious and stress filled day as yesterday I marvel at the peaceful look on her face, the look that I expect to see on all who live in my Empire as this brings warmth in my heart. I start to relax when my spirits alarm me that I am to receive a message from the holders of our master in his penance. That fires up the synthetic blood in my veins as I fight to get a heartbeat once again. What could have happened? I fail to understand why such a message out of the blue? I was just there not that long ago. I had better get to my throne and figure out what is going on. I am ready instantaneously and on my way to my throne. As I rush in the throne is clear as many courts and angels are aligned around the main stage with my armies and special Councils of the Saints awaiting any command that I might have. I immediately assume my humble position in the center of the diamond rich crystal stage and motion for the courts that they may announce to the other dimension that I am ready to join them in their desired conversation. The announcement was made and we all waited in anticipation for their answer. Yes, we all waited, for I knew there was no chance of hiding any information concerning the master of this throne from his throne, and I respected that and absolutely let them see that they indeed had this right. This throne is based on the willing love for their throne and that the throne belongs to them as long as we stay within the range of protocols to keep the dimensions throne from taking us out. I hate how the sweat from waiting soaks the skin and brings on the chills. I am always reluctant to turn up the heat around my throne in case I scare my spirits into thinking an undesirable change is about to occur. A stupid thing such as fear can run away with our minds as mine is now. I hope my spirits catch it before it gets too far away from me. One knows they are in trouble when they hear tick tock, tick tock and they have no clock. Then did the space above us take on shapes as we did see a giant castle that was appearing unexpected sky, yet the sky and castle were two, one being above and one below. This castle was appearing between two dimensions. The one above stood high in the clouds as the one below pointed straight towards my dimension, with a tall tower and a smaller tower with an extended slim tower being shot out of it. This vision now had a red ball growing from my dimension. As the ball continued to grow, I could see who could be a female, in a nice red gown standing and a silver-headed person kneeling before her. My sisters were all beside me now, as Mary commented, "Whoever is wearing that beautiful red gown, beware of the Queen grand-mother for they are the lovers of fine garments and may render her free from the chains of clothing as we are." That was funny; I had not really had much humor from Mary lately so I became excited. This descending matrix had a large gray triangle of space projecting from behind the tall tower. I have learned that things inside these higher throne streams have meanings so I know asked my spirits to translate and open up a path that I may speak to the giver of this gift. A bright light appears before us and a voice speaks out, "Queen Lilith, do you hear me?" I then answered, "I hear a voice but know not who is calling me." The light now started dancing over our sky as a dark solid cloud dropped in the center of it down into my Empire. I then added, "Do you come in war?" as I looked to my Armies and said, "Prepare for an invasion." The voice then said, "Lilith, why do you wish to go to war against me again?" I asked, "When have I attacked you before?" The voice then said, "When you visited your master?" I then ordered my armies to stand down and fell to my knees crying out, "Oh please forgive me for I knew not whom you were and I can take no chances with my master's Empire while he is gone." The voice then run back, "Thou hast done no wrong, for you are still loved among our courts." I then answered, "That brings joy to my hearts and the hearts of those who serve my master. How can I serve you today?" They then said, "You cannot serve us for we are here today to keep our promise to give you a gift during your master's penance. Behold we now bequeath to you two that you may enjoy as you desire from your old dimension. We have made all the arrangements with all thrones involved if you were to decide to keep them for eternity. Until then you will appear with an aristocratic gown. Enjoy and save your armies for when we meet again." We could hear their laughter as they departed. When they departed, I did once again rise, as did my master's servants. I can see now that this is why they serve my throne. It is not the power, which I have over them; it is my ability to save them from the powers above me. As I have told them many times, "As you dance before me as your master, I also dance before others as my master." They seem to worship stronger after witnessing an appearance from a greater throne. We are now trying to guess who the two are that are appearing before us. Then Mary yells out, "I know who they are." Then Joy and Faith yell out, "We also know." Then Ruth asks, "Ann, do you not know who comes before us?" They were all sitting on the surface trying to hide their nudity. I asked them, "Why are you wearing such beautiful red gowns?" They looked at each other and said, "We are free from the chains of clothing however it is you who is wearing the red gown, why do you try to trick us?" I then asked my spirits, "What is going on?" My spirits tell me, "You shall appear as you are to all your servants and all who appear before you except for the two who now arrive. This shall also be with the goddesses Ruth, Mary, Joy, Julia, and Fejér." I then wondered who these two are and why Ruth would call me Ann in front of the throne. Ruth is very tender in her heart and is a very warm emotional loving goddess. She likes to deal head on with things and avoids "beating around the bush." Then I start to stare at the two descending and then everything comes together. This is truly a wonderful gift as I at one time placed this as my number one priority upon returning, however with so many things happening it got put on a back burner. I then motioned for my interested sisters to fall back into the darkness of the stage and await my invitation since I would like to have some fun also. I thus sent the signal to my courts and armies that I was going to have some fun and asked my spirits to get me a special entrance from under my throne to the surface of the clouds where I would greet my new special guest. As they became seated on the cloud stage, I ascended up before them as a young child with birds and stars swerving around me standing on a fantasy pedestal and rainbow wings behind each arm. I looked out and said speaking as a child, "Who enters my kingdom and why hast thou came unto me?" The *thous* and *hasts* were words I learned while sitting between the two now bowed before me. The man answered with his arm holding the woman safely by his side as he used to hold me safely by his side, "You know not our names as we know not where we are." Oh, the way he always answers so wisely and truthfully I am starting to melt. This is the only man that I have ever obeyed in all things and was so thankful for the hard work he had done that provided for my needs. I then answered back, "I am the goddess of now almost 40,000 galaxies as I know all galaxies in all the universes. Which galaxy do you come from?" The stalwart man smiled and relaxingly said, "We are from the Milky Way." I answered back, "I have seen that small galaxy and you look like the life forms from the planet Earth that worships one called "Jesus." He looked at me with a shocking look and said, "Thou are truly a wise goddess who knows all things." I then asked again saying, "I know your name to be Edward and what is the woman's name that stands beside you?" He answered back, "If you know my name you know that I am a good man and that the woman beside me holds my love as I hold hers. How can such a great goddess not know her name as she is filled with love?" I then answered, "I know her name since she also holds in her love for me as do you. Can you tell me my name?" Edward answered, "The spirits have told me you are the great Goddess Queen Lilith, member of the Council of Nykøbing Mors and the holder of the Sword of Justice and servant to the master who holds the Sword of Freedom and the Books of the Gyor-Moson-Sopron." I then asked again, "Yet who do you say that I am?" The woman then answered, "Oh great Goddess Queen Lilith, member of the Council of Nykøbing Mors and the holder of the Sword of Justice and servant to the master who holds the Sword of Freedom and the Books of the Gyor-Moson-Sopron my name are Prudence and I say that one time you were in my womb." All the spirits and Councils of the Saints and armies did start to sound their trumpets as the name and the woman started to tremble. I then stood up as the skies turned bright white and said, "A woman's child can never deceive the one for whom she hath maid in her womb. Prudence, you speak the truth, for many years I was your child Ann for whom you named me after a former queen. I am still flesh of your flesh and my blood did come from you. Empire, behold my mother and father of my penance." Then all began to cheer. I then transformed back to my regular self and had my pedestal lower me to the surface of the clouds and said, "The sisters of Ann, wilt thou join me as we meet once again our parents?" We now appeared to them, as we were the last time they saw us. They began to cry saying, "Our journey to the colonies was so saddened by the death of so many good. Amity was also with us. Prudence asked, "Where is your friend Siusan?" I told her, "I shall tell you all things, yet first we shall go to a special city I have made for us to celebrate this great reunion a day that is consequently very special as some lonely rooms in my heart do now open their doors once again. We did go to the city in the high clouds, as I wanted them to know this was for real. As we all exchanged long kisses, and enjoyed our father's powerful hugs and our mother's tears falling upon our shoulders our joy was reaching levels that before during our earthly days had boundaries. Those boundaries exist no more. I could feel the maternal and fraternal bonds exploding today. They both worked so hard to give us so much. With all of us suddenly leaving, and only my body, receiving a new spirit to receive the love and pain from their broken hearts I know had to be a sad torture. They deserved so much more and from what I have been told had more children and did well in the colonies. I now had to decide how we would bring everyone up to date after all our excitement wore down. We were all looking for the intimate signs to verify we were once again united, however now without the dependency bond I wonder if it will be the same. As I go to talk with my father, I can feel his parental power over me and I enjoy it so. I go running to him, pushing past his other daughters and hug him crying, "Daddy, do you still love me?" He then answered, "Till the same day I had to lay you both the rest." I then asked him, "Daddy, do you remember when your daughters died on the ship going to the colonies?" Sadness now overshadowed his strong body as he answered looking at his other daughters, "Yes, so sad of a day it was, yet I had only a shocked and depressed you to hang on to." I then enlightened him, "Daddy, upon that day I replaced the spirit with Ann with one from the ages as I went into another body to be a Roman slave and beaten everyday till my death." Then my father asked, "Why did you place another body in Ann?" I knew my daddy always wanted to know the why's to any action in order to remove any confusion he might have. So I told him, "We had to go because evil was going to capture us and make us live with them in your lake of fire. We had no choice. That is why our guardians worked hard to make it look like a real accident and placed another soul in my flesh so they would remain focused on me." My mother then answered, "We thought it was the death of your sisters and the transition to the colonies that made your personality change. Even Henrietta Maria withdrew from us, and we blamed the rebellious rumbling of the colonies, for this and having to watch her husband beheaded only to see them beg her son to return to the throne. Such is the total chaotic responses of the Earth maniacs." I then went over to her and let her wrap her arms around me. My entire being melted within my mommy's arms. She was my source of life. I wonder how I was able to survive without her. I then said to them, "You know who I am, now let me introduce your other daughters. I shall begin with our adult guardian the Guardian Goddess Fejér." I know that I change their titles almost daily however; I feel that add to the dynamics of our godhead. Continuing, "The Penance Queen Goddess Faith, the Penance Widowed sister Joy, the Penance sister Goddess Ruth, the Penance sister Goddess Mary, the Penance sister Goddess Amity and not with us today is the Penance Harvey sister Goddess Siusan." Then mommy said, "I am so thankful that so many are here, yet I do worry about Siusan. Is she ok?" I told her, Siusan is going great. I later discovered that she was of a special race of people and was in hiding. I had children of this race on a planet in which I once served as Lord and my children and killed them while I was elsewhere fighting evil. I have always pledged to do good by this race. Siusan is currently in a new human body such as I was. She will bear children and they will show that her blood may be in their genetic pool. When her days are finished, she will become the sole goddess of the Harvey and their protector. All Harvey shall worship her for they will know that she came from among them. She is sister to me and as such will have all my power and support to give into the Harvey that which they never had and that is a safe haven to live and grow in peace of love with no evil to hurt them." My daddy looked at me and said, "I was always so proud to have you as my daughter." I looked at him and my mommy and said, "I shall always as we all who are with you now are your daughters." Without the flesh you made for us to live in, we would not have this blessed Empire to fight and destroy all evil we find. That flesh is burned deep into my soul as it is with your other daughters. You shall be known as the mother and father to the Penance Sisters Goddesses and me." Edward then said, "For us our glory was to know one of our daughters was our Queen, yet now to know that our Ann is greatest among the heavens is a blessing too great for any man to have. I was blessed to give the seed that your mother used to make your flesh of our flesh. You shall always know that even when all others will no longer love you, my daughters will have their mother and father to hold and love them." I looked at him, as I now was secure in his mighty arms holding me and said, "My father and mother, you are a gift that even I am not worthy yet by the mercy of the highest of thrones the great gods have given to me. I know not how to repay them. I do so much hope that you will stay in a special castle that will be beside our Royal Deities Sanctuary. I would have you stay there with us yet the only male, which can be there is our master whom seldom enters, and when he does stays hidden in his special quarters. I know not how to tell you this but just to say it. We all appear free from the chains of clothing before us servant as a gesture that we hide nothing from them and that our love for them is real as we humble ourselves to serve them. We cannot appear in clothing before you, as you are our father, and our nudity would be shame. My spirits clothes us before our parent's eyes. I hope this does not shame you." Then my father is his great wisdom said to us, "My daughters, I lay your flesh that I either gave or cared for in the ground as it is now dust from which it came. Our bodies now we are given by the gods or in your case you, thus I shall not question your divine wisdom. Do that which you must except you must come to us if you need any help." We all once again flooded our parents with hugs and kisses. Our mother said, "It is so special to have the goddesses" love. I think we should retire in the family room in the large castle in the sky and hear a story about your father. What say you?" I then started to cry. My mother whisked me in her arms and as she pet my hair asked, "What's wrong Ann, can mommy make it better?" I then said, "Mommy I miss our servants." I then cried out, "My spirits, can you give into me our penance female servants?" I told mommy, sorry, their brother and India may not enter. I fear that could anger the courts and our master. Daddy said, "That is fine Ann, for you know I too do not like boys around my little girls." We all now felt so good, to know our daddy was still thinking hard about how to protect us. Some things live with a daughter forever and ever. Faith, Joy, Mary, and Ruth always admired how hard they worked to share their home with them as equals and not mercenaries. My spirits then called back to me, "Great goddess, we have four of your penance family servants. The remaining did not make it to the heavens and thus cannot be obtained from the other dimension"'s lakes of fire. Then we saw before us four of our former female servants. They looked so beautiful, yet they had so much feared they were frozen. We all rushed around them and started massaging them telling them it was ok. Then finally one said, "We have done no wrong, so please do not punish us." I looked at them as I motioned for mommy and daddy to come over to us. I asked my spirits in mind talk for which it has been a long time since I did this, "Why do they all look the same?" My spirits told me, "Because we traded for them in their heavens. We will restore their original appearances once they are comfortable here and we can explain to them what we are doing." I told them, "You have done fine and thanks so much." I know sometimes I am hard on them, yet they are my spirits and thus a part of me and I always was hard on myself. Once they saw mommy and daddy they started to ease some. I then appeared to them as Ann and said, "Do you remember me?" They immediately all became happy as they rushed to hug me. Oh their hugs felt so good. We did not just own our domestic help, we lived with them and loved them as they did also live with us and love us. So much of my values on the master servant relationships are based on the relationships my parents had with our servants. It worked out great even though we had to be so careful or we would have faced great punishment. We made it. My higher thrones have supported the relationships we have with our servants, even recommending it to other Empires. I fail to see how they can fault me as this was taught to me during my penance that they gave to me. The mother then said to our found again servants, "Ann has a surprise for you here." They asked what the surprise was as I then returned to my normal appearance and since they were servants, we did appear free from the chains of clothing to them. I said, "We have brought you here to live in our Empire with us." Then one of my new servants asked, "Who are you if you are not Ann." I told her, "I am the Ann you once knew; however, I have always been the great Goddess Queen Lilith. I am a member of the Council of Nykøbing Mors and the holder of the Sword of Justice and number one servant to the master who holds the Sword of Freedom and the Books of the Gyor-Moson-Sopron, my Empire now has over 40,000 galaxies and grows hourly. "You know who I am, now let me introduce your other friends from our days of old. I shall begin with our adult guardian and your most trusted friends the Guardian Goddess Fejér." Continuing, "The Penance Queen Goddess Faith whom you remember as Queen Henrietta Maria, the Penance Wedded sister Joy whom you remember suffering such a tragic death, the Penance sister Goddess Ruth, the Penance sister Goddess Mary. Joining us late and going to the colonies with us is the Penance sister Goddess Amity and not with us today is the Penance Harvey sister Siusan whom we shall visit someday. The four women said to us, "You were always goddesses of good and purity to us and shall always be the masters of our hearts." As we all rushed to hug them and exchange reunion kisses, even mommy and daddy joined in. They were the ones who created the world that this could happen. Then one of the servant girls whispered in my ear, "Ann, does your father know you are nude." I whispered back, "Even though I am strong enough to rule 40,000 galaxies I am not strong enough to appear free from the chains of clothing before my parents, but only to my servants whom love me. Do you love me?" She whispered back, "Ever since that cold day when we pulled you out of your mother you have ruled my heart." Wow this felt accordingly good as it drove nails of love deep inside my soul. The one who held me now was there when I came into their world, as even I no longer remember that day, except for the explosion in my master's throne. Now to put the other servants at ease I asked my mother, "Mommy do you like my blue gown?" She answered by saying, "My daughter got all my good looks and then even some more." Of course, I now feel like a young child who has been starving for this sort of love, ran over to her, and started mobbing her with kisses as all in our gang began laughing. One of the servants looked at Ruth strangely when I had asked my mommy about my dress in which Ruth replied to her, "After all, we are goddesses" in which the servant then winked and smiled at her, "and some things not even goddesses are brave enough to do." The servant shook her head yes agreeing wholeheartedly and appeared so relieved to find some humanity still with us. I could tell that my parents would have Fejér who had always been mommy's friend even back in their university days, plus Faith, Joy, Ruth, and Mary, and some of Amity's time joined by the four servant girls spending a lot of time with them, if not actually living with them, as I could understand so much. I have Empire duties thus like Faith had to move to Buckingham for her Queen responsibilities I would have to spend a lot of time away. Such are the sacrifices a Queen must make to serve the needs of her master. I under no circumstances consider it losing some of my sisters, but as gaining some of my true family. Just to be able to wake up each day and know my father was here was so much a reward for me. I knew that if I am to reach the greatest understanding of the servants of my Empire I would need to learn much more from my father, even though he always stopped what he was doing when I was a child and take the time to show why I needed to do the things I did. That always helped so much, for if my daddy said it needed to be done, I always jumped in to do it. So many times, he would pull me back and tell me, "Now let me show you why good girls do this." It is so strange how such things as this seemed so trivial when I was a child or even at times burdensome yet now are anchors of gold holding my ship on the fierce sea of time. Daddy now asked, "Ann, may we talk for a few minutes." I of course pushed past my sisters and grabbed his arm saying, "Your wish is my command daddy." Our servant girls acted so amazed that such great deity could be so excited over such a small request or even respond to it, yet I only have to say, "You only get one daddy per lifetime in the flesh." As we sat down in a nice talking room in our castle in the sky, he asked me, "Ann what are your views of lakes of fire?" I then told him, "At first I depended upon them as a tool to force compliance by my servants. Yet later discovered that by providing a way for my servants to meet their needs and protecting them from evil and all that evil gives plus established temples that show them that the deity they worship is one of goodness and empathy that I no longer needed the lakes of fire. When good are captured by evil and good abandons them then do not they have the right to abandon good? I no longer need the lakes of fire as for those who were in it have been given new books and lives to see if they can serve good. Those who cannot are eliminated from all matter and mass forever and ever. I have also removed the gardens that evil plants its seeds such as flesh that suffers from diseases and hunger. All my servants, whom I have created our image with our language no longer need food or suffer from pains and evil diseases. I am a goddess of love as is my master or husband as you would say it, we do not need to test the love of our servants. I am the light on the judicious road of life. He who follows my lights shall not walk in darkness. We are divine and can see into their hearts, so there is no need for this make you suffer and fall into evil only to punish you for falling to evil game." My father looked at me and said, "I have surely been blessed with such a fine daughter as you for your wisdom is truly so divine and greater than I have ever known, yet I know what you say is so true." To keep the fantastic mushy stuff rolling I replied, "I too have been blessed with my great parents whom I may now provide for our eternity together. Much of my wisdom was developed from what you taught me daddy. I so much need my daddy to help me stay true to good. I beg that you help me." His answer to me was fast and strong, "A child that is loved by his or her parents shall never need to beg for that which is theirs." Oh, the way his wisdom just flows out in such powerful and natural words still amazes me and likely shall until the end of time. I now just lay in his arms as he pets my hair and tells me, "Annie, everything will be ok because daddy is here now." In my mind, everything will be ok now. What is so amazing is that the creators of the universe told me everything would be ok yet I still had reservations yet just a few words from a spirit who gave up his flesh only a few centuries ago tells me everything will be ok and I cannot in any way now picture anything but everything being ok. Any doubt has been killed and buried so deep that it would be easier to travel back to the beginning of time than to try bringing it back to the surface. How amazing this powerful bond of father and daughter is. The pain of the penance now seems so trivial for the benefits I have received for having such great penance sisters was more than I could have ever created. I now took my parents to my throne and called out to my courts to Harken to my voice. I then told them, "Behold, for the gods of our highest thrones have given back into me my penance mother and penance father. They shall be called, Edward, the Queen's father and Prudence, the Queen's mother. As I have said tell all that they may know and not give into me my spirit of anger." My parents asked me if they did ok. I told them I was very proud of them. They were able to project a very confident look while standing among such a power packed throne. They had drilled into them the aristocratic social postures and it shined through so well today. Yet even if they had appeared weak, I would not have cared. I knew they were working hard to look good for me, thus I can hope for no more. I could feel that they have lived in the spiritual realm for a while, as the fear of being in open space with no surface to support them seemed not to bother them. I do believe they will be ready for some universe sightseeing soon with their daughters soon. Our father now called us all together as we joined in the family room. Our servants have to join us also as we were in no need of refreshments. Then our father told us, "I had told you girls many stories, yet after I lost you I remembered one my father had told me. It was one of my favorite and I so regretted not telling you so I hope you will forgive me and once again my little girls so I can complete one hope that escaped from me during your childhood days." A small tear was pouring down his cheek, which in response I turned all his daughters including myself back into little girls as we now formed a sitting row in front of our parents. There was a time; a poor widow lived in a little cottage with her only son Paul. They lived not far from my grandfather. This story was told to him by his friends for during this year he was staying with some of our relatives who lived in the mountains by the sea. Paul was a giddy, thoughtless boy, but very kind-hearted and caring. They had been through a severe winter, and after it, the poor woman had suffered from fever and flu. Paul did no work yet, and by the quantities, they grew dreadfully poor. The widow saw that there were no means of keeping Paul and herself from starvation but by selling her cow; and then one morning she said to her son, "I am too weak to move myself, Paul, so you must get the cow to market for me, and sell her." Paul liked going to market to sell the cow very much; but as he was on the way, he saw a butcher who owned some beautiful beans in his hand. Paul stopped to look at them, and the butcher told the boy that they were of great value, and persuaded the mindless lad to sell the cow for these beans. When he took them home to his mother instead of the money, she looked for her nice cow; she was very vexed and shed many tears, scolding Paul for his foolishness. He was very sorry, and mother and son went to bed very unhappily and hungry that night; their last hope seemed gone. At daybreak, Paul got up and went out into the garden. "At least," he thought, "I will sow the wonderful beans. Mother says that they are just common scarlet-runners, and nothing else; but I may as well sow them." Therefore, he had a piece of stick, made some holes in the ground, and put in the beans. That day they had very little dinner, and moved sadly to bed, knowing that for the next day there would be none and Paul, unable to sleep from grief and vexation, got up at day-dawn and went out into the garden. What was his amazement to see that the beans had grown up in the night, and climbed up and up until they crossed the high cliff that sheltered the cottage, and disappeared above it! The stalks had twined and twisted themselves together until they built up quite a ladder. "It would be easy to climb it," thought Paul. Furthermore, having thought of the experiment, he at once resolved to carry it out, for Paul was a good climber. However, after his latest mistake about the cow, he thought he had better consult his mother first. So Paul sent for his mother, and they both gazed in silent wonder at the Beanstalk, which was not only of great height, but was thick enough to bear Paul's weight. "I wonder where it ends," said Paul to his mother, "I suppose I will go up and see." His mother wished him not to venture up this strange ladder, but Paul coaxed her to give her consent to the attempt, for he was certain there must be something wonderful in the Beanstalk, hence at last she succumbed to his wishes. Paul instantly began to rise, and went up and up on the ladder, like a bean until everything he had left behind him, the cottage, the village, and even the tall church tower; looked quite little, and still he could not see the top of the Beanstalk. Paul felt a little tired, and thought for a moment that he would go back again; but he was a very tenacious boy, and he knew that the way to succeed in anything is not to quit. Accordingly, after resting for a moment he continued. After climbing higher and higher, till he grew afraid to look down for fear he should be faint, Paul at last reached the crest of the Beanstalk, and found himself in a beautiful country, finely wooded, with beautiful meadows covered with sheep. A crystal stream ran through the pastures; not far from the spot where he held off the Beanstalk stood a fine, strong castle.

Paul wondered very much that he had never heard of or seen this castle before; but when he reflected on the field, he saw that it was as much separated from the village by the perpendicular rock on which it stood as if it were in another country. While Paul was standing looking at the castle, a very strange, looking woman came out of the wood, and advanced towards him. She wore a pointed cap of quilted red satin turned up with ermine, her hair streamed loose over her shoulders, and she walked with a staff. Paul took off his cap and made her a bow. "If you please, ma'am," said he, "is this your house?" "No," said the old woman. "Listen and I will tell you the story of that castle. "Once upon a time, there was a noble knight, who lived in this castle, which is on the borders of Magic land. He had a fair and beloved wife and several lovely children: and as his neighbors, the little people, were very friendly towards him, they bestowed on him many excellent and precious gifts. "Rumor whispered of these treasures; and a colossal giant, who lived at no great distance, and who was a very wicked being, resolved to obtain possession of them. "So he bribed a dishonest servant to let him inside the castle, when the knight was in bed and asleep, and he killed him as he lay.

"Happily for her, the lady was not to be found. She had gone with her infant son, who was just two or three months old, to visit her old nurse, who lived in the valley; and she had been confined all night there by a storm. "The next morning, as soon as it was light, one of the servants at the castle, who had managed to escape, came to tell the poor lady of the sad death of her husband. She could scarcely believe him at first, and was eager at once to go back and share the fate of her dear one; but the old nurse, with many tears, entreated her to remember that she had still a child, and that it was her duty to preserve her life for the sake of the poor innocent. "The lady submitted to this reasoning, and agreed to stay in her nurse's house as the best place of camouflage; for the servant told her that the giant had vowed, if he could find her, he would kill both her and her baby. The years rolled along. The old nurse died, leaving her cottage and the few artifacts of furniture it contained to her poor woman, who dwelt in it, acting as a peasant for her daily bread. Her spinning wheel and the milk of a cow, which she had purchased with the little money she had with her, sufficed for the measly existence of herself and her little son. There was a nice small garden attached to the cottage, in which they cultivated peas, beans, and cabbages, and the woman was not ashamed to go out at harvest time, and glean in the fields to supply her little son's wants. "Paul, that poor lady is your mother. This palace was once your father's, and must again be yours." Paul voiced a cry of surprise. "My mother! Oh, madam, what ought I to do? Oh, my poor father! My precious dear mother!" "Your duty requires you to win it back for your mother. Nevertheless, the task is a very difficult one, and full of danger, Paul. Have you courage to undertake it?" "I fear nothing when I am doing right," said Paul. "And so," said the woman in the red cap, "You are one of those who slay giants. You must go into the castle, and if possible possess yourself of a hen that lays golden eggs and a talking harp. Remember, all the giant possesses is actually yours." As she finished speaking, the woman in the red hat suddenly disappeared, and of course, Paul knew she was a fairy. Paul determined at once to seek the adventure; so he went on, and blew the trumpet, which hung at the castle portal. The door was opened in a minute or two by a frightful giantess, with one great eye in the middle of her forehead. As soon as Paul saw her he turned to run away, but she caught him, and dragged him into the castle. "Ho, ho!" she laughed terribly. "You didn't expect to see me here, that is clear! No, I shall not let you go again. I am weary of my life. I am so overworked, and I do not understand why I should not have a page as well as other women. You shall be my boy. You shall clean the knives; black the boots, make the fires, and help me generally, when the giant is out. When he is at home I must hide you, for he has eaten up all my pages before now, and you would be a delicate morsel, my little lad." While she spoke, she dragged Paul right into the castle. The poor boy was very much frightened; as I am sure, you and I would have been in his place. Nonetheless, he remembered that fear disgraces a man; so he struggled to be brave and make the best of things. "I am quite ready to help you, and do all I can to serve you, madam," he said, "I only beg you will be good enough to conceal me from your husband, for I should not wish to be eaten at all." "That is a good boy," said the Giantess, nodding her head; "it is lucky for you that you did not call out when you saw me, as the other boys who have been here did, for if you had done so my husband would have woken up and have eaten you, as he did them, for breakfast. Come here, child; go into my wardrobe: he never ventures to open that; you will be safe there." She unfolded a huge closet, which stood in the great hall, and shut him into it. Nevertheless, the keyhole was so heavy that it admitted plenty of air, and he could see everything that took place through it. By-and-by he heard a heavy tramp on the stairs, like the lumbering of a great cannon, and then a voice like thunder cried out; "Fe, fa, fi-fo-fum, I smell the hint of an Englishman. Let him be alive or let him be dead, I'll grind his bones to make my bread." "Wife," cried the Giant, "there is a gentleman in the castle. Let me have him for breakfast." "You are growing old and stupid," cried the woman in her loud tones. "It is only a nice fresh steak off an elephant, which I have cooked for you, which you smell. There, sit down and get a good breakfast." In addition, she placed a huge dish before him of savory steaming meat, which greatly pleased him, and made him forget his idea of an Englishman being in the castle. When he had finished eating, he went out for a walk; and then the Giantess opened the door, and made Paul come out to help her. He helped her all day. She fed him well, and when evening came put him back in the closet. The Giant came in to supper. Paul followed him through the keyhole, and was astonished to see him pick a wolf's bone, and put half a fowl at a time into his roomy mouth. When the supper was ended, he bade his wife bring him his hen that laid the golden eggs. "It lays as well as it did when it belonged to that paltry knight," he said; "indeed I think the eggs are heavier than ever." The Giantess went away, and presently came back with a little brown hen, which she laid on the table before her husband. "And now, my dear," she said, "I am going for a walk, if you don't want me any longer." "Go," said the Giant; "I shall be glad to have a nap by-and-by." Then he took up the brown hen and said to her, "Lay!" She instantly laid a golden egg. "Lay!" said the Giant again. Besides she laid another "Lay!" he repeated the third time. Again, a golden egg lay on the table.

Now Paul was sure this hen was that of which the fairy had spoken. By-and-by the Giant put the hen down on the floor, and soon after went fast asleep, snoring so loud that it sounded like thunder. Directly Paul perceived that the Giant was fast asleep, he pushed open the door of the wardrobe and crept out; very softly, he stole across the room, and, seeing the hen, made haste to exit the chamber. He knew the path to the kitchen, the threshold of which he found was left ajar; he opened it, shut and locked it after him, and fled back to the Beanstalk, which he descended as fast as his feet would go. When his mother saw him go into the house, she wept for joy, for she had feared that the fairies had carried him away, or that the Giant had found him. Nevertheless, Paul puts the brown hen down before her, and tells her how he was in the Giant's castle, and all his adventures. She was very happy to see the hen, which would make them rich once more. Paul made another journey up the Beanstalk to the Giant's castle one day while his mother had gone to market; but first he dyed his hair and disguised himself. The old woman did not know him again, and dragged him in as she had done before, to help her to perform the work; but she learned her husband coming, and hid him in the closet, not believing that it was the same boy who had stolen the hen. She wished him stay quite still there, or the Giant would eat him. Then the Giant came in saying: "Fe, fa, fi-fo-fum, I smell the breath of an Englishman. Let him be alive or let him be dead, I'll grind his bones to make my bread." "Nonsense!" said the wife, "it is only a roasted bullock that I thought would be a tit-bit for your supper; sit down, and I will bring it up at once." The Giant sat down, soon his wife brought up a roasted bullock on a large dish, and they began their supper. Paul was amazed to see them pick the bones of the bullock as if it had been a lark. As soon as they had finished their meal, the Giantess rose and said, "Now, my dear, with your leave I am going up to my room to finish the story I am reading. If you want me call for me." "First," answered the Giant, "bring me my money bags, that I may count my gold pieces before I sleep." The Giantess conformed. She lived and presently came back with two heavy bags over her shoulders, which she put down by her husband. "There," she said; "that is all that is left of the knight's money. When you have spent it you must go and take another baron's castle." "That he shall not happen, if I can help it," thought Paul. The Giant, when his wife was gone, took out heaps and oodles of golden pieces, counted them, and put them in piles, until he was tired of the amusement. Then he brushed them all back into their bags, and leaning back in his chair fell fast asleep, snoring so loud that no other sound was audible. Paul stole softly out of the apparel, and taking up the bags of money, which were his very own, because the Giant had stolen them from his father, he ran off, and with great nuisance descending the Beanstalk, laid the bags of gold on his mother's table. She had just returned from town, and was crying at not finding Paul. "There, mother, I have brought you the gold that my father lost." "Oh, Paul! You are a very good boy, but I wish you would not risk your precious life in the Giant's castle. Tell me how you came to go there again." Paul told her all about it. Paul's mother was very glad to get the money, but she did not like him to run any risk for her. Nevertheless after some time Paul made up his mind to go again to the Giant's castle. Accordingly, he climbed the Beanstalk once more, and blew the horn at the Giant's gate. The Giantess soon opened the door; she was very stupid, and did not know him again, but she stopped a minute before she took him in. She feared another robbery; but Paul's fresh face looked so innocent that she could not refuse him, and then she bade him come in, and again hid him away in the closet. After a while the Giant came home, and as soon as he had crossed the doorway he roared out, "Fe, fa, fi-fo-fum, I smell the breath of an Englishman. Let him be alive or let him be dead, I'll grind his bones to make my bread." "You stupid old Giant," said his wife, "you only smell a nice sheep, which I have grilled for your dinner." Furthermore, the Giant sat down, and his wife brought up a whole sheep for his dinner. When he had eaten it all up, he said, "Now bring me my harp, and I will have a little music while you take your walk." The Giantess obeyed, and returned with a beautiful harp. The framework was glittering with diamonds and rubies, and the strings were all of gold. "This is one of the nicest things I took from the knight," said the Giant. "I am very fond of music, and my harp is a faithful servant." He pulled out the harp towards him, and said, "Play!" The harp played a very subdued, sad air. "Play something merrier!" said the Giant. What is more, the harp played a merry tune. "Now play me a lullaby," wailed the Giant; and the harp played a sweet lullaby, to the sound of which its master fell asleep. Then Paul slipped softly out of the closet, and entered the huge kitchen to see if the Giantess had gone out; he found no one there, so he went to the door and opened it softly, for he thought he could not do so with the harp in his hand. in his hand. Then he went into the Giant's room, grabbed the harp, and ran away with it; but as he leaped over the threshold, the harp called out, "Master! Master!"

The Giant woke up. With a tremendous roar, he sprang from his seat, and in two strides reached the door. Nevertheless, Paul was very nimble. He fled like lightning with the harp, talking to it as he went (for he saw it was a fairy), and telling it he was the son of its old master, the knight. Even so, the Giant came on so fast that he was close to poor Paul, and stretched out his great hand to catch him. Nonetheless, luckily, just at that moment he stepped upon a loose stone, stumbled, and fell flat on the ground, where he lay at his full length. This accident gave Paul time to get on the Beanstalk and hasten down it; but even as he reached their garden, he beheld the giant descending after him. "Mother, my mother!" cried Paul, "make haste, and give me the ax." His mother ran to him with a hatchet in her hand, and Paul with one tremendous blow cut through all the Beanstalks except one. "Now, mother, stand out of the way!" he said. Paul's mother shrank back, and it was well she did so, for just as the Giant took hold of the last leg of the Beanstalk, Paul cut the stem quite through, and darted from the office. Down came the Giant with a tremendous crash, and as he fell on his head, he broke his neck, and lay dead at the feet of the woman he possessed so much battered. Before Paul and his mother had recovered from their apprehension and distress, a beautiful woman stood before them. "Paul," said she, "you have done like a brave knight's son, and deserve to have your inheritance restored to you. Dig a grave and bury the Giant, and then go and kill the Giantess." "But," said Paul, "I could not kill anyone unless I was fighting with him; and I could not get my sword upon a woman. Moreover, the Giantess was very kind to me." The Fairy smiled at Paul. "I am very much pleased with your generous feeling," she said. "Nevertheless, return to the castle, and act as you will find needful."

Paul asked the Fairy if she would show him the way to the castle, as the Beanstalk was now down. She told him that she would send him there in her chariot, which was pulled by two peacocks. Paul thanked her, and sat down in the chariot with her. The Fairy drove him a long distance round, until they reached a village, which lay at the bottom of the hill. Here they found a number of miserable-looking men assembled. The Fairy stopped her carriage and addressed them: "My friends," said she, "the cruel giant who oppressed you and ate up all your flocks and herds, is dead, and this young man was the substance of your being delivered from him, and is the son of your kind old master, the knight." The men gave a loud cheer at these words, and pressed forward to say that they would serve Paul as faithfully as they had served his father. The Fairy bade them follow her to the palace, they marched thither in a body, and Paul blew the horn and asked admittance. The old Giantess saw them coming from the turret loophole. She was a good deal frightened, for she thought that something had happened to her husband; and as she came downstairs very fast, she got her foot in her clothes, and cut down from the top to the bottom and broke her neck. When the people found that the outside door was not opened to them, they took crowbars and forced the portal. No one was to be seen, but on leaving the hallway, he or she found the body of the Giantess at the foot of the stairs. Paul took possession of the castle. The Fairy went and took his mother to him, with the hen and the harp. He had the Giantess buried and endeavored as much as use his power to do right to those whom the Giant had robbed.

Before her departure for Magic land, the Fairy explained to Paul that she had sent the butcher to run into him with the beans, in order to hear what sort of fellow he was. If you had looked at the gigantic Beanstalk and only stupidly wondered about it, she said, "I should have left you where misfortune had placed you, only restoring her cow to your mother. But you showed an inquiring mind, and great courage and enterprise, therefore you deserve to rise; and when you mounted the Beanstalk you climbed the Ladder of Fortune." She then departed from Paul and his mother." My father then asked, "My daughters tell me the significance of this story." I began by saying, "Good can defeat evil in the heavens." My father said, "Very good Ann, I never thought about that, yet it is true." Then Faith said, "A good son will revenge those who did wrong to his father." My father looked bewildered but then answered, "A good son indeed should restore honor to their parents." I still marvel how wonderful a diplomatic our daddy is. He can so easily bridge gaps. Then Ruth said, "This story is like David and Goliath that the teacher at our church used to tell us. A little boy can bring down a giant." Our father thought for a second and smiled saying, "My daughters now have such great wisdom for Ruthie, you are so right. You would think a man of the book as I would have made that connection." Then Joy said, "It is good for a son to care for his mother and to have faith in which people tell you such as not seeing poor beans but magic beans." My father then said to Joy, "Spoken as one who would desire to be a mother. It is good when sons or daughters care for their parents though few are as lucky as your mother and I to have so many wonderful daughters. My father looked at Mary and asked, "What do you think about this story Mary?" Mary said, "I believe it has two meanings, the first one being, "It is a good thing when the poor are given back what they had before a good ruler was killed by evil." In addition, the second, "When we hide secrets to hide our laziness we shall lose our most treasured possessions, yet the part I loved the most was how the heavens saw their suffering and tried to help them." We all paused a moment and looked at Mary and together we all give a round of applause. She started to smile then said, "For a moment I thought my ideas were very foolish." Her father replied instantly, "No Mary your ideas were comprehensive and deep. Now your sisters know that I always save the best for last." Our mother joined her daughters as we all now fought to kiss our dynamic Mary. Then Fejér asked, "Do not I get to make an observation?" My father looked at his wife's "blessed" friend who refused to wear a gown to cover her special gifts of the flesh. She was a grown woman, and thus felt she had that right, especially being a goddess. Mother was always close by daddy when Fejér was around now. Our father then said smiling, "Speak your mind Fejér, if you can find it behind your *hidden heart*," although intended as an inside the group joke was referring to what covered her heart. Fejér then said, "The theme of this tale is twofold the first is 'that even a one-eyed woman can find a husband' and the second is 'If you feed a man his dinner he will always go to sleep.'" With this we all laughed, even daddy who commented, "I could never slip anything past you, could I Fejér?" Then mommy added, "I so agree with 'If you feed a man his dinner he will always go to sleep' for when a man has his belly filled he is as fast as a turtle and as bright as midnight." These made us all laugh, as once again, we remembered all the so many times in the family room on a stormy night. Even our servant girls were now rolling on the floor for here they did not have to worry about neighbors peeking in who desired to blackmail our masters. They were such a dirty people in such a dirty time as it was nothing more except people killing each other in the name of their version of heaven with the heavens apparently enjoying it. This was a fertilized garden for evil to prosper. My spirits now tell me my parent's mansion is ready, as many of their daughters will spend much time there, as also our four servants will reside there. We built another mansion for the three queens, which is of course much more elaborate, especially since all three queens are reigning and have our master's blood in them. Nevertheless, if they had their way, they would be sleeping on our surface in the Royal Deities Sanctuary, conversely we do know that our master will have reservations about his sister, mother, and grandmother as he has displayed with his number one servant and her short vacations.

These queens will also be conducting many Empire functions as our courts divvy out our assignments. My spirit and our master's spirits will also be securing the mansions that our parents live in. We will set the solid example and honor our parents. That is a task so easy to do as the Queen Grandmother and Queen Mother and my love Queen Sister are now arriving. The Queen Sister had never officially met my parents as neither had the goddess Máriakémónd. They only appeared in our night world and sometimes our dreams. They knew everything about our parents and of course ran a lot of interference in protecting them. I am so much filled with joy that they will be able to meet them. I introduce the goddess Máriakémónd to my parents, "During our time that our daughters lived with you we had teachers who taught us so many things, things that made it so easy for my sisters to appear as countesses. Our first teacher, who you did know was of course Henrietta whom eventually left your service. She would teach us in our night world, during which time stood still. She turned out to be an evil demon and had to be destroyed. Fearing for our safety, our master selected two more to live with us only in our nighttime world. They served us long and hard and actually saved us on our journeys after our deaths in the ocean. The first for us with names Máriakémónd who was a spirit departed from her flesh. She had lived a painful life with much misery and suffering, yet continued to fight hard to survive. Our courts were so impressed with her inner strength and ability to love and care, many gifts she could not exercise freely while in her flesh. Their faith in her was very much well founded as she came into our hearts and none of us will ever let her go. She has joined Fejér and Julia whom I will introduce in a while as our older sisters and allowing us still to be young girls, a state we so much enjoy when we can. Naturally when we leave our Royal Deities Sanctuary or now our parent's mansions we grow up instantly into the goddesses of the great master's kingdom." My father now stopped me and asked a question as follows, "My Ann, this is so fascinating as your mother and I want to hear the entire story yet as I put this in my mind I wonder three things, the first being how was your mother and I selected for this great honor, the second was the adoption of your sisters planned and lastly why did you have to become human if as I understand you were about to become your master's number one servant?" I told my father, "You were selected and your time was selected based on lowest danger of detection, for if I were to be captured I would have been judged and damned for eternity mainly for entering from another dimension. The dimensional rules have changed much since then. The selection of my sisters was totally by unplanned chance and actually did much to harm my concealment especially after Faith was made Queen Henrietta Maria. It was a magical union of instantaneous and eternal love with such a bonding that we can never part ways. I was made flesh and tested and tortured, most of which was with my second short life as a slave in the Roman Empire, in order to be made a goddess over the powers of evil. I was given the Sword of Justice, which no evil may ever defeat, and now I have been given my name, which no evil can survive after hearing. In order to defeat an evil agent of good must first prove themselves greater than evil. You helped me much on my road to building the fundamental tools to erect the greatest empire of good of which we know of none greater. Only blood saves as you learned through your churches that you attended. It is such a crime that in Europe with all the religious wars, blood was shed on behalf of evil. The third of our guardians is now known as Queen Sister Goddess Julia yet until recently Goddess Julia. She came to us after sometime around the killing of Henrietta. She was selected by our master for his love in the gifts of her spirit of which he could feel yet no one could know. Her scroll showed much suffering and constant danger of punishment. He gave her a new scroll with blank pages and told her to prepare to serve me as a sister. He sent her to us in our night world and we all fell deeply in love with her finding ourselves so dependent on her wisdom. I had to know her history thus went to the Sea of Forgetfulness to find her lost scroll. By divine providence, I did stumble into her scroll while digging in the mud hundreds of miles below the surface of a planet with a frozen core. I discovered that my sister was actually the true and only sister to my master whom we always thought he was without family. The Sea of Wisdom told Julia's mother and exiled queen being chased through eternity by evil that her daughter was safe in her son's Empire. Fate now intervened as my master's, father's old disbanded courts many with members who had now joined our courts notified Queen Grandmother Goddess Tompaládony that Julia had been discovered. She longed to see her granddaughter. For so many millennia, she had served for the mother of my master to kill her in revenge for the death of her son. I discovered a scroll in the Sea of Forgetfulness, which told the story of the Queen's innocence and her son's guilt. He did not create a bad man yet fell into the deceiving clutches of evil, which eventually destroyed him and his empire. This is a secret that I shall hold from the Queen Sister and my Master, with only it only being revealed to the Queen Grandmother for the Queen Mother knows this by suffering through it. When the Queen Grandmother discovered the truth, she begged forgiveness from the Queen Mother who being of a saintly heart did forgive. They are now rebuilding their relationship. All three Queens are ruling Queens as in divine law, the blood relations to the master rule in his absence. All three refuse to take my throne from me and thus risk the destruction of this Empire of Good. I would not fight against divine law, yet the courts and armies would, caring not for the Empire but only for the master's number one servant. Fortunately, we will never travel that road, as our master will be so proud to see how well we work together. I do so much want you to love them for they are truly good and will give you great honor as the Queen's Parents. I do want us all to live in harmony as the Queen Sister shall live with me also as will your daughters for we can never live apart until our master gives us permission in which we have given oath never to ask." Then Queen Grandmother Goddess Tompaládony then asked me, "My number one master, will you and your wonderful parents enjoy a wonderful welcoming party at my mansion to conclude their first day as our honor guests given by the highest of thrones from our sister dimension?" I looked at my parents and they nodded their heads yes, as my mother also added, "May our daughters and their night world guardians also attend?" Then the Queen Sister Goddess Julia answered, "I would beg that they join us in if they did not my soul would be filled with misery." I then said, "Let us enjoy a fine party at the mansion of Three Reigning Heavenly Queens." Little did we know that we were going to be entertained, as we had never been before and exposed to so many new things for us that we actually came on the scene millions of centuries ago. After we all arrived in the "Three Queen's Palace" the saints immediately raised my Queen's flag on the fourth of five poles. The last pole is reserved for our master and is much higher. Thus for now we all had our Queen's Flags up. This is mainly used by the Empire for a sign of the security level required. Queen Grandmother Goddess Tompaládony had redone their Fourth floor as a giant family recreation center. She had it packed with things from her era, as these things seemed once again to have life. She had also installed small escape ports that would take its viewer out into a five dimensional stream. It was better than actually being there in that it was completely safe. Our universe did not look much different back then, as my guest explained that changes occur gradually through time, the only exception being physical life forms, which seem to evolve through many stages until early extension. We all were so excited in the time capsules that our host called them all back in so that we could enjoy each other's company for this "social event" and not "anti-social event." As we all started to return, we discovered the three Queens had my mother surrounded as they were chatting and laughing with great warmth and excitement. That really made me feel good, for my mommy was being accepted naturally and not as a formal jester. Queen Sister Goddess Julia was really filling in the gaps for the newly formed 'mother's club' as they later defined themselves. Julia knew so much about my mother and was still in the beginning stages of getting to know her mother, so mommy was somewhat a 'foster mother' for Julia, since she was the mother of the penance sisters. Julia had always asked me and talked about mommy so much, we just always accepted mommy as being her mommy even though the two had never officially met. The one that I had to spend extra time tonight with is daddy thus giving the girls their breathing room and time to talk girl talk, which between women it apparently does not have barriers between Goddess Queens and humans and the ages. They are all chatting as if they had known each other for eternity. Our space around us changes once again. This time we can see powerful white rays and white lights as some five-point stars blazing through a strobe purple toned space. Our host explains how this was the lights from her father's throne when she was a young goddess. This would have been Julia's great grandfather. She explained that the green and yellow balls were quarantined evil nests. We all now could hear beautiful music, for much better than any I have ever heard to include the wonderful music that introduced me to this dimension. This music was simply created from something I have never been exposed. It was not from anything close to my Empire. I asked the Queen Grandmother, "My master, where did you get this music? It is so wonderful." She answered, "My master, Julia's grandfather discovered it in the space lake of mountains and clouds." I now asked, "Does this place no longer exist, for my spirits know not what you talk about?" She replied, "Have you not read the Books of the Gyor-Moson-Sopron that the Sea of Wisdom gave unto you?" I confessed, "I have yet to read the Books of the Gyor-Moson-Sopron for upon my return we have been so occupied with surprises and my spirits warn me of much danger in them." Then grandmother told me, "The danger is in not reading them my child. After our event you and I shall have an enlightening talk." Then the Queen Mother added, "Once she understands the Books of the Gyor-Moson-Sopron she will know how I have been able to avoid your capture for so many ages." They both agreed as I was now totally lost and my spirits could not pull the information from them. I now feel so guilty to be having such a great time without my other sisters also enjoying themselves. Our grandmother somehow could read this on my face thus, she relieved my guilt by telling me, "Worry not my child, I shall invite our other goddesses here for another special event." I now thanked her as Julia caught my attention. She was smiling with so much joy and excitement as I could see that so many hidden dark rooms inside her were now opening their doors and letting the light enter. This change came during a good time for Julia, for with our parents now here their daughter's attention was now focused on reliving a wonderful childhood. I often think back how we believed the greatest gift for a young pretty girl who survived by letting others enjoy her and giving her pain, yet with such little that she received also supported her three sisters and often times their mother, was to be Queen of England. Yet none in that universe can lay claim to the thrill of sitting in judgment on a throne to over 40,000 galaxies. Yet those sweet little gardens for horrifying insects and viruses to include Fejér who arrived only a few days before her death are now goddesses serving our great throne, as now the daughters of Kings worship them and give all honor and respect to them. My spirits wanted to negotiate for many who tortured and abused Faith. I told them not to do so, for those who died, as saints would not be released, as they have the right to remain in their final resting place. As for those who died in the hands of evil and who burn in the lakes of fire I have no need for them. Their punishment is much worse than what I give, since I now try to give another chance and then completely erase. I actually feel sorry for those souls, as their punishment is far too severe for the flesh left at the mercy of evil and pain. The flesh will do evil unless it has both protection and reward for doing 'good' instead of reward for doing evil. I do not really want to get into this subject again suffice it to say, Faith and our parent's daughters are doing very well now as this wonderful music is mellowing us all inside and outside. Our servant girls, having always been so very creative now are adjusting some of their favorite ballads to this music. We all cannot help but to join in and have one of our family sing-along as we did many times during our childhood. We speak of that brief period as being our childhood as it was now many centuries ago. Time flies in the heavens, much more for the saints than for their rulers. Our hosts are now showing us a wonderful space strobe light show. We are all captivated. This has the makings of a wonderful evening as Julia bonds to her relatives and we back with our parents. I am just floating in the air enjoying the beautiful music and light show. Then the lights stop. The music stops and space turns dark black. Next, a tunnel of pure power drops above this castle and starts spinning us. We are now being spread throughout the inside of this mansion as I hear a large, "Stop in my name." That which came fast was now gone. As we all rushed back to where we were congregated before I was able to determine who gave the command. It was the Queen Grandmother. I marvel that her name still has so much power over even the unknown. Then I wonder if the unknown know her power why do we not know the unknown? I look at this Queen and say, "Thanks so much for saving us. I now know where my master gets his strength from." She tells me, "Oh, it really was not anything more than having dealt with this many times before." I then ask, "What was this thing that you have dealt with many times?" As she was about to answer, my mother started to scream, "Where is Ruth?" I scanned the castle and could not see her and then ask my spirits, "Where is the Goddess Ruth?" They answered me, "We know not." I then said, "Check my Empire." My spirits told me, "We have and she is not in your Empire." I then questioned, "How can that be, for even at my fastest speeds it would take hours to reach my borders, and even more difficult for an alien force since they would have to escape from my security sensors. This cannot be. She is here, find her." Then our Queen Grandmother told me, "My child, your spirits are correct for Ruth is not in your Empire now." I then looked at her and asked, "How can that be my master of love and family." She then said to me, "I so wish your spirits had read the Books of the Gyor-Moson-Sopron, yet we now have no time so you must believe what I tell you to be true if you wish to save our Ruth." I fell to my knees and wrapped my arms around her leg and cried out, "Your words are now my mind our great one of such unlimited mercy." She then said, "I will tell you during our search for Ruth. Prepare for our departure." Then my father fell to his knees and cried out, "Oh great Queen Goddesses, will you have mercy on me and allow me to search with her as her father?" The Queen Grandmother then said, "I can never deny a father of his right to protect his daughter. You may join us, however we must depart now." He looked at us and said, "Let's go, for I fear my little

Ruth could be in danger." Then the Queen Grandmother commanded, "Open and take us in." The twister was now red in color and before I could blink, we were landing on another something. This place was dark and empty as I can see four stars to my upper right as another object is falling to the surface. We are currently alongside a mountain, and I do not know for sure if there is a sea to my left. I see a beast on the ledge with evil wings as it is sending or receiving of the strange spirit in the sky. Our Queen Grandmother now alerts us, "I can see Julia in the eye of Villánykövesd." I now ask, "Who is Villánykövesd and how do you know it?" She tells me, "Villánykövesd is an agent of evil and we did fight him almost daily." Now the questions are flooding my mind, "Why would he want Ruthie?" She answers, "He did not care for whom he took, all die in the same way, begging for the pain to stop." I follow-up, "Then what does it want?" Tompaládony now answers, "He wants the Books of the Gyor-Moson-Sopron, and however we must defend those books with everything up to and including all of our Empire, for if he got those books, evil would be undefeatable." I now pat my arm to my side yet to my shock, I forgot my Sword of Justice. I ask Tompaládony, "Can we go back fast and get my Sword?" She tells me, "Villánykövesd would detect our parting for the guards the poor victims that serve him. He would have Ruth placed into one of the farthest points in the universe before we returned." My questions continue with, "How can he go to the farthest points in the universe?" She tells me, "The same as we did to find him." "Where are we," now becomes my newest question. Tompaládony answers, "We are so far from your Empire that is you traveled at the divine speed for gods it would take you 700 Quintillion (10^{18}) light-years before you would be inside your Empire." I have now spoken softly, "I know not how this is, yet I do now know that my Empire is no longer safe." Tompaládony then told me, "After we rescue Ruthie, I will show you how making your Empire safe again." Then we heard a crashing sound around us. Tompaládony commanded, "Demons have no powers over goddesses." Villánykövesd replied, "I have power over the souls of flesh." He went to pull my father yet Tompaládony stopped him, spun him into a crystal ball, and turned up the heat in the ball. Villánykövesd then said, "You may torture me however your Ruth will suffer more than me." We now could see a blurry image of someone suffering. Tompaládony then said, "Oh you fool, do you not know that if I see her I can free her?" Within a flash, Ruthie was beside us and she did not look good. We could now see billions of armies of demons coming at us. My father grew nervous and cried out, "Beware Lilith, they are attacking." Within an instant Villánykövesd and his armies vanished. Tompaládony then looked shocked as she asked, "What just happened?" I now remembered my gift from the Council of Nykøbing Mors that any evil that heard my name would vanish. Villánykövesd had all his armies tuned into his voice so they could respond to his commands. In doing so they could also hear my father's voice which was to their demise. We could now see light in the sky. Even the beast on the cliff had vanished. We had saved Ruth and prevented my father from being kidnapped. We would now return to my throne and celebrate. As we all were cheering, Queen Grandmother Goddess Tompaládony had a pale look on her face. I asked her, "My great hero, why do you look sad?" She said, "We have no one to hold open this end of our twister hole and as such we cannot safely leave." I then volunteered, "Oh, I will stay back and hold the open hole for you all to return." Tompaládony then said to me, "That will not work my child, for these twister holes are too hard to find on a return as it could take centuries to rescue you." I then asked her, "Then how can we get back to our throne?" She answered, "For I have a return beacon there. I did not bring any beacons with me as I planned on using one of the demons to hold the hole open by taking some prisoner." I then asked her, "What do we do now my Grandmother?" She looked at my father and asked him, "What would you suggest we do?" He answered so swift and smooth as always, "We need to find something or one to hold open the hole." Tompaládony now replied, "Your wisdom is wonderful, for now I know why so many of our goddesses loves you and as even my granddaughter has to greatest honor for you. These we shall do, find someone to hold open the hole. We shall first send out alert beacons that the evil Villánykövesd has perished. We shall monitor the space waves to see who responds. Tompaládony now said, "Let us relax as I shall steal the attention of my little granddaughter Ruthie and help her also to relax." Although the light was starting to appear, it still was not strong enough to bring forth daylight. I still cannot make out what covers the surface although I do suspect it to be demon feces or the remains of any flesh they may have tortured before capturing the victim's soul. I think it would be best to talk with my daddy for a while. I had not noticed that by being so far from my spirits that my gown was no longer visible. My daddy put his arm around me and said, "I am so proud of how healthy my daughters have grown to be and with such independent spirits. You look so much like your mother." I then gave my daddy thanks not knowing that he saw my freedom from the chains of clothing spirit. I was just so lucky to have my daddy beside me, for his confidence gives me great strength. His presence will always make me feel safe, as even he being here now was proof that when his daughters are in danger, even if they be goddesses, he was going to be the first in line to fight for them. I could see this in Ruth also, for as she came to us, she immediately went into her daddy's arms for her salvation. I do believe that is why Grandmother wants to spend some time with her, for all are impressed when so many daughters are so loyal to their daddy who is willing to sacrifice anything for them. One large dark spot in the sky is now being filled with lights. This is like the inside of a big twister with a big bright light in the middle with red, blue, and white veins flowing into its center. Grandmother looks over at it and warns us, "Gang we need to go to another galaxy fast. Hang on and follow me." She whisks us through space as a flashing divine lightning bolt as we sun enters another galaxy. She steers us towards what appears to be a more stable part of this new galaxy and soon we are on a nice beautiful planet. As we are now resting on the surface I tell her, "I hope you are a hijacker and plan to keep us prisoners here until our Empire finds us." Tompaládony replies, "If only we could be that lucky my master. I just want a nice place to get to know your sister as best I can before we go back to our Empire where our Queen's duties will make it so much more difficult." I then asked what must appear to her my millionth question, "What was that in the sky that we had to escape from?" Tompaládony tells us, "The sudden removal of so many demons made that galaxy unstable and when galaxies become unstable the universe contracts them into a dense sand drop and then explodes it and thus a new stable galaxy will be born, and in a couple of billion years will once again begin to show life." This planet has blue peaceful lakes, mountains that reach into the sky and dark pink or light purple vegetation. This world appeared to be in harmony. I asked my Queen Grandmother while she was taking Ruth under her arm and smothering her granny love; "Is there life on this planet?" She answered saying, "Yes, however it is all under the surface because this region has historically been raided so many times from so many directions they could only survive in hiding. They will come to us soon so we can relax, I will care of your sister, and you should care for your daddy." I shook my head in agreement. Daddy put me under his wing, so we two sisters were getting some special big people attended, which was always a treat as a child. Daddy started telling me some stories of his high school days. As he continued to talk, I noticed a new visitor snuggled up beside me. Ruth could not pass up this event as Grandmother sat beside her also thrilled by the stories. I asked her, "My love, I hope this is not boring for you." She immediately responded, "My father would tell me stories when I was older and I so much enjoyed them as I am enjoying this. This is a solid family time. Such time as this departed me so very long ago." She looked at my father and said, "Please continue father, for your daughters and I hunger for your adventures." Little could he have known that those adventures would someday feed three goddesses, two that are also Empire Queens? We do not care about our titles now; we just want to be in a simpler time in a simpler place. Ruth and I of course remember not only the family nights but also the Sunday afternoon adventures. That was our play outside with nature day. We would skin our knees yet not even let a tear out not wanting to waste the time or energy to cry when so much fun was at hand. As his adventures continued, we noticed a sudden change in the sky color as the sea now had an island rising up out of it. We could not identify all that was in it, yet we could see what might be a black haired female walking towards us, and a nice white fence along the upper left hand side of this image. The hopefully a female since it looked like it was wearing a dress that was being held up on the left side to prevent it from getting too dirty in the slushy mud. When it got closer, we could now identify a quite pretty girl approaching us with a warm smile. She asked, "I wish to welcome you to Hódmezovásárhelyi. My name is Szelevény and I have been sent to determine how we may serve you and to beg that you do no harm to us. I looked at her, still wrapped around my daddy and Ruth wrapped around his other side and asked, "Do we look like the ones who would do such a pretty woman as you harm?" Szelevény answered by saying, "We have been visited many times by sheep in wolf's clothing. Our sensors have detected that you have access to great powers." Tompaládony now answered, "I am Queen Grandmother Goddess Tompaládony and I promise to do you no harm, yet there is one also here he is greater than I. She pointed at me and continued, "For she is great the Goddess Queen Lilith, member of the Council of Nykøbing Mors and the holder of the Sword of Justice and number one servant to the master who holds the Sword of Freedom and the Books of the Gyor-Moson-Sopron and beside her is the beautiful young Penance Sister Goddess Ruth, so indeed there is great power here." Szelevény then said, "It is a great honor to be your servants for we have heard great things about you, your council, and your books. You must keep your books a secret for evil will kill to get your books. May I ask who your master that is with you is called?" We all three said as if coming from one mind, "He is our father and master of our family." Tompaládony now continued, "For no good can survive unless they honor their mother and father all the days of their eternity." With this saying, Szelevény's eyes turned bright red as she spoke saying, "You may enter, and we shall serve you as you wish to be served." Her eyes turned back to the way they were previously and she motioned for us to move as she said,

"I shall be your guide oh great powers of the heavens. Please follow me my goddesses." She guided us onto the island and the island did go to the other side of the sea. We then followed her along the shoreline whereas the vegetation kept getting better and better. I wanted to store these images in my mind as Ruth holds on to my arm I could see she was thinking the same thing. I then said to Ruth, "A vacation spot like this in our sanctuary would be a welcome additional would it not." She nodded her head yes as her milky eyes told me this would make us all so good. Then Grandmother said, "I could debate your father on politics in a place such as this, or teach your mother many secrets that a wife in eternity should know." I looked at the senior queen who was now without any doubt the one who was most giving and humble and said, "Or you could spoil Ruth and me by allowing us to enjoy your wonderful company." She reached over, kissed my cheek, and then said to my daddy, "Will you consider protecting me in this new dangerous place we venture to enter?" Daddy looked at her and said, "It is always my great honor to protect my queens." My daddy is so good at giving the most courteous and respectful answer to any question at any time. He would indeed protect Grandma and Ruthie plus myself of course even though he was a spirit from the flesh and we are goddesses, we all did so much want his wisdom and might as part of our defense. We had no fear for one whom we all loved and would obey was with us. Grandma was fostering the same affection for our daddy as Ruthie and I had buried within. Her beauty is still so enticing as her youthful appearance embarrasses me to call her Grandmother. I often feel this is insulting her, yet that is her position of great honor as we wish so much to elevate her, she works so hard to be one of the girls. She performs perfectly as one of the girls and we all love her as both. I can feel that she wants daddy to be her daddy, yet I think mommy could have so reservations about this. Someday we will work it out. As we continue on our way, Szelevény vanishes from our sight. We all grab hold of daddy, as he remains so calm. I wonder how the savior of the goddesses will guide us to our safety. We must have other life forms to hold fast the other end of our space sling shot that will return us to my throne. Daddy tells us, "Szelevény would not have led us here for us to be lost, for she knows the power you goddesses have. I would venture to speculate that she is with her authorities making the final arrangements for our arrival. I would also speculate that the only female to be clothed in our small group has many great stories that she could share with us in the very few years of her young life span." Grandmother blushed as said to Ruthie and me, "Your daddy is equally very wise as I cannot say I have met one as wise as he." Then to our surprise, another host appeared before us. As we viewed her, something was not normal. She had no eyes but holes that apparently ran through her head as we could see on the vegetation that was behind her. I asked her, "Oh kind woman, who are you and why do you appear to us?" She answered, "It is me, Szelevény, and I am to guide you to our wonderful city. My masters wanted me to be fresh and pleasing to your eyes and the eyes of our citizens as we enter our city. They had some concerns about two of you being without garments yet they were able to verify that an Empire, which is so very far away, had some goddesses that did not wear garments. I must ask if you wish to have garments before you enter our city and meet your hosts. We do not want you to be shamed." I then answered Szelevény, "We do not need garments, for we are goddesses that serve our servants as being without shame and hide nothing from them. Szelevény, may I ask why your eyes our different from ours?" Szelevény answered, "Oh great one, our people have lived in the darkness below the surface for so long; we evolved into a race of blind people. When we are on the surface, we must remove our eyes in order not to permanently destroy the organs. We have sensors in the back of our heads that send the images to our empty sockets." Grandmother, then added, "I do so much enjoy your garments with that wonderful necklace. It is as if they were made for this place." Szelevény then smiled and said, "We must go faster now before the darkness makes it difficult for you to see." We then came to the mouth of a small cave. Szelevény was able to move the large rock in front of the opening with just her touch. My daddy then said, "Wow, she has some power in those arms." Szelevény replied, "Not I but those who are on the other end. My movement was simply to trigger the motion detectors for the security forces on the other side. We may now enter." As we went inside the floor below us disappeared and we were all dropping into this deep hole. Szelevény hold Ruthie and my hands as Grandmother held daddy's who held mine and Szelevény was so calm that I saw no need to worry. After a few minutes or eternity in my heart, we started to slow down. Then we gently landed on a hole on the surface. Szelevény now motioned and lights came on. I could see a large flesh made tunnel extending before us. Soon a nice small tunnel jet appeared before us as Szelevény ask us to sit inside of it. With all of us seated, the jet flashed us for about eight minutes as it slowed down. We could see another world through our windows. Dark low cloud camouflaged the ceiling. We could see a large city on the underground cavern's floor in addition to a large city nestled on two large rock towers. Our tunnel would take us to underneath this sky city. We departed the tunnel train and after a short lift on an elevator appeared inside the city. We were met by some unusual vehicles that transported us around this beautiful city. Szelevény now tells us that her people have 107 of these underground cities plus twenty-three underground military cities for our defense. We have no desire to expand considering that, we must live underground, and if we went to another planet we could settle an uninhabited part of the planet and build our station deep under its surface, thus no one would know we were there. We all prefer to stay together here. We now stopped in front of a large palace and proceeded to the doors. The large doors opened and we entered into a large empty room with towers on each side with a throne seat at the other end. Before us appeared a beautiful woman who stood in a graceful stance. Szelevény introduced us to her Queen Ólmod. Queen Ólmod welcomed us to her humble city saying, "It is a great honor to be visited by such bold and free goddesses. I have assembled our people so they may worship you when you so desire. I beg that you let us serve you so you may find goodness in our hearts. Our long history of fighting evil has forced us to live in hiding yet we are so happy to be living that we do not mind. You are the first gods to visit us. My scouts tell me you are gods of good. We are so happy that you found us first and want to thank you for your great victory in our neighbor galaxy which is no more." She dropped to her knees and began worshiping us." Ruthie and I walked over to her and patted her head as I said, "We have found the goodness in your heart and thank you so much for your hard work against evil. I hope someday to be able to fight more evil in this part of the universe since my Empire is so far from here." Queen Ólmod now asked Ruthie, "Oh great goddess Ruth will you bless our people so that their days may be long." Ruthie looked at me and asked, "My goddess, will you give into me some of your blood?" I said to Ruthie, "My sister, my blood is your blood as your blood is my blood. You may bless them with your blood. Those whom you bless will be given new bodies." Queen Ólmod then asked, "What do these bodies do?" Ruthie answered, "They neither hunger nor fall prey to diseases." Queen Ólmod had now fallen to her knees in front of Ruthie and begged her for some blood. Ruthie said to her, "Give me a small knife or needle if you have one." The Queen motioned for her guards, "Give me a needle now my guards." They gave her a needle and she handed it to Ruthie who nervously stuck it in her finger and as her blood came out she wiped it on Queen Ólmod's head and in a flash the Queen turned white, as did her palace behind her. Her guards began to rush before us to defend her. I stuck out my hand and froze them. The Queen was now shouting for joy as her body was being transformed. It took longer than usual since mine on hand power reserves are running low. Actually, Ruthie's power was making the transformation, as this was something new for her also. Soon the lights began to dim as the Queen once again appeared before us. She then once again began worshipping Ruthie. This made Grandmother and me happy in that Ruthie was now getting some well-deserved attention and praise. The Queen now begged Ruthie to stay with them and be their god. Grandmother and I stepped in and explained, "Our Ruthie must stay with us for her love is a rich source of our power. However, someday we plan to return, on that day you will be her people, and she will be your god. However, that may never be unless we get your help in returning us." The queen then asked, "Will our god be able to visit us from time to time to insure that we are still in existence?" I told the queen, "Absolutely, for how can a people worship a god that does not serve them? She will also immediately send you some angels to help you prepare her books and temples." The Queen then rose and yelled out to her guards, which were now 'unfroze', "Blessed be the name of Ruth who is our god and we are her people." Ruth now said, "I shall give more people their heavenly bodies when my priests come to dwell with you." The Queen now said to us, "How may I help my gods?" Grandmother answered by saying, "We need for you to hold open my portal so we may return to our throne. If you secure the portal by the instructions I place in your heart and seal the opening on your side, your god Ruth may visit you in the future and you may send scrolls to her telling her of any special needs you may have." Queen Ólmod opened her mouth and Grandmother feed her the knowledge of the portals. The Queen now said, "I am ready to serve you my gods, so that all will say, the servants of Ruth serve the gods." Ruthie walked over and held the Queen in her arms giving her kisses and saying, "I do love you as my people and shall care for you as my children. Nevertheless, I must now return to the heavens." The portal was now sealed and we jumped in and in a flash were back in the Grandmother's castle. As we stepped out Grandmother commanded, "Portal, you must now serve a new god whom you shall call Ruth. She will find you a secure cave in her Royal Deities Sanctuary. Do and send as she commands." Ruthie now hugged Grandmother saying, "You mercy to me is great, yet I know not how to thank you. I am so afraid, for I never had my own servants before today." Grandmother said, "Repay me with your love and also let me serve you many more times. I remember my first people, and how afraid I was. I shall help you prepare your books, your temple designs, your angels, and priests. We shall have much fun with this if you so agree." Ruthie said, "One thing I know is that I shall so easily give you my love yet as a sister if you so agree." Grandmother said, "Oh my baby, I so much would love that, now let us visit with your mother for a while then we shall get to work." We now walked into Tompaládony's waiting room where all our parties were waiting for us. Julie, Mary, Joy, Faith, mommy, and Máriakémend along with our four servant girls and Queen Julia swarmed Ruth hugging and kissing her to no end as their tears of joy flooded her. Faith then looked at me and asked, "Who found and saved our sister?" I answered by looking at Tompaládony and saying, "Wilt thou answer Faith's question?" Tompaládony answered swiftly and loudly, "Her daddy not only saved her but was strong at all times even when we were filled with fear." Mommy then rushed over and hugged daddy saying, "Thanks so much for your great love of the woman who depend upon you. You have and always will be the best daddy in the entire universe." All his daughters agreed and we all rejoiced saying, "We are so proud to honor our mother and father all the days of eternity."

Chapter 07

Will I sea my missing daughter

O ur joyous reunion was celebrating two important things, first the return of our first kidnapped Goddess, and second the first tragedy that faced our new extended family. We did both wonderfully as Tompaládony stood up and batted hard for Ruth. We worked together if Ruth belonged to both sides of us in which now we all belong together with each other. They all treat our parents as if they too were gods. However, I now had two large tasks ahead of me, first being able to defend against portals and second getting up to speed on the Books of the Gyor-Moson-Sopron. This would be some good missions for my spirits and courts, since they told me that the Books of the Gyor-Moson-Sopron really did not offer any more information relevant to our age. "Spirits, courts, lights and army commanders, meet me in my throne," was my new command. Upon arriving at my throne, I order all to depart for I was to have a top-secret meeting. I then told my security not to let anyone enter during my meeting. Very soon, all who I requested attended. I began by asking, "How is it that the Goddess Ruth was kidnapped and taken out of my Empire in a flash?" No one could answer. I then asked, "How is it that I found her kidnapped by evil on the other side of the universe?" They then asked me, "How do you know you were that far away?" I then said, "I called you here for me to get answers to my questions, and not for you to question my divine judgment. My location was revealed to me by our Queen Grandmother Goddess Tompaládony who was a queen before any here was born in the flesh. I now declare we have no defense against evil and unless we gain our security we will perish." Everyone became very silent and frozen as in a state of shock. I then said, "We have the answer, for our solution is in the Books of the Gyor-Moson-Sopron. We shall enter into a new era where we can go to the farthest ends of the universe in a flash through universe portals, as I went with Queen Grandmother Goddess Tompaládony and my father and we did come back with my kidnapped sister. I want every court to study these books inside and out, for I only know that our defense is in these books. We shall never be invaded again, especially to take a goddess from a castle with four goddess Queens inside. You should have great shame for this. Redeem yourselves and save your Empire for your loved ones could be taken to evil prisons in the far ends of the universe." I then said to my spirits, "Once you have tested the new defense plan in detail implement it and learn how to prepare these space portals for I was to be able to send my armies to fight evil in the far ends of our universe. Even though that evil may never hurt us it will hurt other good races." At this time, Adásztevel approached me and asked, "Mother, may I speak in private with you?" I then said, "Finally someone has given me an easy question to answer. You may have me any time you want me. Join me in our chambers." As we entered and sat down, Adásztevel told me the daughters were upset with me for leaving them without notice. "We searched long and hard and could not find you. Please never forget about the ones who love you and that you gave birth." I walked over to her, gave her a big hug, and answered, "I can now see that what I did was wrong. I actually did not know what was to happen until Tompaládony made it happen, and then it was nothing more than a long hard road to get back. I do so much hope my babies will forgive me." Adásztevel then answered, "We forgave you as you were leaving, and for our blood is our love for you. Mother, are we in as great of a danger as you warned us?" I looked at her and said, "I know not, yet I do know as Tompaládony told me, the Books have the answers." As we were now talking about some things going on in their lives, Sásdi came knocking on the door as I immediately begged for my second visit from a daughter today. Sásdi now asked me, "Are your daughters in danger," and I told her, "I do not believe you are in danger, yet I think it would be good to call back the explorers and insure that two daughters are watching one daughter, thus each daughter will be watching two daughters. If anything happens, notify me immediately and I will rescue you. The good news is that those of you who enjoy exploring will now be able to explore places never before possible once appropriate safeguards are established." Sásdi now told me that she originally had another reason for requesting my audience. She told me, "We have heard rumors that your daughter Atlantis may be in grave danger. We do not know for sure." I then told them, "I will have my spirits try to work out a plan for me, as I am not really all that fond of returning to that hellhole, for I do not even know where she is." Meanwhile, I want you all to tell me what has been happening with my babies." Adásztevel then answered, "Mother, we would prefer you see what is happening with Atlantis first." I then told my daughters, "I will jump back in time and search for her, thus it matters not when I go, I will get there before her troubles begin. First, I need to know what is going on and what we can do about it. A smart rescue is so much better than a foolish failed. Hang on one second. Spirits, my daughters tell me that Atlantis may be in danger. I may have to return to save her. Please tell me what options I have and how I may do this wisely." I then asked, "Now will you update me on anything I should know?" Adásztevel now answered, "Many of your daughters are marrying Saints from your heavens." I then said, "A mother could not hope for better. All who wish to marry our saints may of course do so and enjoy the happiness of love for eternity. I do plan on making a special heaven for daughters that will be connected to my spirits thus we will be linked." Now Cserszegtomaj came climbing out her special tunnel. I do admire her creativity. She wanted to give me an updated report on her sisters. I told her, "I am eager to hear this report." She began by saying, "We have combined our forces, and mingled them into the Saint's Armies as most of us now occupy very high command positions. The saints needed some leaders who have experience in wars, and have been exposed to many outside things in this or any universe. Our relationships are very harmonious and now we can offer you a powerful backup for your armies and also forces to do humanitarian missions if needed." I then said "I am so proud how independent and dependable my daughters have been. I can feel myself living in the part of me I spend the least amount of time with, yet could never have survived without on too many occasions. Know you that our master has great plans in our future around my daughters. You have suffered too long and too much not to be rewarded. You shall be rewarded. They then answered back, "To be the daughters of the great Empire of Good's Master Queen is plenty of reward. For you have shared your powers with us as we now exist so much better than ever dreamed possible. We live in mansions and actually provide for ourselves from the rewards given to us by the Saints. Being surrounded by so much good rebuilds the soul into a fountain of good. Our happiness is the simple privilege of being your daughters with our loyalties established so many times." I then replied, "I feel accordingly sorry for you all sometimes as I was never there for to care for you as a mother should. I am the one who is so fortunate to be your mother, I had a choice of making you, which for most were made as revenge to an unjust god, yet you all had no choice, you were born in the middle of a raging war with your enemies always knocking at your doors. You were always to envy of the spirits, as you were all so smart and fast on your feet. I wonder, which one of my daughters will help me figure out the deal on Atlantis?" The three of them now looked in agreement, as Cserszegtomaj spoke for the group saying, "We had a contest to determine who would babysit our mother while she sticks her head into the lion's jaws in her quest to save Atlantis. We all feel that Agyagosszergény will be the best daughter to save you." Agyagosszergény now spoke, "I am so lucky to have the faith of my sisters in the so challenging task of bringing you back if you so dare to go back into your previous dimension where you we all are fugitives. I shall fight beside you and whatever punishment you get I will demand twice for my failure in saving our greatest purpose for living." I then answered back, "Fear not Agyagosszergény for we shall search the wise plans offered by my lights and courts and armies and Saints who now include my babies. We will go wisely sneaking in and smoothly sneaking out. For I wish to bring you back for your sisters as I could not bear the shame of losing even one daughter. Before we move on to our missions, let me share one great thing with you. You now have another tool in addition to our Sword of Justice. Anytime evil is near or in any way hears my name, they will die. This gift was given by the Council of Nykøbing Mors. It does work, as we accidently spoke my name on the evil Villánykövesd's inter-galactic communication network and all who were evil vanished. The galaxy very soon thereafter collapsed after some mighty empires of good in that region pulled all the good saints out with technology that temporally surpasses that of our spirits who dwell in the flesh. It works; you are always to send out, before your broadcasting sensors that broadcast my name so that you will not enter danger. Moreover, you will be able to make yourselves safe; in case of any physical reactions that occur when there has been a sudden interruption to the harmony since evil so often anchors itself into the harmonious balance where it exists. That is the curse of the ages, as we shall break that harmonious balance even if it destroys the good, for we can round up those spirits and give them new flesh suits along with new places to live. Let my name fight with you, if that is the name of your mother. I shall now take my baby Agyagosszergény and start planning for our very dangerous mission ahead. Goodbye my lovely angels for we shall return." I now go to my throne to talk with my spirits. As I sat on my throne I asked my spirits, "What help can you give to me in another dimension." They answered, "Spirits of Power are forbidden to enter other dimensions. These other universes can freeze out powers and take us into their prisons. We beg that you do not go. We have also received a warning from the god Gyor-Moson-Sopron, the god over our master and his penance. He warns,

"Lilith, do not go into another dimension for you go with limited powers. Our Sword of Justice is only for our universe. Thus, your sword will not work in other universes. You will be a lamb waiting for your slaughter. They still want revenge for your destruction of their throne. If you and Agyagosszergény are caught, you will receive the greatest punishment ever. We will count you as departed forever if you go into that universe." I sat on my throne, looked at my beautiful daughter, and asked her to go back to her sisters. Agyagosszergény fell to her knees and begged that she could have the honor of helping the one she loved the most. Agyagosszergény's petition continued with, "I missed you too much during your 1,000 punishment and I could never live with myself if I let you go unprotected. I came from your womb and shall protect the holder of that womb with all my heart, soul, and spirit." Now the Lights came before us begging, "Oh great queen, let us send in spies and find Atlantis and we will smuggle her back." I then answered them, "Someone has shamed me by taking a revenge for me out on a daughter that has raised her empire under the surface of the oceans. This I must confront and destroy. I will save my daughter even if she refuses me. Once I have, her back then our great spies will go in and bring all her servants back here. Upon this great victory all will know that this Empire has the greatest Queen." Then the Saints came before us saying, "We know not why you would risk never seeing over 3,000 of your daughters here for one. We have rebuilt everything in our system around her mighty daughters. We know that Saints can enter another universe and scout. We cannot in any way rescue you if you are caught. We might be able to plead with you during your judgment. We will send ten Saints to do your searches and then they must return. We will determine which ones go to plead with you if needed." Now my Courts appeared before me saying, "How can you risk so much. We cannot go in with you; however, we can enter if you are on an established path to your universe. We will send seven of our best who have been studying your old empire in absolute detail. They know how to operate all the Earth's transportation devices and have translator sensors planted in their head. We shall also give you both translators." They bowed and departed. Next came before us our highest ranked military angels. They apologized that they could not enter to save me. That is an act of war and so many dimensions or universes would unite and destroy us. Our war against evil would be over with evil the victors. Your spirits assured us that you would not want to jeopardize the greatness of your work in building such a great Empire. Gods from every galaxy in your Empire have volunteered to go in your place. Every angel has begged to go in your place. You are too much love to lose. We will send three top behind the lines fighting angels to escort you. We will not back down from this support except give you more if you want. We need you to keep our Empire together. Do not forsake us greatest Queen Goddess ever to exist." I told them, "Empires are built by great armies and my armies are the greatest and I love everyone in my armies. I wish so much that I could let others suffer my personal will to save Atlantis. Happy good lives exist when they survive their foolish acts returning what they have lost. I do want to have a happy life with my child that is why I will return." I now sat alone with Agyagosszergény and my twenty angel plus saints team. I told the team to wait in the throne's guest chamber with my daughter. Now is the time for me to search my mind considering the wonderful presentations made by the smartest and strongest throne staff ever to exist. This is what makes it so hard because every part of my spirit and I attest to the foolishness of this. I think that maybe a small part of me knows they would rescue me even if it did mean war. Our universe's throne would fight hard to hold together my empire or would they, considering I was warned by their higher throne. I need to process with great caution. I will hide in a galaxy over since their god only rules the Milky Way. Will have to avoid an occasional Mempire warship thus, I should be good to go. We will be doing most of the initial searches deep under the ocean surface. Her children should be able to tell us where she is or was last seen. That is when I will attack, get her, and bring her back even if against her will, as I will have some divine powers. The question is, "Do I have to do this? I am puzzled as to why I am going. She is a special child, whose father was King Mike and later raised by King James (Mike) and Lablonta. She is my claim into the Mempire Empires as a child of their first King. Her childhood was blessed as they kept the identity of her true mother a secret. Then one day while I was Lord of New Venus, they revealed to me that she was my daughter. Like all my daughters, I never knew much about her; except her empire is very secret, and has very limited contact with the planet. Its station is planted. Their big, coming out of their shell, is when they leave their flesh. They all, except a strange one here and there, go to heaven. Atlantis is strong on her flesh children that they are to serve the Lord of their heaven. I never really heard of anyone being punished in that heaven; only know of Lucifer and his gang being kicked out. I suspect she is being punished because of me, as they are using her to pull me into their traps. I will go in and jump out as the snare comes down and rush back with my daughter in my arms. I will send in teams of my saints to pull all those in their stations, as I will build the new stations for them here. Actually, my spirits have already built most of them. They were shocked when they discovered how many galaxies they occupied. They will be provided some of our advanced transportation and travel wherever they want whenever they want. That will make all their stations like extension rooms on one station. They will love that. I will give them my blood showered flesh bodies that have no pain or diseases nor require food. Food is the number one reason they leave their station as many become prey to large sea animals that quickly learn this is the place to feed at the bottom of the ocean. In my galaxies, they can stay safely inside and "light flash" instantaneously to their other destinations, thus have no need to go outside their station except for protecting recreation. I will use these in my arguments with Atlantis if I need to do so. If she is being punished for me than I need to save her and that, I will do. I shall gather my team and we shall go to guerilla warfare now. My team quickly gathered around me and I had a war space ship that had two back rooms packed with Criliton diodes. If someone shoots us, they shall end up three or four galaxies away. I also plan to have it hit the throne if I am captured. Its projected courses are controlled by my mind, thus if I am standing in judgment, that throne will be scattered across the universe. Criliton diodes have another unique feature. If an object has a Ziapon diode in it, the Criliton diodes will simply pass through and around them. Yes, we all have a Ziapon diode placed in many places inside our souls. I plan on the Criliton diodes also to destroy any lakes of fire in the Milky Way. I have many extra to implant in Atlantis and any of her comrades. My gang is here and we are all in my Queen's war ship as I give the command, "Mission starts now," and we are heading for the current gap portal to the destination universe. Tompaládony set this up for us thus; we will pop up inside that universe and not at the guarded seams. We are on our way now. I now have no fear, for I know that fear invites demons. I would like to pop a few billion that pestered me on New Venus. I can now see the hole in front of us. Tompaládony gave me the power over it, thus on my return trip I can open it and close it after some enemy enter into it then close it leaving them between the dimensions which is a sad place to be. In we go and now I can see my former universe in front of me. Out we go, thus we are now in hostile territory. As we are, moving towards a small galaxy probably twelve galaxies below the Milky Way the space turns white and rocks my ship stopping us. Darn, was I caught already? Was this a trap set up by Tompaládony to get another queen on the throne? The military team members are preparing to bolt us out of here. They cannot detect any life forms or spirits in the area, thus this must be a border protection set up by the universe to keep its galaxies from drifting into another universe. Something like when the flesh detects a foreign bacteria or whatever it will try to quarantine it. Bang like to big bang we are now working our way back into the black of space. Now we can land on a planet and set up our missions. My baby Agyagosszergény, military, courts, and saints order me to stay here. Usually I would get offended by such an order; however, I set up, ordained my army, my courts, and reorganized my saints. They are doing what I have told them to do. They are protecting their throne. I must protect the image of the Queen and adhere to the role in order to give them the pride of their positions. Whatever, I will suffer through the beautiful place they landed. I tell them I will stay only if Agyagosszergény stays with me. I need so much to start building experiences with my 3000 babies. I will have to do it one at a time, yet we do have a lot of time. My spirits are watching and protecting them now, which shows all how special they are to their Queen. My court (of seven) tells me the people here are friendly thus enjoy the outside. The ten saints are blending in with the saints of the Milky Way to get information about Atlantis. The courts and army (of three) are getting information from Mempire. I would think the Mempire would fight if one of their Child's Empires. I need to know what they know. The inhabitants of this planet must truly value tranquility as I am holding my daughters and we are walking down a path with benches on the side and leaves forming a ceiling above us. It has a nice white light at the end of it. As we start to enter the white light, my courts warn me not to enter and to rush back to the ship. Naturally, when I got back to my ship I asked the courts for an update. They told me that evil demons were approaching that area and to stay concealed in the ship. I asked them, "Why would demons be here so fast?" My courts told me it was not only here yet they had now flooded the Milky Way. I thought to myself that this would be a good time to get a message out that they should avoid us. I wanted to make sure my name would kill demons in this universe as I was told it would. Thus, I told my baby Agyagosszergény to wait for me that I shall return. She said to me, "No mommy, we shall return." She was serious and had fought demons for millions of years so I shook my head yes, in which she ran to me hugging me saying, "thanks mommy." I can see that she will most likely get her way with me using the 'mommy' weapon. I can never refuse a daughter that calls me mommy. My courts asked me once when I was seated on my throne. I told them the powers of righteousness in my old universe told one daughter from me for every two that I gave birth to and in turn, I took 3000 of Eve's babies. "He takes, I take." Hence, my 3000 daughters represent 9,000 spirits. Anyway that was so many years ago. We now walk down the path and into the light. We are immediately taken by demons. They bind us and rush as back to their throne. I now think this will be better and will destroy more demons. We are now in what appears to be a king's seat. I am bound while Agyagosszergény's left arm is being held by a beam of green light and she is slightly off the floor. I am tied with my hands above my head and bound by two green lights behind me. I guess this is to impress us as the mystery is killing me. I thus yell out, "Who are you?" The voice said, "We are all one, united in all things, as what one sees all see." I then said, "Your power is week if only your eyes are united." The voice thundered back, "We are united in all things. Why do you come here?" I then said, "We have been sent by a Queen of an Empire in another universe to bring back a prisoner called Atlantis. She has done much evil to our people." The voice now said, "She is a mystery to us also, for we have heard of no evil that she committed." I then said, "I know not how she can be free." The voice said, "She is not free, for she is being kept in torture for not revealing her mother to the throne. Her mother was once a Queen of Demons and pretended to be in the arms of good only to destroy the old throne and killing two of their queens." I then said, "Wow, it would be better for me to be your prisoner than to take a chance on running into such a great force of evil." The voice said, "The throne of good is foolish, for they think she still exists. All demons have searched for her to give back her throne, yet none can find her or evil her army of daughters, save Atlantis since the destruction of the old throne for that galaxy. We sadly know she no longer exists." I then said, "My queen will want to know the names of the two Queens that survived, as she may want to kidnap one of them as punishment in revenge for her daughter's capture." The voice said, "The survivors are Lablonta and Eve, we shall not help you capture them and you should not go into that galaxy for their throne is one of hate and revenge in the falsehood of love. They actually kill or help destroy many more times the flesh than evil does. Evil gets so many new servants from the flesh who wishes to be free from the pain inflicted upon them in the name of righteousness." I looked at him and said, "I believe that may very well be true." The voice said, "I shall release you for I see no threat to you." I then said, "Evil is different in this universe than in mine. They would have tortured me claiming they had caught a Queen for their glory." The voice said, "When we have a Queen we shall do that, yet since all know and see this none would believe such a lie. We see and hear and smell and taste as one." I then spoke in a questioning voice tone, "You mean they hear my voice now?" The voice spoke again saying, "They hear your voice, yet love evil more than the weakness of a female, especially ones too poor to have garments." I then said, "I hear a thought saying, what is the name of your Queen?" The voice then replied, "I heard no such thing, you females are all so strange, no wonder so many of the male flesh beg to serve us to be free from the bonds of their females thus oh by the way, what is your Queen's name." I then said, "My queen has erased her name from my memory yet said, if ones asks tell them your Queen is the aunt of Atlantis and a sister of LILITH." The entire galaxy shook as all evil was immediately destroyed. Lucky for us, they were not interwoven with it. The green lights released Agyagosszergény as she rushed to me untying my hands with a shocked look on her face. My baby told me, "Mommy, I can feel the total absence of evil here. Did you not say that your daughters can use your name in the battle against evil?" I rested my hands on her shoulder and said, "Yes, all my babies can. You shall never fear evil again, it is the righteous that we must fear." We then scanned for our ship, which we finally found, and back to it, we did go in peaceful fashion. We could see a few of the planets as the confusion was erased with the help of our ship's homing device. Now we are entering the atmosphere at a much slower speed thanks to the gravity and my ship is below us. It will be nice to rest on it for a while. I always enjoy a break after destroying an evil force, as this is my first break in a short while. The smell of these trees as now the ending is filled with the fresh glow of planetary light from its source star. Now my team has started returning, so I will take that break another time. As they prepared to give me their briefing I spoke first saying, "They only have the Queens Lablonta and Eve plus Atlantis is being held somewhere around the throne for her loyalty to me." They all looked at me in somewhat amazement, as I said, "Am not I your goddess and number one servant of your master?" They answered, "Yes, yet the new throne has no Queens as both Lablonta and Eve resigned. Lablonta went back to King James and Eve went back to Adam. They are now to be judged for disputing a decision made by their throne. Atlantis is guarded solidly as so many demons are trying to take her prisoner." I said, "The demons do not want to take her prisoner. They wish to give her my throne and to rule until my return. I was once the Queen of Evil in this universe." The army members now asked, "How do you know about these things?" I then told them that my baby "Agyagosszergény and I were captured by demons in this peaceful place you put us in and these demons did take us to their headquarters in this galaxy and put us on trial. I told them I was sent by the Queen of another galaxy to capture Atlantis and bring her back for her crimes. They told me that she was being held by the righteous for the transgressions of the erased Lilith. They did not worry about me being a threat since no one can capture Atlantis. In addition, both of the only remaining Queens (Lablonta and Eve) had resigned as queens and were currently in protection awaiting trials. I can tell you that even though I have issues with both of these Queens; I have also had special times with them, in Lablonta giving me Atlantis and Eve serving as my mother, not by design but by agreement, on New Venus. I am not going openly to fight for them, as that would cause them the same treatment as Atlantis. I will however make sure the new throne gets a special blast from my ship." The army team reminded me that if we destroy the ship, it would be a long trip back as I might have to avoid the vortex or portal without the ship's protection. I would however be able to load a space vehicle "borrowed from another galaxy" camouflaged as a peace envoy packed with our special diodes to level the new throne. I do like a staff that when they tell me I cannot do something they tell me why and how we can make it an alternative way. These guys are the best ever. I now asked them about what they discovered. They told me that, "Even though Lablonta and King James know, they are banned from telling their surviving flesh Empire. Your saints were able to discover the memory spirits who hold these memories and to pull copies of these memories into their storage banks. With your permission, we wish to show them to the current King, The King James (989,774). The saints did not make contact with King James or Lablonta as their spirits are very much protected and the souls monitored. That is a one way trip down and an immediate stop to our mission." I told them, "You did well. Continue." They have now focused on Atlantis saying, "Atlantis is being held captive in a distant secure part of the Milky Way's center. We know where she is by tracing your spiritual coding and matching it with hers. It will take a hard fight to get her. We recommend that we have one team to blast the new throne while the other team frees her. The blasting team will exit in our space warships "life boat" and will meet you at the Portal. If there is any delay, you will get out and we will escape through the pathway you established ending your penance. We will have a rescue Army to help us get out since; if the old throne is leveled effectively then no charges will be against us making us innocents trying to return to our dimension, which does qualify for protection. Your team will have some hard fighting; however, we do expect and project many sympathizers considering the release of knowledge that King James and their only Supreme Queen are being held captive along with Eve. The Empire has always claimed a bond with as she did marry one of their native sons and you are trying to save the mother of a Child Empire born from Mempire. We have requested that Mempire begin rescue operations in the underwater cities of Atlantis. They can do most of this underwater and under the radar. The stations will be reprogrammed with some of our special data feeds that will keep it hustling and bustling. The only thing missing will be the daughters. We may send in rescue forces for humanitarian reasons based on their throne's pattern of mistreatment of their top mother spirit. We will put a good show on by first showing our intent in saving the girls is legit. Your spirits are preparing that now, which will show them the greatness of your Empire of Good, and your right to save the flesh of your living daughters. However, for this part you will be on your throne and your courts working as you so command. Of course, the daughters leaving are being video streamed to all their holding ports in Mempire and their arrivals in the new cities under the sea that you have prepared for them. If anything at any time places you and Agyagosszergény in danger, we will get you out. You will be able to fight another day and we hope to have all the evidence we need to petition for a legal war. We will launch operations as soon as we load up the 'life boat' and stage some satellite planets as additional launch sites. We want our reign of destruction to hit hard the first time, and to continue to hit in a scattered range destroying those who try to escape. We are waiting for the saints to return from Mempire. They are doing some manifestations in various non-Christian temples to get the masses excited about the "Return of the Queen of Good to save Atlantis." Two are now doing manifestations on the planet that Atlantis is on, declaring that, "Justice shall soon be here." The natives will consider that to mean that Atlantis will soon be taken to judgment. Oh, what a surprise they will receive. The spirits have just told me that the underwater cities are being by sympathetic spirits and told of their great salvation shall soon be, as Mempire will take them to their temporary sanctuary before going to the greatest Empire of Good. In addition, you will know when to start your team's mission begins when you see a giant explosion followed by another wider spraying pattern of utter destruction. That will put the planet's security forces in disarray and give you a chance to spray another smaller pattern over the planet. Then your saints will take you for a head on battle to get Atlantis. They will determine immediately if she is to offer resistance and if so, they will put her spirit into soul rest and bring her to you." I then said to me, "Army spirit, as all others were now making preparations, you have all done such a wonderful job in making this mission a great success. Our master will be so proud of you for serving his number on servant so faithfully." His spirit glowed as he quickly made his preparations. This is so hard for me just to wait as I can now start to feel my spiritual powers are beginning to weaken. This concealing our activity as it is now in so many places is draining me, however they

Army and the courts are now in their 'life boat' as we all of a sudden are met with a strange powerful royal god warship heading straight for my assault team. This is too close for comfort and I must attack now and keep them safe. Too much is at risk and my spirit flashes before the ship as I am met by a messenger towing the ship. I ask, "Who are you and why are you here?" The messenger said, "I am a servant to the god of the universe in which you destroyed all the demons. He wishes for your team to travel better than in your 'life boat'. He wishes you to accept this, as he will be helping you camouflage your activities as he senses your powers weakening. He will help you if needed, to tell your victory is yours, and he someday shall visit your great Empire of Good and worship you. He will go to war to insure this does take place. May we help you?" I told him, "I really could use your help now, especially if this throne's outer armies deploy. I will have my master bless your god once his penance is served." The messenger, now speaking for his god said, "I had heard your Empire was great yet did not know you are a penance Empire as we have only heard of such things. No throne in this universe has ever been offered penance. Your army and courts and your special threats to your hostile throne are now rushing to complete their mission. I now have one million of my armies invading the Milky Way now, from the opposite side of your expedition to help create a diversion and force this throne to pull in its forces, feeding your special treats and excellent meal. I shall depart, and will be watching and helping you especially on your retreat to your guarded and protected portal." I sincerely thanked him, as this is the time I need some help. Then our ship rocked and spun and flipped and did everything except break as we looked out and saw an explosion as never before seen. I knew that all in this section of the universe either saw this or felt it. My boys have started the war. Next, as they had told me another greater series of massive universe shaking explosions shattered all solar systems in that sector. The saints had told Mempire to announce a Milky Way border simulated battle and had moved their people and equipment away from the destruction. I had never seen so much power released that it could not explode together and had to branch out over so many light years to explode sideways. The light is so packed on the inside that it is white and as it spreads, it is able to feed on enough matter to take its color. I had no idea that Criliton diodes were that powerful, yet what is even better is that we only used two-thirds of them in these bangs and my courts with our army team know how to use them on enemy forces trailing behind. We are now bombarding this planet and destroying their launched primitive ships to meet us. This planet will not exist after I have my daughter on board my warship. The planet is taking a serious beating now, however we do not need to worry about the flesh forces except that they alert any dormant defensive spirit cells who could spell disaster yet I have another unexpected ally. The evil forces in this galaxy are rushing in to enjoy the fresh kill and opportunities. We have now isolated the spirits guarding Atlantis as my divine powers can trip them up better. I can now see her spirit and I do not like what I see. The evil of this righteous throne has made her spirit into a spirit flesh blended shell in order to get maximum pain in the tortures. I think that as we enter my portal, I will send the other ship back to the section where the new throne was and do another blast to make sure they suffer a quadrillion (10^{15}) times more than Atlantis did. All of a sudden, tons of unexpected spiritual forces are surrounding us. My ship is barely holding on as I am trying to send some pop shots out at them for little effect. They must have planned for me to attempt a rescue. To be so close as to see Atlantis's spirit and then have to abort my mission and make a mad run for the portal is so frustrating. I am fighting hard now, slinging every dirty thing that I can at them. We are also sending messages to the demons in the area that some throne's forces are available for their enjoyment without a support force to back them. This is clearly a time for me to rise and shine, yet I do not know how bright my light will be. Then I receive a welcome surprise. My Army and courts are here, they are releasing an array of Criliton individual diodes with spirit tracking devices, and they are popping these spirits left and right. In addition, the god of the neighboring galaxy has massive forces deployed to help pluck away at the now dwindling massive defense force. We are now all back in my warship and have to neighbors warship loaded and heading back to whatever is left over in the old throne's area. This is for a precautionary raid in order to give us more time to get to my portal. Now my combined team is ready for the rescue. They are proceeding to her prison cavern deep inside the planet not far from the core. We must get there fast before her climate control units are disabled. She would not be destroyed if they were disabled, however she would burn, and I do not want her to suffer because of me. The teams are meeting resistance and are employing the spirit zappers with my power in them. Only a god can zap a spirit and I want these resisters vanished forever. Do not want a nuisance that may turn into a thorn later. The king is now warning us that major armies are on their way for a fight. He also has additional armies arriving to meet them. My Army team now suggests that I devote some of the Criliton diodes to zapping them. That is a good idea and since the neighboring king is handling the concealment functions, I can release more of my power into these Criliton diodes and zap the approaching armies. I just have the feeling the more I erase now, the better I will be in the future. A revenge raid could be on the horizon and in the distant horizon when I am off guard as they would not have a portal and thus would have to move their armies through other universes, which would take offense to this. I now have my first vision of Atlantis and this is not good. She has suffered great spiritual punishment yet appears to have remained loyal to me although I do not know what reasons precipitated this loyalty I am sure she will tell me. I am now going to make a normal spiritual light shell, which will remove a lot of her pain or the perception of it. The god of the neighboring galaxy or Adorjás has agreed to take her old flesh mingled suit and have her guided warship head towards a very hostile galaxy about two weeks away. The ship will have the Milky Way emblem, which should cause some hostile revenge after this ship fires upon their throne. The more that fight against this disbanded throne the better off I shall be. We have her loaded and we are now heading for my portal. The Army team is scanning to make sure no hidden tracking devices are implanted in her spirit and that no dormant cells have been embedded. A righteous throne is a dangerously evil throne when it comes to war. The saints are working on her spiritual awareness defects and trying to restore what has been blocked by the tormenting throne. My courts have searched every possible record to determine if she did anything wrong. She has been found to be innocent, as even my intense divine scans attest. This has been a serious wrong, and they did not expect to get the surprise I gave them. She is now walking around my giant ship regaining control over her spirit. I have given her flesh to help her focus and recover. I shall now go and find her and thus remove any unnecessary mistrust or anxiety, as I know she has suffered so much. When she sees me, she cries out while bracing her weak body, "Who goes there?" I answer, "I am your mother the great Goddess Queen Lilith, member of the Council of Nykøbing Mors and the holder of the Sword of Justice and number one servant of the master who holds the Sword of Freedom and the Books of the Gyor-Moson-Sopron." She then answers, "My mother no longer exists as she was destroyed after her attack on the old throne." I replied, "How do you know such a lie?" Atlantis answers, "For the powers of the demons whom she rules told me so." I then fired back, "How do they know?" She then answered, "My mother was a demon and never a goddess." I continued, "That is true for this dying universe but not for the one my great empire is in, can a demon rule saints? Speak into my small band of saints as we rush back to my universe." Atlantis, then questioned, "I cannot leave for someone must protect my children under the sea." This left the door open for me to question, "Who was caring for your children while you were being held prisoner? What crime did you commit?" She told me, "I know not what my children are doing now and I did commit no crime except for being the daughter of my mother whom they wanted." I continued, "Your children are being held by Mempire in highly protected places for fear that the evil throne would harm them. Why would they punish you for hiding a mother that does not exist?" Atlantis continued, "I feel so sad that Lablonta and Eve are to stand judgment for my secret, for I do not want this terrible throne to know about my mother. I get more joy in their fear of her attacking the throne someday again." I then told Atlantis, "They also wish to hold your father King James, yet he stands strong beside Lablonta and Eve. That which you are punishing throne feared, did happen. The new throne is no more and this time I got the escapees and many of their armies. I also have Adorjás, the god of your neighboring empire to monitor a very slow rebuilding." My daughter now asked, "Who is the one that stands behind me and why did you return to save me if you have such a great Empire?" I told her, "The one who stands behind you is your sister Agyagosszergény one of 3000 sisters who now live with me. All my daughters live with my saints in their thousands of heavens. I saved you for what mother of 3000 daughters would not rejoice at saving the one which was lost?" I must now go and prepare the portal or star gate that we are going to pass through to get home. Your sister will guide you and help you know the teams that worked so hard to save you, as by inter-universal law we could have been damned for eternity if we failed." The saints were showing her Mempire delivering the sea daughters to the special portals that Tompaládony had provided for them to take to their new homes. They told her how, "These girls would be given bodies that neither hunger nor get ill. They will also be able to survive under the great pressures of the ocean without becoming dysfunctional and can survive without air. Death in stations will be outdated, as they can exit to another station in a flash. Atlantis asked them, "Why is she doing so much for me? One of the courts answered, "You are blood of her blood. That which she has she gives to those who have her blood in them to flourish and receive great blessings. The power of your empire will be magnified by thousands as also being the only Empire to reign inside her Empire." The nice thing about being divine is that you know what others are saying especially on your ship. Anyway, now is the time for me to get us home. My portal is open and in we go at full speed. I now must slow this ship down and let the portal pull. The slowdown is implemented and the pull is in control. I am now sensing other forces following me. I will deploy my emergency beacons that will transmit my name through all frequencies in the event evil is following us. I have declared the throne I just destroyed also to be of evil and it they would be zapped if in my portal. The zapping is happening now as some of their vessels are now flying out of control. My portal is disintegrating on my entry opening and the ripples are waving towards my ship. I have flashed my ship into super turbo hydro warp as I am heading for my exit. My courts and army teams are with me now as we our senses are picking up our exit. The question remains, can I make it there as the portal is drifting sideways forcing me to move in a V leg pattern, which is taking more time. The sides of my ship are now as molten liquid as my powers are fighting hard to hold it together. She was not built, as was nothing ever so far built to withstand this speed. The thing that saves us is the lack frictional forces in this tunnel. The countdown is on, thirty seconds to exit, and now slowly twenty seconds. We are very close now. Ten seconds and the portal are rapidly deteriorating. As the portal is crashing, we feel a clamp like force grip our ship and pull it sideways. I wonder why we are flying sideways back into the empty portal. Then about five seconds later, we feel ourselves shooting into my Empire and a titanic army waiting. They have my call sensor, yet I wonder how they got so deep into my portal. My courts now tell me that our mission is finished. We are home. I ask them, "What about our sideways flight?" They explain we were actually being pulled up out of the portal, it was the portal that was unstable and moving the matter sideways. Since we were clamped, we went straight out the side of the crippled portal. My courts immediately advise me to release the armies to help get the daughters to their new homes and out of the Milky Way. I order that to be so. The rush is on as I now depend upon Adorjás and Mempire to get the girls in ships and into the many portals, we have open. Adorjás is amazed at these portals, having never even dreamed of such a thing that can bypass universes and plug into a very distant universe. I cannot give them this technology for fear that it ends up in the wrong hands. I now have the Council of the Saints to show Atlantis her flesh daughters being planted in their new cities, which are so much more advanced than the cities they left behind. They each are also equipped with a massive military arsenal and discovery vessels. One city will exist in a galaxy with their instantaneous transports moving them as fast as them going to any of the 1,000 floors on each ship. Their cities are portable, thus they can move them to any planet or solar system they so desire actually anywhere in their host galaxy. They are under the protection of my armies who will provide any support they need. Atlantis was now visiting one of the cities as her children of the flesh were moving in. She was so over moved with joy as continued to ask the saints, "Why is she doing this for us?" They told her, "You are her daughter and she can now give you and all that you have a wonderful safe world ruled by good in her Empire of now over 60,000 galaxies. We have an emergency that requires our armies to rush back into the Milky Way to save your daughters and Mempire from the attacked renegade throne armies. We may not enter unless you declare sanctuary here and then we can bring all that you want here." Atlantis said, "I declare sanctuary" and the universe did rumble as a mighty voice said, "Lilith save the children of Atlantis and protect Mempire. Let no more blood spill." Atlantis now asked, "Who is that who speaks?" The saints told her, "That is the god of our dimensions or for you to understand better of many universes. They have the ultimate power and they do very much love your mother." Atlantis now said, "That is good." The saints now feed her some streams showing the heavens. The host saint said to her, "We have thousands of heavens spread throughout the Empire as any saint may go to any heaven at will. We are now pulling your departed saints, which were removed from your old throne's heavens to your great benefit, for that heaven no longer exists. We now have armies of saints commanded by your sisters dedicated to getting every soul out and into the greatest eternal resting place ever known in all the heavens." Atlantis keeps now saying, "I remember the horrifying day when my father and Lablonta, they only mother I ever had known told me that the Lord of New Venus was my mother. I feared her as being too high above me to want me. Then she vanished and I had no mother. The only thing I had was her memory of being good and that I could not, even if I lost all give up. It was something that had to hold on to the glory of a lord of an entire planet, yet now I wonder how many planets serve her?" The saints told her forty quintillion planets worship her and each planet has thousands of temples, each with an angel in it." Atlantis asked "First, what is a quintillion and second why an angel in each temple and lastly who made these beautiful things under the ocean." The saints started by saying a one billion is 10^9 one quintillion is 10^{18} and second, our goddess demands that our flesh servants be given a personal visible spiritual experience to reduce any suffering. Our servants were given to us to love and not to watch suffer. Lilith has demanded that all the gods of the galaxies make their ocean floors perfect for you." Atlantis, then questioned, "Are the galaxies ruled only by the gods and not any goddesses?" The saint then told her, "There were once six goddesses namely Bárdudvarnok, Tamási, Békéscsaba, Ceglédbercel, Dédestapolcsány, Jakabszállás who are beseeching to be personal servants to your mother as they now dwell in the Royal Deities Sanctuary with the other disciples your mother has approved." Atlantis now asked a personal question, "Why are my mother and sister naked and why do I have such little clothing?" The saints answered, "Your mother believes in sharing all she has and hiding nothing from her servants. She has the power to go free from the chains of clothing as even our master had approved it before she agreed to be his number one servant." Atlantis was still filled with more questions than our universe had stars and asked the saints, "Before she agreed to be his number one servant?" The saints told her, "That is the same as married for the flesh, yet gods do not marry, they pledge their service to each other." The current station was now receiving their new tenants and a smooth transition it was as they appeared through beams of light in their new bodies. The courts now invited Atlantis to the throne for a briefing on how the resettlements were going. They showed her how the flesh daughters were moving quickly to their new homes and how the saints were entering the heavens. She also saw visual streams of Adorjás's armies, fighting to remove any threats to Mempire, and how so many were being resettled in his galaxy. He was actually transporting the residents, and pulling the planets in his galaxy and placing them in good orbits throughout his galaxy. Mempire would once again be restored to the glory it once had. Adorjás was glad to have such an Empire is roaming through his galaxy as it offered a better quality of life for those who lived among them. Atlantis was now very happy, for she had protected a faith that she did not see or know still live. She had held on to the faith that her mother was good and for anyone to attempt to tell her different was evil and not her friend. Even while thinking I was dead and no longer existed she defended my name and a name that was not very popular in that throne. She will be busy for a while as she is getting to know how to manage her new empire's locations. Her flesh daughters have so much more breathing room now and such a better life. They no longer had to leave the stations, except for recreation and curiosity, a trait inbred through me. Their transportation now was completely through Vasvári beams which was instantaneously anywhere in the Empire. The service they provided for the Empire was in their deep-sea research, which was now done with equipment advanced by trillions of millennium. Their claim now was "Atlantis, daughter of Lilith and King James." Many saints recommended that they not emphasis the King James part too much as they would get more by saying, "Atlantis daughter of the number one servant of the master." Atlantis agreed and informed her station commanders. These stations now received random visits from the Armies to insure all was okay. The daughters enjoyed having large ships of future fathers visit them. The galaxy gods enjoyed very much having them in their galaxy as it not only promoted more visits by the armies yet also offered advanced warnings of any potential threats entering from the deep space between the galaxies. The pressure of the ocean reacts different to deep space movement by the method in which it is absorbed by the water. Even though it is so trivial, special equipment for these new stations can detect it and report it. Although the technology had known about this phenomenon for millennium, no one wanted to invest the workforce, or plant the equipment to monitor it. Instead, they relied on the unguarded deep space posted warning sensors. Now with Atlantis under the sea, the empire no longer had to take that risk. No need to go out and armies helping to insure safety plus no longer a need to stay concealed. They had the 'do not touch' brand of the highest Queen Goddess to protect them and naturally, the god of the current galaxy would offer additional protection to show he accepted the honor and responsibility for protecting the only other Empire inside our borders. The other Empire was to be independent and actually bound by a higher force and that is by the blood in their veins. This qualified them as the chosen people, yet this favoritism was not flaunted in front of the other flesh, as they lived in the darkest realms of the planet. Most flesh on the planets considered the Empire's armies as practicing some unknown defensive tactic in the most concealed weakest place on their planets. We believed it was better in the flesh on the planets not to know who are what was living at the bottom of the sea for security reasons. A force angry at the throne would see these spotted planets throughout the Empire as easy targets for shots at the throne. Atlantis now asked the saints, "Why are there so many angels around the throne?" The saints revealed to her, "This is the highest throne in the Empire, the place where the master reveals himself." Atlantis, then fired back, "Where is the master, for I do not wish to appear a fool before him or my mother?" The court angels now guided her to the throne telling her, "By the rules of the Council of Nykøbing Mors as written in the Books of the Gyor-Moson-Sopron on the Mountain of the Rødovre the gods of the greatest kingdom of good must prove their power to hold fast to their will to serve all good must live and die a life of penance. He is now serving his penance with one of your aunts helping him." Atlantis surprisingly questioned, "I have aunts, and I do not know them?" The courts told her, "You have many aunts as your mother will introduce you to them. They all live in the Royal Deities Sanctuary and share time on the throne so your mother may do other things that she so desires." The curious Atlantis fed her investigation by asking, "Are all free from the chains of clothing who are in the Royal Deities Sanctuary?" The Court answered,

"All except the Grandmother Queen and Mother Queen and the servants." Atlantis in excitement articulated, "My mother's mother and her mother are here?" The courts pronounced, "No our child, they are the masters, however you may claim them as many of your sisters have already done so." Now the question and answer series received a shocking disturbance. I was pulled up into a mysterious vacuum to where I do not know. All around the throne were puzzled as the armies immediately tried to enter this mystery tunnel that met them with a solid wall and thrust them back like into a bowling ball hitting its pins tumbling them and scattering. This immediately activated the court, lights, and saints to no avail. Disaster had hit as the thrones number one servant to the master had just been sucked into oblivion. Fear and shock waved through the millions of soldiers, saints, and courts in unbelief that this had happened. The court called upon Queen Grandmother Goddess Tompaládony to set upon the throne to show stability. She sat on it as if she had ruled for billions of years which she of course has yet in pleasing the saints who made no such request she gave on orders, "Temporarily on behalf of the thrones number one servant until she rescinds I order . . . ." Many feared that this would be an opportunity for her to take the throne, which may have tempted her before however not now. They have courted advised her that she could declare the throne hers and have it forever. She declared, "To have the throne would not give pleasure for it would be offset by the misery of not having the love of the Queen who paid the penance price for it." This quickly spreads through all the armies and courts and the saints as all relaxed for fear that if the throne lost Lilith they would also lose the sword of justice, her name and her membership on the Council of Nykøbing Mors. I really felt relieved when I later learned of this loyalty. My hard work and love were paying off great dividends for our servants saving them the terrors and misery of a civil war. Actually, as long as they gave me Royal Deities Sanctuary I would not care, however Bogovi would fight to an unusual extent and I would stand beside him. After all, that is what number one servants do. At this time a messenger did appear from the area of the hole in which I had gone through. She was wearing royal garments with a nice jewel hanging over her eyes. Her hair was covered signifying she belonged to something great. As she appeared, everyone got quiet as she looked out among him or her. Her powerful diamonds shined above her beautiful eyes. The simplicity of her royal gown, which fit her to perfection, was magnified by its unity. She stood in the rushing space light waves that surrounded the throne as if standing in a peaceful field on a windless day. Her eyes were dark and had a piercing focus with her smile that only displayed her top perfect teeth. It was a smile of one, who is a deep thinker. Queen Grandmother Goddess Tompaládony stood tall and Revenant as she walked across the throne to speak to this spirit in the sky. As she began to speak the woman rose out her hand with her palm down. Tompaládony immediately bowed and cried out, "Oh mighty one of mercy, how may the Empire of Good serves you this day." When Tompaládony dropped, everyone also dropped. No one knew what was happening; they only knew that if the wise and time-tested Tompaládony were on her knees, it would be a good idea to get on theirs. The messenger now looked to her right as the Six Great Horses of Ancient Council of Nykøbing Mors charged across the sky. Something was happening here, whatever it was the universe, and the ages were supporting it. Tompaládony now cried out again, "Oh great one blessed by the Mountain of the Rødovre how we shall speak your name if we know it's not?" She now spoke with a voice of love and harmony, "I am Pusztaszentlászló the messenger of Gyor-Moson-Sopron." Tompaládony now after waiting through some silence asked again, "Oh Pusztaszentlászló the messenger of Gyor-Moson-Sopron, how may we serve the master of all ever created?" Pusztaszentlászló then answered, "You all may arise, for I am only the messenger and my message for you today may not be good to your ears. Your number one servant has violated the dimensional laws and must stand trial in accordance with the laws in the Books of the Gyor-Moson-Sopron. The great master Gyor-Moson-Sopron has no choice but to put Lilith on trial before his council of ancient elders. Our wise Queen Grandmother Goddess Tompaládony then cried out, "Do not the books also say that she may be represented by any of her ancient elders?" Pusztaszentlászló then answered, "That is true, however Gyor-Moson-Sopron could not find any of her elders who are familiar with the Books of the Gyor-Moson-Sopron." Tompaládony then declared, "He did not look in the right places and thus our number one servant will have no fair representation. Before, I always believed that Gyor-Moson-Sopron was of good and justice." Pusztaszentlászló then declared, "He is the master of all good and justice, do you know of one who is qualified to represent her?" Tompaládony then stood tall and proud saying, "I am that one and it is my will to represent her and if I fail I shall share her punishment." With this statement, Queen Sister Goddess Julia came running out crying, "Do not leave me the mother of my mother for our master will be saddened if you are not here to greet him." Tompaládony now as she held Julia spoke into her ear saying, "The child of my daughter, do you not know how sad he will be if his number one servant is not here? We will return." The courts, saints and Armies all stood in shock having no idea what was going on and the entire throne hung on the words of their wise and time-tested Queen Grandmother Goddess. They all knew she had knowledge of such great things, as she was able to determine the greatness of this messenger even before she spoke. Julia's grandmother motioned for her to return to her sisters and mother. Tompaládony then said, "Pusztaszentlászló I petition for the right to represent one has the same blood as I." We knew not how she could have the same blood until Queen Mother Goddess Julia told all the other goddesses, "Fear not for she does have the blood of Lilith for when we were visiting the temples, one priest asked us if we loved Lilith. We said yes, then he challenged us, "Then as all others in this Empire, will you be showered in the blood of life and love?" We both fell to our knees before a priest, on some distant planet, and were baptized in her loving blood and did worship her. Tompaládony told me that the Empire may only have one master and he may only have one Number One Servant. The thing we do will unite this empire for my grandson and your son. We shall now be dedicated to building for him and not tempted to take from him.

Queen Mother Goddess Julia said as she was removing her clothing, "The wisdom and majesty of Tompaládony will be the cornerstone of this Empire, and I now shall have no shame and shall stand free from all shame and without hiding behind the chains of clothing, with you before the throne. The servants are my masters." The sisters all were so surprised as Julia was so proud of her mother and all the sisters hugged her. Then in a flash Pusztaszentlászló and Tompaládony went up into the same tunnel that I had gone up. The throne now slowly started to speak again, having seen a negotiation based on the ancient established multi-universal law, a law so far above that they even wondered how Tompaládony knew of such things. The lights then answered their questions by telling them that the law and codes of the protocol are in the Books of the Gyor-Moson-Sopron. Tompaládony was very well versed in these books, a knowledge that may have saved the Empire on this day. Tompaládony would be the only one who could save me, yet she also was the only one that could hold the empire together unless a surprise was to take place. The courts now shouted out, "Who is to have the throne now?" The Queen Mother had been terrified when the Honorable Galaxy Goddess Bárdudvarnok and sisters all told her she had to set upon the throne. All the Goddesses now answered, "The mother of our Master Queen Mother Goddess Julia. Then the Honorable Galaxy Goddess Dédestapolcsány continued, "For any who disobey her orders shall face the anger of her son, our master upon his return. Woe, for it would be better that such a traitor never is born for the punishment our master shall unleash. Is there any among you who wish to challenge our mother to her right to hold the throne for her sons return?" The lights then spoke out, "Let all know that our master's mother has the throne upon her selection by the Royal Deities Sanctuary." At this time, all the Goddesses escorted the Queen mother to her throne as she shocked all with her new wardrobe style. All the sisters formed lines in front of her free from the chains of clothing body with her hair hanging down and no massive makeup on her face. They all bowed crying out their loyalty, "We serve the master's mother." The lights now released a massive show of light works as the entire throne worshiped the sitting goddess. The first words that came out of her mouth was, "Let the courts record that I do declare I shall surrender the throne upon the return of my son, his mother or his number one servant. I shall work hard to hold this throne for them." The entire sister goddesses were impressed with her style and comfort consolidating into a new sense of completeness as she sat upon the throne with her legs crossed. She later told the sisters that the servants had not earned the right to see where our master first entered this universe. The lights dazzled around her complement the beauty of her fit body. She was always doing things to help keep her flesh suit looking good and all the sisters, except Fejér who was exceptionally blessed looked upon her with envy and excitement. Fejér looked upon her with great respect because she was doing what they all needed her to do and that was to project royalty worthy of this throne. The courts were now shouting, "In the name of the mother" as the Queen Mother now released a smile and slowly with style moving her head up and down to show approval. Yet in the back of all our minds was the disturbing question, "Where are Lilith and our grandmother?" This question they did not know. The only thing we knew now was that the throne had style and power sitting on it in Queen Mother Goddess Julia. Even the sisters now had a new sense of loyalty to her. She soon got up, walked across the stage in the middle, and asked, "Is there any business that the Empire needs for me to attend to?" The Court answered, "No oh mighty Queen Goddess for that which took two of our Queens is too advanced and powerful by force and law that we can only wait." Queen Mother Goddess Julia now leaned into the holy tent on the throne and vanished with it. Each ruler may have a special way to depart the throne stage. She was well versed in this custom and floated over her servants and slid into the tent, which has an entrance to the goddesses' special chamber. All the sisters were impressed as she floated closer to her servants keeping her head focused on the throne and slid right out. She was now rejoining with her sisters. Fejér gave Julia a big hug and said, "I will set on your throne in your behalf if you so will?" She then told

Fejér, "I can think of no one better to follow me. I thank you for your respect and loyalty." Fejér quickly replied, "My Queen, you have earned it for my fear of the unknown is no more. It is now filled with my faith in you." Fejér now went out and sat on the throne. This was a very common practice for the throne as I most often only appeared with our master and followed him if he so desired." My spirits always helped the one sitting on the throne so my sisters had no fear of failing. A careless mistake while on the throne will cause major disturbances. The immediate appearance of Fejér after the Queen Mother's exit gave the courts comfort in knowing that the Royal Deities Sanctuary was not only verbally supported her but willing to share this massive responsibility. Most of the work now was the ceremonial annexing of so many new galaxies. I always wanted to give the current reigning god a sign of great respect for their decision to give up their independence for the good of their servants. They would also receive celebrations at each throne level in their support network. They were part of something big, however I also wanted them to feel a part of something comprehensible and that if support were needed they would be able to get it, sometimes even being notified that support was needed. I want them to be a part of and not apart from their new Empire. Yet I find myself now apart from my Empire as I had yet to know that Tompaládony would be with me soon. I was now in total darkness and pinned in tight. What can this ran through my mind repeatedly? Could it be a portal from another universe, which snuck in and kidnapped me? I immediately wondered if there would ever be a sense of security, or would it fall into the hands of every lunatic who got hold of a portal. Finally, the darkness turned into light and I could see this strange planet that now had me trapped. I can see a winding gray single path or maybe even some sort of floating bridge, because it is hard to tell if I have a pink field in front of me or it could be a pink calm lake. The two main pink trees that I see now look so sad as if they were weeping. Nothing moves in this place, not even the branches on the trees and especially me. I still do not know why I am here and where here is. I now scream out, "Who are the evil ones who brought me here?"

No response. My luck, would to be captured by weaklings who not are too afraid or stupid to talk. I do believe this silence and mystery is enough to drive a spirit crazy. I wonder where my spirits are now with all that massive power they have. They are probably wondering why I have not been giving them any orders. The courts have most likely told them by now and they are responding, "We did not know that." I will have to have my Lights figure some way to make them smarter. That will prove to me that miracles can still happen. As I think back on my recent briefings, I do believe that my Armies and lights told me that no portals could kidnap any one from our Empire. I would have hoped that I would be included in that 'anyone'. Now a small section of the field in front of me opened allowing surface from below to rise up before me. The surface has a few little patches of green and some bare trees covered by fog behind. I could see dead vegetation along with some small dirt walls. Then appeared a red haired woman dressed in a low front cut armless light blue gown. She had strange vein filled wing the even draped in small threads along her arm onto the leg part of her gown. She had two shoes and it looked as if some flowers were growing from her head and out of her privates. Her head was tilted to her left as a few strands flowed across her right breast. I asked her, "What is your name stranger?" She then replied, "My name is Heves and I am not a stranger here as you are. I do know your name to be Lilith." I then looked at her and said, "It has been a while since one has only called me Lilith." She quickly responded, "For here you are only a powerless criminal awaiting to be judged." I now in anger replied, "How can I be a powerless criminal when I have done no crime?" Heves then responded also in anger, "The Judges have accused you, and thus you are guilty and shall be punished severely for the remainder of your eternity. They searched for one qualified to represent you, yet could find none. You will wear your flesh during your trial and you will burn thus showing you are evil. Do you know of one who could defend you?" I answered, "You said that the judges could find none qualified. How is one qualified?" Heves answered, "They must have your blood in them and know the Books of the

Gyor-Moson-Sopron. Do you have any blood relatives you know the Books of the Gyor-Moson-Sopron? Do you know the books I speak of?" I retorted, "I know about the books you speak of yet I cannot think of a relative who would know them." Heves then answered, "That proves you are guilty you wicked criminal. I shall enjoy chewing on your burn flesh as your spirit goes into eternal punishment." Then in a twisting windy flash did a familiar face appear in the pink lake before us. The face was so familiar and as the wind calmed and the blue from the sky reappeared I could see this strong face and cried out, "Oh Tompaládony, how did you know where I was?" She told me, "I petition to Gyor-Moson-Sopron to permit me to represent you in your forthcoming trial." Heves looked at me and asked, "How can you be qualified to represent her as Gyor-Moson-Sopron searched all who are qualified and found none. You are a liar and shall be punished with this wicked crime." Tompaládony then said, "Gyor-Moson-Sopron made a mistake and is no longer perfect." Heves screamed out, "That is blaspheme and proves you are evil and must be punished." Tompaládony then said, "It proves you are wrong and thus evil and must be punished." Heves yelled out, "Oh great Gyor-Moson-Sopron, I beg that you take these criminals now to be judged, for they deserve not the right to be free and must be judged accordingly. With the saying of Heves' words, we both were yanked off the small desolate planet a now appeared in a dark stormy space cloud. Tompaládony now stood ahead of me to my right. I stood on the other side of a scattered and frayed white light that divided us. Then did one appear before us, a mighty warrior female. Her hair was perfect as were her firm legs and crossed arms. She actually looked like a goddess as her belt and neckband matched with small silver bars above and below and solid black that ran in the middle. She had three identical large round gemstones with a pair of horns on their tops. She also had a red coat drape on her back. Her eyes were sharp, and her smile extremely serious as if to ask, "Why are you wasting my time?" She began by saying, "I am the senior goddess of our court as you Lilith are to appear today for judgment of your criminal acts of forbidden war and you Tompaládony for blasphemy. How do you plead to your charges Tompaládony?" Tompaládony fired back, "I committed no blasphemy. I only spoke the truth. Gyor-Moson-Sopron did not search for a qualified representative of my god."

Iris: How can she be your goddess when you were the mightiest goddess of a great empire trillions of millenniums before her birth?

Tompaládony: I worship her as my only god and I have surrendered all for her mercy to allow me to serve as her slave for eternity.

Iris: I cannot believe you would belittle yourself to such a low position.

Tompaládony: It is forward a low position, for to kiss her feet and enjoy her walking upon me is a glory beyond my greatest dreams.

Iris: How can you say the greatest god ever Gyor-Moson-Sopron has not searched righteously for a representative for the demon you worship?

Tompaládony: She who calls my god a demon is my enemy. You are my enemy and after this trial, you will stand in my court, which is a real court and not a joke as this one.

Iris: Do you have proof that a qualified representative who meets the criteria as set forth in the Books of the Gyor-Moson-Sopron?

Tompaládony: I do know a qualified representative.

Gyor-Moson-Sopron: Tompaládony, tell me who is more qualified that may give Lilith representation, before I punish her, for her wicked deeds.

Tompaládony: I am she; as if you would have listened to your messenger Pusztaszentlászló, you would have known this.

Gyor-Moson-Sopron: She told me, yet I do not know how you can contest that Lilith has your blood in her.

Tompaládony: Then scan it both now and before she committed your false crime and you will see that the blood codes in her spirit and flesh are the same as mine. As I was born as you say trillions of millenniums before her birth then she must have been born from one that came from my womb. Do you not think a mother can know who her babies are? Your foolishness in the knowledge of women has produced idiot goddesses such as Iris.

Gyor-Moson-Sopron: I have run the scans as you advised me to. I do not understand how she is a child from one who came from your womb, yet the scans support your claim. Lilith is from your seed and as I have known for so long, you are a master at my books so you may represent your criminal child.

Tompaládony: I am surprised that you do not know your books, for your books say that one is innocent until the evidence proves them guilty.

Gyor-Moson-Sopron: I have the evidence.

Tompaládony: Yet according to your books, one is innocent until you prove them guilty and the accused has a chance to prepare a defense for such ridiculous charges.

Gyor-Moson-Sopron: The charges are very serious and if any other had committed them, I would have cast them into my lake of fire immediately. Since Lilith holds our prestigious Sword of Justice and is a member of the Council of Nykøbing Mors.

Tompaládony: As a member are not they entitled to be here with her.

Gyor-Moson-Sopron: Pusztaszentlászló, summon the Council of Nykøbing Mors.

Gyor-Moson-Sopron: Lilith how do you plead to your charges?

Lilith: I know not the charges you have accused me.

Gyor-Moson-Sopron: Iris, read the charges for Lilith's last trial.

Tompaládony: Gyor-Moson-Sopron why do you not play by the rules written in your books?

Gyor-Moson-Sopron: Which rule do you speak?

Tompaládony: You may not speak of the accused being guilty until you pronounce them as such, nor may you make comments that imply that they shall be penalized until the punishment part of the tribulation.t part of the trial.

Iris: Lilith, you are accused of raiding another universe. You are accused of destroying their throne without due cause or reason to believe risk or danger would befall you if the throne were to capture you for a wrongful raid. You also accused of taking from that universe servants who did not wish to leave. You are accused of disobeying a direct command not to enter the other universe. Lastly, you are accused of not knowing you were committing a crime. How do you plead?

Tompaládony: We plead not guilty of all charges.

Gyor-Moson-Sopron: Speak now Lilith.

Lilith: I did not raid another universe. I went there to save my daughter who was being tortured, while being knowingly innocent. Her wrongful punishment resulted in their number one flesh Empire called Mempire to contest the wrongful capture. The remaining two Heavenly Angels are responsible for ensuring righteousness to resign in protest. That throne had armies searching for me to take away my freedom. The capture of the innocent one I spoke of being to bait a trap for me. I took no one who did not want to leave. You did not order me not to invade, you merely informed me of the risks involved. I know not of a crime being committed as I committed no crimes.

Tompaládony: We protest wrongful accusations.

Council of Nykøbing Mors: We request a suspension of this trial until we can completely scan the accused actions.

Gyor-Moson-Sopron: I grant the temporary suspension and shall review the scans.

Tompaládony: I declare it unlawful for you to be burning the flesh of Lilith, whom our Iris or Pusztaszentlászló declared to be just as guilty before this court as Lilith does.

Council of Nykøbing Mors: We also declare it wrong for you to burn flesh that you did not create that has not been declared guilty. We are surprised that such actions would befall on of our members who has worked so hard in defeating evil and is building an empire of good that shall soon be worthy of eternal rest in our realm. Did she destroy all the evil that you must now destroy good?

Iris: Council of Nykøbing Mors you may not speak to Gyor-Moson-Sopron in such a manner.

Council of Nykøbing Mors: Gyor-Moson-Sopron have you not informed you dinky Iris of our power nor do you wish for us to exile you from joining us in your not too distant future?

Gyor-Moson-Sopron: Iris, they have such a right. I shall now represent myself seeing that the Council of Nykøbing Mors wish to join this trial.

Council of Nykøbing Mors: And should we not join a council member who is being accused by one who is not a council member?

Gyor-Moson-Sopron: You should. We shall now recess for a short period.

It felt so good not being burned as the pain was making it so hard for me to concentrate. It was a stinky burn, which had all the pain from a burn, yet the flesh was not destroyed. On my way out of this burning storm, I received a surprise wink from Pusztaszentlászló. I winked back and smiled at her since she was the one who got the Council here. She had to petition in my favor as they arrived knowing about as much as I did. I asked my grandmother who she was and she told me that Pusztaszentlászló was the one who sent her here. Thus, we did owe her a debt of gratitude. I can tell by looking at her eyes and the way she avoids Iris that she is on my side. I cannot wait to get back at Iris if there is a way I can, yet I must also accept that she is doing as she is ordered. I actually think I would like to have her hanging around my throne for a little female punch. I guess it goes one-step at a time. The council is now calling Tompaládony and me to appear with them. As we walk in I ask my special Tompaládony, "How did you pull off that your blood was on me?" She told me something that totally shocked me, "You are my goddess, as the Queen Mother who also worships you. I received your showers of blood from one of your priests in your temple. Thus, your blood is in me meaning the blood is identical in us. Since I am the senior, it was easy to convince them that you were from my seed. That gave me the right to represent you according to the books that your lights and courts are slowly working. I hope that the one I shall worship and serve for my eternity is pleased with the way I am representing you. I so wish that I had strength to be nude and have the power of freedom, yet unlike the Queen Mother who is holding your throne is sitting free from the chains of clothing among all I have too great a fear, yet I would go free from the chains of clothing if you were to command me." I told her, "Tompaládony, I feel I am unworthy of your worship and should worship you as you are so perfect in so many ways and a much wiser goddess than I. You need not walk free from the chains of clothing around my throne, however a little more participation in our Royal Deities Sanctuary would be of great value for all of us, as we share and surrender while serving each other. I marvel at how you are representing me today, as I believe if you were not I would be facing an eternity of torture now. You are my heart and hope now. I love you so much." We now appeared with the council as they had comfortable seats for us to sit in. They began by asking me,

Council of Nykøbing Mors: Lilith, why did you go into your previous throne?

Lilith: I went to save my righteous daughter from wrongful confinement for a crime she did not commit. She had to be freed along with her flesh servants.

Council of Nykøbing Mors: We are now looking at the scans and puzzled why Gyor-Moson-Sopron has not seen this. We are also scanning your attack and searching for any reason you may have felt you were in danger.

Lilith: One reason I was in fear was the warning from Gyor-Moson-Sopron, which left no confusion. In addition, my courts have many records of threat from that rebuilt throne. Moreover, the massive armies they had stationed around a beaten and burning helpless woman proves they were setting traps for me.

Council of Nykøbing Mors: Our scans are verifying what you have said. We are collecting the reports from your courts now and reviewing them.

- 263 -

Tompaládony: I fail to understand why Gyor-Moson-Sopron has not done this search.

Council of Nykøbing Mors: The Books of the Gyor-Moson-Sopron may require that he prosecute without favor to the accused. The rules are simple; the accused waits for the accuser to prove guilt. A quick muscle on a confused defendant many times provides the proof or confession. A very simple, did they do it, and then punishment.

Lilith: It is not simple when the accuser allowed the accused to commit the questionable act.

Pusztaszentlászló: Lilith and honorable quests, our master is ready to resume the hearing.

Council of Nykøbing Mors: Oh precious and lovely Pusztaszentlászló, please tell your master we are putting together our solid defense and should in a few short hours.

Pusztaszentlászló: As you so wish such fine and honorable guests.

She once again smiles at all of us and gracefully departs.

Council of Nykøbing Mors: Lilith, I do believe you have a new fan.

Lilith: And that co-member, a set of ears and mouth to have as an ally as much as she says, and how she feels is visible to Gyor-Moson-Sopron.

Tompaládony: I believe she loves you as all here do.

Council of Nykøbing Mors: We now have the scanned reports and are ready to argue. Tompaládony, stand beside our Lilith and we shall defend her. We must be able to detect if evil is confusing Gyor-Moson-Sopron. Thus, we will begin by arguing that the trial be heard by all people and things in this sector and when we have verified that all can hear we will ask the accused to stand and identify herself. At this time, you are to stand Lilith and say your name. We will use the power of your name to destroy any evil around the throne. Now let us begin our battle to bring you home our fair Queen. Thus, we all entered the trial clouds. This time the clouds were peaceful as was the calm wind. We all found special places for us; however, Tompaládony left her position and sat in a cloud to my right. We had not told Pusztaszentlászló nor had any intention to get her in any trouble so we all just acted, as it was normal and kept our satisfied smiles on our faces.

Pusztaszentlászló: Oh great members before the court, the wrongful charges for the wronging of the great Tompaládony must be seated with honor. Court spirits, prepare a place for Tompaládony beside the mother of all Lilith.

Council of Nykøbing Mors: Pusztaszentlászló, you could not have known as we only announced this change among ourselves prior to exiting our chambers. You have performed honorably as we are all very satisfied.

Gyor-Moson-Sopron: This is not good that you talk to each other in terms to make yourselves happy, for soon you may have tears as this criminal, before us, is judged and punished.

Council of Nykøbing Mors: We protest that you do not address the ACCUSED by her name, for she is a Queen Goddess and number one servant to her Empires master. You will show more respect or we will ban you to exile and curse this throne. You will obey your laws or destroy them. This innocent victim of your foolishness shall address herself now with the dignity her Empire and this council. Come forth and introduce yourself of great innocent one. (I thus went before the court and introduced myself.)

Lilith: I am the great Goddess Queen . . . Court . . . all can hear you have heard your evil speaking of me.

Pusztaszentlászló: Yes my goddess. I have petitioned that all shall hear the name of my new goddess. (This sent a wave through the throne as all now rushed to hear the new name that shall forever be written down in the highest of glories. Pusztaszentlászló walked with me as we hugged and she said to me, "The show is yours now Queen, as I believe you will save us.)

Lilith: I am the great Goddess Queen LILITH member of the Council of Nykøbing Mors and holder of the Sword of Justice and number one servant to the master who holds the Sword of Freedom and the Books of the Gyor-Moson-Sopron. I looked around and could see no changes, as I now believed our gamble had failed and now it was time for plan B. Then I noticed some strange rumblings behind the throne as Gyor-Moson-Sopron immediately declared a recess for twelve hours. Pusztaszentlászló and Iris departed with him. We grouped together and tried to run scans yet could get no information. We noticed that many of the dark clouds were gone and it appeared that more light was getting in. The council attributed that to Gyor-Moson-Sopron trying to remove his apparent prejudice against this case. We were blocked from all contact so to guess who only drive us crazy. Thus, the council demanded the trials resume or the charges be reduced. After twenty minutes, Pusztaszentlászló came rushing in and had the guards secure her entrance as she sat down at my feet and began begging me to be her goddess. I told her that I would have to get her master to ok it yet I would petition hard and give him a fair trade. She then kissed my feet as I asked her, "Why would you want to worship a god who could be punished for eternity and cause you great shame?" She told me, "To serve you can never be shame for I believe you to be innocent and good and to serve innocent and good can never be shamed. The reason I have come to you if to tell you that the court has dropped two charges, namely of disobeying a direct command not to enter the other universe and of not knowing you were committing a crime. The council now petitioned Pusztaszentlászló to tell Gyor-Moson-Sopron that the three remaining charges also need to be dropped for justice to prevail. They also asked her to explain why the court was recessed. Pusztaszentlászló, as she was holding my feet to her heart said, "There were so many explosions in our sector as many occurred in vacant areas and areas seldom frequented. In addition, the sector scans are going crazy. Where there was nothing there is now a more peaceful nothing. We know not why?" The Council told this lovely little future addition to my Royal Deities Sanctuary if I am to survive this kangaroo court, "Tell your master that a countless number of demon cells were destroyed here today." His scans will verify this." She then bowed to all of us and slowly backed out of the room and flashed away with her guards to tell her master the news. Gyor-Moson-Sopron was shocked when he heard this news and became angry that his throne would be accused as having cells of demons. Upon hearing this news Iris in a state or rage flashed out of the throne to her armies and demanded an investigation. One hour later she returned to Gyor-Moson-Sopron with some troubling news.

Iris: Oh, great Gyor-Moson-Sopron I have petitioned your armies to verify the wrongful accusations by the council and they have given me their findings based upon millions of sources of reliable information points.

Gyor-Moson-Sopron: Tell me Iris, what did they find?

Iris: Oh great god of all, our Empire was infested with demon cells awaiting the sentencing of Lilith to destroy all good. They were dangerously concealed into every part of our beings as even to distort all our judgments. We are now using historical models of our beings, running them against projections of our actions, and comparing that against our actions to determine the degree and affect the terrible tragedy that has hurt us so. Some are trying to find evidence if the council or Lilith may have been involved in this.

Pusztaszentlászló: How can Lilith be involved as you brought her here, and did not Gyor-Moson-Sopron request the council attend?

Gyor-Moson-Sopron: This raises many questions that must be answered, Iris continue your great work while I resume this trial while I still have charges pending.

Pusztaszentlászló: I beg oh great master that you let me continue this work and allow Iris to serve you in the courtroom.

Gyor-Moson-Sopron: You now see the futility of your hope.

Pusztaszentlászló: I never see futility in a hope to find justice, as I would hope your heart would lie in finding justice.

Gyor-Moson-Sopron: You are my very wise messenger, do what you need to do and then share with me the fruits of your labors. I shall now resume the trial. This trial shall now resume. The accused may now place take her seat in the clouds. I will listen to the evidence as to be presented by the honorable Council of Nykøbing Mors.

We could feel a different tone in the trial now. The judge did not release it yet, however he was now so much less filled with a one sided blind hatred in all his words. We now had something to work with, yet the chains of his burning hell were still heavy on me. It was now time to place absolute trust in my fellow council members.

Council of Nykøbing Mors: Honorable Gyor-Moson-Sopron, we now have elected with approval from the great goddess of good Queen Lilith to represent her with the tested by the ages to be a foundation for good Queen Grandmother Goddess Tompaládony, as both do rule over our greatest Empire of Good in the fight against Evil.

Gyor-Moson-Sopron: So approved. Begin your arguments with the blessings of this court.

Council of Nykøbing Mors: We do appreciate the now peaceful tone of the court.

Gyor-Moson-Sopron: Has not this court consistently acted in a climate of good and peace?

Council of Nykøbing Mors: No, your greatness.

Gyor-Moson-Sopron: Iris, what does the council speak?

Iris: I, like you can see not where we are in any manner except as guardians of justice, yet for unknown reasons my guards say otherwise. Until I can determine why this inconsistency exists, I will be forced to agree with the council.

Gyor-Moson-Sopron: With this, I do apologize and would like to get this trial back on track as it has lasted way so long.

Council of Nykøbing Mors: We now ask Gyor-Moson-Sopron why you convened this court.

Iris: We wish to protect the innocent universes from the evil greedy powers.

Council of Nykøbing Mors: First, as we present streams you should be familiar with this universe was not innocent. As you can see, they are torturing an innocent angel named Atlantis.

Iris: How can you prove she is innocent and how could she be the cause of an evil invasion?

Council of Nykøbing Mors: Show us the charges against this Atlantis so that we may agree she is not innocent.

Iris: We could find no charges.

Council of Nykøbing Mors: Are we to believe that if you cannot find charges that would prove guilt? How can that be?

Gyor-Moson-Sopron: We will strike the allegation that the raided universe was innocent. We still see no cause for Lilith to protect Atlantis.

Council of Nykøbing Mors: How can you not see cause? Can you really be that foolish as to justify under the very first exemption to the raid clause as listed in your books? Are you even competent to convene a trial?

Gyor-Moson-Sopron: You need to watch how you accuse for the books do give me the power to plus the council on trial.

Council of Nykøbing Mors: Have not you done so by placing one of our council members on trial here? Moreover, to charge one of our council members as being evil is a crime against the foundation of all universes.

Gyor-Moson-Sopron: The murder of so many innocent are worthy of a guilty charge. Tell me how this qualifies as exempt under the clauses outlined in my books.

Council of Nykøbing Mors: Should we not charge you with concealing your knowledge? Atlantis is the daughter of Lilith and King James 1st of Mempire.

Iris: How can we prove this?

Council of Nykøbing Mors: How can you be a court and not know how to prove the parents of a child. Go and ask the spirit of her father and ask the two exiled Queen Angels of that evil throne.

Gyor-Moson-Sopron: Go Iris, back into time and return a few seconds after you departed for I want to give my verdict, and be finished with the case.

Iris: Yes my master.

Iris: (upon returning) Oh great master, I did travel back to the birth date of this victim angel and Lilith is indeed her father. Both Queens and the father petitioned on behalf of Lilith, thus giving her the right to invade. They also claim they helped provide a sanctuary for her to rescue the flesh children of Atlantis.

Gyor-Moson-Sopron: Thank you Iris, thus we now acquit Lilith of the charge of entering another universe as my book does provide exemption for a parent's right to protect their children. I also acquit Lilith of taking from those universe servants who did not wish to leave, based upon the spirit of that throne mightiest king and that throne only two Queen Angels. There can be no higher evidence that the testimony of two Queen Angels. Thus the only charge, yet the most serious remaining is: You are accused of destroying their throne without due cause or reason to believe risk or danger would befall you if the throne were to capture you for an uninvited raid.

Council of Nykøbing Mors: We object to your modification of the charge, "If the throne were to capture you for a wrongful raid" to read, "If the throne were to capture you for an uninvited raid." We are shocked that you would stoop this low and declare a mistrial.

Gyor-Moson-Sopron: We will have no mistrial, as I will remove the disputed part of the charge to read, "You are accused of destroying their throne without due cause or reason to believe risk or danger would befall you."

Council of Nykøbing Mors: We have quit easily found evidence that she had due cause and reason to believe risk or danger. We have many streams of the throne's anger with her. In addition, to show that they imprisoned her innocent daughter, in which she had no contact since her acceptance of divinity in her host universe.

Gyor-Moson-Sopron: I have not seen those streams. Iris, find them.

Pusztaszentlászló: Oh great master, I have found them and shall give them now to you.

Gyor-Moson-Sopron: I have them; Iris explains why I never had them before this joke of an injustice.

Pusztaszentlászló: I may explain master. You and Iris had slowly been reprogrammed over so many centuries. An evil force of demons had invaded the entire throne. They were so securely engraved that none could detect them. When the Queen of Justice and Good announced her name, all the evil were immediately destroyed. Your throne was freed.

Iris: Pusztaszentlászló speaks the truth. I have failed in my responsibilities and shall immediately resign.

Gyor-Moson-Sopron: I can see belief of risk of being captured however; I still cannot see justification for destroying that throne.

Lilith: Gyor-Moson-Sopron, can you not see the battle philosophy of that throne. When they fight, they destroy everything and every part of their enemy. They have no gray in battle. It is either them or nothing. As per the armies they had planted to capture me I was in the nothing part of their equation.

Gyor-Moson-Sopron: I see that now. I now see no viable charge against you. This trial is over. You shall be once again released to your Throne. An injustice has occurred here and I will give unto you any non-penance possession you or the council shall desire.

Council of Nykøbing Mors: We hold you not at fault Gyor-Moson-Sopron as you were the victim of evil's continual battle against good. We encourage you to use this example in cleaning up the empires in your dimensions, as evil surely must have seeds planted. You have a great task ahead of you.

Lilith: I have two requests to receive from your empire.

Gyor-Moson-Sopron: Speak and you may have although no penance person, such as your master, may be included. I wonder if the council will continue to allow me to control penance. Ask and you shall receive.

Council of Nykøbing Mors: Gyor-Moson-Sopron, penance is still yours in accordance with our agreement. We have no issue against you.

Lilith: I request that I may have Pusztaszentlászló and your currently jobless Iris.

Gyor-Moson-Sopron: Do you wish to revenge them for your trial.

Lilith: I wish to have Pusztaszentlászló as my personal love toy and for promotion to a goddess as my spirits will make her divine. I wish to make Iris the special head court goddess for throne security. She will have millions of angels to command.

Iris: What have I done to deserve such mercy from you? Why would you return honor to one who has worked so hard to dishonor you?

Lilith: Actually Iris, you reported the truth even if I brought shame upon you. I do love that loyalty to truth and you can be assured, I shall love you as I do my entire sister goddesses.

Gyor-Moson-Sopron: They are yours to do as you please.

Pusztaszentlászló: I now declare my god to be Lilith, and that I shall worship her all the days of my life and shall share all things and hide nothing to include my flesh suit. My goddess for eternity shall be my master and I her slave.

She now appeared free from the chains of clothing before all in front of me with her body humbled.

Gyor-Moson-Sopron: For love, I shall give unto the cloud heart that all may see you worship a great goddess of good.

Iris: I beg you great goddess of good, not to torment and torture me for eternity. I swear that I shall do my best to serve you as you wish for me to serve you as your slave.

Tompaládony: I do believe you shall soon discover why so many gods surrender their galaxies to this goddess of pure love and why I am now her humble servant as I do worship her all the days of my life. Iris, you have nothing to fear except not asking her for help.

Lilith: Iris and Pusztaszentlászló, the Council of Nykøbing Mors has agreed to give you your divinity with Gyor-Moson-Sopron as witness. You will find none greater to coronate you as goddesses as your divinity will be established in over 150 dimensions. You shall live with me in my Royal Deities Sanctuary.

Iris: My sources tell me you lay with your goddesses in your sanctuary.

Lilith: I lay with those whom love me with the permission of our master. Iris and Pusztaszentlászló, do you love me?

Pusztaszentlászló: I have loved you ever since first seeing you when you brought your sister to lie with and comfort your master. I do love you more than myself and shall love you in any manner you shall want me.

Gyor-Moson-Sopron: At least that explains all the winking during the trial. I think it is good for the sister goddesses to serve each other only if their master knows. I have scanned Bogovi and he does indeed approve and know of the sister's love. No other god may interfere with another god's servant goddesses.

Iris: I feel so ashamed that I could not see the wonders of your Empire. Thus, I shall also serve you, yet I have too much fear and shame to serve you completely unclothed. When you wish to play with me, I shall then of course completely surrender to you. Will you give me the honor to hide some of my shame, for I am not as strong as Pusztaszentlászló and you?

Tompaládony: Iris, as you can witness by looking at me, I too have to great of a fear to bear my shame. Yet, Lilith still loves me.

Lilith: Iris, serve me as you so desire for I must have you happy so you can defend us.

Iris: I shall wear my mighty flesh suit while serving you my only god. I wish now only to be a great benefit to your Empire.

Lilith: I feel so guilty for taking two such great servants from Gyor-Moson-Sopron.

Gyor-Moson-Sopron: You took two servants from me and made them into powerful loyal goddesses. With that, I can only envy your Empire and its future.

Council of Nykøbing Mors: Lilith and your goddesses let us go home. We will now go home. You will have a much better return trip.

Lilith: I petition the council to give me some time to talk with my grandmother first.

Gyor-Moson-Sopron: Go into my castle to the finest visitor's chambers and do that which you must.

I had to ask Tompaládony for more details on the shower of blood thing she told me she had done. Her response was immediate and swift. She dropped to her knees and cried on my feet wiping my feet with her hair. She then unzipped the back of her gown and wiggled it from her flesh. I asked again, what has taken your heart Tompaládony. She answered, "You have my goddess. I swear only to worship you as my master and not my grandson." I asked, "Tompaládony what did I do to deserve that worship from one who I may not even be worthy of worshiping?" She then told me, "You freed me from hate and showed me how the one I hated the most and blamed for all things was so innocent. I have nightmares about catching her and the pain I caused her, yet she is filled with your love. She now has gives her love to me. I cannot think of my life without her. We both have declared you as our god and we shall petition my grandson not to take that away from us. We begged one of your priests to baptize us in your blood. Like it or not, we are your servants until the end of time. We so much hope you can forgive us and at least give us a chance to serve you. Here is my flesh, do with me as you so wish." I then said to her, "Queen Grandmother Goddess Tompaládony, you just save me by your knowledge of the Books of the Gyor-Moson-Sopron. If not for you, I would have nothing at this time. How can I take

from you when all I have should be yours? Tell me my love!"
Tompaládony now answered, "You can repay me by being my
god and allowing me to serve you and drink of your wine and to
share my wine. Is that too much to ask or pray to you for?" I now
told her, "Let me help put your gown back on since I can drink no
wine in this painful place. I will be your master if you let me be
your servant as I demand from all who worship me." Tompaládony
now answered, "I shall agree to anything as long as you are my
goddess. Do you wish for me to kill my fear of being free from
the chains of clothing among your servants? I will obey anything
you wish of me. I told her, "You are the highest ranking as by
divine rules and most experienced with more experience than all
the other goddesses to include me combined. You may continue to
wear your beautiful garments. Since the servants cannot see your
flesh yet can see the flesh of all the other goddesses, they shall lust
more after you, which are the way things, should be. Do as you
wish, and what gives you the greatest peace and happiness. Now,
let us get out of this place for me so long to be in our Royal Deities
Sanctuary." We returned to my two new goddesses as I told them,
"Let us show you your new paradise." I then asked our host, "Gyor-
Moson-Sopron, will you please send us to our home." He told me,
"You four gods shall have a smooth ride back to your Empire.
May those who worship you have been as blessed as I am because
of your goodness?" We four sat very comfortably in our divine
flash ship as the portal powers were so steadily contained with so
much power protecting it. I do believe that either Gyor-Moson-
Sopron or the Council of Nykøbing Mors wanted to make sure we
got back safely. Maybe it is too embarrassing for them to explain
why they did not protect four goddesses. Moreover, suddenly we
were descending upon our throne. We could not land for too many
spirits were packed around and on it to share in the festivities of
our return. Tompaládony escorted Iris, Pusztaszentlászló, and the
very quiet and confused Agyagosszergény to the goddesses' throne
chambers. The massive crowd was roaring so loud that the sound
density in the space was becoming shaky. My courts, army, and
saints now exited and went to the goddesses' throne chambers, as

it was too dangerous for them to be left without the highest degree of security. My throne advised me to wait for a while for it to sink in that I was safe and back home. Iris now told Tompaládony with tears rolling down her cheeks and voice crackling as she wrapped her arms around Tompaládony, "I have never heard of an Empire loving their Queen Goddess this much. Even though I see it, I cannot believe it. She must surely be the greatest loved goddess in all the universes throughout all the ages." The main thing I wanted to see was my daughter from the sea.

Chapter 08

The beginning of the Rødkærsbro War

I patiently wait in the magnificent divine ship that Gyor-Moson-Sopron gave us. I asked him how I should return it, as I could not guarantee a safe trip through our portals. He said to keep it for when I wanted to return and see my master.

This was kind yet I now have waited for days as I am forced to use my armies to escort me into my thrones Goddesses' chambers. Iris continues to look in awe as she asks the so many kind empires' goddesses, "How can so many love her?" Penance Guardian Stuart Goddess Máriakémend asks her, "Do you love our Queen Goddess?" Iris wraps her arms around Máriakémend tenderly and answers, "For the first time in all my existence I truly do love her for her mercy is so great and her heart so filled with grace and love. I truly enjoy worshiping her." Máriakémend is now answering Iris as she is kissing her cheeks, "The serve her because she serves them. Her spirits work so hard to make their divine relationship one that is alive and real. She has taken away their pains, hunger, and loneliness. She loves them as she would love herself." Iris then asks, "Why would she want me when she has so many who wish to serve her?" Máriakémend then answers, "We all have wondered that, yet she continues to serve us with all her special grace. If a goddess needs love as food, then she has enough food to last multiple eternities. Relax and surrender your fears and give unto her all your faith and your rewards shall be greater than any you have ever dreamed." Iris then answered, "She already has by making me a divine goddess. I tried to convict her of a crime she was innocent. I expected to hate and a serious revenge yet she gave me great honor and love. I am so lucky to have met her." Hyrum Trinity Goddess Sabina now joins the conversation by adding, "As we all are very lucky." Master Guardian Goddess Fejér now asks Agyagosszergény, "Would you please bring your sister Atlantis to our chambers?" Agyagosszergény replies, "My aunt, it would be my honor." Soon the courts rushed Atlantis and Agyagosszergény into the chambers. The army was now clearing a pathway for me to make it to my throne's chambers. They were using their harmless spirit displacers to make a path for me to walk through. My heavenly servants could now verify that I had indeed returned. The courts were reporting through my now 75,000-galaxy empire. We are growing so fast, yet our revolutionary layered throne system is keeping everything on track. Our flesh servants are all showered in my blood thus having their new bodies and living on demon free planets. We have to now build our new temples through my spirits and have saints return in the flesh to be priests. We are creating new angels at an unbelievable three trillion for a second in order to provide for temple angels and galaxy armies, which for the most part work on standardizing to our high standards the quality of the social infrastructures for my servants. We provide space ship landing stations, massive road systems, schools and universities, museums and recreational parks and police forces to enforce the laws they establish, plus of course giant temples that work hard to keep their family units strong. Bogovi will be so surprised at the size of his empire when he returns. I shall of course bow before him in the center of our throne's stage and surrender unto him all that the empire has. This way all will know who the master is. However, for now I just want to see my baby Atlantis. We are making steady progress to my chambers, as I only am able to hug Atlantis quickly. I must return to the stage and give my victory speech and warning of how evil can appear in the most unexpected forms and places. I must also announce our two newest goddesses as gifts from the penance god. I can now look over and see Queen Mother Goddess Julia as she has now made it to the throne. She stands up and orders all to make way for our master's number one servant. The masses follow her orders. She must have done a fine job in our absence. This is good, since it adds depth in our divine ranks. With the master, his grandmother and myself gone she stepped in and kept the empire strong and growing. I look over and see her sitting on the throne. I am impressed with her energetic style, as she does not sit high on the stage in her mighty chair; instead, she sits on the right ledge close to the entrance. The servants enter and immediately greeted by her. This shows confidence and courage, and they do not get that security by making the walk down the path to stand before her. Her shyness comes through yet what she shares she have placed in a powerful position. The way she has her head tilted pulled her visitor's in where she wants them. She has done a wonderful job of controlling and using her stage to help her relate and come through as warm, sharing, and approachable to her servants. I wave over to her and give her my thumbs up as the crowd once again cheers. I just told them something they already knew and that is the Queen Mother is fully qualified to rule as a queen and that our master will be greatly pleased when he learns how great she did. The servants love her as do I. Fejér is in position to relieve Julia thus I wave for Julia to join me, and Fejér to set upon the throne. Fejér has always been willing to make the appropriate sacrifices in all situations allowing those who are more worthy to step into her place. We know that Julia had the hot seat, and naturally wants to get my permission to surrender the throne back. Julia comes running to me and gives me a great hug. The courts, armies, lights, and saints now cheer louder as they can now see the Empire will not be torn apart by a civil war for the throne. I now see how lucky I am to have their loyalty. She now bows down to worship me by kissing my feet. Those old timers know how to leave no mystery in their worshipping. I ask her to rise. She stands up in front of me, as all the servants now stand. When the servants see a god or goddess bow, they too bow. They figure if deity is serving than that which they are worshipping must be divine. I marvel at how fast they pick this up. Anyways, Julia now turns around slowly with her hands elevated. As she approaches me, she does a nice little dance strolling around showing me all her new moves. This gave me so much excitement that I just had to raise my hands is joy. With clouds below us to hide the vast galaxies, I could only concentrate on my master's mother. Wow, could this truly be his mother. She had the perfect body to match her amazing moves. I am so flabbergasted with wonder and amazement. I ask her, "Is this my master's mother." She answers, "This is the new complete and the full contented servant of yours. I plan to survive only off your love as I worship you for eternity." I now said, "Oh beautiful queen, your wine bottle has improved with its age, yet I wonder should not I be the one serving my master's mother?" Julia answers, "Not if his mother is your slave, bound by independent oath while sitting on the throne in absolute power. I lived in hiding for fear of my life, having a son of one galaxy who was head over heels with this angel banned from her home galaxy and a daughter who identification was closed forever in the Sea of Forgetfulness. My master's mother had dedicated all she had to destroy me. Moreover, so many times she came so close. When I heard that, you had gone to the Sea of Forgetfulness I had to take a chance on living in this Empire. Then I witnessed your spirit in your temples, and how all people declared you a goddess of love and mercy. I remember once King Abaúj-Hegyközi talking about how someday the prophets told him would rise a goddess who would hold the Sword of Justice. When I heard, you had that sword I knew I had to take a chance. When I was about to make my move Tompaládony moved in ahead of me to gain the favor of my baby girl. I knew all I ever would have was in your hands. Your love changed Tompaládony and me. We are so much happier today than we could have ever dreamed. I was once showered in your blood and when I had another chance to be showered again with Tompaládony, I could not resist. Your spirit freed us from all hate and offered us a home in you for eternity. I so much wish to drink your wine and to share my wine with you. I was so afraid that my work on your throne would shame you and you would not want me again while everyone else was edging me to take the throne. How could I take a throne that belongs to my god? If all inside me belongs to my god, then if I took it would it not still belong to my god? I beg that you forgive me if I did not please you while sitting on your throne, for I so much want to be of great value to you." I now rush over to hold her trembling soft body and tell her, "You did so much better than any of those could believe, for our people know that even if our master, myself and Tompaládony were to perish, you could save them. You are a gift from the heavens, we shall drink wine together however for my sister's, and master's sake it will be I a private place worthy of a Queen Mother Goddess. My heart is filled with such great joy in hearing how you and Tompaládony are now so happy. I do hope that I live up to your expectations. However my love, I need to see my sisters and Atlantis plus make a speech to our throne, so we need to head on back." Julia then asked again refusing to move, "Will you be my god?" I then told her, "If I am the god of servants from 75,000 galaxies should I not allow my master's mother to serve whom she desires? Hold your god's hand and lead me to our chambers." She smiled and away we two queens zipped to our chambers. As we arrived to our chambers, the guard opened the doors and announced our arrival. When we walked in all my sisters were wrapped all over Tompaládony and started to cheer for us. I looked at Tompaládony and commented, "Oh since you saved me do you think that gives you the right to love my sisters?" Tompaládony replies, "You know they are so wonderful that you cannot handle all of them." I just love her logic; it is always so complete and so non-threatening yet shows how the need is being divinely satisfied. I simply respond to my sisters, "I hope you enjoy her as much as I did?" With this, they pounced her as baby cubs would their mother. Then in a flash, the Queen Mother joins the mass mangled laughing bodies. Then I decide why not considering how close I was to loosing this. As I pounce on this bouncing blob, they strategically wiggle in many directions as I soon find myself on bottom with Tompaládony. We hold hands as we are both laughing hysterically from all the tickling and priceless love. Oh what wonderful joy this is. I look at Tompaládony and said, "Thanks for saving me so that I can be with the ones I love so much." A guard has now announced that I have guests waiting in the Queen's waiting room. My sisters wiggle out some space so I can get out and I ask the guard who is waiting for me. They tell who is visiting and I thus summon Atlantis to join me. Her sisters rush her here and in the room, we walk together. I say to Atlantis, "I have some special spirits I wish for you to know." As we walk in, "I say mommy and daddy, I wish for you to meet my greatest daughter, the mother of an empire of the ages. Mommy rushes over, hugs her, and tells her, "We are so glad to finally meet you Atlantis. If you want a grandmother and grandfather we are here for you as many of your sisters have already accepted our offer." Atlantis then says to them, "Edward and Prudence, you are indeed very popular among my sisters and fear not, for I shall also be pestering you." My mommy now smiled and started kissing her saying, "I can see that you are a very wonderful daughter of our Anne and that she must be very proud of you." I then say, "That I am and I cannot wait to get caught up with my visitations with you all." Mommy says, "Child, you will never get caught up visiting with your children or your parents. We are that special part of you that never leaves, that breathes and sleeps with you." I looked at her and while agreeing said, "That is so true mommy and daddy. How do my children fit into this equation?" Mommy said, "My dear Anne, they fit in exactly the same as you, when we see them we see you." I then looked at Atlantis and said, "You and your sisters better start bringing in some new little spirits for me." Then mommy held the both of us as I could see a question bubbling in daddy's head. I then asked, "Daddy is everything ok?" He then said, "Anne, did not I fight with you for Ruth, why would you not take me to fight in this battle?" I then told him, "Because this time I knew my enemy and that the battle would be greater and thus to great of a chance of losing you. I could not take the chance of losing you and destroying mommy at the same time. You both have earned your eternal rest and I cannot risk losing that for you. The number one reason is from the Books of the Gyor-Moson-Sopron, which forbid me taking a spirit from the flesh into battle against the throne that gave them their flesh if that throne has not placed them in danger or risk of danger. Even I have laws that I must obey." Daddy then asked, "What took you away from us and why did you not come back and get me?" I then told him, "Daddy that which took me away would not release me until we won my trial. When I won my trial, I immediately rushed back. Do you understand? You are my daddy and my daughters and I depend upon you to protect us." Atlantis now added, "I am so happy to once again have a daddy to protect me." Daddy walked over and hugged her saying, "I shall protect my girls for all our eternity." I now told my penance parents, "I must beg my pardon for I have an Empire hungry for some answers. I do wish I had more time to give you a personal account however soon I shall be available for some answers. Atlantis, will you join me?" As we floated towards the throne, I asked my spirits to get Tompaládony to join me on the stage. My spirits, before getting her asked me a question, "The Courts, Lights, Armies and Saints have all reviewed your trip reports from their representatives and wish for you to approve a three day jubilee to celebrate you defeating the great Gyor-Moson-Sopron by the rules of his book and the evil that crippled his throne." I told them, "As long as it is called the Tompaládony Jubilee." I now walked with Tompaládony and Atlantis is walking slowly behind me. I asked them, "Why do you walk so slowly?" They told me that this was my day and for me to savor each precious moment. I was now thinking, "What should I tell my servants?" Tompaládony then told me she would begin with the introductions. That was a big relief off my tender shoulders. I must have the guts for to stand with my daughter free from the chains of clothing in front of 75,000 galaxies is not something done every day. Especially since the prominent intelligent life, form on each planet is converted to my flesh suits. Actually, any life forms on any planet that can communicate and has some sort of sign as being higher life form are transformed. They do not know the difference yet however after they see my daughter and me tonight; they will see how I created the other half. Anyway, the show is getting ready to begin. Tompaládony is now motioning for me to stand back some and for Atlantis to stand to my right. She begins with, "Empire of the Good and the holders of the Sword of Justice EGaSOJ; I your Queen Grandmother Goddess Tompaládony do present to you back for good and evil in their greatest war ever fought. On behalf of your great Goddess Queen Lilith, member of the Council of Nykøbing Mors and holder of the Sword of Justice and number one servant of our master who holds the Sword of Freedom and the Books of the Gyor-Moson-Sopron." Wow, she has put me so high I sure hope I do not let these wonderful servants down. It is now time for me to speak as I walk up on stage and of course hug and kiss Atlantis and Tompaládony. I now turn around and the three of us walk to where I will give my speech as one united body. These girls are wonderful. They are protecting their goddess. That is the love between master and servant at the supreme level. By putting my power in love, I now have more love all my gods in this empire combined. Now I need to wiggle my hips a little, blink my eyes, and pull everyone into this message today. I need to get us online with security so tight that not even a mosquito can go undetected. I now lift my hand, which means everyone stops making noise. They stop immediately. I begin by saying, "First, I would like to thank my courts for giving me some space to share my heart with those I love so much. I am proud to have on my right my daughter Atlantis, Queen of her mighty Empire. I took a small band of twenty spirits into darkness and an Empire plagued by evil and we brought back Atlantis, who was being tortured for her love for me. She only asked one thing from life and that was to be free to love her mother whom she believed to be dead. We are now showing the streams of her suffering. She shall no longer suffer, for us all in my kingdom; those who love me shall not suffer. {Long applause} It is my law and my duty. {The applauses continue} As I planned to introduce her to my children, an evil greater than even known by the Council of Nykøbing Mors demanded this I perish in a lake of fire for eternity. They were only waiting for their blinded slave Gyor-Moson-Sopron to pronounce the guilt. While being contained prior to this trial of good versus evil, I saw and heard by prison guard named Heves as she spoke of the joy she would receive watching me suffer in their blasting furnaces. Evil has not progressed such I with regards towards burning lakes of fire. I will not use punishment as a threat to make my servants worship me. Instead, I use love to show them the joys of having me as their heavenly servant. Love always wins or threats of punishment and endless torture. {Loud long applause} (I looked over at Tompaládony and Atlantis as they both gave me a smile and the thumbs up in needed. This really helped, as I was now ready to roll) When will week gods are ever learning that as they need their servants their servants also need them. Be not foolish to think that I do not need you, for this is why we work so hard to serve all who serve us. We protect them from evil, and that which is unholy. Gods from all galaxies were no reporting great applauses from their spirits and from the flesh dwellers. My Empire was now being united by nails that evil will never be able to pull out. They were geared up for our new war ahead.) I would not be here today if not from your brave Queen Grandmother Goddess Tompaládony who fought hard using her great knowledge of the Books of the Gyor-Moson-Sopron. She forced the court to allow me to have as an additional representative along beside her the Council of Nykøbing Mors. I must once again thank you and your love as it has sent a signal to all thrones the power of the servants. They heard your cries for your god to return that you may worship her. I sit upon your throne as all the gods and goddesses of this Empire worshipping you. For whatever you give into me, I shall return many times. Each day I now face without pain I must give thanks to you and to our master's mother and grandmother. I am so filled with happiness in the way your Queen Mother Goddess Julia kept your Empire together for you. {Very long applause, as even I stood up and applauded her} Our master's mother now makes it possible for your heavens to serve you so much better and to help us in our battle against evil. Our master also gave us a great goddess who has ruled over large empires even before this empire was nothing more than dispersed gasses. Her greatness is more than any throne could ever have given by the highest thrones of all the universes. Our master has provided well for his empire during his penance. The great Queen Grandmother Goddess Tompaládony, Queen Mother Goddess Julia and Queen Sister Goddess Julia are in my heart and soul so much that I know not was is of the old me, and the new me blended so tight with our master's blood spirits. We are one and when you see each of us, you see all of us. I serve our master with all I have, as do you and they are part of our master. Queen Grandmother Goddess Tompaládony risked great dangers going into the unknown to bring your number one servant back to you. She fed the Council of Nykøbing Mors what they needed to defeat Gyor-Moson-Sopron who unknowingly had become a slave of evil. Evil has proved that it will work long, patient, and hard slowly to destroy its victim. We have now placed in place an additional safeguard to monitor all changes that take place in our Empire to detect Evil's invasion even if it is one cell or atom at a time. As you have seen me vanish helplessly in front of you in your throne, we now face another great danger. That is a weapon called 'portals' that even took away your Penance sister Goddess Ruth in which Queen Grandmother Goddess Tompaládony guided my penance Father Edward and myself to very a distant part of our universe to fight a giant battle with the great evil demon Villánykövesd. We destroyed his empire to include all that he had and brought back your Penance sister Goddess Ruth. We also were able to destroy all evil in the throne and empire of Gyor-Moson-Sopron, which enabled the return of your Queen Grandmother Goddess Tompaládony and your master's number one servant. We have also destroyed most evil in my old universe, an evil that strives only to destroy me, and any from me, to include your new angel Atlantis. We had the help of an Empire seeking good and love from the galaxy Adorjás, as their servants wish to be as you and live in peace and love. Adorjás is now and shall forever be an alliance galaxy unless someday we can annex them. I am holding back on annexing galaxies from other universes until I can annex all in universe who want to share in our prosperity and rule through love and servitude. Portals can allow small evil forces from anywhere in any universe to invade us. As I invaded the Milky Way, these unknown evil powers can invade us. Your Queen Grandmother Goddess Tompaládony along with a special gift from Gyor-Moson-Sopron shall form a new powerful force to help defend against the threat that can hit anytime anywhere in our Empire. All lights, courts, and the saints shall help them in this highest priority number one mission. Fear not for our armies will protect you and we shall search out and find any evil that attempts to hurt you. I now have a new weapon that any child or servant my use to destroy all evil around them. I have tested this and it works every time. Any of my servants need only to scream out my name and all evil that hears it shall perish instantly. I pray that anytime you see anything that does not look normal simply call out my name. In this manner you will remain safe as it could be evil simply trying to slowly invade you. The greed of evil can be counted upon to make a mistake. When they make this mistake, let us destroy them immediately. Never have a people had this much power against evil as never has an Empire survived with so much purity and love for good. Moreover, never has an Empire been greater than ours has. {Another long applause} With our victory in saving the great higher throne Gyor-Moson-Sopron this great and once again, an almighty god has given us two special gifts. He has given us a goddess of love and a goddess to fight portals both ordained and made divine by the Council of Nykøbing Mors our new Goddesses of Great Love from the Eternal Throne Pusztaszentlászló and Goddess from the Eternal Throne and Ruler of all Portal Security Iris. This new great love and security shall give unto all of us a new greater Empire. The Goddesses of Great Love from the Eternal Throne Pusztaszentlászló did give unto me her heart and love, as I stood worthless a slave bound for eternal damnation. She proved to be a true love and willing to serve and love the lowest among her. This great gift from Gyor-Moson-Sopron shall give us a greater everlasting well of pure grace filled love. As she loves me she also loves each of you. I do believe we shall all enjoy this new deep well of love. The second powerful gift from Gyor-Moson-Sopron is your Goddess from the Eternal

Throne and Ruler of all Portal Security Iris. Her powerful skills are unmatched as she can search hard and long against the enemies of our Empire. All Evil will fear battle with her. She shall be the rock that I stand upon and build our future foundations. I fear not the light with Iris on my side. Truly, this gift shall save so many lives. I must now join my daughter and goddesses in the Royal Deities Sanctuary and prepare for a future visit to our master so that I may give him your worship." Then in the tradition of making everything I do result in a total disaster lightning struck above us. The space had turned purple and smoke flooded the upper parts of it with pure black ruling below. White and purple lightning bolts of power shot everywhere. My courts are telling me that the bolts are causing no damage in my galaxies. It looks as if a giant white hole is trying to stabilize the middle. I yell out to my spirits to block that hole from taking anyone. I just got back twice and I need some lying around and drinking wine with my sister's time. I am so not in the mood for this. Yet I now see another surprise rushing up to the hole and firing our Criliton diodes into the center. Iris is at work and she is fighting hard. She must have discovered the Criliton diodes when she was studying my case for our trial. What she learns, she learns well and has no hesitation in using it to defend those who are in her need. Bolts are flying up at her to no avail. She dances around some and reflects some back into the hole. What a hot computer to be bundled in her wonderful powerful body. I now tell my spirits, "Tell all my Armies, Courts, Saints and Lights to obey their Goddess from the Eternal Throne and Ruler of all Portal Security Iris." I now stepped back and worked to calm those who were before my throne by saying, "My children behold the power of your Goddess from the Eternal Throne and Ruler of all Portal Security Iris. You now can walk in great pride knowing that your heavens have power and might to fight that which is not known. All hale the great Iris, the protector of the gods and their servants." The battles were raging above us as my Armies were doing as Iris commanded them. She had them in very unique layered positions so that as one group fired, and the group would fire in her L formations. She could spray fire directly at them and from one of their flanks causing turmoil behind their lines as they were trying to avoid fire from in front of them. Force them to move and pop them when they moved. She also had a strong force above them that she used to fire in her mega packs of Criliton diodes. She kept this force back a good safe distance and after they would fire, they would scramble to another position as the diodes were dropping in. By the time they hit, the force had been relocated. Gyor-Moson-Sopron had told me she was an excellent warrior and that he brought her to be with him for fear her lack of fear and total comfort in battle would be the cause of her death. I can see what he meant. Of course, I will have a talk with her; however, she does seem to be in front of her fighting force where they can see her as she gives them her commands. The one thing I know is that warriors who fight in front of their forces get much more fight out of their warriors. She has not had enough time to do any training with them and as they have just met, she is doing a wonderful job fighting, standing strong as a goddess of war. No god can match her, as all the gods of my galaxies are now watching in both amazement and envy. She is now adding great confidence in the Royal Deities Sanctuary. She is standing so strong with a helmet on her side to show her confidence in containing and defeating this enemy. Her commands are all given with her mind talk, which remains in the same tone, and pitch so as not to give the enemy any sign of despair or anxiety. Her face remains looked at her enemy only smiling when we have a direct devastating blow. She has added another crafty touch during this battle and that is what she has labeled 'Lilith diodes.' These diodes emit powerful sound waves that echo my name very loud so that all who are being hit with spray Criliton diodes, which are designed to carry Lilith diodes' deep into the enemy reserve forces. She is using this to mysteriously destroy large demon forces in the backgrounds and even on the line as the Criliton, diodes spray these 'Lilith diodes' in a 360 3d fashion such as a big globe destroying the demons on the battle lines while also destroying the reserves from all directions. Thus, in order for the enemy to sustain this fight they are forced to disband and scramble to find a safe haven. She is having these special blended diode missiles shot deep into the white portal above us. The white portal is now showing dark holes in it. This shows me that the portal now has leaks and shall soon become unstable and may shoot all in it into the unknown vast emptiness of the dimensions padding. My lights are preparing a video stream for me to present to my courts after this invasion so our servants will understand what Iris is doing now in this invasion attempt. The vortex is now shooting out debris as it was pouring over my galaxies like rain. We had destroyed it in such detail that the pieces were broken down enough that as they might enter our planet's atmospheres no major destruction would occur. They would actually be adding a wider variety of minerals to our surfaces. My lights tell me this will benefit us in the end. Then a small ball dropped out and crashed upon the stage to my throne. Then a hologram appeared before us as many strange images rotated around her. Her eyes were the eyes of a hypnotic evil of a bewitching demon. Her hair, clothing, and neckband were black. She had a seductive dress on with a jewel that resembled the objects of light that flowed from her hand. She even had a special light that showed her face in a somewhat non-threatening fashion. Then a voice flowed from the objects around her as she copied Iris with a stern strong face. She said, "I am the Queen of a mighty evil empire with many more galaxies than yours. I am called Queen of Pain and Torture Rødkærsbro. I have come today to capture and destroy your sick weak empire of love and good. As we now scramble below your dimension, I shall build another great army and we shall fight again someday. The Queen of Pain and Torture Rødkærsbro shall consume all who worship you and you shall beg me each day to free you from your pain so you may worship me. Enjoy your short future for I promise we shall fight again another day." This left an eerie feeling among those in my galaxy. Iris now had all our armies firing "Lilith diodes style two" into the vortex. This brand of diode would attach itself to a host deep into the vortex and when the host arrives at their home planet will multiply by attaching and reproducing in any life form that it can find. It would study the planet and spread out in such a manner as to get

100% coverage and then mass detonate killing all demons on that planet. If it meets another style two diodes, it will launch itself into space and find another planet. She hopes to give a devastating mysterious blow to our enemies on their home turf. I am so amazed how she was able to coordinate the invention and production, of these diodes while fighting an enemy with an army greater than ours. She was able to keep them bottlenecked at the portals exit and thus not only hit the ones trying to get out but also with her top army fired deep inside destroying armies who could not retreat or see to fight back. With this last for show only weak hologram now vanished and the portal closed, this battle was over however the Rødkærsbro War had just began. This war will need the strongest commander with the greatest army ever known to all in this universe are now prey for this misery seeking demon. The Rødkærsbro War will most likely be a pop and drop guerilla style war with no front lines. Our Empire must now be alert to any deviation and in all things be able to fight with all our might. We will add to our sensors in deep space and everywhere in our Empire our mobilization sensors. These will allow us to put our armies anywhere in an instant. Iris has been here only for a few hours and already saved our empire. I thank my master for my wisdom in forgiving her and bringing her into our family of love. I can see that she wants this also, so I will dedicate some special time for her and me. I must convince her that my love is sincere and has her best interests in mind. I will get the entire Royal Deities Sanctuary. They will come through for me. First, I must return to my throne and give another speech. Can you believe that I have spent all my time on the throne since introducing Atlantis? I so hope that none of my other daughters ever gets lost. Iris returns and asks to meet me in our queen's waiting room. We now walk from the throne to the Queen's waiting room as I hold the entrance allowing her to walk in ahead of me. Many of the courts were wondering if I would permit her in the most sacred waiting room. She is our warrior and as I followed her in, I immediately fell to my knees worshiping her. She leaned over, kissed the top of my head, and then asked me to sit on our special practice throne. I do hope someday to be able to practice a speech before giving it. Iris stand by the closed door staying tuned to the rhythms of our universe while talking with me. She begins by asking me, "Why were you worshiping me? Should I not be the one worshiping you, as you are the master's number one servant and a member of the Council of Nykøbing Mors? I can think of no greater god." I told her, "Remember I told you that I would only allow you in your empire if you let me worship you? I also have another very special request." Iris then asks, "What special request do you have?" I then nervously asked her, "That you would let me worship your body and drink your wine." Iris tells me, "I have never given wine to another male or female, yet if you want this of me I shall very shyly submit myself to you." I then told her, "Tonight you will join me in the master's bed and I shall reward you with all my heart. You are a dream come true as you have only been here for a few hours and you have defeated an attack against Rødkærsbro. During the battle, you invented new weapons that worked so effectively. You stood in front of all, which I shall never allow you to do again without the special army that my spirits are now creating. For only you can see this massive guard force as they will protect you and have special weapons to give you an extra immediate front line punch. I shall never allow you to be unprotected in another battle, even though I know you might probably survive. Iris, I can lose this empire and win it back in war, however I cannot lose you. I hope you understand the depth and sincerity of my love for you. You shall know after I worship your soul tonight. I hope you can forgive me for being as weak as not want an empire without you. With you, we have hope. Without you, we have nothing. Please forgive me for my selfishness. Iris, my love for you is too great. Do you understand?" Iris now dropped her helmet and rush before me with tear filled eyes as she was hugging and kissing my head frantically she said, "I refused to fight for Gyor-Moson-Sopron protected, yet for you I will fight as you so desire. Lilith, this is the first time I ever felt love enter me from outside. This is such a wonderful feeling. I am so ashamed that demons controlled me and almost cost all the dimensions the greatest goddess of love. After tonight, I shall be travelling your Empire organizing our security and training your armies." I raised my hand to stop her saying, "Iris this is our Empire and all the armies are yours. I shall announce your promotion and absolute control of your armies with me only having a few garrisons to protect our throne. You shall be known as Goddess from the Eternal Throne and all our Armies Iris, Commander of the Rødkærsbro War." Iris then looked me straight in my eyes asking me, "How can you trust me with so much power?" I looked at her and said, "Oh, honey it's a little thing called love. Shall we now go to the stage?" She paused for a few seconds in her powerful stare and then said to me, "I have our presentation about the dimensions and how we plan to fight them." I looked at her and said, "Such a wonderful gift that Gyor-Moson-Sopron has given us. He would be so proud of you now if he knew." Then another surprising earthquake like thunder as a voice said to us, "Iris, I have seen and am so proud of you. I shall tell all about your great battle today and your new promotion. Lilith, you outsmarted me on this one, however it gives me joy that you have such a fine gift, which still leaves me owing you a great debt for the injustice I gave to you. With Iris and do not forget the bundle of love I gave you in Pusztaszentlászló the debt will be reduced some. You have all my blessings." Then Gyor-Moson-Sopron voice ended as guards and alarms were sounding off. Iris casually walks outside, raises her hand, and tells all, "Fear not, that was just the greatest Gyor-Moson-Sopron congratulating us on our great battle victory today." I then walked over to her and asked her to join me on our large stage for her promotion. She agreed in a shockingly timid and shy manner. She can destroy the Armies yet is shy when being praised. Either way, she is getting this promotion and being honored. She paid the price and it is hers. I have never had someone serve me as good as she did today. I shall shudder during my rest times thinking about how fierce and calm she was, as our empire was at the threads of disaster, she simply made some new strings to tie it back together. I look at this new living part of my heart and ask her, "Will you escort your queen to the stage?" She smiles and gently grabs hold of my hand and with her other hand smoothly opens the door and we now slowly walk to our giant stage. I am petitioning my spirits to assemble all the goddesses on our giant stage. Our throne was once against packed as all were waiting for the beginning of our new the new every 400 days Tompaládony & Iris three day jubilee. This jubilee will now celebrate not only Tompaládony saving the master's Queen but Iris is saving the Empire and the beginning of a new and very long Rødkærsbro War. Knowing all my Royal Deities Sanctuary stands behind me I am ready to begin. Moreover, I do say my Royal Deities Sanctuary, as I do not share them, except with our master of course. They do perform many functions for our Empire however this is on a volunteer bases unless I gracefully and strategically volunteer them. All my lights, courts, and saints know these goddesses are mine. They perform as me when on missions. I will maybe talk more about this in a later book or chapter. With the rapid expanse of this Empire, we all do keep very busy. It is good that they get their glories especially with Ruth is now having servants. I plan for a lot more of this in the future such as the new galaxies getting to pick their goddess from the Royal Deities Sanctuary as they shall all have one god our master and a goddess of their choice excluding our Rødkærsbro War commanders. I now walk across this giant stage alone. My lights give me a special introduction as our stage glows in wonder. I begin by saying, "The warning I spoke about is upon us. We are now at war with evil that encompasses our empire. We are dedicated to searching out, finding and destroying all evil for anywhere there is evil there are also innocent good suffering, as so many of you have memories in your days of old. We now have greater tools and weapons and as we fight this Rødkærsbro War we shall not only hit her where she is but where she was and where she shall be. She signed the death warrant for her and all that serve her when she hit this throne. As we prepare for this long and fruitful war, we have chosen two of our experienced goddesses to command this war. I then looked back and motioned for Tompaládony and Iris to come forward and as they came to me, I motioned for them to stand beside me with me being in the middle. I now said, oh Empire of the Good and the holders of the Sword of Justice EGaSOJ behold your mighty Goddess from the Eternal Throne and of all our Armies Iris, Commander of the Rødkærsbro War and our number one goddess Queen Grandmother Goddess Tompaládony, and Vice Commander of the Rødkærsbro War. Together we will become the greatest threat and power over all possible portals within our reach as revealed by the Books of the Gyor-Moson-Sopron. The great Iris will command all armies. The armies belong to and shall worship her. My sister Iris will protect us as she did in her first battle with us. She shall now be given time to organize her armies and with the information provided by our Grandmother exploit the portals to provide us the ability to protect and attack at will throughout this great galaxy. I now give the stage to your war commanders." At this, I did return with all the remaining from the Royal Deities Sanctuary to our goddesses' chamber. Tompaládony began by speaking, "I want to first thank my goddess for her great faith in me as I so much want to save this empire so that I may worship her all the days of my eternity. We are a united Empire with one supreme king and his number one servant, the Master's Queen. I have great pride in who my grandson picked to be his number one servant, as few are so lucky to find the greatest, as did he. Iris and I agreed that we must work together in order to provide us the ability to rage a war against evil as never heard of even been possible before. To learn all that is in the eternal Books of the Gyor-Moson-Sopron takes millions of years, as it did for me, even for the greatest of gods. We have not that time available nor should we have to wait, as we have given all that we have and our to our master's number one Queen and servant. Thus, I have given her this knowledge, as she wants me to share it with the great Iris in this war. I will put her armies and weapons where she wants them when she wants them. We will fight evil in all the parts of our galaxy, as I will briefly introduce to the real wormhole structures. We need not have the fear that we have had recently. Portals may only exist where there is negative energy and negative energy may not exist in any universe. The Books of the Gyor-Moson-Sopron provides the tools to locate negative energy to include a method of changing it into positive energy and vice versa. We will place sensors in between the conveyor belt of our universe. Portals exist that can jump to different parts of our universe and to other universes or dimensions. They all must start at a point A on the belt and exit at point B on the belt or in another dimension. Dimensional travel has its own point A inside the same point A in an inter-universal portal that leads to a point B into another universe. A packed negative energy throat connects the two funnel points. As seen from my diagram a universe is only infinite in two dimensions and that infinity only exists in terms of a gigantic conveyer belt that even the greatest Empires have yet to travel its parameter going east to meet the west. I also wish to point out the square boxes along the belt. During each east, west click of the belt each square block also shifts north south. Even the most advanced travel produced by the greatest of gods can travel one of these squares prior to the next click, which creates the illusion of an infinite north-south span to accompany the east-west span. The wormhole in our giant diagram is zoned for our visual purposes only. An actually wormhole would be as a small piece of thread connecting points A and B. I shall map all negative energy traveling between our conveyer belt, as that space is empty and anything different can be detected with ease. Once the coordinates are mapped, we will condense the energy making it positive and transport it to a site on our belt for future possible military use. Our master's number one servant has given me as many lights, courts and saints as needed to accomplish this task and coordinate with our Rødkærsbro War Commander whom I now introduce. The commander of all armies in this empire the Great Goddess Iris shall now speak to you." She walks on the beams as if she were in a total spirit suit. She walks as one who has no fear. No male spirit will chance this powerhouse in battle. She begins by saying, "My greatest hope in all my eternity is to have our master's number one servant as my goddess to worship in honor in all things that I do. I accept this dangerous role only as a means to work hard to keep my goddess on her throne." Let there also be no mistake in my love for our grandmother. The help she is giving us is such that without it, the empire would fall. I have known about portals and have traveled with them on behalf of Gyor-Moson-Sopron, yet he has not dedicated as much time as our Queen Grandmother Goddess Tompaládony whose skills and depth of knowledge will put the Empire ahead of any other existing in any realm. I just must make sure to obey the laws she teaches us. Our master's number one servant, our Master's Queen has given one of her greatest spirits. As also so many of our galaxies have combined enough to make another densely packed with 78,000 spirits which gives us more than enough power to create all the new weapons and Criliton diodes plus "Lilith diodes" and Ziapon diodes for any possible recon missions that may be required. The "Lilith Diodes" combined with distributed Criliton diodes to project them to our target areas and provide maximum dispersion for host multiplication will be our number one weapon shot into our forward target areas. Every demon that we can discover will hear the name of Lilith as they fall to their final death. We will also launch Good Savers to explore any newly cleaned of evil planets for any prisoners to set them free. We currently have four Armies in the negative energy zone closing all portals. I also have four Armies within our Empire scanning for any negative energy and any possible evil staging points. We will be replacing the negative energy with our sabotage negative energies. We will be reopening the portals we closed with this sabotage energy, which will invite demon armies inside them once they are all in, and a few thousand light years from the portal, entrance the sabotage energy will lock them into place. Then pre-staged Lilith diodes will detonate and once every demon is killed the portal will send the evil free armadas to our entrance, as we will scan them for advanced technology possible and then convert what we can to supplement our forces and for possible future sabotage missions. We are constantly upgrading our forces, tactics, and Armies. The Saints have asked to be a part of our force and we welcome them in honor of our Master's Queen with their excellent time tested and approved commanders who are also the daughters of our Master's Queen. As we rush to get our forces into the negative realm, we must all share in our security by reporting anything different or strange. Our galaxy's gods have assured me they will investigate everything reported. We are at war and we are not going to sit back helplessly fearing an attack from Rødkærsbro. We are taking the war to her and any evil in between. We will hit her from every angle and be waiting for her as she tries to escape. Portals are a knowledge that no living demon may have. Any who have this knowledge will have some negative energy scattered in their spirits. We will also have roaming battalions with giant positive collection cells. These cells will activate the negative residue inside these evil spirits and thus pulls the positive cells and their attached Criliton diode and zap the target. The local army will deploy and clean the roaming fleet of evil. The empty enemy equipment will be sent to the nearest portal to return to our holding areas. We actually already have many fleets in holding and plan to supplement our forces with these vessels as special transmitters with some of our Master's Queen's blood attached to it will identify our equipment as I can see within a few months our fleets will all be thirty percent composed of these special refitted war ships. I always enjoyed destroying the enemy by using their equipment. I shall discuss these plans with the Master's Queen this evening and with her permission proceed to our assault level. We must hit now as we are gaining tactical control. I understand that our Queen has given me her Armies however her armies are still her armies as I am only using them for her glory. No member of the army shall ever swear an oath to serve only me and must reaffirm their loyalty to our King and Queen as I so every day. I now place this law in the military laws. If they do not follow me, they will be punished in the names of our King and Queen. This Empire shall always serve only one Master and his number one Servant. Let there be no fear of a mutiny or coup in this Empire as my Armies and I defend the King and Queen with all we have. Tomorrow is the beginning of a long road for our Queen Grandmother Goddess Tompaládony and me as we will set up both perfect protection and deployed armies fighting in an ever-changing front line? May all our heavens and flesh dwellers serve and love our King and Queen." With this, she raised her hand and walked over to me as we hugged each other and I could not stop kissing her cheeks and forehead. I once again took a giant gamble in giving her the armies of law. She could have so easily demanded my divinity and placed me in an awful pain stricken prison in a deep dungeon never to be seen or heard again. Inside she pledges the armies to be mine and establishes laws making the armies reaffirm their loyalty to me. She claims control of the armies only to bring honor to our master and myself. What a wonderful goddess. She has once again added as did the Queen grandmother and mother to the unity of the Royal Deities Sanctuary as bound by true love. Some have claimed I have special glasses or spells I use in the sanctuary to hypnotize them, yet the Seonji all have testified that so such thing exists in there. They testify that we all behave as normal spirits would, we play games, wrestle, run races, go hiking, camping, hang out in both small groups and large groups in a totally random fashion, even asking them (Seonji) to join. They also testify that the goddesses will on occasion invite angels or my daughters for some fun sports games that will result in a winner and loser. They play on equal terms and powers and do naturally lose about as much as they win. All are betting that when Iris joins them after the war, the goddesses will begin winning much more. Iris is now strolling towards me as I motion for my Royal space carriage as we head to Nørresundby Palace, a nice new Palace that the Master's spirits built for us. This really makes me feel good in that my master's spirit approves of my actions, which when declaring war encompass a look of considerations and always elicits a lot of emotions and arguments. My lights tell me that by declaring the commanders first and letting them explain the situation of the danger and how they would keep us not only out of danger but keep our children out of danger also. It is something that must be done and now all know why it must be done. I am heralded as the one who ensures all keeps running smooth with minimum impact. We are striving for no deaths from this war and very limited safety error related deaths behind our lines. Iris agrees that no member of our empire need to suffer from this war, especially since we have such advanced radar-sensing equipment. We spot the danger, my name blast it, remove any evil, then announce we mean no harm to any who are not evil, put up our shields and move on. The dangers occur when non-evil Trojan horses lure us on good ships for humanitarian reasons. That is why Iris implemented a "No boarding unknown ship without the support of a war ship watching." We send in our warriors first. If the host ship is not honoring their request for help, they will pay with their existence; the warship ran millions of scans, usually before boarding and knew every inch of the host ship. Entry is during the verification of any movements or changes, and then they get out. Another rescue method is to have those who need help board our ships and then tow their host ship quarantined a safe distance behind. We will protect our own and try to save any innocent caught in the crossfire. With Iris's new "Lilith diodes," evil will be taking the direct hit. Thus undoing what evil has done will be the priority in the brief salvage operations. As they may need more of our help, we must remember that many others ahead are also suffering. My task has now been to attempt to make it to my Nørresundby Palace. Nevertheless, I must have my spirits release the sister goddesses and Queens. Nørresundby Palace is only a few galaxies from the Royal Deities Sanctuary, thus we will be able to move back and forth at will. After tonight, I will invite them for a viewing. I will most likely get a stream viewing tonight and an official with Atlantis and Agyagosszergény in the morning. Agyagosszergény and Atlantis have grown fond of each other, as Atlantis has asked her for help in ruling her empire. I will not deny that this is a smart move on Atlantis's part since her sister knows this empire inside out plus as one of the top six can produce instant armies if needed. Agyagosszergény is also now working hard with my spirits in establishing an eternal resting place for the saints of Atlantis who have passed on to our side of the line. We have been able, with the help of Mempire successfully to rescue Atlantis's lost spirits, as many occupied the Mempire heavens sanctioned off by the Supreme Heavenly Angel Lablonta. The saints return to their new heavens speaking highly of this Heavenly Angel. I never really met her much except for a brief tangle when I was trying to wipe out what I considered at that time insects on the planet Lamenta. A thousand years in the furnace convinced me otherwise. I have always been thankful for her giving Atlantis to me. She had really worked hard taking care of Atlantis loving her even though Atlantis father was her husband. At the time, I believed she was doing it for revenge against me. However, all works out for the best in the end. I do rather feel sorry for her now, nonetheless I do not think she lost too much sleep over me in the furnace. That was a long time ago and I have my baby getting her reward for all the shame that I put her under and even of so much more value; she is blending in with her sisters. It should take some time to get to know all 3,000 of them however; she has the time now as long as Iris keeps us safe. Tonight is my spirits night with Iris. My working flesh suit is too exhausted so I must put on a spare for tonight, the same wine just another bottle. I ask Iris if she in not tired and she tell me, "My love and goddess, I have fought in wars where today was like unto a holiday in the midst of years of nonstop fighting. That is what happens when they make it through the portal. Today was lucky, the fools hit in the middle of a high security divine ceremony. It is like breaking into a bank with a police ceremony going on inside. I kept them in the portal and thus it was easy pickings as long as we hit hard and fast without stopping. I then chronicled to her, we need to say Goodnight to the sisters. I do not know if they are going to like the idea of Iris having her own palace for she shall live in the Yudashkin (Юдашкин) War Palace. Many of her activities must be kept secret so as not to cause any harm to the Empire's interests. She will of course be permitted to visit the Royal Deities Sanctuary, as I will escort her first maybe dozen times until I feel she is bonding with the sisters. That will be important for her. Her palace will be located in highly secure lightly populated areas. The castle will be mobile as she can move it as she wishes. I have given her a new law that revises what I have already told. I just want to make sure she and her armies know this. Thus, I have many of her top commanders here now. I say, "Yudashkin (Юдашкин) War Palace is never, as with Iris ever to be placed in an insecure place.

Iris is the lifeblood of this empire and we cannot take any chance she might be lost. She may not go into a portal unless escorted by a member of the Royal Deities Sanctuary accompanies her. I have included this clause in her activation of the armies' orders. She may declare war at will and of course always request additional resources from my spirits. She has two of our greatest spirits at her command. They will not allow her in a dangerous situation. The Armies understood these orders and embraced them wholeheartedly, since it is a great shame for an army to lose a high-ranking officer in a battle, let alone one who has Empire throne power. Iris now complains to me that, "This will hurt my ability to launch attacks taking advantage of opportunities as they occur." I tell her, "This cannot in any way cripple your exploitation of opportunities as they occur. You must work through your commanders. You can study the scenario and give your orders for the protection of Yudashkin (Юдашкин) War Palace that my spirits have given you the best equipment known available. You must consider yourself to be our empire and thus if you were to be captured or killed our empire would cease to exist. Anyway, you know gods cannot fight in spiritual wars however we can help our side in the war." Now, let us finally say Goodnight to our sisters and head for Nørresundby Palace." My spirits had previously updated the girls on what would happen this evening, thus they were now actively involved in their celebration of the three day jubilee. Iris has asked me to keep the scheduling of the Tompaládony random and the current choice a secret only notifying one month in advance. This gives her plenty of time to prepare the armies for our defense as holidays and festivals are opportune times for invasion. I enter the Royal Deities Sanctuary and introduce each one to Iris. Many are startled by her powerful looking body and eyes. She keeps such great control over her face most think it to be fake. That is when she loves to attack. Iris gives each goddess a kiss on each cheek hugs them and tells them, "As I love you very much I shall defend you." This is the first step that she is taking to bond with her sisters. I am once again so proud of her method of controlling any situation, this time with love and warmth. Each sister just collapses in her arms telling her how great and wonderful she is. Iris is now, without question, a member of our gang. I need only place her in a situation, she apparently read my mind and before me I see what I was thinking manifest. All the queens and sisters feel so much safer with Iris in our Empire and want her to have special privileges, as she is the one that have the least amount of time to play and with the heaviest burden. I know that my Nørresundby Palace shall give me my greatest gift tonight when I remove her special emerald that holds together her gold waistband. My insides want to explode with barely the thinking of it as I wish so much to hurry with my new great prize to our new Palace. Iris confuses me with an unusual request. She asks me, "So that I may serve my master greater tonight may we walk among this beauty as I try to unwind myself? I wish to know more about the goddess I love so much." I agree and as we lock hands, we begin walking. She tells me, "Sabina told me about some wonderful views on top of this nearby mountain. I tell her, "I know the place she speaks of, for I built her a nice small cabin among the hillsides of red flowers, I shall take us there now." I took us there, as the beauty was breathtaking. Iris says, "Oh master, how could you have made such a beautiful place?" I confess to her, "My love, I must tell you that my master was the one that made this place for us. He has great pride in his goddesses as so many gods envy him for not only our beauty but strong ruling skills and now because of you, we might in war." Iris requests verification from me, "Master Sabina tells me that you gave your twin sister to sleep with our master during his penance. Why would you give him such forbidden fruit?" I answer her, "Iris I can trust my master through faith, just as you trust me and I trust you. I am forbidden to sleep with him during his penance, for they fear the empire would be in danger and they wanted that lose to be part of his sufferings as he does so much suffer. Drusilla is my twin sister for she saved me in my penance and suffered as much if not more for my wellbeing, giving her living life to protect me as be she could and she shared my penance death with me as our blood mingled together on us ground below our died beaten flesh. She did not want to do this for me however, I begged her. Her only weakness is she can never refuse a request for me, even giving up her precious fruits to bring me joy." Iris then asks, "What if they fall in love for the chains of love are hard to break." I tell her, "Then I would have great joy that my master has found a better love for him. Gyor-Moson-Sopron would divide the Empire fairly and I would live in my new Empire with you and my sisters. Nevertheless, I believe my master's love for me is endless and my twin sister's loyalty to me is too great. Therefore, I worry not. I want what is best for my master." Iris then tells me, "You are truly the greatest goddess of pure love. Yet master, my heart is so burdened now." I thought oh no, she is going to put the lid on her cookie jar. However, I must know and I ask her, "Iris, do you fear our wine drinking tonight for I promise to serve you well?" Iris replies, "Oh no master, however I do not feel worthy of such a great gift. My fear is that I may lose this war and you will hate me for letting you down." I tell her, "Iris I do so much believe you will be the best wine bottle I ever opened and that the mighty heavens are giving me the greatest wine in you. No one knows how a war will end, for if he or she would not continue to fight or start the fight if they know they are too loose. You have the greatest equipped spiritual and flesh armies ever to exist with the best saints, courts, and lights to advise you. If at any time you need a break, Tompaládony can relieve you. Do not take chances; if you need a break take it as I shall try hard to be your personal servant. So please relax and let me give you this great honor with all my faith you shall be wonderful." She then tells me, "Master I would like to see the Nørresundby Palace if you would be so kind." I instantly flashed us there. Iris then says, "Wow master that was quick." I told her, "My lust wants to open your bottle and enjoy the beauty of its creation." I then say, "If it were that easy, we must first watch a stream about this palace, and then in the morning when you go off to war, I must take a guided tour." We sat with me on her big lap and watched the stream. She pets my hair and lightly massages me with her big strong, yet soft fingers. Soon the video was over and she easily carries me as she would a baby up these seemingly endless stairs. I plan to do a lot of floating in this palace, because these steps shall not cut it with me. I can appreciate their beauty while floating up and floating down. In addition, I would want to save my energy for the sanctuary. I can appreciate the attention to detail that was put into this giant palace that floats in space. I was nice of them to give me a nice concrete front yard. Maybe someday our master and I shall sit out here and spot for our many galaxies. My spirits tell me that in the wake of the Rødkærsbro War, we now have 93,000 galaxies and 35,000 alliance galaxies, as with the war effort we cannot assimilate them as fast as before. We do want to have as many in our borders as possible to give us more friendly space territory to search the upper realms for possible enemy cells. Notwithstanding, the only cells I want to worry about now are Iris cells. We both look over the directories that are posted along the hallways until we get used to them. I plan to leave them up until Bogovi gets used to them, for it is a sad thing for the master to get lost in his palace. The palace has a physical flesh layout with a spiritual layout inside. We are diffidently in the physical side now. Iris now prepares for our spiritual melding; this feels so good to be in the hands of power and strength. She then asks me, "How may I serve my goddess?" I tell her, "Please give me your red emerald." She reaches down and unhooks it giving it to me. Her golden waist robe falls to our sparkling floor. I lay her red emerald beside the lamp on our nightstand. I motion for her to rest with me on the bed. As I touch her, I can feel her trembling with fear. I tell her, "Iris fear not for I shall not hurt you, yet instead I shall strive hard even on my knees to please you." I then slowly run my hand over her perfect wine bottle while kissing her arms and then belly. She is starting to relax. I then perform my skills to perfection, as this is my greatest victory. To have a former enemy surrendered and willingly submitting to me now is so wonderful. I think she is giving me all the wine she has ever made. She explodes in such excitement and ecstasy as she tells me, "My master, this is the first time I have released my wine, that which I feared as harmful is actually wonderful. Now lay back and we shall see if I am a fast learner." I did not hesitate and she soon proved how fast a learner she really was. The palace was getting a thrill tonight for in it now laid a completely satisfied Queen. Iris then asked me, "Master, which do you better like, your master or your sisters?" I told her, "My master Iris, for once a woman is bound to her master that love becomes the foundation for the greatest event in life and that is reproduction. A sister's love complements that experience and does not compete against it. That is why the sisters never say anything when my master calls me. I was lucky to get a strong caring master who permits me to stay intimate with my sisters. This is the greatest bonding I have been given and I plan to obey our master in all he says. I have reproduced over 7,000 times, with an evil throne taking fifty-seven percent of them. No matter how many you have each lose hurts bitterly and locks hate into an empty room inside you. Our master searched each room and defeated that trapped hate. A sister's love could never do that. You will have some opportunities and if you cannot find them order your commanders to give you some fine specimens. In thinking ahead, I put the provision in your army law giving you that power. Use this power of right, as it will make your soldiers honor you more in knowing you have feelings and long as they do." Iris then thanks me by saying, "I am so lucky to have a master who knows about these things and cares more about our needs than some public image." I now told her, "I created you, or actually recreated you when your commanders showered you with my blood, and as for public image you can go no lower than my complete nudity in front of them. Are you ready to hold me while we rest?" She agreed to hold me lightly kissing me with her wonderful massages saying, "Good night my goddess and might my service to you be worthy." Then we both fell fast to sleep as giving speeches on the throne are energy draining. I have finally reached my plateau although with all this drama lately I may still be in a valley somewhere wriggling my way out of a hole in the ground. I go aggressive to save Ruth, went after Atlantis came back were hauled off to a witch trial and then came back and ended in a war. Yet through it all my girls came through for me. I really think it would be nice to stay low for a while yet now another great fear rocks my soul. What happens if I lose Iris, or for as far as that goes if I lost any of them? I hate the thought of having my heart in so many different places. I would hate even worse is not to have my heart in others. The only thing I can do is keep-fighting evil for with evil out of the scene less tragic things happen. Moreover, as long as evil wants to keep pestering me, they shall suffer. Now that my name has been put into diodes an invention of the beautiful mind in this master creation beside me now, evil will continue to suffer at levels they never knew possible. The biggest advantage I have now is the evil is not yet advanced enough, as neither is good enough to communicate the warnings to all. We cannot say all good as evil, or can we report all evil. Iris's plans of dropping my diodes into all the portals, as I now understand simultaneously will put a thunderbolt into the evil heart as never shot before. Evil will suffer such a large blow and yet not know where it came from, as the wormholes will be diverted to a stage two outlet. Oh the wonderful productions of the mind of Tompaládony, which is another treat I shall soon enjoy with her wonderful consent as already, promised. I owe them all so much yet they continuously give to me. I am lucky in some things; however, I do not feel lucky now. Soon Iris will get up, take her red emerald and fasten on her golden waistband, take her helmet and walk out the door. She slowly wakes up as I immediately start kissing her as fast as I can. My hero must remember waking up to her goddess kisses. She then picks me up, her red emerald and golden clothes and takes me over to the wonderful sofa that sits behind the columns in front of my bed. She sits beside me and says, "My goddess, your gift here has been the great love gift I have ever received. I wish you to know that I shall confess my love and loyalty to you every day for the rest of eternity and will declare every victory in battle to the name of the great goddess of the heavens, Lilith." I then looked at her with tear-filled eyes and asked her, "Do you wish to please your master?" She immediately rose up and then bowed to her knees wrapping her arms around me and while crying, "More than my life itself, my divine master. I serve and only worship you." I then said to my greatest servant, "I am too weak to let you go. For I feel now my life must have you at my side," She then starts kissing me again saying, "My love for you makes it hard to leave you, yet we must remember I am a gift from Gyor-Moson-Sopron to serve and suffer for you on the battlefields." I immediately begged, "Oh Iris promise me you will not suffer, please your goddess begs this of you." Iris then surprised me by saying, "I shall not suffer for I wish to be able to serve all your needs of the return from our victories." I started hugging and laughing in great excitement saying, "That is the way I want my Iris to think. Always remember you live first in my heart then second in some stupid war." Iris now stood up and holding her red emerald wrapped her golden clothes around her waist and fastened it. She then said with such a force and stair that there could be no doubt, "My goddess, I shall return with your victories." She then walked out of our room. The muscles of her powerful built body looked as wonderful as she gave me a new appreciation for gold. Then faster than I could leap across the room and hold on to her begging her not to leave she was gone. How low and cruel could I be to send her off to do my job? Am not I the champion against evil? I then yelled for my spirits, "Make sure Iris has my Sword of Justice at her side." They instantly showed me a stream of them attaching the sword to her side. She looked back and blew me a kiss. How can I put so much love in a war? I now ask my lights, "Am I a week and selfish goddess to put such a wonderful servant into war in my place, is not this evil?" The lights then answered, "We know not why things happen as they do, we only know what things have happened. We know that Gyor-Moson-Sopron gave Iris to you. His lights tell us he so dearly still and always will love her as his greatest servant. We know that she loves to fight. We know that she can be trusted with great powers and that her loyalty in unquestionable. We know that she always puts her god before her. We have seen, and thus know she can kick ass in war. This could be the perfect thing to insure we can fight in these new everywhere all the time wars. We have run the most possible scenarios with her in the war and she always wins and returns. She will return to her master." I argued back, I understand all the logic for having her in command of our armies for I am not foolish enough to think I could do better. She is greater than I am and I would worship her as my god anytime for as long as she should so desire. I feel ashamed to be the Master's Queen while others fight in my place." The lights then said to me, "Oh mighty Queen, all fight in your place." I thought, "Wow that is true." My power shall be to do what is right, and that is to make sure she gets all the glory for her sacrifice and abilities. As long as I keep telling everyone, "She did it and not me." They will all have heard it so many times they will just ignore it as yesterday's news. Thus, I will not have the danger of letting pride destroy me. This whole debate is not about who is the best; she is. Case closed. Case reopened. The debate is my guilt in waiting something I love walk out on me. She leaves on my orders. May my spirits work with and protect her. It is time for me to see what all is in the big empty castle floating in space. The rooms feel as if they grew one hundred times not including all the emptiness of space. So much love was here such a short time ago. Now I have some nice nervous female servants showing me this castle that they are so proud to be part of such a great divine structure. We have no male servants as Bogovi has forbidden them. He feels that is an unnecessary avenue to allow evil to invade and harm me. I know today that I will ask for mommy and daddy to move in. They always try to take care of their little Anne. I should be thankful for this peace as it has been so long since I have enjoyed it. I ask my servants, "Do you think that 4,000 penthouse suites are enough?" She answers, "No my master, not one who is quickly approaching 100,000 galaxies." I look at this little thing and ask her, "Why are some of you free from the chains of clothing and others not?" She tells me, "The courts let us decide, those who love you with all their heart and soul and trust you in all things will be free to go free from the chains of clothing if they pass the test from the lights." I now ask, "What is your name and tell me more about the test from the lights?" She tells me, "Master, my name is Yudachyov and the test from the lights includes a detailed scan of all the thoughts in my life plus a pain test in which we must declare our love for you while being tortured." I now started to get angry and said, "Yudachyov, I have forbidden anyone to suffer for my name."

Yudachyov quickly adds, "Oh no master, this was from our begging to take this test since we want no one serving you who are not completely loyal. The pain did hurt, however I now have the pride of knowing I will endure anything for your namesake." I then said, "Oh Yudachyov, this causes great pain in me. I can never allow anything that gives pain into my servants. I must forbid this." She then replied, "Oh master, please give unto your servants a chance to give you a greater love. Is this not fair? For so many wishes to serve you and our master, should not only those of the greatest love be allowed to serve you? At any time during the test, we can stop it. We suffer because we want to. Please do not punish those who love you." I looked at Yudachyov and said, "I like your style and your logic, for you have defeated me in our first debate." She then frantically lowers herself beside me causing me to jump back. She holds my back with both hands keeping me up, yet she maintains her balance. I strangely continue to look down one of our massive hallways keeping my ear towards her to hear her speaking. Yudachyov says to me, "Oh forgive me master for defeating you. I will surrender myself to the lights to be put into prison for eternity." I now turned around and actually looked at her thinking the court sure knows what I like. The loneliness that burdened me earlier was now gone. I said to her while holding her head, "Yudachyov, why would you do something foolish like that? Also, how can you stay balanced in that position so easily?" Lastly, are you flesh or spirit?" She then says, "Master I am both spirit and flesh, as in the flesh my years were many and in all my days before every meal and rest I prayed out to the heavens, "Lilith is my god and only her do I worship and serve. I spent many days in your temples begging you to give me ways to serve you. Your spirits heard me and made me young and when I passed the court's tests, they gave me this new body and allowed me to cross over the line of death to serve you for eternity. They asked me if I liked this body as they told me you would find favor in it. I could hold this position easily for in my young days I played a hitting the ball game with my brothers and they made me catch the balls they would throw for the other team to hit. I offered to surrender myself for hurting the goddess I love the most. I cannot live with myself knowing I have hurt you." I then said, "Oh Yudachyov you spent too much time praying and not enough time reading my holy books. For in those books you would have discovered that when my servants defeat me in anything, except war of course, I find great happiness and joy in it. I want my children to be the best creation that ever existed. You brought so much joy to me, I will ask to the courts to give you to me as my chamber maiden if you so desire." Yudachyov asks curiously, "I shall serve you any way you want, by the way master, what is a chamber maiden?" I told her, "Due to my many tasks, you will be a special kind of chamber maiden only responsible for my domestic functions. You will live in this palace as you currently do; however, anytime I enter my bedroom you shall be there with me. You and only you may serve me when in my chambers and you will sleep with your god when she sleeps here. My bedroom is your place of work. Do you understand?" Yudachyov then asked, "What shall I do when our master sleeps in your room? I then told her, "When I have guests, you may sleep in your personal penthouse. I shall give you the greatest penthouse I can in this palace, for when I am away I want no one to bother you. All shall know you as my chamber maiden. If you decide to marry someday, we will give back to you your current position as long as I get to attend the wedding. Do you have any reservations such as how to serve me in my chamber?" Yudachyov asked me, "Would it be like you and Iris last night?" I asked her, "How did you know about that my love?" She told me, "Oh I was so worried about you. Do you want me to serve you as Iris did?" I then hugged her and said, "Yes, that would make me so happy." Yudachyov told me, "In all the many years of my long life I have never done like that, however when I watched you last night I did envy Iris as being the luckiest creation in this empire. I do hope you make me lucky also." I then kissed her and said, "What if we hurry up this tour as you can teach me more in our chamber and I can announce to the courts that you are my chamber maiden. Congratulations, you live in the same room as your heavenly queen." Yudachyov then told me, "Everyone told me you are the creator of all kinds of loves and that all love comes from you. They told me the truth." I then hugged her and wrapped my arm around her shoulder saying, "I had better be careful for you might make me think I am greater than I am." Yudachyov stands bold and strong and says, "There is none greater than you and you are my goddess as you have been all the days of my wonderful life." I could only hold her and say, "Thanks now show me what you want me to see, ok love." She rushes me into a nearby penthouse as I tell her, "Relax Yudachyov, we have plenty of time." Yudachyov tells me, "I always dreamed of a kitchen like this. We would see them in some streams in our town centers." I asked, "Yudachyov these are available to any who serve me, why did you not ask your temple?" Yudachyov answers, "Our galaxy was way behind the others for evil really pounded as hard over the last few millenniums. We had so much to learn in order to move into a new era. We actually just recently came out of our caves. We are truly so thankful for the great gifts you have given all of us. Yet your greatest gift is the gift of hope. With you we have a tomorrow and it will be better than today." My heart is now getting mushy so I say to Yudachyov, "My dream is that all my children live good challenging and rewarding lives. I depend upon so many thrones to help my spirits. We have a long way to go, yet we have come such a long way. I can see our empire someday with millions of galaxies and all living their lives as I have created them to live. I so must be the goddess of the great love and mercy for I have a history of great evil to pay for." Yudachyov looks at me and says, "I refuse to ever believe you were evil." I told her, "My innocent child, times change people, and this universe has changed me for the better." Yudachyov then adds, "My god, the greatest day in this universe was when it received you." I once again kiss this little thing and ask, "Yudachyov, are all the penthouses the same as this?" She answered, "Oh no god. They are of many designs and styles." I ask, "Yudachyov, if there is one you want, take it for it is yours. I shall now call my spirits to announce you as my love toy. Spirits Harken, be it known that Yudachyov is here and now until revoked at her will my chamber maiden, to serve your queen in my chamber. This is now also her chamber and when our master wishes to be here, she will have her own penthouse of her choice in this palace. She is the protector of my dark hours. My stamp is upon her soul. No one may see her again without seeing me in her soul. When all speak to her, they are speaking to me. As I have said it is done." I then asked her, "Yudachyov let us go to our chambers and see what you learned last night while watching Iris?" She answers, "Yes, with love my master. I shall serve you better than did Iris. You will be served so well that you may wish never to leave your chambers." I kissed her hard and said, "Let us go now and see this mystery I have discovered." Indeed, I had discovered a diamond in the ruff. She had no shyness and did not lack confidence and put her precious little heart into loving her goddess. I was very surprised as in two nights two rookies had hit home runs. I am not one to take advantage of these gifts as I also feel I must serve, thus I had a Yudachyov rest upon our bed as I did serve her. Her young fresh flesh suit thundered with joy as its creator revealed the creator's secrets. When our wine glasses became empty the hours in the day were still early, yet our flesh was absent of any energy thus we both did fall into a peaceful sleep. The willing love from a servant is the best love in all creations. Oh, the peace that is flowing through my body as both Iris and Yudachyov has placed their god in a new heaven. I must commend myself in my excellent creations. This is truly going to be an excellent place to serve my creations. Each specimen created has its unique features as Yudachyov serves by enduring patience, faith, hope and an attitude of gratitude. I am so glad my courts found her and passed her my way. She has everything I marvel in my servants and the glow of peace upon her face as her god holds her now is breathtaking. She will make simple boring things exciting as even I now like that blue kitchen she showed me. With her in my chamber, the Empire and Royal Deities Sanctuary will get a better Queen. A whole day without any major dramas is a special gift within itself. I wonder now how I was able to survive such crap and why we must be at war. I know why we must be at war so I should rephrase that and ask why there is not any other empire that can fight this war. Yet evil must pay as even the gift in bed beside me tells of how her planet and galaxy suffered so. I just do not understand how it has been allowed to exist for so long. An uphill climb keeps getting steeper. Where would I be without Iris to be my bloodhound and chase them down? As the peace of the night opens my soul to some reflections it is suddenly broken by alarms. My spirits now awaken me, "Master, we have some trouble? I ask, "My spirits, what are the alarms about?" They answer, "We have some foreign material in our Empire that could be a prelude to an evil invasion." I thought, "Oh no, Rødkærsbro has brought the Rødkærsbro War home to me when my Armies are fighting in the portals. What shall we do?"

Chapter 09

The eve of a new beginning

As I leave a panic stricken Yudachyov I tell her, "My child, your god will protect you." I say this not knowing if I really can because this is a new type of war, which has new rules that I still do not completely know. The two who know are collecting negative energy between dimensions and in the empty space of this universes conveyer belt. I rush to my throne as most members of the Royal Deities Sanctuary are already in place. The courts are here as are all the saint's armies. My daughters are on their toes for this one. I must start at the top and work down since I believe that Rødkærsbro enjoys starting at the top first. I ask Fejér if all the goddesses and queens are accounted for, which she tells me all except for Medica. She has the Seonji searching the Sanctuary for her. She then rushes to me and tells me the Seonji have found her and she is ok. I flinch for a second thinking it strange that the hero of Ereshkigal's great demon wars would miss this yet I have too many other things on my mind now. Galaxies are activating their armies as I have a whole empire with almost 100,000 galactic armies setting in docks waiting to be deployed. I have to think of something fast. I scream out, "Lights and courts give me your recommendations." The lights answer first, "We have narrowed the galactic disturbance to this galaxy and feel that about twenty of the surrounding galactic armies should be enough to contain them. We recommend that you allow the other galaxies to stand down and concentrate on their immediate security." I then say, "I do not contain invasions, I destroy them. Give me thirty armies and allow the rest to stand down." The saints then add, "Oh great queen, we can give you the thirty armies and thus you can allow all the remaining galaxies to maintain high alert." I tell them, "Make it so. I know I can count on the armies commanded by my daughters." I then say, "Ok throne, let us find this little bug, and squash it" while smiling. I now begin to hum a nice little lullaby trying to bring stability to my throne. I can now see the action calming down and focusing. At this time, my sisters and the two other remaining queens come out to join me on the stage. They ask, "Oh great lover, would you not prefer to take us to your queen's waiting room and have some fun?" I look at them laughing and say, "No I think I would be safer out in the open than trapped in a room with you girls." Then Mary says, "True, we are neither the big tall warrior type, nor the little innocent human types anymore, so I guess you will dispose of us." I reached over to her and started tickling her saying, "I could never give up this little bundle of joy." The courts send me a message saying, "Good job Queens and goddesses, the empire is relaxing as the fear of an invasion is fading." Then the queen mother comes over beside me and says, "Oh I thank my son that this did not happen while you were away, for I would have fainted under such a crisis. My son is so lucky to have a number one servant like you my master." I then go over and kiss her saying in her ear, "When do I get to share some wine with you." She looks at me and says, "Your sisters tell me I would have to make a reservation far in advance." I had to laugh at this one; the old woman was quick on her feet and now so much like us I do not believe any could tell the difference. I then smiled at her and said, "I allow the old ones to move to the front of the line in case they are not still with us when their number hits." She smiles while kissing me, "That is so kind of you my master." The gang appears to be relaxing up now so we can head inside to the court's command centers. Upon arriving inside, the courts give us news that puts us all back on our toes. "Master, the disturbance is in the Royal Deities Sanctuary." I ask the girls, "Did you goddesses notice or detect anything strange?" Máriakéménd answers, "Yes master and Medica researched it and said she fixed it." I then said to the courts, "Mobilize are your sensors on the Sanctuary and slowly start packing some of your armies in that vicinity. We will use our return to the Sanctuary as warranting the extra security precautions." I then call over to the Saint's commanders, "Daughters, we are going to do more search in our master's special command post in the sanctuary, so if you need something call upon me. In the meantime, hold down our fort, ok girls." They answer, "Yes mother." This last exchange was working well to my benefit as it sends a strong signal to the empire of my faith in my daughters, which is of course very true. Now it is time to clear our sanctuary. As we enter in, Medica is relaxing in their recent camp. I ask her, "Medica darling, have you noticed anything unusual?" She answers, "Master I did earlier however it proved to be a false alarm thus I felt it was a glitch in our sensors." Next, my lights updated me, "Master, the distortion is no longer in this Sanctuary nevertheless it now appears to be imitating from your Nørresundby Palace!" I then responded, "Get the saints there to quarantine it as I shall be there soon. All who wish to join me can, and even get a sneak preview of our master's quarters. Medica, has things been ok with you lately?" Medica answers, "Except for now wars, things are ok?" Then my mind started to focus on what may be the problem, "What do you mean no wars? And why are you not giving me updated reports on how you are deploying the thirty armies that are defending us?" Medica jumped up with a big smile and said, "I did not know." Thus, I replied, "Now get to work and save us. Spirits, why have you not informed Medica that she is our homeland commander, and order her to start saving us?" Now my spirits are starting to understand my soul as they respond, "Oh master please forgive us, this was a serious infraction on our part. We will run our diagnostics and fix the error." I am then smiling said to my spirits, "I trust you will do a fine job, have the courts get their new homeland security commander all the intelligence that she needs." Medica now smiled and jumped up and flashed out of

sight. Maybe she was not so disappointed after all as she stopped
by my palace to introduce herself to Yudachyov and thank her for
taking such good care of me. This indeed did impress me as I was
informed of her visit by my lights. Yudachyov may now actually
start getting credit when I am perceived as being in a good mood.
When I am in a bad mood, I will have to double the guards around
her for safety purposes. As I arrive at my palace all the Royal
Deities Sanctuary including the Seonji are putting the palace staff
to work giving them tours. Maybe I should start tossing up a few
palaces in the Sanctuary with plenty of kitchens and dining rooms
with lavish ballrooms. Even though they are divine, they were
created as all females and still have that basic instinctive desire to
serve guests. I will get my spirits starting on that. Everyone is here
now except for my new commanding god who is busy at work.
Something about war gets puts my girls on the ball, which I guess
is good. I will have Ruth or Mary bring our parents over for a
special tour. As I greet them, I give each a special key to my palace
and ask for their support on a few things of a personal nature,
"Please do not pester our master when he is here. The Sanctuary is
your home turf as this palace is his, not mine home turf. Also,
please do not hurt my special toy Yudashkin since she is new to
this side of the line. I do hope you will be like Medica as earlier she
introduced herself to Yudachyov, yet be careful with your jokes, as
she is still very innocent and shy. I do thank you so much for
respecting my wishes on these few requests, as our love shall reign
over us for eternity." The lights now flash indicating an update. I
looked at them and they said, "Master, the disruption is coming
from your master bedroom." I then added, "Let us go there now
and seal off the room." With the room sealed, the lights ran the
scans again and the distortion still existed so we entered the room.
Immediately my shy little bundle of love rushed over behind our
soda. I sat down, front of her, and introduced her to my lights
telling her, "Yudachyov, I would like to introduce you to our
thrones lights. Each throne has lights, which contain the
summation of all our knowledge and any captured knowledge.
Lights only communicate with courts of gods, unless a god tells

them otherwise. The lights would like to talk with us. So, remember you are my chamber maiden and I am responsible for your safety. Ok, my love?" She nervously shook her head yes. My lights were alarmed by her nervousness, however I told them this is a part of her being and among the major reasons, and I selected her. The lights now ask, "Yudachyov, are you a member of any evil force that wishes to harm our Empire?" She immediately put her head on my shoulder and begins to cry saying to me, "Master, do you not know my heart?" I tell her, "I do know your heart and I am so sorry my love." I look at my lights and say, "She is loyal to me and only to me." The lights ask me, "How do you know?" I tell them, "Excuse me, am I not the Master's Queen goddess?" The lights then ask again, "Master, we need to scan her to make sure." I tell them, "No one touches my Yudachyov. Remember she belongs to me such as my hand belongs to me. Scan me instead." Yudachyov hugs me and says, "I knew you know all things in my heart and mind, for you have always been and shall always be my only god." I gently kiss her and wipe away her tears from her reddened sorrow filled face. The lights then ask, "Master, is it worth placing your Empire in risk?" I say to them, "Do not I place my life in her hands each time we sleep together. I do because of my faith in her. She is loyal to me so I am not placing my Empire at risk." Then the lights flash that an update is forthcoming, "Master, the disturbance is once again in the sanctuary." I then told them, "For security purposes and for Yudachyov's protection, scan this room again." They scanned it and came up with an "All clear." I then tell my lights, "When I live in someone's heart such as Yudachyov, I know her mind and deeds through faith. If a god demands faith from the servants, then cannot the servants receive faith from the one whom they worship?" The lights agree and ask if they can rush back to the Sanctuary. I tell them to keep the palace sealed. They agree, implement, and vanish all instantly. I now tell Yudachyov, "My child, I must also go to the sanctuary, however I shall return. Remember, you are mine bound by your love for me and my unwavering faith in you." Her starry eyes gave me a relieved tight hug and smothered my face with kisses." I then kiss her, get up waving goodbye, and vanish. I must confess I felt sorry for her. I did not expect the lights to follow that line of questions. I would have hoped that the requests I gave to my goddesses and queens would apply to them. I will have my spirits talk to them. I do not want her placed in that position again. I am supposed to be her protector, not her prosecutor. I must get back to those running in circle game, except I hope with quarantining to have closed half the circle. I am going to continue monitoring my palace because now the thing that is bothering me is how it jumps between my intimate places. Is it showing me that I am vulnerable anywhere I may be. I will have my lights study this for me, although I cannot think of any connection between my master bedroom and the Royal Deities Sanctuary. This shall be another mission for my lights. As I approach my sanctuary, my lights tell me the disturbance is now around my throne. I ask, "Who is on my throne now?" The Lights reply, "Oh do not worry Master, the Commanding God of Homeland Security is there. She will fix this for us." It now hits me, Medica was alone with the disturbance in the sanctuary, she went to my master bedroom to meet my toy Yudachyov, and she is on the throne now. Ok, time to bring the mystery visitor or whatever out of its hole. I then say to my lights, please tell my Medica that I need her in my palace in the Queen's number one receiving room. I now had a special hunch that I might make me a catch with this hideaway getting a sudden surprise. Either way I can justify her visit here since my security is tighter than that around the throne. She arrives quickly and since she missed this morning tour with her sisters, she has some of our staff escort to my receiving room, as they summon me. I rush quickly into the room, yelling at my staff making sure Medica can hear, "Darn, do you know we may not have a commanding godly idle during a war?" I rush into the room and apologize, saying, "Oh love, I am so sorry, they are a new staff." Medica then replies, "This room is so beautiful, for I have never been in one such as this." I told her, "You missed the Royal Deities Sanctuary tour this morning because of the war." Medica replies, "I know, I do hope you will give me a special one, or you will allow that precious

Yudachyov to guide us." I smile and say, "That is a good idea; I keep forgetting that at one time you did live inside me." Medica then replies, "And such a happy time it was." I remind her, "I shall stand by my promise to let you live in my spirit anytime you wish." Medica utters back, "I do appreciate that invitation master; however I enjoy living as I was created and modified by you of course. How may I serve you today?" I then ask her, "Medica, do you love me and would you always tell me the truth?" Medica falls to her knees and cries out, "Oh master my love for you is endless, as I hope you remember, I risked eternal damnation to serve you when you were but a forgotten lord of New Venus. Have I ever not told the truth to you my god?" I pause for a moment realizing that so many are now calling me god and I ask her, "My love, why do you call me god?" Medica answers, "You must also be our god when our master is away." I walk over and kiss her, yet her kiss is a little reserved so I ask, "Tell me Medica is anything different about you today than a few days ago?" She pauses for a moment remaining silent and then confesses, "My god, I know what the disturbance is and I swear it will harm no one. Will you believe and trust me?" I told her, "My special love, I believe and trust you in all things without question. I also know in all things you will obey me without hesitation and that you would share all your things with me as I have shared all my things with you. Now, show me the disturbance, since we both have so much work to do." She froze and before I did a female appear on the floor with her head on my knees. Medica was frozen I think for fear of my anger so I asked her, "Medica, why do you look so rigid?" She said, "I think maybe you will no longer love me." I smiled and said to her, "Medica, you are mine forever to love and cherish are you not?" Medica replies, "That is my prayer and my hope filled dream my goddess." I then motioned for her to come to me and I hugged her kissing my love with great feeling. I then answered her by saying, "Then your prayers are answered. I do hope you understand that you may have anyone you wish to lay with as long as it is also his or her free will. Now, please introduce me to your new special secret toy." Medica then updates me, "My master, she is not my secret toy although I would wish so. You already know her. Speak to her for she wishes to worship you." I then wrap Medica in my arms with her back to this stranger and say to the stranger, "May I know who wishes to share my love" while kissing Medica. The servant answers, "I am one who has journeyed long and hard to worship you." I then said to her, "First, pull yourself into this chamber for your safety also where did you travel from and have we ever met before?" The stranger answered, "I can as a prisoner from an evil empire, and we have met before and were many times with each other, for I have always loved you, yet you changed and returned to me hate for which I am innocent." I looked her over and said, "Well you do prove that I have good taste yet please tell me your name because we must finish this quickly so Medica can go back to her war seat. Medica, today speak with my courts for you shall have your own palace as the homeland war commanding god." She stranger on the floor then answered, "I could only pray that your hate for me would not throw me into one of your lakes of fire." I looked at her and said, "Stranger, I hate no one who is not evil and I am a strong god of good and love, thus I need no lakes of fire. Tell me your name." Her face was now filled with tears as she cried out, "You called me Eve when you loved me." I looked at her in shock. I then said, "My child how did you make it hers, you must have mastered inter dimensional travel." Eve told me, "I professed you as my god to many along the way and luckily one was a trader with your Empire. When I got here, I begged Medica, whom I also always loved since I cried in pain many days when I saw her torn body half eaten by the sea beasts wash up on my shore. I did beg her so much not to leave me, yet she had to serve her husband and departed from my womb. I do hope you will forgive her for saving me." I then looked at Eve and said, "You are mine, for we shall talk and work out our differences thus Medica honey, you may go and serve your Empire. I have an old acquaintance to visit with." Medica then kissed Eve and me thus vanishing. I now said to Eve, "We shall go to my Royal Deities Sanctuary where you can update me." Eve said, "Take me where you will my goddess and do with me what you wish." I now took her to one of my favorite flower fields. Eve was trembling with fear as her fingers were spread apart gripping her legs. She could not look me in the face. She stood in the path of our misty light from our candlelight star nearby. The light shined off her beautiful sandy blond hair and enlightened her right breast, which stole my eyes and lightly over the left side of her abdomen and a few thin patches along her legs. I could start to feel why I may have loved her at one time. I then said to her, "Eve, why do you fear me?" Eve then said, "Many of your spirits told me that when you vanished you cursed me saying that you had great hate for me. I feared a god who ruled but one galaxy, should I not fear one who rules 100,000 much more?" I then told Eve, "My child, as in any relationship that involves a male when it ends it is so much easier to hate other females for victory over them is more probable. It was wrong of me and for that I must ask your forgiveness." Eve then says, "How may one such mighty god as you ask for forgiveness from a fugitive like me for even the dirt we stand upon is greater than I?" I then went over and held her saying, "In my Empire, even the dirt is mightier than I since I rule not from my servant's fear but from their love. Please remember, like you I am also a fugitive from the same evil righteousness. Will you take my blood as your blood and worship me as your god?" Eve fell to her knees and cried out, "Oh great master, drown me in your blood that the old I shall die and if I have life it will be in your holy blood. I then pulled a small knife out of my sky, cut my finger, and gave her my hand. She eagerly wiped the blood over her and did suck upon my finger praying, "Oh master do not give me all your blood for I must have you to worship." I smiled at her and said, "Fear not my child for as I have created all who live in my Empire I also created their blood. I shall make sure I have enough holy blood to keep this flesh suit functioning. My blood did transform her and she now had the body that I created for her, with some retractable wings. We now walked in the shade of some of my favorite trees when she did drop to the ground and cry out, "My goddess, as I lay upon these red leaves in the shade of such beautiful trees I beg that you take me and enjoy that which you have given me." I told her, "Eve, as I enjoyed you over the last few million years I shall once again enjoy you many times, yet today I want our minds and hearts to unite and remove any painful memories as I feel much sorrow and pain in your soul. Please know that I have created you to a perfection that will bring great joy to many to include myself. Now tell me what you have been up to for such a long time." She began by saying, "I was one of four who were originally promoted to the heavenly angels. Shortly after you vanished, our throne was shattered by something that no one knew. Later, some space traders told us it was you. This made the throne very angry and they vowed to punish all angels from New Venus as revenge. They placed all four of us in deep dark dungeons for demons to enjoy. Boudica and Tianshire may have perished quickly, more from the absence from their lord and the punishment while being innocent. They only knew of love and good. When the lord sent them to be out of his presence, and to be enjoyed by evil their souls completely vanished. They were your greatest creations of New Venus and they did so much love you. We three would join in secret and worship you. Lablonta and I survived because of hate; we had learned about pain and misery and believed that at the end would become known. That light did not come. The throne promoted more angels only to destroy them for small infractions. Soon no angels wanted to be promoted and when they thought they might be promoted vanished into nearby galaxies thanks to a great discovery by King James. He discovered other gods ruling in other galaxies. In addition, our salvation would come from leaving the Milky Way. He always talked so highly of a god named Adorjás who actually gave them some solar systems slowly to start migrating to the future home of Mempire. The throne discovered this and put a halt to it. The Empire had already transferred about thirty percent as Adorjás found many more planets and solar systems for them. He was actually helping Mempire backfill the empty planets they were leaving with evil civilizations he no longer wanted. Fair trade we all thought." I then motioned for her to put her back against my chest as I was firmly supported by one of these strong trees. We both stretched out our legs and I held her in my arms, for I wanted to feel her pain leave a nice new body I created for her. It is always such a joy to see how happy spirits are when I place them in my A+ flesh suits as I place all of them in. I cannot justify giving those suits that diseases kill or have defective parts. How cruel and evil. I now get the joy of holding one of these nice suits with a spirit inside it that goes back a long way with me. I then start slowly to run my hand over her soft hair and lightly kiss her strawberry cheeks saying, "Please continue?" Eve continues saying, "The Mempire of Adorjás did provide you much support during your recent rescue of your lovely daughter Atlantis. Every man, woman and child begged to join the campaign they called, "Unite Atlantis with her mother." King James was so proud of them, as he did find many who were fighting in the Milky Way to tell them of his great love and pride for them. King James had petitioned all the saints, prophets and the throne to free the love angels Lablonta and myself. At first, I did not know why he also saved me although later he told me that Lablonta confessed to him her great respect and love for me and that we both went or none would go. After you put your double charge on the new throne, Adorjás was able to get all of Mempire back to his galaxy. He even created a new solar system exactly like the home galaxy that gave birth to Mempire. He was able to get the help of some neighboring galaxy gods, and took apart Lamenta and rebuilt it in the new solar system. They are only transferring the populated places with their exact landscape copies filling in the vacant areas. The only thing different will be the night stars. They will be reunited on the other side of Adorjás to help provide concealment from the Milky Way. They are in a big rush now as reconstruction of the throne will be in the deep distant future for after you ripped the "poop" out of them. For some strange reason a galaxy not too far away is launching a blistering continuous attack on them, yet at the same time sparing any flesh life forms and rescuing any lost spirits who so desire. King James had provided sanctuary for us protecting us from the throne, which had vowed to capture us and destroy us in a special lake of fire. Oh god, how could a throne hate us so?" I told her, "My love, I know not why and am of course so saddened when I hear about it. My attack on that evil throne almost lost me my empire for an illegal attack across dimensional lines." Eve asks, "How did you save your empire?" I told her, "With the help of mighty friends of the ages." Eve then responds by saying, "At least you are safe, for you are my only hope for salvation." I then ask her, "What about Lablonta and Mempire?" Eve then says, "The inclusion of Lablonta in the Mempire equation causes great division against those who fashion hAyonjE and those who claim that Lablonta was also a Hersonian Queen. Her death at the hands of a Hersonian Queen sealed her death with Mempire also. I begged for her to join me in my escape, yet she said you most likely hated her more for raising Atlantis in secret before giving her to you." I looked at Eve and said, "I know that many of my days were as a servant of evil, yet I do not hate you or Lablonta. You served me well and did give me much good love. You mothered, for my glory the first Garden of Eden that died without the stains of sin. I have so much missed you over the many millenniums that have separated us. I do beg that you give me a chance to love you again. In addition, Lablonta gave Atlantis to me without prejudice to my horrible evil past. She saved Atlantis from my evil. How could I be justified in hating such a great deed? I do not know Lablonta yet I often find myself ruling as she did." Eve then put her hand up against my mouth and starting kissing me and crying, "I want to be a slave to your love my master. I want all to say, "Eve truly loves her goddess." I then said to Eve, "Let us go up this hill a little ways beside a nice stream where we shall once again share the burning love inside of us. I shall make you the mother of love in our Empire, for you shall wonder the galaxies looking for those who have no love and making their lives filled with love again. I shall give your many lights to help you. You may give all love except our master whom you may only worship. I know that if he got love from you he would want me no more." Eve wrapped her arms around me and said, "You flatter me with lies, I took what you cast aside once and do not intend to do so again." I then told her, "You did get a raw deal with Adam didn't you? I regret bringing him as a toy from Lamenta. That toy turned out to be a big headache for me. Whatever happened with him in his gold

old boy's network?" Eve then said, "He was captured by some demons and taken away to an unknown place. Traders told us in confidence that he had really made some leader angry and was caste into a dungeon." I then said, "I truly do not like to hear of anyone suffering even my enemies." Eve then said to me, "Master, why do you make me suffer now?" We were walking beside a nice rock bed stream as she sat down along the side letting some of her toes cool off in the water. I asked her, "My champion of love, how do I make you suffer?" Eve said, "By depriving me of the touch of your hands and lips as I remember you had such great skills." I then sat beside her and told her, "My great Eve, mother of so many worlds, you shall suffer no more for your goddess shall now serve you." In addition, the happy times of old flooded both of our minds as the stupidity and jealousy of mine was now craving for her forgiveness. I owe this creation so much for she had always truly served me and loved me even when I was a cast away. As the memories of my cruelty towards her punishes my soul I wonder, why she always loved me so. I now pull my lips away from hers as she is so desperately trying to share the waste air that is coming out of my mouth I ask her, "Eve I have been cruel and evil towards you so many times, why can you still love me?" As she squeezed me so tight with her wonderful mothering arms, she said, "Because the times you loved me were so much greater than the few times you did not give me your love. Your love account with me has always had a high balance, now let me replace that which I lost." Eve always had a way of controlling me because she always puts her heart on the table and gives me the knives and permission to destroy if so desired. How could I ever hurt one so loyal? Maybe I should be in that dungeon instead of Adam. I now wonder why I could not be submissive to him, yet I can barely stay on my feet with my master, as I seem always to be pulling him down to cover me with the warmth of his power and love. I think it was because Adam demanded it, whereas Bogovi never demands and is always so willing to sacrifice and give all that he has. He is so much greater than Adam personality wise. I may secretly send some warrior spirits to find him and release him and tell them do not let him know from whence you came. After all, because of him I have to meet and love the creation that now is chocking the air out of me with her intense display of deep love. Eve is the mother of deep love as evidenced by the way she was loved by those who were in her family, to even include recently to have Medica willing to sacrifice all for her. I so understand Medica's feelings. Love shall flow in my 113,000 galaxies and we now have a waiting list of 67,000. The list is much that the galaxies have volunteered to donate more power spirits as my lights will combine them to make hopefully two more throne-level power spirits. These two will cut very hard at the waiting list and allow my spirits to work more on raising the quality of living for all my children so that I have fewer if not rare cases of a child who longs to have what was promised such as my blessed toy Yudachyov. I have heard of some grumbling in my courts about me calling her my toy as being degrading. I think maybe my courts need some more work, however to address that complaint let me say, she is my toy and we do play together. I shall never play with her rights and feelings. She is treated, as among my greatest creations, for in my chambers there is not flesh dweller and goddess, there is Lilith and Yudachyov equals. She is protected by my love. She is free to leave at any time. If she needs, forget when she needs some excitement or adventure we will provide it for her. Her quality of life is also of such great importance. This is getting crazy now, three days and three outstanding embalmment exotic thrilling love amalgamations. The I three days ago is not the me today. I have been defeated by Iris, Yudachyov and Eve, from a very somewhat shy goddess of power to a flesh dweller consumed by shyness to what may have been my first true love and one who absolute controls me. I thank Gyor-Moson-Sopron for putting me on a roller coaster that may require me to build a larger palace as 4,000 penthouses may not be enough. I still yet have the goddess of love and my master's grandmother and mother, as the latter two must be confidential and before our master's return. I owe them this, for if they truly want it from me they have earned that right. With the master's mother and grandmother I will be completely the servant because I do not care what they say, they outrank me. They are my gods, yet it is hard to worship a god who fights to see which ones can get their knees the lowest to serve. This is a wonderful problem indeed. Oh, how my flesh is burning with love now, for Eve knows how to pull from me everything and she is so great about cleaning it up and putting it back into place. She is the architectural constructionist in the application and conception of love, especially concerning my love. I remember the dew on the vividly green leaves and as they sucked in all the wonderful aromas from the copious array of flowers that flooded the garden we first met in. I remember looking in shock and amazement that another almost like me existed, the only thing different was she was built in perfection, which is understandable as she came from dirt and all things dirty tend to produce greater rewards at least in the short run, the only exception being Eve. I was made in the image of my creator, later recorded as Adam's creator. Luckily, my creator is from a distant universe. I know not from whence I came nor even my mother. I would search hard for her, yet I now shall accept as my mother and father Edward and Prudence. My spirits have updated me in that time with them was not a true penance but a sanctuary against evil and was added to penance time since I was deprived of my throne and divinity. The blood and guts of my penance was with Drusilla, whom I also miss so much. I think Eve's penetrating love is opening some deeply buried rooms inside my soul. The winds are cooler now and with our bodies being drenched in sweet I create and place over us a nice quilt with her head flower as the center peace. I include my red flowers representing my protection of her and a vine of green to represent the birth of two planets of humans that I know of (old old Earth and the old New Venus) Eve tells me that New Venus was completely destroyed after I departed. So sad, a race that did not sin in the Garden except for one son whom later joined the saints and produced two-throne level saints, one of which became a heavenly angel. New Venus ended up producing three heavenly angels. Although most of my time there was dedicated to fighting an unheard of invasion of demons, as none of the quintillion planets I now rule have in their histories records of such invasions.

I bear in mind that throne never had any solid evidence, with only reports coming from traders who illegally smuggled products across dimensions. I cannot conceive why that could justify destroying a planet with so much goodness in it, yet I still am mystified that the old ancient Mars who had a perfect race was destroyed. I cannot change what they did; I believe I have put a stop to it for a long time, especially with a couple of neighboring galaxies vested in its ruin. The priority task assigned to my spirit is too make sure it does not happen in the soon to be over 200,000 galaxies in my master's kingdom. My flesh suit and soul have now been recharged by the master of recharging. I shall now rightly assigned and reward my team of love since their mission is as important, if not more importance than that which I dedicated to war lavish palaces one called Siyangulov (Сиянгулов) Palace for the Goddess of Great Love from the Eternal Throne Pusztaszentlászló and the other for Eve, the Mother of Love called Siyalov (Сиялов) Palace. They call be not too far (say less than two million light years or a less than one second flash in our new flash drives) from our Royal Deities Sanctuary. The new flash transporters are working to perfection for the flesh children of Atlantis. These palaces will be placed in uninhabited solar systems in which we will find a few dying ones, give them a new star and begin creating new planets in these systems. All gods in my empire will be required to visit these palaces. I want to get a love fever burning in my children, and I shall start at the top and we will work our way down as we work our way towards the greatest empire of good and love ever to have existed. As Eve and I continue walking, I get an alert to report to the throne immediately. I tell my spirits to take Eve and Pusztaszentlászló to their new palaces. To say goodbye to Eve as follows, "So sorry my rediscovered love of the ages, I must respond to this emergency. Go now with my deepest love and meet your new servants who will help you with your missions. I now hop into my personal flash drive and shoot for my throne.

Chapter 10

Mothers discover their new home

As I walk down the vast audience flooring so many thoughts are rushing through my mind. I felt this thus elected not to arrive in front of my courts as I can see them waiting ahead. I have yet to hear anything from Iris and it looks like Medica is in the field. When that girl goes to war, she gets smartly involved. I have not received any updates on my new enemy in these wars Rødkærsbro. I may have to brace myself, as they will lay all this on me at once. I have had a few rewarding encounters over the last few days, so maybe it is time for me to get working. The courts have now spotted me as the lights gave away my position. The courts urge me, "Master, please hurry!" Thus, I zap in front of them and ask, "Who is on the throne now?" An answer from a new source replies' "Master It is I your humble Goddess from Our Higher Throne Bácsalmás." I then ask my courts, "Is not Bácsalmás qualified to handle this?" Bácsalmás answers, "My goddess, I believe you will want to see this." I walk over, hold her hand smiling at her, and say to my throne, "Show me this mystery?" Then I saw one before me who has been beaten and cut with the stitches running over her back and she is asking for something not to speak. Her bruised and beaten eyes were fighting to keep her soul from escaping to its freedom. I then asked, "I hope this is not who I think it is?" Bácsalmás wrapped her arms around me as I placed my head on her shoulder, she told, "It is our master." I then said to my courts, "Bring me Tápiószolos from Balatonföldvári." The courts then said, "On his way master, sadly we have more to show you." I then said to Bácsalmás, "Will you save your goddess now Bácsalmás?" Bácsalmás whispers back, "I shall save you because I can never love and worship a god as great as you ever again. If you fall, it will be on my back as I shall be worshipping you, I will take you back to our sanctuary where we may all worship you." The courts showed me the next stream as my Suisan was crying out on a poorly made cross that had her hands and feet tied to it. I heard her say, "I now return to you Lilith, receive my soul my sister." Moreover, at this did the people cast stones upon her saying, "You are a blasphemer, for Lilith's sisters live in the Royal Deities Sanctuary. She came and blessed us once and now with your terrible deeds she may return. Die you demon from the hells." Just as she died some of our priests made it to her. They did not know until too late that this horrible murder had been committed. They cursed the people there and demanded that all your blood that could be found poured out on this sight. And they did pour your blood all over the sight declaring that no one ever enter this ground again to keep it holy yelling to the people "For here today we have committed a terrible sin and shall receive the wrath of our master." I then said, "Put all who are there back again, and make a strong force to keep them in. Let not their feet touch the ground for that ground shall be declared by me to be holy. Find me the soul of my sister and bring me to her." As I see the great pain on her face I question my decision to give the Harvey a special goddess, for now Siusan will most likely not want to let them serve her. I with my garrison army arrive at Sasdi as Tápiószolos comes slowly and casually singing salutations with arms open to greet me. I yell at him, "Do you not harken to my calls to report to our master's throne?" Tápiószolos then answers, "Well the master was not their so I figured I would get around to it someday." I yelled back as I froze his armies, "Fool, I was your master, for you shall be vanished now and I shall give a new god to this galaxy." Tápiószolos seeing his armies froze and all his allies running away fell to his knees crying, "Forgive me oh great master." I then had the lights to stream this to all my galaxies, "Let him who defies my commands see this for I am your master's number one servant. Obey my commands or I shall destroy you and give your galaxy to someone new. It is better for Tápiószolos that I destroy him today for if Bogovi were here he would punish him without mercy all the days of eternity." Just then I saw to more flashes arrive, Queen Mother Goddess Julia and Queen Sister Goddess Julia each standing on my sides. The Queen Mother screamed out, "I am the mother of our master and I beg my master's number one servant to punish this evil god without mercy for eternity." Then did Queen Sister Goddess Julia scream out, "Any who disobey my god shall parish by the blood of our master." They then whispered in my ear, "Do with him what you wish my god" as one raised my right hand and the other my left hand. I did then yell out, "Because I am the goddess of good and love today Tápiószolos you shall vanish and I shall give your galaxy a new god. Vanish and never be seen or heard of again as your soul shall be spread in small lights the over my Empire." I now thought about the video stream from my lights, and asked, "Is there any other who wishes to challenge me today? We are at war so send me more armies with equipment so I may give them to Iris and Medica." I figured to be able to skim and build a few armies to monitor Balatonföldvári until the new throne got everything intact. I am going to give all Balatonföldvári's armies to Iris so I never have to worry about a religious rebellion. Those armies will be on the front lines. Slowly eliminate possible trouble and keep those who are loyal to me a little longer. Let them die for their dead god and my servants live for me. I like my way of thinking. This may sound hard; yet one little bad weed seed can eventually overtake the entire garden. Why should a garden suffer when a seed can be removed? I also tell my courts to round up all Tápiószolos immediate family including parents, such as wives and all sons for a court sponsored streamed execution. Finally, the courts reported they had the soul of Siusan and that she was resisting returning to me. I then said, "Tell Siusan her sister begs to see her, and if that does not work bring her to me for I must see her." Within a few seconds, she appeared in front of me. I rushed over to her frigid soul and happened to look behind me and saw a heart shaped cloud. Then did our Queen Sister Goddess Julia say unto me, "If your servant Queen Grandmother Goddess Tompaládony were here today she would wish you to have this. Take your time her for our mother and I shall help Bácsalmás on the throne. Worry about nothing for we will handle it. We think you will need some time to diffuse any hard feelings or hurts so we will tell Iris, Eve, and Yudachyov you shall return in a few days." They both were giggling as I went over and wrapped my arms around them kissing their cheeks saying, "You are the best Queens an Empire could dream of. Keep giggling; remember you are in my rotation also." Then the Queen Mother answered, "A reward that I pray will soon befall upon me." I smiled and said, "I am so sorry mother, you are a big priority and must happen before your son returns." She smiled and agreed as the Queen Sister spoke, "Lilith, and my mother?" I then looked at Julia and said, "Your mother loves me as you do, should I punish her for being good in the past and saving her children from evil and death?" Julia looked at her mother and asked, "Is this your wish mother? The Queen Mother than answered, "It is the greatest prayer of not only me but my mother also, for we want to drink wine from the fountain of the greatest goddesses of good. Is this wrong for us my daughter? Would you not want for us to enjoy the greatest wine ever in the heavens?" Julia then said, "I have drank that wine and I can promise you that never shall either of find better and I pray also that you have that bottle in your hands soon and please before my brother returns. I fear not what my brother may say to me for I will say unto him, did you not give me to serve her?" We both looked at her as her mother said, "Truly my daughter is a great goddess of love, good, and wisdom for she loves with empathy through the hearts of others." I then said, "She has been a lifeboat for me many times as I have seen her wisdom pull me out of the belly of the ancient earth. She lives in my heart also and for eternity." Then Julia said, "Mother let us give leave to our master for she has some fences to mend." Then they did vanish. I looked over at what was one time a bubbly happy go lucky special friend. She stood tall and frigid and had a far off stair refusing to look at me. I rested my hands upon my hips and stared at her. She finally said, "Master, why did you forsake me?" I told her, "Whatever has happened to you I am the blame and I am so sorry. Please believe me that I love you so much and must have you in my life for eternity. Will you forgive me?" Siusan looked at me and said, "I cannot forgive what I did not hate for I loved you even as the stones pounded my flesh and freed my soul." Then I asked her, "Why did you not want to see me when our courts discovered you?" Siusan answered, "For my soul is beaten as my face is scared and ruined. I have so much shame standing beside you today my goddess." I looked at her and said, "Do you not remember that I can make you whole again?" Siusan then replied, "Master, I failed you for no man would take me to be his wife and I have no blood running in the Harvey." I then said to her, "That is their loss not yours for you are now a penance goddess who may live with me in this universe forever and your people did have you among them yet they chose to beat and kill you." Siusan quickly replied, "Master my people do not love me so why should you love me?" I then answered her by saying, "Do you not remember that we are blood of our blood for you are in me and I am in you. Will you let me tell you what happened? Siusan then answered, "If it be your will my master." I then told her that I trusted Tápiószolos and tasked him to watch you carefully and to contact my spirit if any trouble should arise. Tápiószolos foolishly thought that since our master is away doing his penance he was under no obligation to obey my commands. That was the last mistake he shall ever make for I have destroyed him forever and my courts our now executing his entire family. His armies are now fighting in our war under our commanding god Iris as she is sending three armies back to guard Balatonföldvári and serve their new galaxy god." Siusan asked, "Whom did you select as Balatonföldvári's new god?" I told her, "I have yet to decide and I must have you help me select one who will protect the Harvey and allow them to expand in this galaxy. Will you please search your heart and soul for one whom you would like to see on this throne?" Siusan looked at me as she was almost starting to break a smile that she quickly pulled back saying, "Would you at least let me be a servant in that throne my master?" I then looked at her and said, "Never, the only way I will let you serve in that throne is as their goddess! Now you either accept being the goddess of Balatonföldvári or you come back with me!" Siusan then fell to her knees, which really does not do that much when you are high in the sky and with tears said to me, "My master would you give me such a great honor even though the Harvey hate me?" I then looked at her and said, "My love, your people love you, for after your death they flood the area with my blood and declared it to be holy ground forever. Love, I owe you so much more because I let you down, one who means so much to me that I truly missed. I have returned all who cast stones upon you and judged you to the area where you died. I have them one foot off the ground so that they may not touch this holy ground. I shall now have you stand beside me and I shall judge and destroy them." Siusan then said, "Master how can we destroy them for I had no proof that you were in me except my words. They were afraid you would punish them for the words I spoke about you. Can we punish the blind for being blind? Let me forgive them." I then looked at her and said, "I gave unto Sásdi a child goddess and they gave me back a complete goddess, aged greater than even I so full of love and mercy. Siusan, do unto your servants as you desire. Do you wish for me to join you?" Siusan said, "No master this I must do for my people." I thought to myself how could one grow so wise in such a few years, although her years went by much faster than mine she has gained the divinity of many millennium. The people of Balatonföldvári are very lucky indeed. She then appeared before those who killed or were involved in her death and said, "Fear not those who took away my life for I am your goddess Siusan. Tell my people that I shall love and care for them as my master loves and cares for her servants. Lilith has given all of Balatonföldvári to me so I shall be very busy. Call out my name when you need me and I shall send an angel to you." Then did one female among them cry out, "Oh master will you forgive my foolish husband and spare his life for I need for him to provide for our six children least we starve in the streets?" Siusan looked at the woman and said, "Woman your husband is lucky to have you petition for him for he is forgiven, as I shall also forgive all of you. Your deaths will not serve a gain for the Harvey people. Go and tell my children that I am a goddess of love and mercy." Then I appeared behind her saying nothing. I then bowed to her as the people were horrified and ran as fast as they could screaming in the streets, "We now have a Harvey goddess named Siusan who is blessed and loved by Lilith." While Siusan was talking, I had my lights, and courts quickly add Siusan's statues beside mine in the entire galaxy starting with Sásdi. The priests were briefed that Siusan was the new goddess of Balatonföldvári and that those who worship her are worshipping me. She is the only galaxy god or goddess that can be worshipped in my name. Siusan returned to me looking much better saying to me, "I do believe the joy of forgiving outweighs the hate of their hurt." Wow is all I could think. How can I let her live so far away. Wait, I do not have too. I now showed her our new flash drives so she can travel from her throne to my palace or her true home the Royal Deities Sanctuary instantly. She was so amazed telling me, "Master so many things have changed I feel as a stranger now. I saw Julia with a woman I know not and they spoke of an Iris, Eve, and Yudachyov that I know not." I then looked at Siusan and said, "Yes my child many good things and many bad things have happened yet fear not for you know me and my spirits will show you all things my love." That which you missed is not as great as you being missed are. I still remember how excited I was when discovering that one I loved was Harvey. Once I had you in my heart I would never again set you free." Siusan than cried out to me, "Master keep me as your slave, and never curse me by taking away my chains of slavery." I was now thinking to myself that this wise goddess might even be able to teach Tompaládony a few lines. I then said to my Harvey diamond, "My spirits will give many new solar systems packed with life sustaining orbiting planets to Balatonföldvári and we shall call out to all dimensions for the return of the Harvey to their goddess. I

will talk to Gyor-Moson-Sopron and ask him for helpppp . . ."
Gyor-Moson-Sopron then answers unexpected (sorry Harvies) "I
have seen the suffering of the Harvey which is so sad, for they
were created to be living flowers for the gods. Sadly, only one
goddess could appreciate their beauty thus I shall petition all
dimensions for the return of the Harvey to their new sacred
homeland." Then as fast as he showed up he was gone. It now hit
me that I must be careful when I speak his name for to do so is to
invite his presence. Would hate to do that unexpectedly now during
my 'hot nights' winning streak that I have a feeling shall continue
in a few short hours, I do so hope since these put be completely of
free will. Siusan asked me, "Who was that voice . . . . ?" I told her,
"The mighty god of many universes. My saints are putting new
doors on all the temples of Sásdi, and soon will complete all
temples in Balatonföldvári. Let me show you my treasure. All the
doors shall be red to show all that our divinity was earned through
the blood of sacrifice." Siusan then begged, "Master, allow me to
be the one kneeling and sitting behind you." I then said to her, "No
Siusan, I am your servant and protector as all must know of our
union. They must know that what you say is the same as what I say.
My temple books are adding the complete history of our love."
Then Siusan said, "I hope you did not include the wine drinking." I
reassured her, "My love that is for the Royal Deities Sanctuary."
Sadness now overshadowed her beautiful blue face as she said to
me, "I wish I could spend some time in the Royal Deities
Sanctuary for I do miss my sisters and their wine so much." I then
wrapped my arms around her and told her, "You will have our flash
drives and may enter and leave as you wish. One second you are
here, the next you are in the Royal Deities Sanctuary. You may
have all your loves and serve your servants also." She then asked
the words I have been longing for ever sense the courts mentioned
her name, "Master will I ever have your wine again?" I told her,
"Only if you stay in our river of salivation where the wine flows."
She then, showing her new confidence in negotiating skills asked,
"Master would now be ok?" I told her, "My love I do not think I
could have lasted much longer. I have some nice red clouds

prepared for us. Come lay for me now my treasure." She now rested her blue soul upon the soft clouds. The clouds looked so happy to have her upon them allowing her soul to mold into a sensual position. Her eyes looked up at me with my invitation in them. As I now slowly roamed, my greedy fingers over her soul memories of how the descendants of Eve's sisters massacred all the Harvey on my New Venus rushed through my head. As I have recently had too much trust in others to care for Siusan, my faith in the descendants proved to be ill founded as the Harvey's blood covered the hard cold lands they fought with to survive. I can still hear their blood called, "Oh Lord wilt thou save us?" They got no answer as their souls rush back to join their ancestors. Even in the midst of this war with Rødkærsbro, we shall establish a security for them that my spirits will monitor them. I may have let them down too many times yet my spirits will not let them down. They had received the same reward living on a planet that I was lord of as their brothers and sisters received living on planets ruled by evil, and that was their blood flowing upon the surfaces. Siusan has been so different in that she mixes logic and forgiveness into her actions. She had learned to live as a non-blue hiding herself under different colors, and then we discovered her to be Harvey; she was willing to give her life for the sin of being a Harvey. That was when I knew this sacrificial lamb was mine. I was too much in love with here and Amity that there could be no turning back. She has always undervalued herself too much and always forgives those who strike her, often times offering to let them strike her more for their pleasure as pain for her is a normal cost associated with each breath. My courts and lights understand the priority I have placed on Siusan and no stupid Rødkærsbro war is going to force her to undergo any more sacrifice. Any rebellions from non-Harvey in the Balatonföldvári galaxy will meet my armies fully loaded for immediate genocide. The non-Harvey will of course be permitted to continue their lives as is and with all the same upgrades and rights as all others in the universe. Once they see this in action, the rebellions will cease. That will be Siusan's first priority in establishing faith in the non-Harvey in which she will be able to

accomplish with ease. Wow, Siusan is putting her famous blueprint
on me. She is pulling wine out of my sealed wine cellars that Iris,
Eve, and Yudachyov did not find. We always call this her blueprint
since she appears to know exactly how everything is laid out and
how it functions. We often ask her how she can do this as she
simply says, "By listening to the heart." Wow, oh my goodness, if
this does not end I will never again function yet I plead that it
never ends. She has now repositioned in such a way I have access
to her wine bottle and may now start enjoying her wine. Harvey
wine is so . . . . ooo fine and this wine is aged and as usual well
made. Siusan was always very meticulous about what she ate,
concentrating on herbs and spices that excited the glands to
produce the "whatever" she wanted. Now with the foodless bodies
she continues this practice now using additional external means for
the digestion and extraction. When she makes up her mind to do
something, it is done, just as she now has her master in total
submission not wanting to be freed. The queen of the blueprints
has no mercy on those who drink wine with her, for she
concentrates so much on servitude and requests so little in return
and so sadly those sharing this experience with her having nothing
left to give in return. Yet I am so lucky to have spirits that can feed
me a few extra batteries so I can keep on charging. I refuse not to
fairly give back to one who always gives and gives without asking
to receive. I also know that all who love her in the Royal Deities
Sanctuary, which is of course all who have met her, feel the same.
She is that important to us. She has me feeling so good that I could
stand in front of my armies in the middle of a raging battle and still
feel this good. Wow, my blueprint has been discovered. I now look
over and see the star to the local planet hitting the places we just
departed. Could it be morning already? Oh, I hope Julia did tell
Yudachyov about the urgency of this crisis. I now ask Siusan if we
can talk a few minutes before I return to my palace and work on
some throne matters. Siusan then replies, "Speak as you wish my
master." I ask her, "Please promise me we shall meet sooner next
time." She answers, "With this new flash drive device you gave me
I do believe we shall meet quit often." I responded, "Siusan, my

courts will be calling you often to appear on the throne with us as you are first a sacred member of the Royal Deities Sanctuary and prime exposure with the other goddesses will suppress many challenges and reward those who follow you by sharing in your glory. I know you will do an outstanding job, as you must first gain the trust of the non-Harvey, as no others have ever worshiped a Harvey goddess. My spirits are with you this time. Even as I may off, somewhere doing something my spirits will be with you. Call upon them, for they are with you always. I must now depart with the image of your beauty outshining the red clouds that worship you in this sky." Siusan then said, "Remember master, I am always worshiping and serving you and that I know your blueprint." I then said to Siusan, "You absolutely know my blueprint and without reservation I can say, 'no other knows me as you do my love.'" As I started to leave, she began to cry as a terrible loneliness tore through her newly revived divine soul. I said to her, "Oh Siusan, we must get back out in space before you flood this planet." She looked down and was surprised to see the rivers starting to fill. We jumped back into space as she said to me, "Master, I have been alone for so long, I just do not want to be alone now." I reached over, put her in my arms, and asked her, "Would you like to go back to the Royal Deities Sanctuary and meet your sisters and any new sisters or queens." Siusan looked at me with the look she had when we were children and I was solving some big problem she was facing. It is a trusting looked packed with fear however energized by faith. She shook that beautiful face yes and reached out for me. I would take her back home. I know the sisters want so much to see her and this will be good for our Royal Deities Sanctuary. Siusan asks me, "Master, what about my galaxy?" I told her, "Fear not for it will take some time to redo the temple doors, build additional statues of you and to add you to the holy books. The armies are loyal to you, and are prepared. They have written on the backs of their uniforms "Siusan's Army with a picture of you. My spirits will tell your servants that you are with your sisters and the masters Queen in the Royal Deities Sanctuary. Bear in mind, there is no greater place a goddess may be then in the

Sanctuary from which comes those who sit upon the throne. You will sit on the throne before you go back. We will insure that all see you on the throne as soon the Queen Grandmother will return and all four Queens will bow before you and say, "Holy is the name of Siusan in which we give all our eternal love." Every galaxy will see that, as we will have a ceremony demoting you to your home galaxy to care for the Harvey and their friends. I did not want to tell her that one empire, which controlled a solar system already, announced session and once the acting throne verified it; we spun the planets out into the darkness of between them and the next solar system far from any suns. They all should be frozen within a few days, as we will slowly bring them in to the outer limits of their solar system until we can verify collection of all the souls. Once verified they will return to their original orbits as the animal life will be restored and Mother Nature will clean the planet for us allowing for future Harvey seeking sanctuary from other universes. I know I did not stutter when I explained the new rules; however, there is that percentage that must challenge. I understand that now all the children were guilty, that is why they will naturally be judged. The innocent ones will join the saints and the guilty be punished. We have something to special here to throw away. As Siusan enters the Royal Deities Sanctuary all the sisters go frantic especially the ones that Siusan has their blueprints. The excitement is so frantic that the Queen Mother rushes to me and asks, "What is this that even my daughter are fighting to touch." I told her, "You would be wise to join the fight for Siusan is the creator of all love. Pusztaszentlászló, join the fight also so you can enjoy a joy unspeakable that is charged by love that has been created in the pits of hate and misery and purified by mercy and forgiveness. There can be no greater gift that I can make plain to you, that as your sisters and confirm. Since I was her slave last night, I shall go and sit upon the throne." Upon the throne sat Amity who asked me, "Master why do you come here now?" I then told her, "My dearest Amity, "I brought a surprise back for you." Amity jumped for joy smothering me with kisses and hugs to the degree that it scared the courts around the throne saying, "It is true, you have saved Siusan.

All my dreams are now true. I have the greatest master ever. May I please go and serve our sister now?" As I said go, a flash streaked across the throne, as Amity was gone. As I sat down the court reported, "Master there is craziness being reported from the Royal Deities Sanctuary as the energy levels are approaching dangerous levels." I told them, "All is well, for that which was lost is now found as your Royal Deities Sanctuary is once again made complete." I now sat back to relax the normal way souls do and try to recover from the last four days. These four days have been the greatest in my memory and I am truly dazed. The adventure and lack of control over my partner has given back the humanity in this fulfillment process. I need to stop thinking because even my thinking is being garbled. I can honestly say I have my starting lineup in place now and it is packed with starters who need no relievers. It looks like the courts, lights, and saints have our ship running on course as I can expect to be here for a while as this time the first sisters to exit the sanctuary will be still dazed. I now ask the lights for an update on the Empire's status. They give me the highlights; Medica and Iris are reporting that they are ahead of schedule, as Medica is bringing back the excess enemy war equipment apprehended for use in her homeland security. That is Medica, a scrounger to get what she needs to win. We now have the two new spirits up and producing. Our galaxy count now is 128,000 with 56,000 more waiting or 184,000 up from 180,000 with waiting down 11,000 galaxies. We expect a faster process rate with the two new spirits online, with them dedicating sixty percent of their time to processing and forty percent to upgrading current galaxies. We are making great progress in Balatonföldvári adding Siusan to the doors, statues, temple books and indoctrinating the priests. The armies are functioning and in place now with their new uniforms. Penance reports that our master is progressing excellently and that his sacrificial execution shall soon be accomplished. I now stopped them and asked, "A sacrificial execution, no one said anything about this and what about my twin sister?" The courts responded, "We will now feed you the streams from that throne as this is above our influence. Drusilla is scheduled to begin her trip home later this week. She is now in spirit form visiting our master in his mind only. She reports that his mind is tormented yet strong enough to pay the price for good. We have fed all other information to your spirits." I now thought, "Why does not evil have to sacrifice have to sacrifice for their right to be evil as good must sacrifice for the right to protect good?" I have argued this to no end only to be told this is the rule from our ancestors, which leads me no doubt, why they no longer exist. I then told my courts "Make the arrangements for me to bring Drusilla and our master back, for I do not want them to suffer as I did in the emptiness and confusion of my return trip not even knowing where I was going. Our master will be surprised at all that has changed. Now let us hold the fort down so he actually has something worth returning to rule." As I was now scanning the special reports prepared by my spirits, the Court of Fun and Dance began playing some special music for me. This music is truly worthy of any throne. This throne seat now feels as if it is turning soft as my soul is mellowed with it as to form a new unity. I hope they are not too attached because I need to bounce around and shake up a few week points in my chains. I can wait for a few more songs as we must find someone to hold the throne as I go out and I do not want to take away from my sister's joyous reunion, because when it is all said and done, that is all they truly have. The courts are flashing some beautiful scenery pictures taken from some of our new galaxies. I get a special kick in knowing that good and loving people who have showered in my blood may now enjoy this beauty as all initial scans transmit my name to every part of each planet in order to destroy any dormant evil cells, as those tend to regain life at the worse possible times. All of a sudden, as it seems every time I am around the throne all the emergency lights are now activating from several galaxies. "Unknown energy reading!" Oh no as I first ask, "Where is Medica?" The courts tell me, "She is in a portal below our universe." I now think, darn this one could be for real. Is it time for my enemy Rødkærsbro to strike again? Let me have some surprises for her. I now command, "Alert those galaxies to execute for alert. If any moves, we must know about it.

We need to get our homeland armies consolidated in the quickest places and get them high power flash drives so we can put them where Rødkærsbro may be trying to enter. What is the status of the jumps within my Empire?" The courts now tell me, "Strangely, every time we lock a scan on it, it jumps to another place as if it knows where it is going." I now ask, "You say it, and not them. Could this be an Invasion Force?" The lights jump in now and say, "Master, it is not an Invasion Force because it moves to fast and with too much accuracy." I then ask, "What dangers could this thing present and we do not have time for the Master Protocol?" The lights respond, "It could be an individual front runner to open a receiving portal." I then asked, "Could a portal be sat up in so many places?" The lights respond, "The jumps could be to get us off track while another sets up a portal elsewhere." I now command, "Then we must have a blanket scan in progress. Also alert Iris as she can watch out for the portal's point B starting point and maybe suffocate them in transit. Run some detailed equations as we must discover the relationship between these points." It appears as if a billion lights are flashing now as silence is upon my throne. Then my Aide for Destruction comes out to me saying, "We now believe the mystery of the random points is evident." I look at him and say, "Well are you going to tell me now or after we have dinner and watch a movie?" Now the first time in the last hour I hear laughter throughout the throne. Good, I have loosened things up. The aide now tells me, "The points all come from cities in the Atlantis Empire." I knew the aide was 100% confident in his analysis, since he was doing what I created him to do so I said to him, "Very good work Aide. I need strong aides like you to tell what is and not fear telling me the truth. Thank you. Now can we plug in all the cities and see if our scans can predict the next jump?" The lights now told me, "Yes we can." I then said to my spirit, "Take me to Atlantis and work with the lights so we can meet at a place where the stranger jumps. I want to catch this beast that endangers my daughter's empire." My spirits sent me through their internal omnipresent flash drives to Atlantis. I find myself at her bedroom door. I knock on the door. She asks, "Who is it?" I tell her, "It is your mother, may I enter." She answers, "Yes, give me one minute to finish this transmission." I am now briefed by my courts, "We have the intruder." I tell them, "Secure it, and bring it to me after I have a talk with my daughter." Atlantis now tells me to enter. As I walk in she is beside her stowaway bed with her hands above her back touching her glass window. Then I hear a noise that startles me from the other side of her room. She tells me, "Do not worry mother, it is just the city settling. I ask her, "Why are your hands against the window?" She looks at me and answers, "Mother, we get very little exercise down here so we use little tricks like this to keep toned." I then laughed and said, "Well it must work, for I have never seen any of your flesh daughters who were not beautiful. By the way, what brings you to this city?" She then told me, "I am famous for surprise visits." I then said, "Why is this room so small?" She then tells me, "Mother I always stay in small rooms for I do not want a large room for just a seldom random visit. That space is better used by those who live here." I then told her, "Very kind, my daughter I am impressed. I do feel guilty that I have not spent much time with you since we have returned. Is everything going good for you?" She then answers, "Everything is almost completely perfect. I am working out the small kinks. The cities are wonderful and my children love their new bodies. We have yet to lose a daughter, which is already a great achievement for us. Safe, secure and able to move around as most families now have their children working in other cities, yet still living with them. You did great mother." I then asked her, "Have you noticed anything strange today my daughter?" Atlantis now answers, "Is this visit for personal reasons or for work?" I told her both. She then said, "I am confused about what you mean by unusual as everything down here every day is unusual." Ok, my daughter "Is there anything here that we did not bring?" She looks at me and then a small tear starts to run down her cheek. She says, "Maybe mommy." Oh craps, she is pulling the mommy card on me and that card always wins. I then say, "It is ok, mommy is here. You can tell me so that way I can make sure it is not a weapon by Rødkærsbro." Oh mommy, she is not a weapon for Rødkærsbro, however we fear you may hate her and have her punished. She has nowhere to go." I then said, "This is not one of your famous stray pets is it daughter." She says, "Oh no mommy, do not worry I will take care of her and you will have nothing to worry about." I then said, "Well at least let me see her as she will be under your shield ok daughter." Atlantis closes her eyes thinking hard and opens her eyes crying, "Mommy I lost her." I then said, "It is ok daughter, for I have found her, is this whom you had?" She looks over and says, "Yes mommy, can I have her please?" We are processing her now, making sure that Rødkærsbro has not planted something in her. She shall be released soon. I must say daughter you have amazing taste." She looks at me strangely and says, "Mother do you know who she is?" I looked and then told her, "I have never seen this woman before?" She answers back begging and negotiating as all children do, "At least let us go and talk to her." I then said to her, "Atlantis, you go talk to her and keep her for I must get the Empire off full alert." Atlantis then says, "Mommy, have your spirits do that for you and pleasssssssssse come with me as I want to introduce her to you and for you to not hate her anymore." I then said, "Spirits have the Empire stand down and tell the throne I will be there soon. I need some time with Atlantis." She hugs me and kisses me telling me, "You're the greatest mommy ever" all the things a kid does when they are setting you up for the kill." I flash us to her holding room. Atlantis begins by asking, "Are you ok?" She looks at me and says, "I hope so Atlantis. Did you tell her who I am?" Atlantis looks at her, then looks at me, and says, "Mommy, promise me I can keep her. Please mommy." I look at her and say, "Of course Atlantis, you are a very special daughter and I am so proud of your judgment and running your empire. You may keep her, now I should go." Atlantis says, "Please wait mommy and look at her again then I will tell you her name." I look at her and say, "I am sorry honey; I do not know who this is. However, the mystery is starting to get me curious and I hate asking my spirits. You may tell me." She wraps her arms around me as I can feel her heart beating and says, "Mommy this is Lablonta." I look at her again and say, "How can you say that she is Lablonta?" Lablonta then says, "Oh great master, I am Lablonta and I have come here to beg you to be my god." She now steps forward and drops to her knees with her hands still confined. I flash her hands free as she says, "Oh thank you great goddess of all things, I am here to suffer punishment for the hate you against me. You may punish me for your amusement and brag to all that you have captured me. I care not. I just wanted to see Atlantis before I cease to exist." I then ask, "Why would you cease to exist for are you not the Supreme Queen of Mempire, Lablonta, Queen of Cumber Lablonta Empire, Queen of Onivac Lablonta Empire, Hersonia 8th? She then answers, "My throne wants to destroy me because I challenged them for wanting to hurt our Atlantis. When Atlantis escaped, they decided that I should be punished in her place. Thus, Eve and I escaped. We found a trader to get us over into your universe. A demon altered the trader's navigation devices and we ended up in a demon trap. The trader had only one extra space in his escape pod so I bound Eve and told the trader to take her. I had to bind her for she would never go and leave me behind. They vanished and I never saw them again. I pray to you that she be found and saved for I have heard you are the greatest god of mercy and love. The demons tortured me for some time until a group of lost angels snuck in and saved me. They told me they could sense my wings from very far away. They were able to bring me to your borders; however, we could not get in. I gave Atlantis a special set of earrings that she could activate if she were ever to be in trouble. I activated them and she found me and brought me to one of her underwater cities. Then we started setting off alarms from someone's scans. We did not know if it was from the demons that had me as prisoner, or my prior throne wanting to bring me back to their sick form of justice. We were terrified because the alarms kept going off everywhere I went until finally a force apprehended me. I asked them to whom was I a prisoner of and they said, 'You are the prisoner of the great Goddess Queen Lilith, number one servant of our master, member of the Council of Nykøbing Mors, holder of the Sword of Justice and holder of the Books of Gyor-Moson-Sopron.' This brought me joy for now I could be punish by one who is worthy to punish and my pain and suffering would bring my Atlantis's mother great joy." I then said to her, "Lablonta, relax for my belly has drank enough blood today." Atlantis then looked at me sternly and said, "Mother." I then looked at Lablonta and said, "Sorry, just having some fun, I do not drink blood yet those who worship me are showered in my blood." Lablonta then said, "One of your saints told us during your rescue of Atlantis that you baptize your servants in your blood so that they may have your life in them as they may also have their lives in you. I pray Lilith, baptize me, and fear not for I shall submit to your punishment and let my suffering bring you great joy." I then looked seriously at her and said, "You have done no wrong so why would I punish you?" She then said, "The throne picked me as a Heavenly Queen before you and I concealed that Atlantis was your baby. You have earned the right to punish me severely." I looked at her and said, "Atlantis, give me that small knife lying on the table behind you." She says, "Mommy there is no kniiiiiiii, . . . how did that get there? I thought I checked everything so you would not kill Lablonta!" I then said to Atlantis, I could not kill a spirit with a knife, "Give me the knife please." Lablonta then says to Atlantis, "Give her the knife so I can suffer for a great god of good. Please . . . ." Atlantis hands me the knife and I say to Lablonta, "Lablonta, do you love me and will you make me your god?" She falls flat on the floor and cries out, "I shall always love you Lilith and I wish so much for you to be my God for ever and ever. I shall serve you any way you wish. For I have done evil to you and deserve to be punished." I then said, "Lablonta will you please be quiet. She stopped talking and then I took the knife and cut a big cut across my wrists and my blood came gushing out. I poured it all over Lablonta as Atlantis then asked, "Mother will you shower me also." I then motioned for her to lie on the concrete floor and as she showered her. My spirits then warned, "Your blood level is getting too low." I then said to them, "Give me more and fix my wrist." I could feel the new blood flooding into my body as my wrist was fixed instantaneously. Then my blood took effect and both Lablonta and Atlantis were made new. As the great white lights slowly vanished they both jumped up and hugged each other and then bowed to me one saying, "I love you mommy" and the other saying, "I beg that you be my goddess and let me suffer great things in your name." I looked at Lablonta and said, "Too late strange one, I am now your god. I am the goddess of love and good. My servants do not suffer in my name. They live lives free from pain, misery, and evil. A god who makes his servants suffer is not righteous. I now ask that you work for good to your brothers and sisters in your new family of love, go forth, and be happy." Lablonta then said, "Oh master will you help me find Eve since she does want so much to serve you also?" I looked at Lablonta and said, "I will not search for Eve." Lablonta looked sad and pale as she bowed her head in submission. Atlantis once again scolded me saying, "Motherrrrrr!" I then said, "Sorry Lablonta, it is just too much fun playing with you . . . I will take you to Siyalov (Сиялов) Palace where Eve now lives. Come with me and hold on girl because we are going to flash there if Atlantis no longer wishes to entertain you." Atlantis, then said, "Take her mother however please go easy on her since she has a great fear of you." I looked at Lablonta and said, "Why do you fear me?" Lablonta said, "Is it not a great thing to fear your god and his punishments?" I looked at her and said, "Only for week gods, however gods of love who take care of their children need no fear to get their worship and punishment I only reserve for special reasons." Lablonta then said, "The angels who brought me here said that you froze all people in a solar system and then brought the planets back to their original places and let the animals eat their dead flesh." I told Lablonta, "I told them not to do something and they challenged me and did it. All the innocents who died were given saints spirits and sent to their heavens. The evil wrongdoers like their god were banished forever." Lablonta then asked, "You have no burning lakes?" I told her, "Lablonta, burning lakes do nothing but needlessly punish. I spent one thousand years in a lake of fire and upon my release; I only searched for evil revenge. It festers evil by putting evil with evil and giving them a united enemy in which someday they may fight thus all the lakes of fire we found in the Milky Way were destroyed and we released all except for Lucifer. We put him in a portal and shot his way to the distant parts of that universe. I do not want him to find me for Bogovi will not have the mercy on him such as I do. I now shall have my spirits tell you about a new tool that you may use anytime evil is near you." She quickly went into a trance and came back out saying, "Never did I ever dream your name would have so much power." I told her, "I get my power by serving my servants. I will earn your love my dear." That girl is going to need extra knees for she dropped again crying out, "I have given you all that I am, and I beg to be nothing if giving myself can make you greater." I then told her, "Lablonta die not for me but live for you. Now let us take a walk in a forest nearby on the surface. I am so confused as to why you and Eve thought I hated you. How can a goddess of such a great empire of good hate such heavenly angels as you and Eve?" Lablonta then said, "We saw only hate and punishment as righteous would only make a small mistake and be cast away. We never saw forgiveness as evil would always prosper and the good suffer. How could we even think you would be so great as to have mercy upon us?" Lablonta, "You shall soon see the love I have for Eve. Walk with me. Let me tell you how I see things. At first I could not understand the foolishness you had in helping the poor and innocent. You were a royal white as none could stand with you in their presence yet you worked hard with a dream of them having families, homes, and security. I wondered what pleasure or gain you could be getting from that stupidity until I saw your memorial service. I saw flesh suits crying in great pain at your premature death as your enemy entered into your sanctuary and took your life. That memory tormented me for such a long time as I soon realized that the champions of good were suffering at the hands of evil. Why did you suffer so much for the innocent who could give you nothing?" Lablonta then said, "I hope you consider what I say not to be of blasphemy however I do believe you have discovered that answer." I looked at her and said, "You are truly as wise as your tales report. It was your example of being a queen that guided me on my throne in Ereshkigal and the rest is simply their hunger for a mother in the heavens that loves them. You, above all others have influenced my style of divinity as it seems such a shame that you are not here instead of me." Lablonta quickly adds, "I had not the strength to put faith in another universe and throne as you did. You always were a challenger and a get down and dirty fighter of which I always admired." I then said, "Lablonta, why are you no longer white?" She answered, "The throne took that away from us saying that we must give all honor to them and that the white made us less humble and in possession of a love apart from them." I looked at her and said, "Honey, oh is it ok if I call you honey." Lablonta then said, "Master I came here with the dream of serving and submitting to you. Eve told me that you were a lover of wine. My wine is yours if you so desire, my goddess. Take all that you want whenever you want." I was so surprised and shocked to hear this, for I can only think of many hundred thousands of servants screaming, "Supreme Queen of Mempire, Lablonta, Queen of Cumber Lablonta Empire, Queen of Onivac Lablonta Empire, Hersonia 8th, a title that I often thought was higher than a god." What happened to the first ever, Heavenly Queen of our old throne? What is this before me? I then asked her, "I have never had a wine so fine as yours for your wine may be better than that which I may have. I may have to get permission for my higher thrones. Will you wait while I get permission?" Lablonta said, "No, I pray that you have mercy on me and at least let me drink your wine. If your gods deny you from enjoying me, which you have created, I shall petition and beg all in your Empire until you have mercy on me and let me worship you by drinking your wine." I then said, "Lablonta I must have some time to think about it, for I owe you so much." Lablonta fired back, "You owe me nothing, yet I owe you so much for saving me from my former evil throne and an eternity of punishment for something I am innocent." Lablonta, you saved Atlantis and took her when many would have cast her to rot with the demons. You love and care for her as if she came from your womb. In addition, as I departed and vanished in haste leaving your universe you took her back and cared for her as a true mother would. I would be so foolish and cruel to not beg you to stay very active in her life as her 'other mother' a title you paid for in your tears alone. Will you also continue to forgive me and love Atlantis? With great joy, Lablonta rushed to me holding me tight with her trembling body and kissing my cheeks without reservation saying, "Oh thank you master, for you are truly the greatest goddess of good ever to exist in all the ages. You are my goddess forever and ever." I told her, "It is such a great pleasure to be in your arms." Lablonta now looked serious at me and confessed, "My goddess, I have longed for the first time in heard about you to have you in my arms. I envied the power you had in controlling both men and women getting great pleasure from them while also giving back to them great pleasure. That is when I knew without a doubt that inside you burned a fire of love and good. I first only cared for Atlantis in hopes of meeting you hoping that you would take me and do unto me that which you had done into so many others. Yet strangely, I feel so deeply in love for your Atlantis so much that I could not face life without her. I hope you forgive me for this." I then for the first time kissed her and said, "How can a goddess hate a servant for confessing her great love? I beg that this love never ends my precious Lablonta. I still have one more question by an angel, and that is what happened with you and your Mempire and King James?" Lablonta now held her head down as she said, "All still loved me however no-one needed me. They kept busy and did not include me in what they were doing. As time went on, I had my missions and they had theirs. When I was promoted to Heavenly Queen, the throne shifted me away from Mempire as we went our separate ways. I became a great name in the books and stories of the beginning. For most, I ended at the hands of my mother in law while supposedly in the protection of my husband. I am a hero of the old days, something nice to include in a photo. I slowly became so low that the only way to go was to the lake of fire to burn with the other trash. Soon we must go, for I know Eve will want to see you. Lablonta, why did you come to me nude? I know you had so many gorgeous gowns as all men would look upon you as looking upon the heavens." Master, Eve told me, "We would be much safer to surrender all before as we fall to our knees. Our glory is gone and we go there for her glory. She is a kind lover of women and if we are to be blessed maybe, she will look up us and wish to enjoy our bottle as she drinks out wine. My wine began flowing then just thinking of you enjoying it. Master, we have such a nice empty field here. Can we get our bottles ready for our wine? This is the first time I have given my wine to another female. Will you teach me how I may serve you and release my love into your soul? I beg this of my goddess." I then said, "It is so amazing that we both wanted each other yet our chains kept us apart. I do believe you as you talk and I think it is such a shame that one of your godly wisdom, beauty and of course love should not be given a chance to care for her fellow family members in the empire." She had now fallen upon me as her clumsiness attested to her innocence and lack of skills for this type of drink. Her hands continued to tremble as her heart was beating excessively fast. She has desire as I look upon her now and the majesty of a true royal white. I gently ran my hands through her hair and asked, "Lablonta are you sure you wish to do this? Moreover, is this completely of your own free will knowing that either way you are not going to receive. In addition, none of your privileges will be influenced either way. I do not want you ever to do something you do not want to do. This is so important to me that you not sell yourself short to one as low as me." Lablonta then said to me, "Master I would want your wine even if you told me to spend one millennium in a lake of fire. I have lusted after you are chasing you in my dreams for over one million years. You have always represented to free side on my running independently on the edge. When you chose to serve good it then proved to me that the path I had taken was indeed a wise one, for now I might be able to meet you. I love you with all my heart, soul, and spirit, and into your hands, I surrender them. I feel so stupid now, there is so much I want to do, yet I do not know how properly to get your wine. Please help me my goddess, I really need to do this correct or I may never forgive myself. I want it to be as in my so many trillions of dreams about my powerful bad girl." I then said to her, "Lablonta, your heart must now be your master. Listen and do as your heart tells you and you shall be proud of your great gift to me this night." The goody girl that always wanted to be bad but could not surrender to her "bad girl" for the sake of good. Now, tell me if that does not rattle the brains some. The innocent girl that was selected for the bride of the Queen's old son, yet took her mission so seriously that she went against the bitter laws, which when broken would mean death, refused to eat human flesh. Instead, she was eating grass and weeds, instead with her rebel prince, and fled to an unknown land filled with savages and help build so many great empires, most which were still going strong during my last invasion. Oh, I now long for my master to return for I have been enjoying too much well brewed wine and soon my tongue and lips will touch the without any doubt greatest queen ever to rule while in flesh. Yet even with all that glory, she stayed focused on the poor and hungry. Sure, I am heralded as being the goddess of good, yet all I have done is created monumental power regenerating spirits who are omnipresent and do all the work while I lay around playing with some of the best wine bottles ever to have been created. Her heart is now in control of her and she is creating a wine extractor that already has my resupply of wine that my spirits gave me today. I got a resupply in case I got too busy before Bogovi returned. She now represents something else for me, and that is the powerful loyalty and responsibility Atlantis display in saving one who gave her so much. She could have told Lablonta to leave knowing that her future was solid now, however she took the chance and when interrogated refused to lie to me keeping my trust in the one that I risked so much for, yet still have not bonded with her or any of her sisters. I am of course proud of my daughters who have taken her under their wing and bonded successfully. Each cool wind that brushes over my body helps to fight the tremendous amount of heat my body has generated. I am now starting to think that I am truly being rewarded by some great remuneration as the heavens now flow in my veins and the flesh suit I created has performed its sensual functions way beyond my expectations. I now motion for Lablonta to roll over and allow me to enjoy her tea. She begs me to let her continue for "I wish only to serve you. I am of no value and you should not waste your time on me." I told her, "Lablonta, am I not your goddess and if you serve me, cannot I serve you? Is it not fair? Would you hate me so that you would not want my lips to touch you?" Lablonta then said to me, "Master, please forgive me for all my days I worked only to please others and no one ever even once offered to help me with my feelings or pleasures. I did all the caring and giving." As she spoke, she stood up with her back to me. I thought to myself, what a shame that I was not the first one to create a being as beautiful as this one. I was able to recopy her and bring her back to her greatest bloom. Whoever created this was even perfect on both sides. In addition, to think that wonderful exotic creation just took all my wine and would have gotten more if my spirits would have given me more for my flesh craved her love. When she gave in to her heart, it was the end of my reservations. Notwithstanding, I must serve her, for this is as a prime steak waiting to be consumed. It is cooked perfect with all the right spices; however, I am going to have to do some work to get past her chattered broken and almost dead feelings of self-worth. I so want her to leave her tonight having been served, as she deserves. The thought that if she would have stayed in Hersonia she would have ended up weighting anywhere between 700 to 1000 pounds as she was next in line to be Queen and Queens had to be larger than the aristocrats in that Empire. What a blessing that she escaped, although only to give up any hope of having her necessities met. Her king was way too busy being involved in the bloodiest hate filled war ever to be recorded on Lamenta and then afterwards to create an entirely revolutionary style of government and started building a new Empire with sticks and stones and savages. Blessed Lablonta was caught in the crossfire and faded as a legend in the ages. She never faded with me. I always automatically assumed that at the end of the highest pedestal of mercy I would find Lablonta. I am going to get inside her feelings tonight. I start my attack by saying, "Lablonta, I will tell you that I serve my servants and if you want me to be your goddess you must let me serve you. You mean so much to me and I want you in my empire. I beg that you allow me to serve you as I have so many others. I have great shame in that my spirits have never created a being as beautiful as you have. The value that you bring to my Empire is great. My spirits have searched your soul and they tell me that indeed, you got a bad deal notwithstanding my Lablonta for now I own you and the bad deal stuff has been cast into the Sea of Forgetfulness. It is time for you to start the best deal and that will start with your goddess on her knees giving back to you what you gave her. I so much hope that you, my servant will accept me as your servant for now I must and shall provide and protect you. Now please let me begin as I am on my knees before you. How long will you punish me and make me beg you?" I could see her legs now start to quiver as she was trying to walk towards me a few steps then walk backwards a few steps. Her poor mind was very confused yet I could see she wanted me to get her wine so much. She all of a sudden became stick and her body marched in front of me as she laid down and opened her bottle and said, "I am yours my god. Please yourself." There was no need to ask if this was from her heart for I could see this was a dream come true for her. I immediately started working in the wine. I think it may have truly been over one million years since she released some of her wine. Her wine was flowing now and I am the luckiest god ever to be enjoying this as human-to-human. I may be the only god that spends so much time in the flesh, yet with what has happened to me these last five days is even for me unbelievable. The conquer a conqueror, to free a bound servant, to surrender my blueprint, to love one you are loving and now to enjoy the greatest gift of all humans and without question my greatest conquest. We are now in midafternoon at this event is approaching twenty-four hours and yet I cannot stop. My adrenaline has this flesh suit pumped up. I think I could jump over the mountain before us without any supernatural help although since I do not want to lose this flesh suit that is getting packed with Lablonta wine for this flesh is now fortified with the best that could ever enter a flesh suit. Moreover, the fortification is not ending soon. I must give her my greatest performance because this being is worth so much and I bought her at a rock bottom price. What a foolish market! I am so happy, yet I do not have anyone to thank because I do not want 'you know who' to be here and if I mention his name he will be here. The Lablonta's body is reacting so exotic in response to my actions. These responses are in perfect rhythm as she just moans in complete ecstasy. The Supreme Queen of Mempire, Queen of Cumber Lablonta Empire, Queen of Onivac Lablonta Empire, and Hersonia 8th is now at her coronation celebration. I am having this title posted all through her palace and any official streams involving this great one will have her title. I love her skin, how it reacts to my touch as if it were a magnet not wanting to lose my fingers. Now this is absolutely the greatest experience even greater than the last four nights as this one now is passing two days. She has just now fallen fast asleep and the sight of her sleeping has sent a signal to my flesh suit that it is time to end this 'heavenly event'. I now lay beside her and fall instantly into sleep so deep that there will be no dreams to this day. We rewarded our love beaten bodies with two days of rest. My Empire as the first was puzzled, however my spirits were in tune with me and covered for me by saying, "Our master is receiving great honors and rewards" which is true so I must confess my spirits are on the ball now. It is time now to tell about the new position she is to occupy. At this time, I feel myself becoming dizzy and wobbly just from one look at this creation before me. I wonder, "How can she be this beautiful in the morning." I look at her and say, "Good morning my love" and extend my hands out showing her that a hug is needed. She jumps into my arms and says, "Master, thanks so much for making my dreams come true, for truly I have a goddess of love and good with a home in the real true heavens." I then said to her, "Lablonta, as you are now forming to such a high perfection you shall have many of our sisters and even predictably Eve sharing your wines. As you share with them, giving and receiving your mercy you will bring great joy to them. I beg of you to open up and allow others to give to you, for you have proven to me that giving to you is an unspeakable wonderful joy." She kissed me and said, "I thank you for saving my hopeless soul and making it a well of love." I then asked her, "Lablonta, the thing I need so much in my throne is a mother of mercy. Until now, I could never find someone I thought who gave mercy to my children. Would you please accept this great honorable position and give life to its title?" Lablonta then replied, "If it is you will it is my will. I am your mother of mercy. Now please tell me how to begin and what to do." I told her, "First let me take you to the house of the mother of mercy, your Meshcheryakov (Мещеряков) Palace." I flashed us to in front of it. She just looks so amazed and asks me, "Master, are you sure?" I told her, "I have never been surer. I need you so much in our Empire, for it is also yours my love. In shame, I must confess that I do plan to visit you during the rest times for more of your wine if you will share it with me. I now tell her, "We have just notified Eve that you are here and safe getting ready to enter your new palace. Please remember, my spirit is always with you and I do very much love you. I am so glad to have you on my team." Eve had now arrived and they stood together as I asked them, "My wonderful lovers, may your servant please talk with you for a minute?" Both consented and I said to them, "Eve and Lablonta I am so truly blessed to have you on my team and to have bonded with a wine meeting. The future is yours, as I now know that my children will have another source of love and mercy. I do know that since you are not goddess you cannot help all of our children in our quickly approaching 200,000 galaxies. Just do what you can comfortably do and make sure you keep a lot of free time in your schedule for joy and love. You may love any spirit that consents, which with both of you that will most likely be an immediate response. There is no requirement that you be free from the chains of clothing as you are not a goddess, yet if you do decide to share your blessings with the Empire, you of course may do so. My spirits shall always be with you. I must now go back to my throne and rule again since I have dedicated too much time with wonderful wine parties this week. Please forgive me of my love." I now flashed back to my throne feeling very lonely and empty inside. My time with Eve and Lablonta were so wonderful, yet of even greater value, they have joined my Empire giving it such power packed depth. My courts are already wondering why I have not made them divine. My difficulty now is finding enough extra power to transform them. All our power is being used now in upgrading galaxies, in processing galaxies, and the war. I will promote them when the time is good. They are divine material. Eve is now busy with Lablonta, season is tearing up our sanctuary sharing great joy before going back to Balatonföldvári as a goddess from the highest throne, and Iris is breaking down our enemy's infrastructure, while my chamber is nice and cozy with my blessed Yudachyov. My Empire now feels so real with Eve and Lablonta, comprehensive with a Harvey homeland and their goddess, powerful with the warrior Iris with everything sandwiched by a place to rest in peace, with Yudachyov. Oh, I forgot to say that I missed my master although not during the last five days. I will hold down my throne while my sisters continue their private jubilee. These winds feel very good as the massage me and the ice keeps my temperature down. I now ask my lights and courts how things are going. The lights start flashing and a court yells out, "Incoming message for our Master's Queen." Oh no, what now?

Chapter II

Come home

The courts now sound the alarms as they tell me an intruding object is approaching our borders. I immediately ask my Court Angel for Dimensional Travel to contact Iris for me. Instantaneously, Iris is online with me. I ask her, "Do you know of any threat objects that might be approaching our Empire?" She then tells me that the object has been tracked and is not a threat, actually coming from my old boss before I saw your light Master." I then said, "Thanks so much love, by the way, when do I get to see your light again?" Iris tells me, "Soon master, we have actually been chasing Rødkærsbro lately destroying as much as possible in front of her and behind her. Her threat ability now is a joke; I just want to bring her back to be judged by my greatest love." I now say in front of all proudly, "Iris you are a well of great news today, please hurry back so I may fall before you on my knees and beg for your mercy." Iris is in a much better mood since she had been deployed, and responds, "I do not think you will have to beg too hard, unless you want another special wine drinking ceremony." I told her, "Well in that case I will be begging hard, got to go love, keep up your great work." As she gets off the line, our throne erupts in great cheers. I then said to all of them, "He who faces Iris in war is facing his doom." The cheers went on and on as I had to stop them, "Hey guys we need to get that incoming transmission and object. We would not want to look bad for my boss." Then the Court Revealer of the Spirits reports, "The incoming object is your Hyrum Twin Sister Goddess Drusilla and the incoming transmission reads as follows: "Oh great master and my twin sister, may I please come home and serve you again?" I told the throne, "Transmit, Come Home," and "Send some escorts to bring her home as fast as you can safely because I want to see my twin sister." Then as the raging clouds of space slowly revealed my Drusilla was appearing. She was somewhat slimmer than before as we caught her making last minute adjustments to her hair. Her feet were hanging down, eager to land on the old throne that she shared in ruling. As she landed all the courts became silent as we all were in awl not knowing what to expect. She took a few steps and fell to her knees saying, "Oh great master, will you hear the prayers of your twin sister?" This was usually her way of wanting to talk privately, and since I did put her in an intimate situation with our master, it would be good to talk in private. I then said, "Wilt thou join me in the Queen's waiting chambers?" We then went to my chambers with a goal to talk about whatever needed talking about. As we entered and started to make ourselves at ease she started crying. I had to rush over and hold her as I had so many times in our days of flesh as we would attempt to comfort each other's miseries. I had to ask her, "Dear sister, will you tell me what is wrong?" She answered, "Oh great master, everything is wrong and nothing is right." I then asked her to tell me the whole story. She began by saying, "At first I wanted to serve you and your master with all my love however I now so greatly hate your master. After we visit for a short while and I say goodbye to our sisters I shall flee into another dimension." I looked at her in shock since she never asked to go anywhere without me, "Why Drusilla?" She answered, "Because your master hates me and never did like me." This was such a shock since Bogovi had never showed me signs of any hostilities with any in the sanctuary, and once again, I asked, "Why Drusilla, would you think that?" Drusilla then added, "The blame is also yours for you should have never placed me there to be intimate with that monster and you

promised to visit regularly." I responded, "Drusilla the penance
throne sent back reports each day that you were all doing fine and
not to visit or worry." Drusilla angrily replies, "Oh great another
throne that lies. I do not even know why I am telling you this, for
your master will deny all things and revenge me." I looked at her
and said, "Drusilla, the master does not have the years of pain that
bonded us together. Tell me the truth and I will handle this." She
then says, "He tried to make love to me, with of course the
permission you gave us, yet he could not do the man thing thus he
blamed me saying I had cursed him and was working with the
penance demons. He looked me into a room in his dirty little house
and refused to talk with me. He only fed me garbage from the trash
cans and many times would bring in sticks or belts and beat me." I
then said, "Hold it love, Gyor-Moson-Sopron." No response as I
looked at Drusilla and said, "Girl you just scored a run, Gyor-
Moson-Sopron though evil and unjust spirit appear to me now or I
will ask to convene a meeting with the Council of Nykøbing
Mors." Then Gyor-Moson-Sopron answered, "Why do you disturb
me?" I replied, "Oh I am so sorry to have disturbed you, go back to
what you were doing, I will get the Council of Nykøbing Mors to
explain why my sister was abused and you did not help her." Gyor-
Moson-Sopron then replied, "Since I am already here I will listen."
I then looked at him and said, "Go to hell you bastard,
Council . . . ." He stopped me, blocked my transmission, and
appeared before me getting serious, "I am sorry, please forgive me
as you do have my undivided attention." I then said, "Explain what
Drusilla just told me and do not play any games for you know the
truth." Gyor-Moson-Sopron, "I must confess that we have allowed
punishment and suffering of Drusilla to add to Bogovi's torment
and pressure to give up." I the then reminded him, "Your promise
was that no harm would come upon Drusilla and that if anything
happened you would tell me immediately. I think Iris would be
more than willing to do some serious damage here with the new
equipment she has found in the negative energy space." Gyor-
Moson-Sopron then said to Drusilla, "I am so sorry to have done
this to you, for you truly are so special. When I saw the suffering

you went through with Lilith in her penance years I did not think this would be hard for you, yet it did get out of control for I should have stopped Bogovi. How can I repay you?" Drusilla said, "I want Bogovi's head on a platter." Gyor-Moson-Sopron told her, "that I cannot do, however I will erase these memories from your soul and your master's soul so you will have no fear of revenge. I shall also give you a special honor for you shall have the Crown of Sopron. This was my mother's crown, who was also a healer. You shall also be the healer. You will be able to heal all physical and emotional troubles in not only the flesh but in other gods and goddesses. This crown shall be yours to keep and enjoy as your powers are now three fold. You will be at peace with your master and yet still be able to give her master back to your master healed and purified. Your divinity is now recorded with my throne. Does this find favor with you, Crown of Sopron Hyrum Twin Sister the Healing Goddess Drusilla as none will ever know why you have it and you can know now that Bogovi tormented himself with great pain in guilt because of his love for you?" As Drusilla felt a divine peace take over her body, she looked at me and said, "Your master is my master." I then looked at Gyor-Moson-Sopron and said, "If she is at peace with this than so am I. She spent too many nights cleaning me from my beatings during your penance games." Gyor-Moson-Sopron then said to Drusilla, "I will present a copy of the crown as you will have the original before your throne as loyalty to my throne. My servants will take you back now as I must speak with Lilith." She departed as he now said to me, Gyor-Moson-Sopron, "Lilith I know this has been hard on you especially trying to rebuild your empire and fight a war. I do have a debt also to you, for I so want you to always trust me. I shall give you the power to make divine with my name Eve and Lablonta. They do deserve this. In addition, I should deliver to Iris Rødkærsbro so that she may bring her armies home. I shall also give to you 100 armies and another power spirit to help with your Empire's expansion. Lastly, I will tell you that your master did suffer greatly and he may not have handled it the best way for Drusilla, for he was fighting so hard to remain loyal and faithful to you. This battle with his longing to be with you was released on Drusilla. I truly believe he should be forgiven and you should allow me to erase this from your memory. This memory can never work for good, yet you could allow evil to plant a seed in you. May I erase this memory?" I then looked at him and said, "If I truly be a goddess of love and mercy for good this memory must die." Gyor-Moson-Sopron then replied, "It is now dead. I shall send Bogovi back to you soon; however I owe you the option to see his final hours." I then asked, "Will he know I am with him?" He answered, "Sorry, we cannot allow that." I then asked Gyor-Moson-Sopron then will you let me bring him home?" He said, "I shall hold him here and bring you to him. You shall soon have the greatest god that any goddess could ever dream to have." I told him, "I always had that. Our days of friendship will be many, now I have to decide where these one hundred armies shall go. How many days before my man will be with us again?" Gyor-Moson-Sopron said, "You have three days, so make sure you reward his mother and grandmother as you promised." I then asked him, "That is private and they have the right to be honored for their love as the other queens and sisters." He then told me, "Fear not, for I promise never to watch you during intimacy and never to speak of any such thing to others. I simply was trying to remind you that they do deserve priority and preferential treatment now. Let your Sanctuary take care of Drusilla." I told him, "That which you say is true and wise. Well you escort me to my throne?" He then said, "Let's go . . . ." Instantly we were at my throne, as if I was coming home yet I knew my time would come with Bogovi. As I sat upon my stage in front of my Empire Gyor-Moson-Sopron flashed his power behind me. I then said to my courts and lights "Alert my Empire that we have a very special reward to present coming from Gyor-Moson-Sopron." They were all petrified and scrambling to do their best to get everyone online. I then said to them, "Fear not and have no stress for this is a good thing." Gyor-Moson-Sopron now laughed and said, "Fear not for I am here to give you great blessing and to share my love with your great Empire." I can see them bragging to all their friends tonight, "We handle Gyor-Moson-Sopron with ease." Oh-well as three-foot fish always sounds better than a three inches. If it makes them happy and does not hurt anyone then why worry about it. I also said, "Give unto me Eve and Lablonta and assemble the queens and goddesses of the Royal Deities Sanctuary now. The courts then answered as the three queens came out to be with me and the Sanctuary was now being filled. We put Drusilla on hold. Now my lights said, "Begin!" Gyor-Moson-Sopron now said, "Behold Empire of the Good and the holders of the Sword of Justice and Freedom EGaSOJAF, I have great tidings for you today. First, your master shall return three days from now. I will have your master's Queen held in their palace, only to be visited by Queens until he returns so she shall be holy and clean to receive another penance god for your Empire. You now have the Sword of Freedom as Iris shall be able to use it in her battles now." Oh wow I thought, first I just felt that he did not know our empire and mistakenly added the 'and Freedom with the AF' at the end, yet now I can see he was giving us our Sword of Freedom. He began again saying, "Your goddess Drusilla was called to my Empire to help us with our penance work. She performed so far beyond our expectations that my other has offered her the Crown of Sopron and all the Healing power that goes with it. She will be able to help the children of your Empire by healing hurt memories preventing evil from planting its seeds. Your master endured greater sufferings than any other penance god did during his penance. He shall be given a special reward of 100 powerful armies in which we shall send to Iris so she can clean up your war before your master shall come home. As I place the crown upon Drusilla now I also place her divinity also under my name as in all places that she goes she shall be a goddess of power as she now harness three times her original power. I am also giving you another super power spirit to assist in your Empire's growth. Great things are happening to your Empire and greater things shall happen in the future, as we have been fortunate to receive two wonderful spirits of the ages. I now call before me Eve and Lablonta. Your great deeds of good have been seen. Your sufferings are being avenged. Yet your great deeds of good are now beginning. Today, because of your love for Lilith and the good we give you your divine powers of a goddess. Your powers are four times greater than your previous throne, which will never be permitted to harm you. Even thinking about harming you will bring them great punishments and destructions. Eve, you shall be called, Throne Supreme Goddess of Intimacy Mother Eve considering your motherhood of many worlds and loves and Lablonta, Throne Supreme Goddess of Blessings Lablonta in that you always gave and never received and always forgave as others did you harm, blessing. All who have ever met? You return to your castles as goddess and any who challenge you shall answer to me. The three of you are great additions to our dimensions. Let all now bow to you." I stood out in front of all and bowed to them as everyone else rushed to get to their knees. We Queens now hugged our newly promoted family. I then looked out and said, "Let all my empire now bow to the great and honorable Gyor-Moson-Sopron." The Queens and my sisters were now standing behind us, bowed as all in the Empire did. This did bring great pleasure to Gyor-Moson-Sopron who had so honorably confessed to his wrongs, whatever they may be and rewarded us so greatly. Another power spirit and this is a superpower spirit that I shall assign to our master as he will surely want to process and upgrade our galaxies. My lights are predicting now with all our power spirits running at peak performance and the addition of Gyor-Moson-Sopron's supreme power spirit that our galaxy numbers for the return of our master will be 173,000 (most of which have been upgraded to at least 75% of our goals) with only 27,000 waiting. That means we concerted 45,000 and reduced the waiting list by 29,000. I have my 200,000 that was my goal. Our master will be shocked, especially when he sees how they all have new bodies, schools, roads advanced production equipment and temples packed with our statues, books, and priests. His priests are being notified to get their uniforms cleaned and dust off their books. They of course had all the freedom to do as they wished and we gave them everything they wanted, yet many wanted to fade in the background waiting for him to return to provide them guidance. His spirits approved it, so we made sure not to do anything we knew we should not do. My priests began all their teachings and sermons 'in the name of our master and his number one servant' as I want everything here, except my sisters to be his. Speaking of my master our three, other queens are waiting for me now at the Nørresundby Palace as they have smoothly placed Yudachyov in a deep sleep. I do not want to hurt her feelings however this thing I must do as I can blame it on you know who (do not want to mention his name and have him appear). Somehow I have a feeling he heard that. Oh well, let me bring Iris up to date and I will go and have some more fun since it has been three days (two of which I slept) since I had some fun. "Courts please connect me with our War Commanding Goddess . . . ." Iris joins the line saying, "My, I must be getting popular again." I tell her, "Sugar, mommy is sending you some more candy, like in the line of 100 super equipped and trained Armies." Iris then asks, "And why am I getting so much candy to my master?" I told her, "Iris, our master will come home in three days and I would like to give me Rødkærsbro head on a platter. Can you make this happen for me safely my love?" Iris then answers, "I do believe with 100 more armies I can make that happen. I will try my best my master." I then told her, "Your best is better than all the rest, go and remember be safe, as I do plan to be conquered by you many times." Iris then answers, "Oh master, I would never do anything like that unless you ordered me. I am your servant in the war, serving the great goddess." She is such a great field commander, as I can now see the Armies mobilizing and being sucked into her portals. Rødkærsbro is not going to have a nice next three days, although she does not know it yet. Off to my Nørresundby Palace where my master's family awaits me. As I arrive, I behold my sleeping beauty Yudachyov dressed in a nice gown waiting for my return. The armies are positioned around this palace, as it is now a highly secured site with all four queens inside, which is natural, as all know our master returns soon. Tompaládony greats me at the door and tells me to follow her. We walk past a special private waiting room where I am greeted by the other two queens. My sister, as I will always keep this for me although she will simultaneously have her rightful title as the master's sister, begs me "Oh master forget me not." I reach over and put her in my arms and say, "I could never forget you as you shall always also be MY sister." She now hugged me tighter and said, "I shall always be YOUR sister my master and goddess whom I worship." I then told her, "No worshipping now, but animal playing ok." All three now say, "Yes master." I then say to Julia, "Am I right not to allow you with me when caring for your mother or grandmother?" Julia kissed me and said, "That truly would be best as it gives extra protection from my brother's scans." I then told Julia, "As usual you are my rock for salvation in wisdom." Tompaládony then said, "Let us go here." She guided me to a servant's room as the servant had gladly consented to loan her room to two gods. In our secrecy and privacy, she once again enjoyed the fruit from the trees of too many ages prior, with the energy of a young teen. We enjoyed ten hours of play and I got eight hours of rest as I was then transferred to another room. My master's family has unconstrained power over me, which is the way of things since I am very lucky that they love me so much. If they did not, as many master's queens find themselves, their love would be spoiled by misery and trivial obstacles. Our faithful new mother now joined me, starting with such a wonderful massage, one like Prudence always gave me after we played in the park for a whole afternoon. My flesh was like a sponge now as she first set free her "bad girl" fantasies. She was somewhat harsh in the beginning as if she thought someone was going to end it. Then when she realized that, she had the floor to this stage things started to flow much better as my expectations with both of them had been blown through the roof. Apparently, grandmother and mother had primed the required knowledge out of their newest generation and honed it to a T. When mother had finished giving and received, she called for my sister to rescue me. Having some fun I told Julia, "I did not know they were such experienced professionals." Julia quickly responded, "Master, you are their first since I taught them feeding their hungry hearts." I then told her, "Julia, I may need you to train some new friends for me in the future." She then said, "Sure Master, with my brother's help of course." Oh she got me,

"Julia, why are you always so far ahead of me?" She calmly answered, "Master, someone must make sure you walk the right path and care for you." I then seriously told her, "It was a great day for me when we met my love. Where will you guide me now?" She calmly told me, "In their little tiger." In addition, there was indeed a jungle. I had sixty hours of drinking the best Queen's wines produced in the heavens. The last few hours that we rested the mother and Tompaládony joined us. This was so special in that for the first time I felt like I was actually a part of them. They of course had always been generous, courteous, and so eager to serve yet we never had the time where our hair was a mess and in our unique special awkward sleeping positions. I guess I mean no borders were up. No trying to serve or gain acceptance. This was bonded sisterhood something my daughters got however never me. As we took turns rolling over and accidentally kicking each other, no one cared and just shrugged it off in the sisterhood. What made this even so much more rewarding is how each of them gave up a greater power over me. Some have stated that they did not want civil war, however I would die to serve them and never do anything but just enjoy the crap out of them. I hope they recognize this, yet I believe the old women did know it. They wanted to be in the Royal Deities Sanctuary, our exclusive club in which bonding is in each blood cell. I am so lucky that wisdom taught me the sharing of blood, although if I were to trace it back hard it had to be a brainchild from Fejér, Máriakéménd, and Julia. This is a mystery that I truly never fancy to solve, given it is instituted in love. I at first had concerns about showering our servants in my blood that Bogovi would become angry. He told me, "Do as you will, for I care not. The people need something to believe in so give it to them." That is when I packed my temples with his statues added and combined his books, which were few and combined his priests. He never had angels in his temples so we use mine. He modified and updated his temples to add my books, priests, and statues. It can occasionally be confusing trying to figure which temple one is looking. Anyway, his sister, mother, and grandmother are living inside me as I live inside of them. They are so much a part of the

Royal Deities Sanctuary that when they wake up in the palaces in the morning they rush to the Sanctuary and return prior to going to bed, leaving it only to sit on the throne or attend Ceremonies or attend to Empire business. If it were not for the divine laws that a master queen must sleep in a palace they, as most likely even I, would live exclusively in the Sanctuary. Those laws were for the protection of the Queen, so we cannot complain. I feel at peace flowing over me that is as if I were elated. The one thing that helps save us is that the heavenly wine contains no alcohol or we would never be able to stand on our feet. My flesh suit is regaining its energy quickly as the peace of this palace calms all my senses. Then as my lucky streak continues an alarm sounds and the courts urge me, "Queens, please report to the throne." We floor jump up snap our fingers which makes us clean and presentable as flash off onto the throne. What we were about to see was so wonderful, the best news I have had in so long. High above us was a powerful spirit with the great warrior Iris and someone tied down beside her. As we appear she says, "Mighty Queens of our Master, may I present to you Rødkærsbro?" There in the tranquil blue sky above us, which is being brought forth by the power spirit, is one with her hands securely tied to some sort of a yoke and feet secured behind her, I would say with rope or chains connected to the yoke. Her face is battered and a scarf tied around her lower face. The mountain Iris stands so strong, as she always does. She did what I asked her to do and more important she returned safely. I sincerely believe that having her in my empire or even around, it allows my flesh suits to take a breather at night in this new portal hijacking style of warfare. One so mighty with so many armies, with plans of great conquering now hangs above me defeated awaiting her doom. I wonder why I feel sorry for her yet I must be careful for in my evil days I also used that card which gave me many hands. However, I will be after judging her, simply vanish her from existence. To leave her in a torture zone somewhere always runs the risk of escape with a newly fully motivated army such as the gift I unleashed on my prior throne. I now command, "Call forth the Judges of our Court and let them judge one named

Rødkærsbro. I charge her with raging war upon my Empire with the intent of killing or torturing my servants. One judge asks me, "Why do you believe this was her intent?" I tell him, "From her words as spoken above my throne" as I show him the stream. He asks Rødkærsbro, "Are these your words?" She answers, "They were, are, and shall always be." The judge then asked her, "Did you intend to wage war against this empire?" Rødkærsbro answered, "I intended to win which may be delayed a short time." The judge now asks her, "Is there any reason this court should not hold you guilty as charged." Rødkærsbro said nothing. The judges talked among themselves and then read, "Let all about justice and righteousness record the events of today as the Judges of the Queen's Court (they could not say my name for to do so would vanish Rødkærsbro) could find no evidence of Rødkærsbro's innocence of the charges as charged. The master's number one servant may pronounce the punishment. I then look at Rødkærsbro and say, "Before all who are here today, do you have anything to say before I give to you your punishment?" Rødkærsbro then says, "You are not strong enough to punish me, for I have many hundreds of armies that shall rescue me." I look at Iris and she shakes her head no, telling me in mind talk, "Master those armies were destroyed." Rødkærsbro continues, "I shall chain you and flaunt your before all who foolishly believe in good. You shall perish, for good has never in the history of all dimensions won over evil. Evil shall always deliver the goods. Today is your day, which shall be short-lived for your future, shall be filled with great pain and misery. My future will see me assign upon your throne only long enough to destroy all in our foolish empire. Any who worship me now shall be spared." She looked around and no one answered. I then said, "Today you have been defeated by Lilith." With that, she vanished. Iris had ended the war and took back home before I was summoned to escort our master, as he shall come home. Iris then told me that she and medics were going to establish a powerful defense against portals and an easier way to identify intrusions. I told her, "As long as both are here the worship our master when I bring him home." They both shook their heads yes and vanished. I get the feeling that they will turn out to be very close sisters which is always beneficial in defense matters. Great cheer now sounded over the Empire as I lifted my hand and told them, "Hold fast your cheer as we are approaching the hour of our master's return." Then, as the power spirit departed, a new much stronger power spirit painted the sky. I knew exactly what that meant. My long wait, having suffered it twice was soon to be over. To be hit when you are low has been the way I was forced to endure. However, soon it will be over and I shall enjoy the real purpose my empire gave us the Nørresundby Palace as I fear Yudachyov when she wakes up to find she is decades old. I will talk to our master begging to hold her. Wars, invasions, trials, so many things have happened so fast I just do not know if my soul can comprehend it entirely. I am so thankful I created so many power spirits first from my mighty generator, which someday will once again be making spirits as it is now upgrading galaxies. Gyor-Moson-Sopron now puts out his handwriting and says, "Lilith his time is near and even though you did not want to be there, he does need you." Out went my hands grabbing his hand and bammo (wow, this person has a power pack super-duper flasher) I look out and what I see cannot be for real. My spouse is exhausted to the point of deformity as worse than one would his most hated enemies. I ask Gyor-Moson-Sopron. "Why?" He tells me, "Demons got into our little world and tried to make him curse all gods and give all that he had with them. Without knowing, what he had and only holding on to the rain blasted small light of the good he stood firm. He has the greatest victory of any god in penance and shall be given even more power than me. I would not even think of Rødkærsbro little speech as she can never get past him and I since we are bonded in power till you sit upon your seat in the Council of Nykøbing Mors. His name need not be heard to destroy demons for wherever his name travels in the depths of your universe evil will die. Thus, anytime his name is spoken evil somewhere will eventually fail. Bogovi now surprised us as he pronounced the greatest works I have ever heard, "Lilith I now Come Home." As his body suit ceased to function, I grabbed his spirit as it flashed by me. His soul was badly damaged as I said to Gyor-Moson-Sopron, "I must get him home to fix him." I did not even blink my eye as I was in our Nørresundby Palace with my head courts and the other three Queens. The Queens immediately went into frenzy as I yelled at them, "Stay calm since we shall save him." Then I called upon the Crown of Sopron Hyrum Twin Sister the Healing Goddess Drusilla who immediately came out and touched him with both hands as she began crying. I reckon they must have been close during her brief stay in the penance prison. I could see her glow as new lights were now shining in his psyche. I can feel him starting to heal. Drusilla told me and the other Queens as we all were touching his soul, "It shall be a very short time now." He will be back in control of all his spirits and his intellect. Next, his lights would get bright then dim out then bright again. Drusilla now told us, "He is exercising his control and will be with us . . ." Bogovi says, "Now. He looked at Drusilla and said, "I always knew there was something special about you. I do hope you visit Lilith often." Drusilla then quickly said, "Or master, you let her visit me . . . ," as she blinked her eyes and smiled. Bogovi quickly shut his eyes saying, "I dread looking into your eyes, lest I give unto you my small empire." Now Tompaládony sweetly said, "Oh you are a king of a great empire." Bogovi looks at her then me and asks, "Who are those two with your penance gift I gave you?" Tompaládony quickly answers, "I am your mothers mother," and the queen mother quickly says, "And you young man are my son," as she kisses his cheek. Then Julia says, "I need you, why you gave Lilith me, your sister?" Bogovi looks at me and says, "How is she my sister?" I told him, "While digging deep into the mug beneath the Sea of Forgetfulness, Tompaládony made available to me your sister's hidden scroll. She risked all by trusting me." Bogovi looks at her and says, "Indeed, my mother's mother is called Tompaládony, for she always told us wonderful stories about you." Tompaládony then looked at the Queen mother and said, "Is that true?" The Queen mother responds, "Yes, I could see you in the distant future as we are now," as she winks at Tompaládony who rushes over and kisses her. Bogovi then apologized to Julia saying,

"Believe me, if I would have known," as Julia puts her hand over his mouth and says, "If you would not have given me to my goddess I would have as I did." Then Tompaládony and the Queen mother quickly added, "As we did also." Bogovi looks at me and shakes his head, "I am so sorry to have so much foolishness in my family. I never realized that when you talked my pants off you would pursue the rest of my house," as he now smiled and gave me my first kiss. The family Queens all clapped with delight and we all did hug each other as I told my master, "I talked your pants off before and I will again, however this time they are staying off for a long time." Bogovi laughs and says, "Mother, could a master ask more from such this number one servant?" The queen mother kisses him and then me and says, "Truly she is the love of all of our lives, for when we were lonely she made us her friends and when I wore garments she made me unsheathed (at this we all started laughing to include our master). Seriously, when I needed love she gave me, love and when I needed trust and mercy and goodness she gave all to me asking nothing in return. I do hope you forgive my son, for I did beg her priest to shower me in her blood and make her my goddess." Immediately, Tompaládony added, "As did I my grandson." Then Julia added, "I can never revoke the promise I made for her to be my god." Then Bogovi surprised us all and laughingly says, "Darn, I get no one to worship me in my family, at which time I jumped in his arms and said, "I shall worship you as my only master all the days of our great new beginning." This is the beginning of eternity.

Next of the Great Ones: Who is Tianshire?

Other adventures available

The Lilith Series
Mempire, Born in Blood
Penance on Earth
Lord of New Venus
Rachmanism in Ereshkigal
Sisterhood, Blood of our Blood

The Great Ones Series
Prikhodko, Dream of Nagykanizsai
Tianshire, Life in the Light

Author Bio

James Hendershot, D.D. was born on July 12, 1957, living in old wooden houses with no running water until his father obtained work with a construction company that built Interstate 77 from Cleveland, Ohio to Marietta Ohio. He made friends in each of the new towns that his family moved to during this time. The family finally settled in Caldwell, Ohio where he eventually attended a school for auto mechanics. Being of the lover of parties more than study, he graduated at the bottom of his class. After barely graduating, he served four years in the Air Force and graduated Magna Cum Laude, with three majors from the prestigious Marietta College. He then served until retirement in the US Army during which time he obtained his Masters of Science degree from Central Michigan University and his third degree in Computer Programing from Central Texas College. His final degree was the honorary degree of Doctors of Divinity from Kingsway Bible College, which provided him with keen insight into the divine nature of man.

After retiring from the US Army, he accepted a visiting professor position with Korea University in Seoul, South Korea. Upon returning to a small hometown close to his mother's childhood home, he served as a personnel director for Kollar Enterprises. Eleven years later, he moved to a suburb of Seattle to finish his life-long search for Mempire and the goddess Lilith, only to find them in his fingers and not with his eyes. It is now time for Earth to learn about the great mysteries not only deep in our universe but also in the universes or dimensions beyond. Listen to his fingers as they are sharing these mysteries with you.

Index

Tompaládony & Iris three day jubilee
    296
Tompaládony Jubilee 285
Trojan horse 135

V

Valley of Giant Flowers 163
Vasvári 248
Veszprém 10, 79
Villánykövesd 213, 288

Y

Yanaba 2, 72
Yudachyov 311, 317, 336, 370
Yudashkin (Юдашкин) War Palace
    303

Z

Ziapon diode 233